ISTANBUL
IN WOMEN'S SHORT STORIES

Edited by HANDE ÖĞÜT

Milet Publishing
Smallfields Cottage, Cox Green
Rudgwick, Horsham, West Sussex
RH12 3DE England
info@milet.com
www.milet.com
www.milet.co.uk

First English edition published by Milet Publishing in 2012

Copyright © Milet Publishing, 2012

ISBN 978 1 84059 680 9

First published in Turkish as *Kadın Öykülerinde İstanbul* in 2008

"Fig Seed" by Feryal Tilmaç previously published in "T32: New Prose Fiction from Turkey" (November 2009), *Transcript: European Internet Review of Books and Writing*

With thanks to the Cunda International Workshop for Translators of Turkish Literature (CWTTL/TEÇCA) for bringing together the translators and thus launching this collaboration

Funded by the Turkish Ministry of Culture and Tourism TEDA Project

Printed and bound in Turkey by Ertem Matbaası

Contents

From Foreword to Turkish Edition

The women writers who have contributed to this collection each share with us the faces of their own Istanbul, of women and Istanbul, and being a woman in Istanbul. Every woman writer from each generation is bound to have journeyed through Tarlabaşı, and taken a breather in one of the patisseries in Beyoğlu. Some perished in this city, some withered away in its *pavyons*. Some filled the ferries that cross the Bosphorus, and some wrapped their love for it around a kitten... But they all loved Istanbul because they knew how to put up a fight, to walk side by side, and because they all cherished freedom.

—Hande Öğüt
Translated by İdil Aydoğan

Foreword to English Edition

This collection does not present its reader with an idealized Istanbul where "East meets West". Rather, Istanbul is a place where, over the centuries, East and West have engaged in a testy relationship, pushing and pulling, repelling and attracting, with the ebb and flow of the Bosporus, leaving its inhabitants in a constant struggle—a struggle for their identities, those they express for all to see and those they feel inside, deeply. Some writers here engage subtly with the East–West paradigm; others obliterate it by consciously rejecting its determinant role, or simply by not paying attention to it. The struggle manifests in the feelings of disbelief and despair that rear up, vividly, in some of the stories and characters. Yet it also yields rewards, among which is creative and critical cultural expression, brilliantly evidenced by the works here. Some of what appears in these stories may feel particular to Turkey; some may feel like it could happen almost anywhere—after all, women are women, right? If only it were so easy...

With contributors born mainly between 1940 and 1970, who are not just from Turkish but also Greek, Kurdish and Armenian ethnic backgrounds, this collection of contemporary women's short fiction translated from Turkish represents the works of different generations and cultural groups. Some contributors are well-established authors, while several are journalists or film directors who have stories to tell of Istanbul. All except three stories were written for this collection. The women in these stories work, they study, they translate books, they laugh, they mourn loves lost to natural death or to murder, they cover their heads, they put on makeup and black lace, they revel in each other's company, and in the company of men. Most of all, they scream at the top of their lungs that this city is not a woman to be possessed, and that it will speak its mind (and they will too). Istanbul is more than just a setting: it is itself the protagonist—or antagonist—of the stories. In either case, it is never less than alive.

— İdil Aydoğan and Patricia Billings

Editorial Notes

Throughout the stories in this collection, we have retained the Turkish for several types of terms, including personal names, some honorifics, place names, foods, and musical forms, among others. We have used the English spelling of Istanbul, rather than its Turkish spelling, İstanbul, because the English version is so commonly known. For the Turkish terms, we have used italics in their first instance in each story and then normal text for subsequent instances in the same story. We have not italicized the Turkish terms of respect that form part of a name, such as Bey and Hanım, to avoid splitting the name visually with a style change. A glossary of Turkish terms that appear in this book follows overleaf.

Among the translators represented here, some write primarily in British English and some in American English. In this edition, we have aimed for a 'mid-Atlantic' pitch, using terms and idioms from both dialects, but mainly US spellings.

Guide to Turkish Pronunciation

Turkish letters that appear in the stories and which may be unfamiliar are shown below, with a guide to their pronunciation.

c as *j* in 'just'
ç as *ch* in 'child'
ğ silent, but lengthens the preceding vowel
ı as *a* in 'along'
ö as German *ö* in 'Köln', or French *oe* in 'oeuf'
ş as *sh* in 'ship'
ü as German *ü* in 'fünf', or French *u* in 'tu'
ˆ accent over vowel: syllable is stressed, as *â* in 'Leylâ'

Glossary of Turkish Terms

Ağabey (Colloquial: abi): Older brother, also used as an honorific for men.

Abla: Older sister, also used as an honorific for women.

Akide: Ottoman rock candy.

Aşure: A Turkish pudding with grains, fruits and nuts.

Ayran: A yoghurt drink.

Bayan: Lady.

Bayram: Holiday, in this case an Islamic holiday.

Bay: A respectful term of address used before a man's name, like Mr.

Bey: A respectful term of address used after a man's first name.

Cezve: A long-handled Turkish coffee pot.

Dolma: Vegetables, mainly bell peppers, stuffed with a filling of either rice or minced meat.

Dolmuş: A shared minibus or taxi that follows a set route within a city.

Efendi: A title of courtesy, equivalent to the English 'sir', literally meaning lord or master.

Ezan: The call to prayer.

Fasıl: A suite in Ottoman and Turkish classical music comprising a sequence of musical forms.

Gecekondu: A house put up quickly without proper permissions; a squatter's house.

Halal (Turkish: helal): Lawful according to Islamic law.

Hamam: A Turkish bath.

Hanım: A respectful term of address used after a woman's first name.

Hanımefendi: A respectful way of addressing a woman without using her first name.

Hodja (Turkish: hoca): Mostly used as a synonym for imam; religious leader of a mosque.

İftar: The meal at sunset that breaks the day's fast during Ramadan.

Kaytan: A hook moustache.

Kelle-paça: A soup made with the meat from around the head and feet of a lamb.

Kemal Paşa: A syrupy dessert made with dough and cheese which is shaped into small balls and then fried.

Keşkül: A type of milk pudding.

Kilim: A tapestry-woven rug.

Kokoreç: A dish consisting of animal intestines, usually lamb, seasoned and commonly served in a sandwich.

Köfte: Meatballs.

Köşk: A mansion.

Lahmacun: A thin pizza-like base with a seasoned minced meat topping.

Lodos: A southwest wind.

Lokum: Turkish delight.

Medrese: An educational institution teaching mainly Islamic theology.

Meyhane: A restaurant which serves *meze* and alcoholic beverages, similar to a tapas bar.

Meze: Small dishes served especially with alcoholic beverages, primarily *rakı*.

Müezzin: A person who sings the call to prayer.

Oud (Turkish: ut): A stringed musical instrument similar to a lute.

Paşa: A high military rank. Also used as an honorary title.

Pavyon: A nightclub where drinks are served; there is generally a woman singing for entertainment, and women who work there are treated to paid drinks to accompany men at their tables.

Pide: A flatbread which can also be served with a topping, akin to pizza.

Piyaz: A salad made with beans and various vegetables.

Poyraz: A northeast wind.

Rakı: An anise-flavored strong alcoholic drink, akin to the Greek ouzo.

Sarma: A dish made by rolling grape leaves around a filling of rice or minced meat.

Saz: A stringed musical instrument in the lute family.

Simit: A baked ring of bread covered with sesame seeds, often sold on the street.

Şalvar: Traditional, pyjama-like baggy trousers.

Şam Baba: A syrupy sponge cake.

Teyze: Aunt, also used to express respect.

The Music of the Ox Horn

Berat Alanyalı

Translated by Mark Wyers

I alighted in a large square. It was crowded, chaotic. Because of all of the pushing, nobody could get anywhere. Everyone was being spun around, as if they were in a whirlpool. The faces in the crowd were sullen. The others of my sex were either so few as to be lost in the crowd, or the square was reserved solely for men. *Wait,* I told myself, *you will surely find a place for yourself in this city.* Before long the whirlpool pulled me in as well.

It was so packed I couldn't even turn to see who was beside me. Like the others, I had to get used to being pressed up against the person in front of me and taking a step when the person behind me heaved forward. The heat was oppressive. The sun hammered down, as if its full fury had been unleashed on the square to ensure that nothing remained in shadow. Nobody spoke with anyone else, but there was a murmur arising from the depths of the crowd that was utterly undecipherable. And that smell… I couldn't place it, like a battery that had leaked acid, or burnt wires.

As I struggled forward, an arched gateway came into view; what lay beyond was shrouded in darkness. The structure resembled an old bazaar: domed, monumental. The coolness within refreshed my spirits. Inside, at least I would be able to catch my breath.

The First Gate

As I drew nearer, I saw a relief carved into the stone archway: the tensed body of a lion, with a head that was human. The lion had reared up and leaned back against the trunk of a grape vine, plump grapes dangling from its tangled branches. It held a drawn bow, the arrow poised. But that face... it was ghastly! It stared straight into the eyes of the beholder. The thin creased brows, the eyes flashing anger, the pursed lips... Of course, it was only a carving, but that stare, that burning stare. It was petrifying. I quickly gathered my wits. It could have been a hundred, maybe even a thousand years old. But isn't it indeed the case that only stone could bear such anger down through the ages?

If it weren't for that stare, that face framed with curled locks of hair and those full cheeks could have belonged to a cute child, or woman, or man. Yes, it could have been any of those. That face carved into stone expressed emotion; but it bore no traces of age or gender. The admiration I felt for the fine workmanship brought tears to my eyes. In my mind, I ventured through time and kissed the hand of the master who carved that stone and pressed it to my forehead out of respect.

Who ordered such anger to be carved into stone? Why had they wanted it? My eyes locked on the carving, I had become lost in thought. I suddenly noticed that it was not as crowded as it had been before. A chill ran down my spine. Out of instinct I turned. That human-headed lion stood behind me, in flesh and blood. It glowered at me with the same fury as in the carving, as it stood among the branches of the grape vine climbing the mosque wall. It had drawn its bow, and aimed the arrow straight at me. My blood froze in fear, and then was set aflame, pounding through my heart, ears and head. Such moments of anxiety, as we discover later, become inscribed on our bodies. Was the stone relief carving still there? I desperately wanted to look. But if I had dared to do so, I would not be here now, nor would you be hearing this story. Sometimes, we can be swifter than an arrow. My instincts howled at me to bolt. The adrenaline pumping in my veins exploded through my legs, and at the last moment I dashed through the gate.

The Second Gate

I don't know how long I cowered there. When I regained my senses, the first thing I noticed was that inside was just as stifling as outside. As my eyes grew accustomed to the dark, I began to make out people dashing here and there, and row upon row of shops. Nobody took heed of me. They were in such a bustle that even had I fainted nobody would have stopped to lend a helping hand. They went in and out of the shops, as if they were carrying things. But their hands, arms and backs bore nothing. When I stood up and looked around, I noticed that the shops were empty, from the display cases to the shelves. In spite of this, money exchanged hands at a frantic rate; the rustle of banknotes and the jingle of change echoed in the vaults of the bazaar, rising in a crescendo. It was stuffy. The air was clammy. The stench of rotting meat hung in the air. There wasn't a single window. My stomach churned with nausea. I had to get out of there, as quickly as possible. Perhaps that poised arrow awaited me, but I had to do something, anything, to get out of the bazaar. The moment I leaped to my feet, I saw stars and collapsed. My knees were gashed open. Blood trickled down my calves. As I vomited on the base of the column I clung to, I glanced in the direction from where I had come. There was no gate, no passageway.

There had to be an exit. Even though my knees were throbbing, I limped into the darkness of the bazaar. In the corridors that led off from the right and left of the passageway, I looked for any kind of opening letting in the light of the sun. As I wandered, I began to understand that the bazaar was far from what it appeared to be. From the square, it appeared to be a single-story bazaar, but inside there were stairs. Leading off from the corridors, behind the passageway gates, these absurd stairways conjoined, and then led nowhere. The steps were worn to an angle by the tread of feet continually plying up and down. They were good for nothing except making you traipse around the bazaar like a workhorse. No doors, no openings.

The bazaar was holding me captive.

—Come here!

My mother, standing at the base of a large column, looked smaller than her usual self. She was leaning on a crutch, and shifted her weight away from the leg that was bound in a plaster cast. I limped towards her. Wearily, she held something towards me. A glass of water and a bundle of gauze.

—Take these, pull yourself together.

—Mother, what kind of place is this, I can't find the exit…

—We'll go down to the parking garage, through the fire escape. I couldn't find your father, but his car is parked below.

I followed her. She led me through a door which I hadn't noticed before.

The Third Gate

The parking garage was a jumble. From somewhere above, sunlight trickled down. Beneath the ceiling beams, everything was caked in dust. The cars were parked right up against each other, in such a way that they couldn't even be moved. Concrete blocks from the ceiling to the floor left little room for maneuvering. All of the cars were old. Old models, old paint jobs, old tires…It was as if we were in a car cemetery. But we couldn't find my father's car. My mother, dragging her cast-bound leg, carefully examined each car with patience, and hope. Lamenting that she hadn't found it, she would start back at the beginning, and start looking again. My patience running out, I clambered atop the nearest car, and leaping from car to car, headed towards the light. A steep flight of stairs led to a narrow door up near the ceiling.

—Mother, stop! Look, they built a flight of stairs here. How will we get the car out? How will it fit through the door? Mother! Mother?

The Fourth Gate

I returned to the bazaar to find my mother. Frantic preparations were underway in the passageways. The shops were being swept out, the windows polished, the floors mopped. Nonetheless, the stench had grown worse. When I entered the main passage, I saw television crews, and red, white and blue flags, and cloth banners hung from wall to wall:

WELCOME, ESTEEMED PRESIDENT!
– Bazaar Administration

PRESIDENT THOMAS WHITMORE, PAY US A VISIT TOO!
– Bazaar Junior League

THOMAS, OUR PRESIDENT! WE WILL NOT GIVE IN!
– Bazaar Sports League

ESTEEMED THOMAS, DO NOT LEAVE, STAY FOR THE NIGHT!
– Bazaar Industrialist Union

The crowd pressing around the television crew resembled lepers trying to touch a messianic healer. As soon as the officials pushing and shoving them turned their backs, the throng jostled forward again, leering into the cameras and lights. They aped famous people, made grotesque faces, craned their necks towards microphones to blurt out freakish songs. They paid heed to neither warnings nor reproach. With their pathetic fervor and harrowing hope, they were deaf as stone. I was filled with such a sense of shame that I bit my lip, my hands pressed to my ears. Ignoring the pain in my knees, I fled. I had to find my mother as soon as possible.

As I rushed down the other passageway, I saw her. No, it wasn't her. I never found her again. What I had seen was a child. A young boy, by himself. He was crouched down at the base of the wall, watching the tumult.

—Young boy, are you alone?

His arms twitched uncontrollably. Forcing open his twisted mouth, he spoke:

—My father is at the movies.

—And you?

— ...

I wiped the spittle from his lips, and held him to my chest. His heart was pounding like a drum. There was no way I could leave him.

—Where do you live?

—Around the center...

—Don't be afraid, we will find your father.

To find his father, we had to find the movie theater.

—Where is the movie theater?

With jerky movements, he pointed behind him. Where the autowalk began, I saw the posters. The theater had eight screens, and the same film was playing on all eight: *Independence Day*.

Suddenly sirens sounded, and an immediate commotion ensued. The sound of the pounding of feet and a mechanical banging thundered through the vaults of the bazaar. People scampered away, and the din quieted down. Armed guards swarmed in and took up their assigned posts. A woman's languorous voice announced:

—Attention, please. Thomas Whitmore, esteemed president of our exalted ally the United States of Shadows, will presently enter our bazaar to make his planned visit. Please turn off your cell phones and extinguish your cigarettes.

At that moment, an old man beside us suddenly sneezed. The guards cocked their guns with simultaneous clacks, and aimed at the poor man. Clutching the young boy, I bolted for the autowalk. He was screaming uncontrollably. Which theater was his father in? What kind of a father was he! At the same time, I was keeping an eye out for my mother. The passage continued on and on. The theater doors were nowhere to be seen. The young boy continued wailing, a single piercing howl. My bandages came loose, and my wounds began bleeding again. I looked over the side: a black void. The floor under the autowalk had disappeared. The autowalk began making turns, dips, lurching up, gathering speed. We were about to smash into a wall that appeared straight in front of us. I was trembling from head to toe. Suddenly a door opened in the wall, and the autowalk, like a garbage chute, hurled us into the light of day.

The Fifth Gate

I opened my eyes and found myself on a grassy knoll. I looked at the calm, blue sky, and wept. From below arose the sound of the sea, splashing. Seagulls fluttered around the ferryboats. The scent of seagrass mingled with redbud blossoms. Bleating red goats leaped from one edge of the sky to the other. They were still so many of them. On the grassy knoll, I closed my eyes.

"There is no town square… No arrow… No bazaar."

I slept, and woke, and slept. For who knows how many years.

The grassy knoll began where the road ended. The grass on the knoll was always green. When we were not sleeping, we watered the grass. We, the wounded from the bazaar in the square. The bandaged, the crippled, the counters of goats. There were enough of us to keep the grass green with our weeping.

I first saw the weeping three-breasted dwarf there, at a time when we had fallen silent. She played music for us on an ox horn. When it was time for us to be treated, we would gather around the oxcart on the lower slope of the knoll. The three-breasted dwarf would place the yoke over her head, and blow into the horn of the ox skeleton. Music like that has never been heard anywhere in the world. The doors of the east and the west opened for that melody, and took us in. We were lulled in its embrace, gathered up. Suddenly we were transformed into dolphins soaring upwards from the depths. We became the hovering of the crane, the ascent of the eagle. A crisp, fresh melon would crack open inside of us, and we would be refreshed. When she played the horn, the three-breasted dwarf would be transformed into a tall, slender woman. She would clothe her nakedness in her tears. Her tears were like immense pearls; she cleansed the pain we carried within. Afterwards, she would tell us the tale of a fairy tale city. Her tale was an elixir. It whetted our desire. It flowed, like a long river. It was such a city that the tales about it went on for thousands and thousands of years.

The Open Gate

If, in the middle of this square, I can relate my story to you today, it is thanks to what I learned from the three-breasted dwarf. I cannot express to you the music of the ox horn, but I can convey the essence of the tale:

On the shores of that azure passage, a city was founded on the edges of two continents, shrouded in mystery. Master of miracles, virtuoso of contradictions, shah of beauties. In the past they called it the Gate of

Felicity, and today, it is known as the Gate of Bereavement. This fairy tale is the tale of that city.

This is a venerable city, its fair visage vaster than its dark. But its dark is so dark that its shadow falls across its fairness. It is a broken balance scale. On its pans, forever out of balance, time is weighed against money. The divine and delirium, and carnage and clemency, sleep bosom to bosom in its ancient bed. No matter what the city is, its mirror shines back a true reflection of whoever looks upon its surface. Entering the city's innumerable gates, the innumerable new denizens thought that what they saw in the mirror was the city itself. The shadows of the city are so weighty, so barbarous, that the newcomers were stricken with fear. At that moment they began to curse the city. All who heard, came to the city, and all who came, settled down. As more people came, the shadows flourished, the maledictions gushed forth. The mirror grew darker and darker, and in the end shattered in darkness.

—Ah, vulgarity! I shall be even crueler to your worshippers. Though their countenances fill my spirit and their natures become my nature, I shall possess ninety-nine souls. I shall saunter appareled as I please, and torment their pointless lives. May they all behold my dark side! Let this curse be perpetuated, until the reign of the grateful.

From past to present, this city has always been a grinder of human souls. It devours those who stumble, disgorges those lodged in its throat. And waits, for the day when those who will break the curse have risen.

Bayan Naciye House

Esmahan Aykol

Translated by Ruth Whitehouse

I.

The first thing I remember about that house is the coffin rest that was visible through the window. I'd sometimes wake up early to the voice of the *müezzin* when it was only half light. While dull, dissonant calls to prayer emanated from other minarets in the city, our müezzin recited the *ezan* with a passion as though he were whispering a love poem into the ear of his dearly beloved wife, as though he wanted to soothe the fire in his heart. That's how our müezzin was: a young man, passionately in love with his wife.

My ex-husband came to the house that evening. With a torn photo of me. In bits. He was clutching the pieces tightly. I was nineteen in that picture, and I remember where it was taken. We were in the garden café of a museum but had no money to pay for coffee. Abroad, in Tallinn. We were back-packing tourists then, and very much in love.

The first thing he said was, my wife wanted to tear up your photo. She not only wanted to do it, she had done it. I was looking at it. That's what new wives are like—they're jealous of the old ones. What they miss out on is youth, their husband's youth; there's nothing they can do about it and for that reason they're jealous.

I touched his cheek to comfort him, unthinkingly, as a reflex from the past. His beard had grown a little. He'd obviously shaved that morning but, as always, it had grown again by evening. I knew. From experience. My chin used to hurt from rubbing against his beard when we kissed. My chin would bear the marks of long kissing sessions like the stains on the foreheads of Egyptians after their prostrations. In those days…

My hand was on his cheek, my ex-husband's large hand on mine. When I say ex, I really mean ex. It had been eight and a half years since we divorced. Almost nine. But I couldn't be bothered to count the months, years and days just then. I realized I'd missed his skin. My heart skipped a beat when he kissed the palm of the hand that had been touching his cheek. We had never made love since we divorced. Our love life during the last stages of our marriage was not worth talking about. The final days of our relationship had left a bad taste in my mouth.

He pressed his body against mine. The raincoat he was wearing smelled of the street. I buried my nose in his shoulder, inhaling a mixture of smells: earth, exhaust fumes, coal. But it was good. I was briefly distracted by the smell of coal, and then I thought about his lips again… Strangely, this didn't bring back any bad memories. Otherwise I might have pushed him away. I couldn't even remember what had happened, apart from the usual excuse that I gave everyone, which was that our love was over. He put his hands inside my jacket. What he did felt very familiar. Yet he seemed not to realize. I mean, not to realize how we'd left things. It was better like that. We kissed with a calmness that belied the beating of our hearts, as if wishing to wipe away traces of having touched other lips. He smiled ruefully as he scattered like confetti the pieces of photograph in his hand. Come and sit on the sofa, he said.

At that time, I was translating *Şehriyar's Ring—A Love Story,* by the Bosnian writer Cevad Karahasan. My ex wandered around the house stark naked, just like the old days, meddling with papers on my desk: translations of the novel in a few languages I knew, a dictionary of Sufi terms, some Goethe texts...

He read aloud from the computer screen the section I'd been translating when he rang my doorbell:

> *In the mornings, before taking a shower, when your soul resists having to get up, when having someone to think about whose very existence delights you—although she knew for a fact that he was a very good person... On a grey, dank morning in Sarajevo, when you feel with every fiber of your body that the world has no purpose or meaning, and never will have... On such a morning, a single glance through the window at you and your existence in the world, while reminding yourself of the countless bad things about this horrendous hole that is still proud enough to call itself a town, on such a morning, before taking a shower, before putting on makeup, before all those little things you do to persuade yourself that you can participate in the day—on such a morning, thinking of someone else makes you feel there is a valid reason, even a powerful reason, for the day to start. The clouds radiating that smell which pervades Sarajevo are almost penetrated by a ray of sunlight. I'd be afraid of such a love in real life. It must be as unlikely as a ray of sunlight in Sarajevo, but maybe it would be good to be gripped by such a love. However, that person is definitely not Faruk. Grey, life-sustaining Faruk. Oh, stop this, for God's sake!*
>
> *If true love has this effect, then she definitely did not love Faruk. Or put it this way: if, as is claimed, true love really has this effect, then she could never be in love with Faruk.*

Doesn't she love Faruk, he asked. I don't know either. You know I never read a book before translating it. It seems like a good book, he murmured, as he rummaged around in the fridge.

That night, the bad taste of past lovemaking was wiped from my lips.

Replaced by a taste like that of discovering how to kiss for the first time: a fresh, unsullied taste that was eager for life. I'd fallen in love again, without knowing which I missed most: my youth or him.

My ex-husband didn't go back to his wife.

There's something about falling in love with the same man again that is different from a brand new love. *Şehriyar's Ring* lay untouched and unopened for weeks. Yet I should have been working: the translation was supposed to be ready in time for the November book fair.

I spent the days going out for long walks. Along roads and streets, down steep slopes and past waterside cafés, sometimes having a glass of tea beneath the bridge before returning home. I'd recall our walks through the streets of Tallinn, Rome and Barcelona, cities we'd roamed together, hand in hand, believing in eternal love. And in the final episode of our relationship…I'd given him a slap, he'd pushed me; I'd thrown a couple of plates, he'd punched the wall with his fist…We were gradually killing ourselves and our love, and what's more, we were enjoying it.

He divorced his wife quickly; if there were any problems, he didn't tell me about them.

I was on the verge of finishing *Şehriyar's Ring*. To make up for lost time, I was translating for as many hours as I possibly could. Like Sisyphus, I kept going back and checking all the pages I'd previously translated.

In the evenings, my ex would sit on the sofa watching me as I worked. In his hand, he'd have a few files he'd brought back from the office. His laptop and a glass of *rakı* would sit side by side on the coffee table. I thought then that this must be happiness. I understood why we hadn't managed to make this relationship work previously, and why we would be able to do it now. Or perhaps I should say that I thought I understood.

II.

One evening, my landlord, Hacı Bey, knocked on the door. Instead of the remaining twenty-eight pages waiting to be translated, which I simply couldn't face, I had another book on my desk. Hacı Bey said I had to move out because his youngest son was getting married and would be moving in here. After he left, I stood gazing at the coffin rest, waiting for the afternoon ezan. Was it chilly? The thought of moving had given me the shivers. I thought about where I'd like to live—where I wanted to make love, to work and to live.

What about Bebek, my ex asked that evening on the sofa as I stretched out my feet on his lap. It's near my work. Going back and forth from here is difficult anyway.

He was the managing director in Turkey of an international pharmaceutical company based in Levent. A great achievement for a man of his age, his mother used to say.

Why don't we buy an apartment, just to spite the landlords, he said, maybe as a joke. But it made me realize how scared I was at the thought of buying a place. It was like a blatant request for us to put down roots, and there was something unacceptable, even sullying about it... It would mean bargaining, arguments with land registry officials, dealing with real estate agents... Are you prepared to dirty your hands, asked a voice inside me. An ex-husband and a new house. Bebek would be good. And you like walking by the sea. As he spoke, he was caressing my calves. I giggled involuntarily. But my mind was elsewhere. I'd been talked into buying an apartment. He didn't wait for me to think it out for myself. You'll spill your rakı, I said as he crawled towards me on his knees. So what, he said. If we can make love without worrying about spilt rakı, broken glasses or crumpled clothes, then we should be able to put down a few roots, I thought.

I started to look at apartments in Bebek. Sometimes I'd go out before the mist had lifted from the strait. Whenever I phoned my ex at work, he'd give me a few words of advice, even though he was very busy. After all, I was the one who spent the most time at home. We'll buy or rent, I'd say to the real estate agents. They insisted on trying to find out what my budget was. They'd try to size me up by studying the quality of the boots, jacket or coat I was wearing. You're just coming up against the realities of life, babe, my ex would say. It's a world where you are what you wear. If it's to be a rental, can you pay the rent? Are you going to try and negotiate a lower commission? How serious are you about buying?

If I was claiming to have so much money, why was my hair brown? Why wasn't it blonde or highlighted like rich women? If we were going to live there as a couple, where was my partner? If I was married, why didn't I have a wedding ring? Or better still, why no big rock on my finger?

When I heard an eager agent say that she had just what I was looking for, I conjured up dreams of boarding the ferry at Beşiktaş and, despite the damp cold that froze my cheeks, sitting alone on the deck, sipping tea and gazing out at Çırağan Palace, Esma Sultan or one of the other villas. In these fantasies, I was still nineteen, new to love and sex. We were discovering them together. My body was carrying odors of the previous night's lovemaking; my skin smelled of my lover; my hair had rippled between his legs… I was getting off the ferry at Bebek and taking a short walk around the garden of the beautiful mosque designed by Kemalettin. My eyebrows still retained the tension of prolonged lovemaking. I was in love with a former lover. I was in love once again. A love that seemed eternal.

He hadn't exactly aged, but he had changed. And I liked the changes in him. The tattoo, which he'd gotten despite all my objections, had been removed, leaving a mark which was faint but still clear enough that it didn't escape my watchful eye. He shaved twice a day now. I'd lean against the bathroom door watching him in the evening and he'd wink at me in the mirror. Why did I never think of this before, he'd say. There was an imperative tone to his voice when he wanted something done, even when asking a favor. The days of yelling and fighting were over. Whenever he thought we were heading towards any sort of tension, he'd disappear until we both calmed down.

The apartment shown to us that day by the red-lipped, buxom agent was on the left, the sea-facing side, of a stepped street intersecting the bottom of the steep slope running up from Bebek to Etiler. It was in Bayan Naciye House which, despite being squeezed between rows of tall apartment blocks, had lost none of its dignity. The name of the building had immediately aroused my interest, even more than the architecture. Endeavour Apartments, Patience Apartments, New Life Apartments— they were common enough names. But Bayan Naciye House! Who was Bayan Naciye? Just under the name were the words 'Built in 1934'. I stood as far away as possible in the narrow street, staring at the building for a long time. If I'm going to put down roots, it has to be somewhere like this, I thought. That building was calling me, inviting me to settle and put down roots.

The horizontal windows remind me of Corbusier, said Mother the next day when we went there together. Very simple. Purist. Early Republican era… Sedad Hakkı Eldem built an apartment block like that in Maçka. At that time, master builders used to copy buildings designed by great architects. It must be one of those. It's a good imitation.

The entrance hall and stairway were broad and striking. A section that had been used as a laundry while the building was being constructed had later been converted into a small flat. Including this, the block consisted of five apartments. The one for sale was a top floor apartment with terrace. The living room, which had a dining area separated by a glass partition, was at the front of the building overlooking the street. It's a typical feature of that era, said Mother. In the old days, people thought a view meant being able to see passersby. Back then living rooms were always made to overlook the street. Thank goodness they haven't ruined it with some frightful conversion. Make sure you don't change it either.

Of course, I don't know what your budget is, the lady agent had said the previous day, scrutinizing me from head to toe yet again. I patted my hair with a hand that was now sporting a platinum-mounted diamond ring given to me on my wedding day by my ex-mother-in-law, who had never dared to ask for it back after the divorce. I immediately despised myself for trying to ingratiate myself with this chain-smoking woman, with her unpleasant job and shiny red lipstick.

Keep looking; after all, you're not going to make a decision on your own, said Mother. I mean, do you like it? What do you mean, do I like it—I love it. But the bathroom and kitchen need a good going over. And the roof isn't in great shape. It needs money spent on it, of course. I expect there's commission to pay as well, isn't there?

Semiha Hanım, the owner and Bayan Naciye's daughter, used to live in the apartment. When she passed on, her children put it up for sale. She was old and unable to look after the place, said the agent, without any mention of commission.

Fine, said my ex on the phone. I don't need to see it. We'll buy it if you like it. Come and take a look at it. How can I make a decision on my own? You're not on your own—your mother's with you. She knows much more about these things than I do. She's a woman and an architect. Anyway, I have no time today, as I said this morning. I'm busy with some men who've just arrived from Switzerland. Take some photos of the place and send them to me if it makes you feel better.

It's a middle class area compared with other parts of Bebek, said the agent, as I was taking photos. That accounts for the price. But it's a bargain at the moment. This district is gradually changing, of course. I recently sold the fourth floor of that yellow building. To the woman who plays Rezzan in the TV series, *Voices from the Supernatural*. What's her name? Oh, it doesn't matter. Single women really like our area. Nobody bothers about who comes and goes. But of course, you're not single…

What if I call you tomorrow and let you know… I hadn't paid much attention to what she'd been saying, or to the equivocal smile on her red lips. This evening would be better. The house has only just gone on the market, but you never know. There's a lot of interest in our area. As she spoke, she blinked her clumpy mascara-coated eyelashes. Of course, I'd love you to buy it. Was this woman flirting with me or what? I thought I saw in her eyes an illusion of wintry sun streaking into a freezing cold room. I wasn't yet experienced enough to interpret her look in any other way.

As we went down the stairs, the door of the ground floor apartment opened. It was an elderly woman. With her body inside and her head stretched out into the landing, she epitomized curiosity. Good day, Miss Perihan, is the apartment being bought by the lady? She meant my mother. No, said the agent, this young lady is going to buy it. The woman smiled, covering her lips with the edge of her white headscarf. I wish you well. We're very neighborly in our block. Why not come in for coffee before you go. We must beat the evening rush, retorted Mother. She hates doorstep conversations and gossiping with neighbors. Any children, asked the elderly woman, seeming not to mind my mother's rejection of her coffee invitation. No. Ah well, you're still young, my dear. There's time yet, God willing. My children are all married. They come and see me from time to time. Everyone's struggling to get by. Do you work? I work at home. I used to work at home too when I was young, but my fingers are all arthritic now. She held out her hand through the open door. It was like an eagle's claw. I did piecework embroidery for wholesalers at the Grand Bazaar for about fifty years. You can call me Aunt Hanife. I'm an aunt to everyone in this district. I smiled. I hate all that auntie talk. But of course I said nothing, not on the first day. Please excuse us, the traffic... Not at all, it's you who must forgive me. I've kept you standing there. If only you'd had one of my coffees. We'll drink your coffee another time. God willing, God willing. As we went out into the street, I felt Hanife Hanım following us with her eyes. I didn't look up.

III.

One day, my ex-husband's ex-wife called. I must see you, she said, I've been stabbed in the back. Where did you find my number? I'd never had any contact with her before that day. Why are you calling me? You've been hanging over our relationship like the sword of Damocles and now you're back together with him, she said. You used me to bring some excitement back into your relationship... She would have continued if I'd let her, and the level of insults was clearly going to escalate. I put the phone down without saying anything in reply. What could I say? No, we didn't use you. And I didn't like the 'sword of Damocles' metaphor at all. If she'd been one of the writers I was translating, I would have abandoned the book immediately.

The book I'd started translating months ago, before moving to the new house, was full of metaphors and symbols. Perhaps that's why I didn't like it. For instance, the hero bought a cuckoo clock for his wife instead of the canary she wanted…I didn't like that novel. It seemed to be festering in my hands. I looked at the author's photo on the back cover. A beautiful brown-haired woman with a seductive expression on her lips that she'd obviously adopted for the photograph. Or maybe she was always seductive. Her photo said nothing to me. Every so often, the nice woman editor at the publishing house would ask how the translation was going. That's all. The sum of my relationship with the novel was the voice of a female editor on the telephone.

The ex-wife of my ex-husband kept calling me that day. I didn't pick up the phone. When he came home in the evening, my ex didn't seem bothered. Had it not been an ego stroke for him? That's all I need, he murmured at one point when I kept bringing up the subject over dinner. As I lay tensely by his side before going to sleep, he suddenly turned towards me, put his leg between mine and said, come on, let's make a baby. Let's make space in our lives for a baby. Don't take the pills anymore. Little pink pills. One every day. After brushing my teeth.

Then he put his hand on my knee. Give the devil his due, he knew where and how to touch a woman. As his other ex-wife would have said, Render onto Caesar the things which are Caesar's. No, not tonight, I don't feel like it, I murmured. Well, the real job is to make you feel like it, babe. Smiling, he kissed me. I couldn't see his face in the dark, but I knew him well enough to know that the smile on the lips touching mine was not genuine. Leave me alone. He suddenly turned, switched on the bedside lamp and took a deep breath. What's the matter now? Do you think I told her to call you? No, but you could at least try to find a way to stop her calling me again. I'll get you a new mobile number tomorrow. Okay? Fine. Simple solutions to complex problems. That's how my ex-husband is. Are we going to sleep feeling mad at each other? I said, are we going to sleep feeling mad at each other? Oh well, as you like!

No, we're not going to go to sleep feeling mad at each other.

We didn't go to sleep feeling mad at each other.

My most difficult decision in the new apartment was where to put my desk. After many years, I had a study for the first time. Something quite unnecessary for anyone living alone. It made me feel totally cut off from the world. I only resorted to it when my ex was watching a match on television. Any other time, I'd be on the sofa, at the dining table, in bed… I'd work wherever I fancied that day. My back was aching badly. That was why, a few months after we moved in, I found a couple of porters and had my unwieldy desk moved into the large room overlooking the street. One of the changes we made to the apartment, despite Mother's bleating, was to remove the glass partition separating the dining area from the living room. Of course, it was the first thing she noticed the moment she set foot in the apartment again. But before telling you about her, I have to relate the events that had happened before. In order.

By sheer force of will, I'd managed to get through the first 100 pages of the festering novel. Psychologically, that was a watershed number for me. I'd never given up on a novel if I'd translated the first hundred pages. However, it was just at that time that my father went into another alcoholic coma and was taken off to the emergency room. From there he was packed off to Balıklı Rum Hospital for further investigation, treated for alcoholism, and put on a drip.

I was now very much aware that the relationship with my ex-husband was dwindling. Yet again. And I felt there was nothing we could do to stop it. In my mind, I had a definite image of the moment my ex's presence stopped giving me pleasure: a momentary image. That night. The night after his ex-wife called me. As we lay side by side in bed after making love, I was seized with despair at the thought of a joint future, of a child we might have, and the next time we made love. That night, I knew before I went to sleep. We'd fall asleep and wake up as two people whose paths had separated. And that's what happened. At least that's how it felt to me.

The next morning, I went out for a long walk along the Bosphorus, took the ferry to Yeniköy and back, did a few rounds of the mosque garden, sat around on benches and in cafés, and tried my best to shrug off the weight of the past and my suffocating thoughts. How on earth had I been tempted to let our lives become entangled again? Why had I made room in my wardrobe for the shirts, jackets and multicolored ties he had brought from the house he shared with his wife? Why hadn't my heart murmured when I was moving the silver dish holding my hair clips, which sat in front of the bathroom mirror and which I liked having there, in order to make a space for his shaving kit? Why had I behaved so harshly toward myself? History had repeated itself. The first time was a tragedy, the second a farce. Come on, you have to laugh. I wanted to howl. How could I laugh?

My ex eventually started coming home late. Father was still in hospital and Mother said she couldn't sit at home worrying on her own, so she was usually with us, wandering around and looking as if she was about to burst into tears at any moment. She'd taken up smoking again. It was thirty-two years since she had given it up. She'd sit out on the terrace trying to prove that she had no difficulty chain-smoking five cigarettes. It got on my nerves. They both did. And my father. All three of them.

IV.

At that time, if there'd been anywhere I could have escaped to, I'm certain I would have done so without a second thought. For instance, if Jenny had been somewhere sensible instead of Malawi. Or if a new opportunity had come up for me in another country. I wanted to leave everyone and everything behind me and get away. I needed some breathing space.

One day, when for some reason Mother had decided to stay over at my brother's, I returned home in the early evening after a long walk and, as I went up the stairs, I heard the door to the apartment in the ground floor extension open. Hanife Hanım. No, it's Aunt Hanife, she corrected me. This forced familiarity… It's so irritating. If you're at home, Aysel and I would like to come and see you. I didn't ask who Aysel was. She had to be someone who lived either in the apartment block or the neighborhood. When? Now. You put the tea on. I've made some pastries. Have you tried leek pastries? It's one of our specialties. Whose? I'm Albanian, from Kumanova. At that moment I wasn't interested in either Albanians or leek pastries. But I couldn't tell them not to come. After all I'm a Turk. Hospitable. We'll come up in half an hour.

Aysel was beautiful. She'd been widowed young and left with two children and a mother-in-law… Without much emotion, she related how and when her husband died. Who knows how many times she had told that story, or how many times Hanife Hanım had heard it. I couldn't have cared less, but I listened all the same. You're at home alone all day and you have no children. You must get bored. Why don't you ever come down and see us, she asked. No, I don't have time to get bored. I work at home. Translating. I translate novels from foreign languages. Your husband's never at home, he must be very busy, said Hanife Hanım. Meaningfully. Oh, Aunt Hanife, you are a one, giggled Aysel. What's wrong with that, my girl? Naturally, a real man has to work, to bring home the bread. And she's young. Pretty, a good figure—everything in the right place. Why shouldn't she go out and enjoy herself. I didn't like them talking about me as if I wasn't there. But as I said before, I'm a Turk, and I didn't want to be rude to anyone who came into my home.

The next day, again when I was alone in the apartment, the doorbell rang. I couldn't help it, my dear. I know it's the wrong time, but I made a special *aşure* pudding and I wanted to give you some. Of course it was Hanife Hanım. Thank you so much, you shouldn't have. What do you mean? It was no trouble. Let me just get my breath. Reluctantly, I asked her to come inside. As we drank our coffee, she loosened her muslin headscarf and said, take no notice of Aysel, she's jealous of you. She never stops talking. Why should Aysel be jealous of me? All the best-looking scallywags are after you. She keeps me up to date. Were you sitting in the mosque garden or something? You were seen from a distance. My guy told me. Hang on a minute. Who's following me? Who's your guy? She let out a throaty laugh. Almost indecent. She covered her lips with the edge of her headscarf. You know nothing about the world, my dear. Don't you have any friends, anyone you go and meet for a chat? You've been cooped up at home too long. I don't understand what you're trying to say. Don't be offended, but Perihan said you were naive. And who's Perihan? Don't you remember the person who sold the apartment to you? The real estate agent? Oh yes, the real estate agent. I dropped a few hints, but she didn't cotton on. Either her husband's madly in love with her, or she's as naive as a newborn child, she said. Look, don't take offense. I'm the same age as your mother. I don't understand what you're talking about. Well then say so, my dear. If you say you don't understand, I'll explain. Why did you move here? My ex-husband wanted to. What do you mean, your ex-husband? Well, my husband. What a pimp. So it was him who wanted it. Just a minute, who saw me sitting in the mosque garden? Who do you think? One of the men who come from the Bosphorus. The men who come from the Bosphorus? Yes, the men who come from the Bosphorus. Have you never heard about the men who come from the Bosphorus? She seemed to think it unbelievable that I'd never heard of them. She was even scornful. So you thought the coast was clear of studs and the like. A man coming from the throat-like strait, I thought. What kind of man is that? What kind of throat? Instinctively, I put my hand to my throat. Hanife Hanım laughed maniacally. Good luck to you, my dear. You really know nothing! You must go around with your eyes shut. Have you never heard of them? No, I haven't. What is this, some sort of secret code? She stared at me vacantly and started laughing. She was puzzled more than anything now. Why do you think it's only women who move to the Bosphorus? You mean the Boğaziçi area? I mean the Bosphorus, she said. The sea. Because they want to live somewhere nice. She pursed her lips at my reply. Fine, but why do you think the Bosphorus districts are so expensive? Why? Why are the women living in these districts so happy? Why? Are you the only one who knows nothing about this business, my dear? What business?

My head was spinning. When Hanife Hanım left, I poured myself a drink for the first time since my father went into the hospital. I went out onto the terrace and stretched out on the recliner. If this wasn't a time to have a drink, when was?

My guy has a thin pointed moustache, a *kaytan* moustache. Oh, I'm a sucker for moustaches! My Kaytan! I went inside and turned on some music. While the woman was speaking, I'd been wandering around in my head among the unknowns of the apartment and the district. Doing the tango. To a tango from the Fifties. One woman. One man. Making barefaced love before my eyes.

He comes round early in the evening. Twice, three times a week… I know it's him from the way he knocks on the door. It's not like my husband's pounding or the little tap of my neighbors, and not at all like the children. The knock of my young man is completely different. Would you like another coffee, Hanife Hanım? I want to be alone in the kitchen.

To digest what she's saying. She doesn't want any more coffee. I'd better go now, she says. No, stay a bit longer. Have some tea? Or a cold drink? Oh well, I'll have a soda, if you insist. It is light soda, isn't it? I never touch dark soda. The soda fizzes in the glass. I fix my eyes on the bubbles. What kind of nonsense is this? Men coming from the Bosphorus! After all, she'd never say she'd found herself a lover or that she was flirting with the grocer on the corner. She'd just made up a cover story for her lover.

You don't believe me, says Hanife Hanım. She's in the kitchen doorway now. It is all rather confusing and difficult to believe. I can't believe you moved here without knowing about the men who come from the Bosphorus. In that case, why did you pay out so much money for this apartment? Isn't there anywhere else to live? It's the first time I've ever seen anyone like you. How long have you been in Istanbul? I was born here. I went to school here, fell in love here and lived here. You've lived here, but don't you have a husband or any friends? I have to admit that I'm not really into friendships. But of course, I didn't say that to Hanife Hanım. I said nothing. Where does your mother live? I choked on my soda and had a long fit of coughing. Anadoluhisarı. See now, she's a woman who knows a thing or two. I could see that straight away. Typical mother, eh? She didn't tell you anything. Aren't people meant to tell their children about these things? Should they leave them ignorant of life's pleasures? She'll never move away from there. And me... God forbid that I should ever have to move from here. She said this with a conviction that impressed me. It's funny really. Why? Well, wouldn't your Kaytan go running after you wherever you went? He wouldn't come after me, my dear. Oh, my poor ignorant darling. Their hearts are no bigger than the nail on my little finger. He wouldn't bother. He needs to smell the sea air to stay alive. But not any sea, it must be the Bosphorus. Why do think they only live on the Bosphorus? My Kaytan says the smell of the Bosphorus is completely different. They won't climb up slopes or get on buses… Are they like us? They never age, they're never born and never die. My Kaytan told me recently that he had a lover in the time of Sultan Murat. The things this woman knows. The things she gets up to… Which Murat? How should I know which Murat. Are there lots of Murats? When's your Kaytan coming again? I think I should meet him.

She laughed lewdly at this suggestion. This time without covering her mouth with her scarf. Among her teeth, a few gold ones glinted. Her tongue was pink. Why don't people's tongues age? The lines around her lips seemed to soften and her calcified bones loosen. Her eagle claw. The hand clutching the soda glass. She undid three of the buttons on her blouse. Her breasts were plump and fresh. She lifted her elasticized long print skirt slightly. Was this woman wearing garters? Today is my Kaytan's day. He'll be here soon. I can't stay long with you. I have to go.

Hanife Hanım!

Well, my dear. This is a world of death. Do you blame me? No, I never blame anyone. Thanks be to God that He brought me to this apartment. I can never thank Him enough. I've been a tenant in the same apartment for fifty years. I never fall behind with the rent. I couldn't live anywhere else. God forbid. I'll go now. As I said, he'll be here soon. Any moment now. If he doesn't find me there, he won't wait. He'll turn around and leave. Can I meet him? He won't show himself to you, my dear. He doesn't show himself to anyone. I'm the only one who sees him. And he sees no one else but me. More laughter. Of the sauciest kind. She undid another button on her blouse. Her skin was bare right down to her stomach. How firm. Take no notice of my age, there's still a lot left in me. I must go. But you haven't finished your soda. Don't go yet. Tell me a bit more. I can't. I have to go. Hanife Hanım gets up. Silently, she almost floats down the stairs. Like a shadow.

Another whiskey on the recliner. Why did my ex-husband want to move to Bebek? Did he know, if not about the men coming from the Bosphorus, that women living by the Bosphorus are happier? And Mother? What was the real reason she'd stayed on in Anadoluhisarı? Why did she resist so much when my father wanted to move to Kemerburgaz? I must smell the Bosphorus air. Is that what she'd said? No way. The woman was making it all up. The story was so far-fetched that, if it had been in a novel I was translating, I'd have said the writer must be off his head. Or that the writer hadn't had a lover for a long time and consoled himself with such fantasies.

And supposing there are men coming from the Bosphorus, then why aren't there women coming from the Bosphorus? Maybe there are, but women don't know about them. Does my ex-husband come home late every night because he has fixed himself up with one of them? That's got you worried, my girl!

I was completely drunk when my ex came home. I was watching an awful TV program with the sound turned off. What's happened? His first question. He isn't used to seeing me drunk. I downed a couple of mouthfuls. You did the right thing. It calms the nerves. Yes, he knows about these things. He knocks back a couple every night himself. I'm going for a shower. Why? Why the hurry for a shower? Or do you smell of the sea? Which sea smell? Oh, for God's sake. I've been working like a dog all day… And who's in the sea? The Marmara Sea? The Bosphorus? That's it. I swam over to the opposite shore before coming home. He starts to loosen his tie. Don't take a shower tonight. I don't want to smell soap when we make love. Peach shower gel. It's your favorite smell, isn't it? His lips twist with lust. I can see what's coming. Not tonight. Tonight, my favorite is the smell of your skin. Oooh, babe, you should have a couple of drinks every night. You haven't spoken like that to me for years. Come here. Where? Again, that lustful twist on his lips. On the sofa. He leans his elbow against the doorframe, one hand in his hair, eyes narrowed. He watches me. Get undressed. He switches off the light. In the light of the television. I take off my T-shirt. Looking straight into his eyes. I'm waiting. Get undressed, he repeats. Get on with it. My shorts. Get undressed. Again. I am getting undressed. Now touch yourself. He's still dressed and on his feet. I moisten my finger in my mouth. He unfastens his belt. His trouser buttons. Someone coughs. The sitting room windows are open. From the street. Finally, he removes his shirt. I've missed this, he says, as he goes down on his knees in front of me. He pushes away my hand. His lips. His tongue.

Apparently there are men who come from the Bosphorus. They visit women living in the areas on the shores of the Bosphorus once a week. Twice. Three times. I have to prove Hanife Hanım's story. Or disprove it. What a strange story. Complete fiction.

'Scarlet lips' is what my ex called the real estate woman the first time he saw her. Some people use so much makeup. It can make you feel sick. Now, as I talk to the woman, I am staring at her lips. I don't know how to broach the subject. In fact, I wait for her to get around to it. Would you like another tea, she says again. There's nothing to talk about. What is there to say to a female real estate agent if you're not looking for a house? I just dropped by as I was passing, I'd better go. You must be very busy. Drop in again when you're passing by, she says. She has no idea how I'm squirming inside. Or perhaps she does. She says nothing.

I go down to the seashore. To the mosque garden. Fishermen! They're men who come from the Bosphorus. One of them must have made Hanife Hanım believe he comes from the Bosphorus. One of those swarthy types with a pencil moustache. Yet none of them are like that. They're tiny. And no moustaches. One is bearded. Are you looking for someone, Miss? It's a child. Fourteen. Fifteen at most. No, I'm just taking a walk. But you're not walking. You're making us laugh. I just stopped for a bit to have a rest. Do you live here? No. Over there. He points to over there. Wherever that is over there. My school's here. The schools aren't open yet. No, they're not. I came to see my friends. What's your name? Deniz[1]. Deniz? My big brother gave me that name. It's a good name, isn't it? There are supposed to be men who come from the sea, have you heard about that, Deniz? Am I crazy? The kid is staring at me intently trying to understand. He says nothing. Deniz! I call after him. He doesn't turn round.

I think of calling my mother, but decide not to. These aren't mother–daughter things. At least, not for us. And anyway, I'm upset with her. If this is all true, why didn't she tell me? What about going to see the friendly woman editor at the publishing house? But we're still on formal terms with each other. Father? It's not visiting day. Anyway, we never talk. We just remain silent. Maybe the poor man was reduced to this state because he knew Mother had a man who came from the Bosphorus. Poor thing. He couldn't compete. It would make anyone seek consolation in a bottle. My brother? Definitely not! His wife? She's too feeble. What man coming from the Bosphorus would have anything to do with her? I doubt whether she even has a sex life with her husband. I love to exaggerate. After all, they do have two children. But what does continuing the family line have to do with a sex life? Özlem? From our department. The wildest of us. The last time I saw her she was complaining because she didn't have a lover. Would she live in Nişantaşı if she knew about the men who come from the Bosphorus? Ayşe Konyalı? There were several girls called Ayşe in our class, so we called them by their surnames. Where was she living? Was it Etiler? Or maybe Ulus. What was the name of that girl who

---

[1] The name Deniz means 'sea' in Turkish.

only wore black? She became a journalist. How can I find the telephone number of someone if I can't even remember her name? The woman who comes to do the cleaning. Fatma? No. She lives in Fatih. Her daughter-in-law? She lives in their basement. My classmates from high school? We have a meal together once a year, if nothing else. Didn't Çiğdem say she was living in Maçka? Would that count, I wonder? But you have to climb up a slope to get there. And these men don't go up slopes. Elif. Didn't we all comment on how she looks younger than the rest of us? She hasn't gained any weight since graduation. Okay, so I haven't either, but she does some kind of sport four days a week. And she's definitely getting Botox. Yes, Elif's a good idea. I can find her number easily. The Alumni Association will have it. Oh, and there's that woman. The lawyer who represented me at my divorce. Bennu. She was living in Beylerbeyi. She's uninhibited enough for me to ask if she has someone else. And she had no qualms about asking why I was divorcing him. The truth is I shouldn't have. So why did you divorce him, you idiot?

My ex-husband called. But he never calls during the day. How are you? I'm fine. Just fine? Of course, I know what he means. Yesterday evening… But still I ask. What do you mean? I don't know, just… how are you? Well… I'm fine. I went out for a walk. Sooo? My legs are aching. It's too much lovemaking, babe. Are you having a couple again tonight? A throaty laugh. That's how he laughs when he's aroused. What time will you be back? What time shall I come? Haven't you got work to do? Loads. Well then…? But I'll come back early, if you like. Yes, come early. Let's go out for a meal first. In that case, I'll make a reservation. Do that. Where? It doesn't matter. Put your hair up. You look like Helena when you do that. Okay. Is eight alright? Fine.

I'm excited. What was that about men coming from the Bosphorus? I've forgotten all about them. They have very small lungs, can't climb up slopes, and can't live without the smell of the Bosphorus. They make women 'happy' once a week. Twice. Three times. Nonsense! No one sees them except women. And they have eyes only for women. Or at any rate, Hanife Hanım's guy has eyes only for Hanife Hanım. Whatever. My eyes, including my third eye, are only for my ex-husband at the moment. I'm thinking about what to wear that evening. I'm shivering. It's a summer's day. My ex's touch. He traces his finger down my back. Don't touch me! But I want to touch you. Not now! He jumps from the bed and wanders over to me. Is it forbidden to kiss? It's not that. We kiss. My tongue is in his mouth. He sucks on it. Then he kisses my neck. He lifts his head. What happened then, he asks. Nothing. What do you mean, nothing. I don't know. Yet I do know. My skin is sensitive to his skin. So sensitive that his touch hurts me sometimes. It's unbearable. I can't tell him that. I feel ashamed and say nothing. He caresses my breasts, his eyes gaze into mine. Don't touch! Am I going to say it again? Out of curiosity, or maybe anxiety. I say nothing. I turn slightly and open my legs to let his hand slide into me.

Over here, young lady, I'll tell your fortune for five. Look at you, child, lost in thought. I can tell you what your problem is… Where has this woman suddenly appeared from? I know what my problem is, and I don't need you to tell me. I get up and walk away quickly, leaving the woman and the bench behind me. My ex-husband—he's my problem.

Should I tell him what's bothering me over dinner this evening? Even if it means we have an argument? Even if he blames me for ruining the evening, and the moment we get home, he takes his pillow and his shirt and trousers for the next day from the bedroom and sleeps on the sofa in the living room? Even if he sits up late drinking and watching TV, and passes out drunk and exhausted? Even if the following evening he comes back so late it's hardly worth it and he's so drunk that I wonder how he managed to find his way home? And the same thing the next night. Over and over again. Didn't we go through all this ten years ago? Why do it again? Why, I ask myself, as we lick each other's wounds. Why do it again? What power was in the house overlooking the coffin rest that night? What power made us believe we could do it all again, not from where we left off but from where we started.

Loneliness?

Yes? asks the waiter. I look blankly for a moment. Yes? Again. What was it you wanted? I came into this café to get away from the fortune-teller. I'd like my coffee *az şekerli*. Just a little sugar. Not too much. Do they use sugar cubes? He nods his head. In that case, half a sugar cube.

I hadn't been in a relationship for three years when my ex-husband knocked on the door. Three years of loneliness. I'm not the sort of person who can establish relationships easily. I'd met Murat at a Turkish Translators' Association dinner. For some reason, I'd actually made the effort to go to that dinner. We just happened to find ourselves sitting next to each other. Later I'd learned that it wasn't coincidence at all. He'd specifically asked to sit next to me. Apparently, he found me mysterious. And very beautiful. I'd translated a Croatian novel for the publisher for whom he worked as an editor. He'd noticed me going in and out of the office. We'd spoken about what happened to the book I'd translated. At that time, there was no interest in Balkan writers, nor is there now. I don't know why that is. We've lived alongside each other for hundreds of years, yet at the moment no one is interested in what those people are doing. Everybody reads the Anglo-Saxon writers. The whole world.

He had a strange mobile. With a screen you could write on with a pencil. It was the first time I'd seen one of those.

High tech. He liked things like that. Like the latest cars. But he had no money to buy them. He wrote down my number. I'll call you, he said. We were casual with each other right at the start of the evening, hours before exchanging telephone numbers. We had so much to talk about: literature, translation, favorite authors, little-known writers, good but sidelined writers... Things I was never going to discuss with my ex-husband. He wouldn't know or be interested. He never read except on holiday. He didn't have the time.

He'd called the next day. So soon. I hadn't expected it, actually. Shall we meet for a drink? I wasn't in love or anything. It was never like that. From the first day to the last. Never. Not for a moment. Don't people think, if only for a moment, that they're in love when they're in a relationship? Well, they don't have to. Which means it happens. Before Murat, there'd been no one in my life for a long time. Mother had not yet given up on me. She kept urging me to go out. If you sit at home, who's going to find you? Well, my ex-husband did. He found me when I was sitting at home, didn't he? *Let him go*, said Jenny when she saw the huge poster-sized picture of my ex-husband I'd stuck on the back of the door. That was all she said. *LET HIM GO!* I'd added, *he's already gone anyway,* when I took the picture down from behind the door. Jenny's my closest friend. Not geographically close. We met in Bosnia. During the war. Now, she's in Africa. But that's a long story.

Did Dursun take your order? The waiter smirks. It takes a long time to split a sugar lump in two. He always has a ready answer. After waiting so long, I hope my coffee really is az şekerli when it comes. It's an obsession. It upsets me if things aren't exactly as I want them. For instance: my coffee must be az şekerli, my steak rare to medium rare, my pasta al dente, my salad finely chopped with lots of dressing, my dessert preferably with chocolate or peaches in it, otherwise tiramisu.

Is it alright, asks my ex-husband. The way you wanted it? Not bad. It could have been taken off the stove one minute earlier. I was worried when you ordered steak, in case they didn't do it the way you like. I can see that he really is worried. You've done your makeup beautifully, he says. He notices such things. How I put my hair up, the color of my underwear, whether it's lace, how my makeup is, if I've used too much blush... You're exhausting. And you? You seem to think you're not. Am I? You've never told me that before. You know I don't comment on things I can't change. I know. You are what you are. I loved you for what you are, right from the start.

I was nineteen when you loved me. Right at the beginning.

I'm wearing a backless mauve dress. Actually, I wish I hadn't. It's chilly. What's the matter? I'm a bit cold. Shall we go inside? He reaches for my foot under the table. Oooh, your feet are cold, babe. He removes my sandal and takes my foot between his hands. I glance sideways at the next table. An elderly man and a young woman. From their manner, they're definitely flirting with each other. They have no interest in where my foot is. My ex could have found a much younger woman than me. A twenty-something bimbo. Why did you come back to me? Have I come back? I didn't leave you. Have you forgotten? It was you who left me. He continues to stroke my foot. What you said isn't entirely true. You left me no option but to leave you. He puts my foot between his legs. See? I'm crazy for you. Shall we go? That's his tactic. Talk, then lovemaking. Not yet. Let's talk for a bit. What shall we talk about? The state of the world? Us...? Immediately, he becomes engrossed with the hard bits on the soles of my feet. He hates world affairs. It's us that he likes. But he doesn't like talking about us. You're doing the same thing again. Going over everything with a fine-tooth comb. Why did this happen? What's going to happen now? Can't we just let this relationship run its course? If only you'd find something else to think about. How's the translation going? Are you proposing some occupational therapy for me? Is my idleness affecting our relationship? I didn't mean that. He certainly did… As long as there's no fight. He'll change his tune now. Fine, let's go then. Let's go home and make love. Like the sun and the moon. You ignite me and I'll freeze you out. Hey, you put that very well, you have indeed frozen me out. It would be better if I went to the office and did some work. No, not tonight, please! I know that whatever I say now will make no difference. How many times have I had to put up with this? Waiter, the check! He raises his hand. I'll drop you off at home. He's not coming home. He's not going to take his pillow into the living room and sleep on the sofa. That's what he used to do. When he didn't have an office with a shower and all. I'll get a cab if you're not coming home. As I say that, I feel rage seething in my groin. It rises. Towards my heart. It keeps clutching with its claws. An animal anger. With icy tentacles that envelop me. An anger that extends to the tips of my fingernails. I'm going to scream, but my cries will not be heard. The sirens of the Bosphorus ferries will drown my voice. Do I even have a voice?

You want to get a taxi? When you ask me like that, of course I want to get a taxi. He opens the door and sits me down inside. Do you have any money? I nod my head. He turns away immediately. He tells some guys to run and get his car. I close my eyes and look at my heart: it's in shreds.

Whatever this relationship is, it can only survive if the past is not allowed to extend into the future. And that includes this apartment, the restaurants we go to together, where we go for holidays, other countries… This relationship is like a fishbone that has stuck in my throat. Ugh, that's a horrible metaphor. It would be over the top even for the saucy writer of that book I'm translating. But that's how it is. We swallow, but can't get rid of it. We cough, but it won't budge. Eat soft bread, Mother says. No, it's no good whatever I do. This fishbone is stuck there. A fish. In my throat.

V.

It's early and I'm in the mosque garden. People are going to work, running for a ferry or a bus; I'm sitting on the end of a bench. I couldn't sleep. Before I knew it, it was getting light. I woke up with a nightmare. Is it possible to fall in love all over again? I'm cold. The early morning Bosphorus air. My eyes are fixed on my hands that are clasped in my lap. I sit, unable to stir. My body is almost numb. It's a miracle I was able to get here. I feel sick from hunger. I haven't eaten since yesterday morning. I'd only eaten a couple of mouthfuls of my steak when we left the restaurant. Wine. And whiskey when I got home. Whiskey finishes me off. Maybe I should sit in one of the cafés here and have some breakfast. A huge breakfast to celebrate the impossible rekindling of a love. Like a hermit. I'm a hermit. A fugitive from humankind. I sit, staring at my hands in my lap. Man, she's asleep, says some kid. They walk around the bench. I can see their feet without raising my head. Shabby, worn sneakers. No, man, she's not asleep, says another. He leans towards me and stares into my face. We come eye to eye. He laughs and runs away. I watch him as he goes. He could have been my son. I was twenty-five when I became pregnant. I'd cried. If you really want it, why don't we have it, my ex-husband had said. I did want it, but yet again I didn't. A child. Mine. My thoughts at that time were like those of most twenty-five-year-olds. Should a child be brought into this world of wars and aggression, a world where people and animals are massacred? Children are born every second, so what? But I'm not doing it. We're not having a child in this situation.

You are very sad, my dear. Shall I tell your fortune? The woman from yesterday again. She's a pest. I've got no money, I say, just to make her go away. Later, give it to me later. No. I don't like owing money. For free then, dear. No. No way. She sits down next to me. On the bench. She has a cloth bag tied round her middle. It's filled with beans. You're in a bad way, my dear. Shame on them for making you sad. They're disgraceful. The bastards around here making lovely ladies cry. And you've cried a lot, dear. There's a man. Is it your husband? It's my ex-husband. There's another man in your destiny. You haven't seen him yet, but he sees you. Every day, on this bench. The woman slides closer towards me on the bench. The beans in her lap. She touches my hand, then puts her arm round my shoulders. Dearie me! You really are in a bad way. What's bothering you, darling? I don't want any fortune-telling. Wait, I haven't told you what's wrong yet. I know what's wrong—you just told me. My ex-husband's my problem. Not him, he's not your problem. It's the other one. The one who doesn't show himself. He just follows you around quietly. No, there isn't anyone like that. That's a fairy tale, nothing to do with real life. An old woman's fantasy. Oh, but there is. Look, see, there he is. She points at the beans in her lap. Green. I want to laugh. Your husband loves you very much. Look, I don't have much money with me, so let's end all this fortune-telling now. As you wish, she says, shrugging her shoulders. Always money, money, money. Is it only money the world runs on? What else if not money? Love. Without love, we all die in the end.

Crude philosophy! Of course, any fortune-teller who turned up in front of me was bound to be like that. Is anything normal in my life?

What is it? Doesn't matter. Did you hear what I said to you? I've got the solution to your problem. So tell me what to do. Show me how much money you've got. I put my hand in my jacket pocket. A bit of cash. So, you can order me some breakfast then. My throat's dry from all this talking. She winks. This woman is beginning to interest me. What's your name? Leyla. Right, Leyla Hanım, let's have coffee. That's more like it, she says as we walk side by side towards the café. She pushes back her embroidery-edged, white muslin headscarf. Red hair. Hennaed. A straggly ponytail. Now ask me, she says as we sit down. What? About your problem. Which one? My father? My ex-husband? My mother? The festering novel I'm still translating? Is that all? She tosses her ponytail. And there's the matter of the men who come from the Bosphorus. Ah yes! Ask me about them. Ask me about the men who come from the Bosphorus. Ask and I'll tell you, my dear. Your heart is as green as one of these beans. A green bean falls from her hand on to the table. No, Leyla Hanım, you too? Is this story true? Whatever you believe in, darling, that's what the truth is.

Crude philosophy, I say.

Now do you believe?

I still don't believe, but my head's all mixed up. Even more so. Don't you worry your lovely head. Go home, get freshened up, and wait. I'll tell him to come to you tonight. You have a little nap. Take this and drink it. You'll sleep like an angel. She presses a tiny translucent thing into my hand. It's a fruit kernel. What's this? I get it from far, far away. You can't find it around here. Swallow it with a sip of coffee. With coffee. I swallow. I feel it going down my throat. Tiny, translucent. And the bone? The one that's always in my throat? The bone that's suspended in my throat latches on to the translucent body and goes down. Unwittingly, I hold my throat. How was that? She winks. I'd never give you anything bad. Go now. Get.

Why did you say 'get' to me?

Don't let him go! It'll all happen at Bayan Naciye House. Your ex-husband. The man from the Bosphorus. Once a week, twice, three times. As often as you want. Translation during the day. Hospital visits once a week. Your father. Your mother, who seems to be disintegrating by the day. Why are you so sad, Mother? I didn't know you loved Father so much. Do you think I'd have stayed with him all these years if I didn't love him?

Of course I love him. But you were always fighting. You got upset by his drinking. He wasn't always like that. He was young. The memories of those days show in the lines around your eyes. I didn't know you, Mother. I didn't know you at all. My heart trembles. Oh, MOTHER! Long-term relationships are like that. You're the same, my love. It's tedious. And seductive at the same time. It comes from knowing each other so well. Doesn't your ex-husband still come home late? What do you mean by 'still'? You were at our place only three days ago, Mother. Didn't he come home late? I'll ask, I said yet again. Ask. Mother. Ask me all those questions I dare not even ask myself. Isn't that what motherhood is all about?

Don't let him go, calls out Jenny from behind me. I'm fast asleep. Building up strength. Lots of peach-scented shower gel. Creams. Lay it on thick. My hair. My hands tremble as I dress. I pour a whiskey. In this heat. The streets are burning hot. I sit cross-legged on the sofa. Ice cubes. Ice cubes jingle in the glass. Soon the doorbell will ring. What will he be like? Music. Tango. Always the same tango. What if he's not like my husband? What if he has a beard. Green eyes. Brown hair. Or what if he is like him? Dark eyes. Broad-shouldered. Black hair.

My body feels weighed down by my thoughts. You're so beautiful, he said to me. I've been in love with you ever since I first saw you. Where did you first see me? On the bench, in the mosque garden. Next to the coffin rest. Your hair had fallen across your face. A book in your hand. But you weren't looking at the book. You were staring at the opposite shore. What made you fall in love with me? A feeling. A feeling that it wasn't really possible to touch you. It's true. I now know that, even if we make love for a lifetime, it's something that will never change. I couldn't be touched. You didn't even let me near you. You're never going to let me in. How do you do that? What? Do you take pleasure in creating that wall around you? He traces round my mouth with his finger. My heart races. This isn't lovemaking, he says. It's adoration. It's me imploring you to take me. Making love with you isn't a two-way thing. It's all about you. Your wishes, your desires. Me? How do you do it? What? You crush me, and then bring me to life with a single touch. That's what love is. Coming up against a wall again and again, and never giving up. Each time, complaining that the other person hasn't yielded completely. Knowing you haven't fully possessed that person. That's love. Hazel eyes. The sun's setting. Time to go. I was here once before. Before I met you. At this house. Bayan Naciye's daughter, Semiha. He shakes his head sadly. People die... We're living. Go now. When shall I come? I'll send for you. Am I really going to send for him? At that moment, I don't know. How are you going to send for me? How? Sit on the bench and I'll see you. Any day you want to see me, sit on the bench. Fine. I'll sit on the bench. By the coffin rest.

When he leaves, I go into the shower again. I use peach-scented shampoo to wash away the smell of the man from the Bosphorus. *Life is a trade-off,* says Jenny. *You can't have it all. Oh yes, I can. And I will, Jenny darling. I will.* My ex-husband won't come tonight. If he hasn't arrived by now... It's past eleven o'clock. I search the apartment for Mother's cigarettes. None. Not a single cigarette. I go to the corner shop. On the way, I make a decision. I'll call. Let him come. We'll talk. Or we'll make love without talking at all. Just the words uttered during lovemaking. Groans. Cries. Let them come forth from our lips. Aren't you coming home? I'm working. His voice is ice cold. I realize you're working. I'm asking whether or not you're coming home. Do you want me to come? He softens. I do want it. I want you. Fine, then I'll come.

I even put on a little makeup. My hair is still damp. I pour myself another whiskey on the rocks. For my father. Tomorrow is visiting day.

Once a week. We never talk. I always take a book. I read him a short story. When we're tired of our silence. One of my favorites. A longish one. To fill the time. So that I can spend more time with him. His liver is ruined, say the doctors. The specialists. They show me pictures in thick, hard-bound books. Pictures of ruined livers. The liver is able to repair itself faster than any other organ, they say. Why, then? It's too late. He was in the hospital before… Nobody told us it was so serious. Nobody told me my father would die one day. Oh, FATHER. Your liver is ruined, and so is my heart. Did we ever love each other? Miss each other? A baby cries. The windows of a house are open. You can't bear crying babies. I can't work because of you! You worked so hard, Father. You drank so much. You were very young. Did you love Mother? As much as she loved you…? Did you love and hide it as much as she did? Your cheeks are hollow. You have a few days' growth. A barber comes to your room. How often, did they say? Every two days. Three. The veins on your hands stand out. You had such lovely hands, Father. I should have been a pianist instead of an engineer, you used to say. We didn't grow up with private lessons like you. We didn't go to private schools. In the melon fields… at Alaçatı. Father! You're dying in front of my very eyes. There is no village beyond death, you used to tell me. If ever there was some difficulty in my life. In your life. In your room at the university. When I came to talk to you. When I told you I was going to divorce my husband. You stood in front of the window so as not to look at my face. Your back was turned towards me. Have you told your mother? I have. She knows. Fine then, you said. I'll give you whatever financial support you need. That's all you said. Don't worry about that side of things. I'm not, Father. I don't worry about that at all. Do you make any money from translating those books? Well, enough to get by on. Do you have a lawyer? Shall I call up Refik? No, don't call him, Father. I have a lawyer. Bennu. What about the property? Have you discussed that? What property, Father? There isn't any property. That's better then. There'll be no problems when you divorce. There aren't any children. That's good. Fine. Didn't you realize how terrified I was, Father? When I got up to go, when I held out my hand to you. That was the only time. You looked at me like a child in a melon field. You pulled me towards you and kissed me. Tell me, did you ever love me? You have no idea. Father. You don't talk. You don't have the answers to my questions. In my heart. Your liver and my heart are destroyed, Father.

A key turning in the lock to the door of your heart. Click. I hear your voice from the terrace. A silent night. The baby's not crying now. Maybe they closed the window. Forget about those old loves now. They took up nine years of our lives. Your ex-wife. Murat. Forget about the future loves too. That is, if there's anyone worthwhile out there. Forget about the man from the Bosphorus. Come to me. Stand behind me and put your arms around my waist. Let it be as it was before. As it was right at the start. Be nineteen again, you say. Let's walk through the streets spreading love. Hand in hand. My heart is yours. Your heart is mine. A poem. From Nazim Hikmet. I'm kissing another man. My eyes are on you. I lean against the terrace wall, naked from the waist down. You smell my arms, my hair. That beautiful smell of the sea, you say. It's lovely. No, it's the smell of peaches. I exchanged the smell of the sea for the smell of peaches before you came. No, this is a wonderful smell of the sea. Is it a new perfume? Don't change it, ever. You must always smell of the sea. Remind me of the heat between your legs. The depths into which we glide. Lovemaking in the sea. The beaches of the Adriatic. Remind me. The nights when you came out of the sea naked and freezing. The nights when you pressed your cold skin against mine. Remind me. I love you.

The beans said you loved me. Green. Is green the color of love?

Let's go on vacation. Right away, tomorrow. In the morning. Where do you want to go? To Alaçatı. To the melon fields. From there to Skopje. To where my grandmother was born. We'll go wherever you want to go. His lips are on my neck. The nape of my neck. His hand, on my thigh. Let's make a baby. His name will be Deniz and his mother will smell of the sea. I touch the faint outline of his tattoo. A mermaid. It used to have a red and green tail. Before. Now it's just a colorless hint of a mermaid. My ex-husband, why am I unable to give you up? Unable to forget you? Love. He says. It will be happen along the shores of the Bosphorus. In Bayan Naciye's house.

I cannot hear his last sentence. His voice is already stifled on my lips.

A Brief Sadness

Erendiz Atasü

Translated by İdil Aydoğan

The slope near the Anatolian Castle met the Bosphorus with a steep drop. Dense vegetation softened the hard rock. In early May, the hillside was covered with redbuds and all shades of green. Silence. The sound of twittering birds did not disturb the silence, but rather deepened the serenity, just like a string of pearls would emphasize the simplicity of a plain dress. A murmur in the background of silence. The uniform mumble consisting of hundreds of sounds of the giant machine that crushed human beings… Distant and harmless for now. The redbuds couldn't care less for the ferocity of the metropolis. The woman touched the pearls around her neck. *Nor do I*, she thought. *But it is always there, never to disappear; it will remain when the branches of the redbuds are naked.* And when the woman would be far away. Exhaust fumes, gases that hills of garbage spewed out, drowning out the noises of humans, the whimpering of the sick, the sobs of the abandoned… Who ever hears the cries of a starving baby or the sighs of those with no future?

I don't either, the woman thought. Her hand still placed on her pearls, *am I too dressed up*, she wondered. After all it was just a garden café. She enjoyed taking special care of how she looked for any occasion. Didn't this mean she cared for both herself and the person she was meeting?

Her daughter paid no attention to things like this. She had pulled her jeans on and slipped on her espadrilles; her messy hair was tactlessly tied up in what was supposedly a ponytail, her face without makeup. *This suits her too,* she thought. She wanted to touch her child, she shied away.

Clink, clink, clink... Her daughter mixed the sugar in her tea. The sound of the spoon hitting the tulip-shaped glass had lasted too long; clink, clink, clink... *She's tired of me,* the woman said to herself. She remembered her own youth. She too would grow weary of her own mother expecting attention.

"I wanted to show you this place," she said to her daughter, "one of the rare spots that witnessed the Istanbul before it expanded so drastically."

"It's very nice," said the young woman, "it really is, very relaxing." For a moment, she moved her hand away from the spoon, shut her eyes and listened to the silence.

Clink, clink... She had begun stirring her tea again. It seemed as if the silence was being sliced into two with a knife.

"I'm glad you like it," her mother said, still playing with her necklace. The young woman knew this hand gesture and this attitude, which were her mother's habit since her daughter was a child. If her mother wanted to say something important, or rather, something she believed to be important, first she'd dress up, then she'd take you to a nice place, and while she struggled to open the topic, she'd play with the dangling bits of her clothing. What was the point in all this pretense, all this ceremoniousness!

"What is it you want to talk to me about?" the young woman asked unreservedly.

Just like that, out of the blue, said the mother to herself, *she's always in a hurry.*

"Nothing. I just wanted us to enjoy this beauty together."

"What do you mean, nothing! Is that why we've come all this way!"

"Yes, I wanted you to see the places where I spent my childhood once again."

"Mother dearest, I already know all this. The house in the side street to the castle, the Kandilli Girls' School, the captain that was in love with you, you know, the one who sounded the boat whistle as a greeting."

The mother smiled; she mustn't reveal she was hurt. Or was she really? It seemed she had learned to take less heed of her daughter in these last years. Motherhood was something akin to servitude; it made one forget the very notion of pride.

"I am not about to tell you any of those stories, I just wanted you to share with me this view worth a lifetime."

Her daughter gave her an empty stare.

"Alright, let's go ahead and share it then," she said.

The mother had shut her eyes and was relishing the breeze stroking her skin. It seemed there really was nothing to say… She was too tired to tolerate hesitant answers, ruthless questionings. Besides, there wasn't enough time left, enough time to quarrel.

Her daughter suddenly became worried, the clink, clink stopped. But the divided silence couldn't be mended, an invisible cut carving its way deeper under serenity.

"You're not ill or anything, are you?"

The mother managed to smile.

"No."

"Okay," said the young woman. She seemed relieved.

That is the only piece of compassion you will receive today, the mother said to herself, and smiled with forbearance. *Is her concern really for my health, or is it merely the fear of having to fit the burden of my illness into her busy life already crammed as full as a storeroom?* Reason pointed to the second option. The mother silenced reason.

Her daughter worked too hard, her son-in-law worked too hard. All young people worked too hard; to make a certain group of invisible people wealthier. They didn't know what they were working for. They thought they were working for a 'good' life. 'Good' meant 'prosperous' in their vocabulary. The gaps in meaning between words had been erased in their fast lives. In reality, they weren't working for a more prosperous life, in reality... Their lives seemed as smooth and clear as a straight line drawn with a ruler, but this line was nothing but a tightrope: below was an abyss no one was quite sure about. And all efforts rolled into that horrifying void, the void that made the future obscure; holding onto a tight, narrow life, tooth and nail...

Yes, yes, it would be best to explain the situation after she had left, with a short letter or phone call. That would be easier. No one need be so distressed.

The woman liked continuous moments, moments when the invisible membranes splitting time into factitious segments dissolved and life reached the infinite. Like the redbud woods that reached the Bosphorus and from there the wide horizon of the Black Sea... Like aged elephants retiring to a quiet corner of the droning jungle to die, what the elderly needed to do was retreat from this cramped city. Far, far away from the propellers that thought they were dancing joyfully, attracted by the mountain of light surrounding skyscrapers... As the time the woman had ahead of her had shortened, it had simultaneously expanded and become lucid. Her gaze had become deeper. She could see: the artificial mountains were an illusion of light. In reality, only bulldozers existed; and it was all a death dance that spiraled around them...

A small town on the Aegean coast. A nursing home, not deprived of compassion. Welcoming continuous time alone, without helplessly expecting crumbs of attention from your nearest and dearest... Life took away everything from you, except for your honor. She had been withdrawing from her close ones for a long time now; getting tangled in the twister formed by the woods, the slope and the sea together, as if being sucked in by a vortex... She was no longer hurt, she was no longer offended. There was no time for any of this... All that existed was the silence of nature. Yes, it was best to tell her after she had left.

With a sudden movement the old woman took off the pearl necklace she was wearing and put it around her daughter's neck. The young woman was surprised.

"I want you to have this, as a gift. It will look prettier on you."

"But why?"

Her daughter was truly surprised. Resting on her shabby T-shirt, the pearl necklace looked borrowed.

"But you really like this."

"So, I want to give the necklace I really like to my daughter I love more than anything in this world. What's wrong with that?"

"But why?"

Her daughter had become hesitant again. The hole carved in serenity had seemed as if it had been filled for a minute, but it hadn't. "Are you not well?" she was about to ask, but she fell silent. She'd already asked that a while ago. Perhaps she was afraid of hearing a possible 'yes'.

The mother smiled. The poor thing couldn't think of anything else to say besides "But why?"! How she'd chatter away as a child... In her fast life, she had shot up high in the sky like a jet and dropped her words; and since she hadn't had time to stop, kneel down and pick them up, she had left her words to scatter like the pearls of a broken necklace...

"Take good care of it," said the mother, pointing to the necklace, "a keepsake handed down from me to you, don't let it fall apart."

"Oh, Mom, quit the moving speech."

Her daughter's ill temper was a sign that she had been touched. For a moment, the woman was sad she had made her daughter sad; but then she decided not to be. As soon as she was back at work, her daughter would forget this brief sadness; in fact, perhaps even before that… before parting from the view of the redbud slope.

Break of Dawn in Tarlabaşı
(The World's State of Exile)

Sevinç Çokum

Translated by Mark Wyers

With my thin, narrow shoulders, I began my first venture into unknown streets. That's how I grew accustomed to the scent of mold.
Whenever I arrived there, in the distance I would hear the fish mongers'
boisterous cries in the market. Like a fragmented song of the sea, pounding and striking the shore. A clamor of voices, all in unison. The crabs
would come to life and take to their feet, and the oysters would pry open
their shells ever so slightly and peer out. When the seller of sheep-head
soup on the corner would throw bloody sheep heads into the pot to boil,
their ponderous black eyes would stare out, human in their gaze, and
then the light would fade from their eyes.

Abandoned houses, and colorless, rusted-out walls. I don't know what
has become of the lives there, most of which were mired in poverty. Poor,
but warm-hearted. That's how the cards fall; a flicker and all is gone. Now,
in some of the windows of these run-down houses, queers look out onto
the street, resembling pantomimists.

Ednan, awaking at odd hours of the day, would pull on a loose silken
dressing gown which didn't conceal how truly thin he was. He would
wander about, his eyes which were accustomed to night heavy with languor.
His skin was suffused with the musty scent of the Grand London Hotel,

and Pianist Ednan would sometimes suddenly be ensnared. Ensnared, unable to escape. His underwear showed through the opening of his dressing gown. Sometimes he would open the door, by pulling a string that ran to the door latch.

—Sadiye Hanım, Sadiye Hanım (shouting upstairs), your brother is here! And I thought it was the milkman. Are you the youngest or the middle child? Your big sister Sadiye was going to bring me a kitten. She must have forgotten. Remind her when you see her…

I am falling in love with the pianist Ednan's ivory hands. I place him on a pedestal in my heart. I am the youngest. Sadiye Hanım's little sister.

Ednan's sheep-like eyes are so tender, humane. His face is sallow. Towards the break of dawn he would go out to smoke his last cigarette, under the streetlight. Utterly worn out. "Kiss of Fire" or some other song ringing in his ears. Sometimes Ednan stayed here in Tarlabaşı, at Kanite's place, before going home to his family in Bostanüstü, near the district of Beşiktaş. Kanite was always fussing about in her transparent morning gown, trying to cover her breasts. Maybe her name was in fact Katina, but some country bumpkin, finding it easier to say Kanite called her that and it stuck, who knows? Or perhaps there was another Katina aside from Kanite? She would open the door with its broken stained glass panes, cursing, "What, are we busted?" But it was Ednan, returning from the London Grand Club. It was a matter of graciousness to call him Ednan rather than Adnan, his real name.

Just as the morning call to prayer echoed out, Pianist Ednan with his red kerchief and hands in his pockets would pass down the slope of our street, the soot and peals of laughter from the London Club clinging to his clothes. Throughout the day the soot and peals would linger and at night add layer upon layer. He was a prisoner: a prisoner of the London Club. Kanite's prisoner. A prisoner of the night. There was this paranoid thug who was obsessed with Kanite. Whenever he showed up, cursing and shouting was sure to follow.

Feeding her children bowl upon bowl of soup made from the broth of boiled sheep heads, Ulviye Hanım managed to get all of them into university. Some nights after her sons had gone to bed, when she felt she was alone with God, Ulviye Hanım would weep on her prayer rug. Her rug would become sodden, and then dry out. She was separated from her husband. Her heart was an internal sea, at low tide. She was wracked by a thousand woes; she had three sons to raise. Forty years later, her oldest son, an architect, would commit suicide for no reason at all. No, there was a reason. He saw much of what we could not see. From within a dark swathe of grief. He saw the truth, while we were living in a fairy tale.

In those days, our diet was bereft of protein; I would visit frequently. Ulviye Hanım would cook green beans in a huge pot. We would chat and carefully prepare the tomato salad with onions. Dip our bread in the sauce. The chickpeas were the same way. Searching for bits of meat among the chickpeas. After the meal, searching for a sliver of fruit, a half-eaten apple. Ulviye Hanım was going sell tickets for the ball at Kervansaray and get her cut.

The room I entered was like the ruins of a palace. The doorway and window were arched, the cracked windowpanes covered over with packaging paper. There was a full-length mirror, the frame engraved with roses, in Ulviye Hanım's slightly chilly back room. People would make love there. In that mirror, a man and a woman would intertwine their limbs; standing, they would fall into each other, and pass into the mirror. Nobody saw them. They disappeared into the mirror and then the mirror broke.

The drawings of the architect who had decided to commit suicide… Later, he would in fact commit suicide. Forty years later. Saying, "What is there to live for?"

—What is there to live for?

—Don't talk that way.

—But that's how it is. Maybe for you... But for me? I cannot get over my mother's death. (Ulviye Hanım's death from cancer. She had said, "Even my last wisps of hair have given in to the cancer." Remembering her hair that her husband had rent from her scalp.)

—Everybody's mother can die.

—True, but I cannot accept it. I want something to make this easier, the architect said. I want to reach a point, a place that will make it easier for death to become real. Show me the way. Show me the way to my death.

This must be a joke. Is death such a laughing matter?

No. He doesn't say it, but his eyes do. In his eyes, I see the horror of life as if it were the dark mouth of a cave. I think of Ednan's hands. Some take life with their touch, and some give life. Is this life on earth merely a joke played by God?

From here, I pass the old hotels on the way to Tepebaşı, my raincoat misted with rain. Taking the small ferries on the Golden Horn on the way to my aunt and uncle's, blowing into the mouth of the clay Eyüp jug like a whistle. Boxes of sweets and *lokum*. Bridges pungent with the exhaust of the ferries. My uncle would write his poems that had neither beginning nor end while gazing upon the waters of the Golden Horn. With the noise of the shipyards, the workers and foremen calling out to each other, the sound of the beating wings of seagulls and pigeons in his ears, thinking of Sabite. The water made him write. Like a mother, teaching her mother tongue.

Some evenings I open those majestic doors and see Ulviye Hanım cooking green beans in an enormous aluminum pot. The boys upstairs,

Ulviye Hanım's sons, strut about heatedly, engorged with testosterone to the bursting point. They are ready to break up fights, to put out fires, to die for the sake of the women they have fallen for, to kill for them.

The piano in Kanite's hall is a remnant of the old vaudeville days, the festive days of yore. Before she was killed by that drunk paranoid thug who obsessed over her. But after she died she would still come and visit once in a while. A material presence. Ulviye Hanım would say, "Kanite comes in the evenings. She wanders around, and leaves; it's no harm to anyone."

The architect works on his drawings until morning; the tracing paper spread over his desk, bags under his eyes, energy pills, the rancorous hate for a distant father. We are becoming modern. The children may not be getting enough protein, but they sure know their math. They have to know. They know love, too, and loyalty.

All along the length of the wall of the British embassy there are prostitutes, taxi drivers, shoe shiners and cats who scrawl on the walls. On the other side of the wall, a different type of people. The English, who are never seen. The English, never seen but existing. But Kanite Hanım's legs were always wide apart. Just like how cavalry rider's walk, that's how she walked. Ulviye Hanım would tell the neighbors when she made her rounds selling tickets for the Justice Party ball about why Kanite's legs were bowed. Because she slept with so many men. Kanite's voice took on a male huskiness when one of her ovaries was removed. "It was rotten," she said of the ovary. Two odd beings, her and her spayed cat. You know how it is, how cats become human once they are spayed.

Was Ednan forgotten? With those beautiful Lizst fingers, playing Chopin's "Second Piano Concerto" and Beethoven's "Moonlight Sonata" on the piano in Kanite's hall. You know how he transformed the streets of Tarlabaşı into Polish nights, Warsaw boulevards. Sometimes he played

Tatyos Efendi's "Kürdili Hicazkâr Saz Semaisi". That's when Istanbul's true velvet curtain would rise. The men who lived on the top floor of Kanite's apartment were always wearing swimming trunks. Ulviye Hanım's sons. They wore latex swim trunks and ambled about, their bodies triangular, dark-skinned. Peonies, the last remains of the garden... Dark, cavernous streets. Ulviye Hanım's cancerous bed. Her way of becoming distant and hiding from view, and becoming a stranger to us as death drew near. Our estrangement. The world's state of exile.

The peonies outside the window. The extinct, dark pink flowers and beyond those, a city of ruins: the umbrella seller Mordo's Yüksek Kaldırım Street and Galata. Black and squalid, the Galata Tower, never wearying of its darkness and filth. Its sagacious ascent; ancient, reclusive tower. Traces that say, "Give me the experience of life!"—footprints, shards of glass.

What happened to your hair, Auntie Ulviye Hanım, your fiery auburn hair? "Eat green beans and grow strong," she would say, favoring my plate over the others'. Or she would, without asking, take a pear from one of the ferociously hungry children, and pass it to me.

I smoke in the latrine. There is no toilet proper; just a ceramic hole, a relic of the past. Before the young men of the house moved upstairs, a singer lived there; she was like a wilted peony. In her later days, she would sing her song, "Is This What I Was to Become?" But the stage was hers. She was blonde in a way that was different from everyone else. Before I came into this world, she acted in an Anatolian film which resembled nothing of Anatolia. Then she became a city woman. All she had left in the end was a bundle of belongings. A patchwork bundle of a life.

She related bits and pieces of her life. "I was never anyone's slave," she said, as she reclined on the mattress on the floor. Coming home drunk at night, she would stumble on every step. She had scars on her face, arms and knees. "I may have lost everything, but I still have my pride."

My hunchbacked cars, my long-winged cars. I could see the rear garden from the bathroom, and the peonies, mementoes of Kanite Hanım. It was as if they were made from paper, fold upon fold of deep pink. They were nothing like her misdeeds. I could see the city beyond the peonies. They stretched toward the Golden Horn.

Looking at the columns and sculptures on the façade of the Grand London Hotel, Ednan smokes a cigarette. With its ivory hue, the hotel is like a country founded unto itself. You turn the corner, and it continues on with its dark and dusty windows. Ednan dreams of hoisting one of the sculptures onto his shoulder and taking it home. In her masculine voice, Kanite shoos dogs away, as they are the enemy of cats, and she hurls curses at her paranoid lover on those evenings when he comes breaking down the doors.

In darkness, Ulviye prays on her prayer rug, which smells of the countryside. Her husband comes and goes like a stranger, swearing at his sons who amble about in their latex swimsuits; the entirety of darkness relinquishes its light, a loaf of bread under his arm to make peace with Ulviye, a few pounds of bananas or oranges. The crabs come alive, and at one point in the night, those sheep eyes, the eyes of a sheep, peer open and weep—it is a vile world that they see, and they pity humankind, but not themselves.

Two people who have separated can never really come back together; Ulviye, and her ex-husband. Rent collected from the ramshackle houses of Beyoğlu, the weary breathing of drunks and singers, their coughs congealed as tar; the soiled handrails of stairs, the dark windows bearing nothing inside—where is my magnolia, my women in magnolia skirts…

Today I saw Ednan's dressing gown at the flea market. A tuxedo, a fedora hat and the dressing gown. It gleamed, with its honeycomb pattern.

Didn't Ednan used to smoke his last cigarette under the streetlight? Is Ednan dead? What is left of Ednan? A cloud of dust.

In the days when we went to the Tepebaşı Club to see the woman that my uncle had fallen in love with, he was married and a father of three. As the voice of this woman who he loved, and for a while was seeing, rose up towards the Golden Horn… Ah those songs—Sabite, wearing a petticoat that a girl about to marry would wear, had not become famous yet; that love happened before my uncle was sent to the dungeons of Camialtı for reading *Marko Paşa*, the newspaper that dared critique the government.

Kanite came that night. She wandered around the house, her steps resounding on the floor. The floor was wood and in some places creaked like the rasping of teeth.

—Did you hear that? I said quietly to my sister. Somebody is walking around. Don't you think it must be Ulviye Hanım?

—No, it's not! It's Kanite. Don't open your eyes! She will go away soon.

I held my breath. What is her face like? A toothless mouth and blind sockets for eyes? What should I do?

—Don't move, my sister whispered.

We were under a bedcover, a thick cotton blanket encased in blue satin. Where had Kanite, killed by her lover, come from? I felt a moist wind, perhaps a breeze scented with briar soil, blow through the room. She approached and straightened the blanket over our feet. Then I felt her breath on my face. Halfway between bay leaves and rosemary. I blinked ever so slightly and peered open my eyes. She was wearing a broad-necked nightgown. Her hair was disheveled. I could not make out her face, but perhaps she did not have one. It was as if she had wafted the smoke of incense over us with a silver thurible in her hand. Her movements were quite methodical; she closed the window. She straightened the lace curtains, which were always in a tangle, and everything was put in order. Ednan's song "Kisas Kisas" was a whistle, skipping across the street.

Kanite would tell Halil Bey, the health official, about her ex-lover: "One day he is going to kill me." "You should have seen her when he was seventeen," the health official would say. "Kanite couldn't even pass through Beyoğlu. She was that beautiful."

The health official Halil Bey, who the Greeks called Halilâki, was one of the old sergeants; with a durable, black leather case, a fedora hat and a fur-lined topcoat, he would set off at five in the morning for his rounds, which took him to every corner of the district of Beyoğlu. He would punctually do his rounds, giving booster injections of Phosfostim, Calcibronate or Calcium-Sandoz for the French, Italian and English embassy gentry.

The injections he gave to the wives of the officers, who usually lay naked under the bedsheets, had long become habit. The wives would be asleep at those hours. Halilâki would, without eliciting a sound from them, sweep the sheets from their bodies in a single swipe, and with a glance and a touch he would quickly find the needle's destination on the women's ivory white posteriors, leaving them to drift back to sleep. Years ago he had become indifferent to the naked bodies of these women.

"For me, full-body ablutions for prayer are pointless; every day I see tens of legs, butts and sexual parts: which should be considered? What's the point, they haven't tempted me to the devil." If the patients were Turkish or Greek and still asleep at nine or ten in the morning, he would chide them: "The whole lot of you snooze like those rich wives of Kadıköy."

After the rich wives, it was Kanite's turn. In those days she was being treated for a gynecological affliction. Halilâki knew her heart, and it was only with her that he would drink coffee during work hours. Coffee with plenty of sugar, in a violet cup. It was different when Kanite, with her hazel eyes, said "Halilâki."

Ulviye Hanım's unhappiness was written on her face, line by line. When her eyes were lowered to the floor, something was extinguished. It was as if a novelist from her hometown had written the story of her life. She was a girl from the south who had been married off early. Weren't there any happy memories? She wanted to separate the beautiful parts of her life into a bundle. But there were so few.

This was a different face of Istanbul. I am polishing an old, musty mirror. Ulviye is gone, as well as the architect, Kanite and Ednan. Not one, nobody is left. Recently, somebody even made off with the iron door of the house, with its upper panes of glass.

Mi Hatice

Gaye Boralıoğlu

Translated by Jonathan Ross

Today she got to the station a bit earlier than usual, having finished her work in good time. As always, Hatice started to wait for her husband at one end of Sirkeci Station, in front of the lockers, where the air was thick with the wafting smell of boiling hot dogs. She waited as she had done yesterday, the day before, and the day before that. As she had done on days too numerous to remember.

When the *müezzin* sounded the call to afternoon prayer, Hatice's hand instinctively reached up to her headscarf and with a well-practiced maneuver, she tightened the knot under her neck with just one hand. Then she bowed her head and waited. As she looked towards the ground, her eyes fell on her toes, which were poking out from the front of her sandals. Her thin stocking had laddered next to her big toe. She drew her feet back inside her sandals. Not that she needed to; no one had noticed the ladder.

Hatice's mind was fixed on the call to prayer. She was doing her utmost to work out what the *hodja* was chanting. But it was no good. She actually knew the *ezan* by heart, having learned it as a child, but that was no use to her now. She just couldn't catch the words. Perhaps, she thought, this was because the words were meaningless; but then she was horrified that she could even think this. As if the words of Allah could be meaningless! The problem was that these words were in another language, a language that Hatice didn't understand. And yet the meaning was the same regardless of the language, so Hatice could have felt it in her heart had she wanted to. Wasn't that what her grandpa had always said? That even if you didn't understand, you'd be able to feel it in your heart. For Hatice to feel the meaning in her soul, she needed to be seized by the ezan, as if it were a huge, cloud-shaped hand, and lifted up and up, far above all those people rushing around, yelling their heads off, above the minarets, buildings and satellite dishes, above the smell of hot dogs. The smell of hot dogs. But this didn't happen. Hatice had sincerely hoped that she would be able to go beyond the words and be carried away by the ezan's sublime melody, yet her hopes were in vain. The ezan simply brushed past her and was gone, leaving even less of an impact than the smell of hot dogs.

At this moment, Hatice had a strange feeling of being abandoned. This didn't upset her though; on the contrary, it relieved her somewhat, making her feel as if the burden she was carrying had become a little lighter. Yet all these feelings in turn disturbed Hatice, and she did what she always did in such circumstances: she started to think of her grandpa. He was a giant of a man, with thick bones and a harsh demeanor. When he took Hatice to school, he would walk along speechless, an anxious look on his face, all the while clasping Hatice's tiny hand and pressing it against his chest, as if he were determined to protect her from a danger that might suddenly spring up. In fact, Hatice adored that perturbed expression, preferring it even to her grandpa's smile. She would complain to him that her arm was aching and ask him to let go of her hand, but he would take no notice and walk her right up to the gate of the primary school and wait there until she had vanished from sight. When the bell rang for home time, Hatice would be one of the first pupils to appear at the door. Scanning the playground with lightning speed, she would be sure to spot her grandpa somewhere or other. He never disappointed her. Even so, whenever the time for the bell approached, Hatice would be seized by a pang of anxiety, which would only abate once she had spotted her grandpa, rushed outside, and planted her hand in his immense palm. Hatice shut her eyes for a second or two, attempting to recapture that instant in all its detail. When she opened her eyes, it was Sacit she found standing in front of her. For a moment, she contemplated smiling and suspected that she did actually do so. In reality though, her face remained motionless. Sacit, for his part, didn't smile at Hatice either.

Having noticed Sacit, Hatice became aware that there were hundreds of other people in the station too: people with sweaty faces, bowed shoulders, piercing glances, white hair, high heels, double-breasted jackets, briefcases, garment bags, slit skirts, caps, hands gripping plastic bags and feet almost too tired to move. Feet. Sacit had already walked off, and Hatice quickened her pace to keep up with him. Without saying a word, they bought their tickets and proceeded to walk quickly along platform three. They passed by half-empty compartments, but even when there were seats available they didn't enter the train to make use of them. By accident, a man in the platform throng trod on Hatice's sandal, and she stumbled. Everyone in the crowd continued pushing forwards, however, as if nothing had happened. The whistle blew, and Sacit stepped into the final carriage, Hatice right behind him. The train pulled away.

Now Hatice and Sacit were sitting next to each other by the window, facing the rear of the train. Hatice couldn't stand travelling like this, forced to watch the world fade into the distance. She felt queasy. As the train jolted along the rails, Sacit and Hatice jiggled here and there, and their wobbling knees came to touch. Yet neither of them noticed this. Nor did any of the passengers in the carriage. Mosques, palaces and seagulls were left ever further behind as the train headed away from the center, rattling calmly as it went.

The first station it stopped at was Cankurtaran, where no one got off. Some passengers did get on, and the carriage became extremely crowded. It was hot. Droplets of sweat accumulated underneath Hatice's headscarf. Just when the train was leaving Cankurtaran, Hatice noticed an odd smell. For days, weeks and years this journey had followed the same pattern, but this time, today, there was an entirely unfamiliar smell. Hatice tried to open the window next to her. With all her strength she pulled the handles, but the dust that had built up over the last century made it impossible for her to open the window. She looked at Sacit. His half-open eyes were fixed on a certain point and he had allowed his body to be swayed however the rocking train saw fit. Hatice looked around for someone else who could help her open the window. It was clear, though, that no one else was bothered by the smell. Perhaps she was the only person to notice it. When she stood up to open the window, her eyes met those of another passenger: a woman around the same age as her who was ogling Hatice's place with eyes that said, 'If you're not going to sit, get out of the way 'cause I will.' Hatice gave up on the window and sat down again. It was not long before she had forgotten about the smell and turned all her attention to her hands. Hatice's hands didn't look like those of a cleaner. She had long fingers, with nails that were short but in good condition. The smoothness of her skin revealed that she was actually very young. Hatice's eyes homed in on the hands of the girl sitting right opposite her. One of them was resting limply on her knee, the other nestled between the palms of the young man by her side. Hatice started to think about whether or not she'd held hands with Sacit.

She couldn't remember ever doing so. Then her eyes shifted once more to her own hands. With these hands she longed to cuddle her grandpa, just as she longed to cling to his trousers, to cry out, 'Don't leave me, Grandpa, please don't leave me.' She balled her hands into fists, which she held against her chest. She gulped. And when she gulped, her throat hurt.

The train suddenly jolted, bringing Hatice back to her senses. For no particular reason, the train had come to a standstill somewhere between Yenikapı and Kocamustafapaşa. There was no station in sight and no another train, and nothing out of the ordinary appeared to be happening. As the train slowed down, so too did the wind. It became uncomfortably hot in the carriage. Nobody asked what the matter was. Although Sacit was sighing deeply, he too didn't bring himself to open his mouth and say something. Hatice also remained silent. The only people to do anything were a couple of youngsters who forced open the door they were standing next to, stuck their heads out and waited. Despite the stifling heat, the lack of a breeze and the intense body odor emanating from Sacit, Hatice was happy not to be moving. Being stationary and no longer having to travel facing the wrong direction meant that she didn't feel so queasy anymore. Her eyes roamed over the carriage's dilapidated lighting fixtures, over its dirty green walls. The carriage itself was sweating; from underneath the windows and from the gaps between the ceiling panels oozed beads of dusty grey sweat. A few times it seemed as if the train was contemplating moving again but then gave up on the idea, leaving the passengers to be jogged to and fro in accordance with the train's game. Meanwhile, the beads of sweat seeping from the walls changed their direction. Fifteen minutes later, the train set off again, as inexplicably as it had stopped, and moved along with its familiar rhythm.

By the time they had arrived at Kocamustafapaşa, Sacit had fallen asleep. Hatice took a sideways glance at his face. His cheeks were flushed and drooping and a small gap had opened up between his lips. It looked as if his eyes were not completely shut, but Hatice was still sure that he was sleeping. After all, Sacit had been oblivious to the man selling lemon squeezers for a lira who had got on at Kocamustafapaşa, to the youngster hawking stuffed toy puppets who came on at Yedikule, and to the comb-selling girl who joined the train at Zeytinburnu. With each station they reached, Sacit's snoring got a little louder. By the time they got to Yenimahalle, he could no longer keep his head upright. It was swinging from right to left at a far more rigorous pace than that of the train. His legs were spread wide and his arms had flopped down by his sides. From the corner of her eye, Hatice glanced at the sweat dripping down his arms. She was embarrassed of him. I'm glad we didn't talk, she thought to herself. No one would have realized that they were husband and wife or suspected that they even knew each other.

Hatice remembered her first journey on this train. She had got on at Menekşe. At the time, she and her family had been living with her grandpa in a ground floor apartment near Highlife Beach. Hatice started thinking about the smells of her childhood: the smell of moss, sand and pebbles, the sweet fragrance of honeysuckle, the smell of a tabby cat, a blonde baby, and those small flip-flops with frayed edges. After her grandpa had died and she had married Sacit, they moved to shabby Halkalı, and from then on it was Sirkeci to Halkalı, Halkalı to Sirkeci, every single day. The intervening stations Hatice had only ever seen out of the window of a train.

After Kocamustafapaşa, the number of people getting on decreased, while the number leaving the train rose. Hatice started to imagine what kind of sound would emerge if each of these passengers were a single musical note. It would be chaotic and noisy to begin with; then the notes would exchange places, and after that the individual sounds would fade away: an ever-diminishing melody.

So what kind of note would Hatice be? And Sacit? When Hatice was in her fifth year at primary school, her grandpa had bought her a flute. With his huge hands, he had had no difficulty covering the holes in the flute, and when he puffed up his cheeks and blew into the flute you could hear the pleasant sound of the notes being played in succession. Try as she might, Hatice couldn't quite manage to position her tiny fingers over the holes and thus avoid producing rasping sounds. Patiently and carefully, the old man showed Hatice what to do, repeating himself over and over. When Hatice became inseparable from the flute, taking it wherever she went, the instrument got used to her small fingers. 'Do re mi'. Just before her grandpa died, Hatice had reached the position where she was finally able to produce the right sounds. The only one she always had problems with, for some reason or other, was 'mi'. Once more, Hatice thought about the notes of the flute, about herself and Sacit. She likened Sacit to 'do'—solid, powerful and loud, with all the fingers clasped tightly. Herself she compared to 'mi'—always rasping, hesitant and insecure, incapable of coming out flawless.

At Bakırköy, most of the notes left the train. The couple sitting across from Hatice also got off. Now there were few enough people in the carriage to be able to count them. No one was standing and there were a lot of empty seats. Just as the train was heading for Yeşilyurt, Sacit's body began to shake bizarrely, out of step with the rhythm of the train, a note that had been sounded incorrectly. From his throat came a strange rattle, and at the same time he clung to Hatice's leg. Hatice's heart began to pound. She glanced around her. There was hardly anyone left who could see them. Because they had chosen to sit at the very end of the carriage, there were just a few seats opposite theirs, and these had been vacated at Bakırköy in any case. The rest of the passengers were at the other end, minding their own business; no one was interested in Hatice and Sacit. Sacit's fingers were squeezing Hatice's knee with all their might. His face had turned deep purple. Hatice was dumbfounded. She just sat there without blinking, budging an inch or saying a word. The train stopped at Florya. Again, some people got off and others got on. Now Sacit was simply sitting there motionless. The train started moving yet another time, on its way out of the station. Sacit's head dropped backwards. He was not snoring anymore and neither did he smell. His grip on Hatice's knee had loosened. And that loosening gradually spread to Hatice's soul. All of a sudden, Hatice became a flawless, faultless 'mi' note. Soon she felt that she had become not just 'mi' but also 'ti', even 'fa' and 'so'. Within her, all the notes were having a ball, colliding for no purpose and with no sense of harmony in the passages of her mind. All that remained in her head was her own music, an impenetrable symphony in which there was no place for 'do'.

At Menekşe Station, Hatice stood up. As she rose, Sacit's hand flopped down to his side. No one noticed that Sacit was no longer breathing and would never again share his breath with the world, and no one saw Hatice getting off the train. As Hatice walked along the platform towards the exit, all the notes coalesced, forming a knot in her throat. Instinctively, she reached up to her throat. Undid that knot. The scarf on her head slid slowly down from her shoulders and cascaded to the floor. Leaving the scarf behind, she walked on calmly and vanished into the streets of Menekşe.

An-bul-ist

Karin Karakaşlı

*Translated by **Ruth Whitehouse***

They watch not the rose, but death
from the first day I knew, yet still I waited
they watch not the rose, but death
the rose is kin to death because in our poem
one gives the other blood and
death is greater, redder than the rose
it cannot be contained by any grave
death they watch, not the roses

—Turgut Uyar, *A Coincidence in Many a Death*[1]

When the archangel Michael entered her room, she felt his presence on her skin like a sudden breeze on a sticky Istanbul summer night. "What are you doing?" he asked. The voice of conscience was recognizable for its sincere interest in her reply and its seraphic quality. "I'm trying to write a story about Istanbul and women," said the young woman. There was no paper or pen to be seen. No computer screen or keyboard. She was just sitting there, holding a paperclip, which unwittingly she had straightened out into a length of wire. She kept poking this wire into

---

[1] *Birçok Ölüm İçin Rastlantı*

various little cracks and holes, creating small piles of dust in front of her. As if this was her most important task in life. As if all the words she had been unable to find were to be found in those particles of dust. The archangel was her only witness.

"Don't try so hard. Just start writing, and then the lines should flow like water," said the voice of conscience. Up to a certain point, sorrows are cried over. After that, one has to laugh. The woman laughed.

"I'm learning everything all over again," she said, "especially how to write."

Words would come together but hover without making sentences, or perch, refusing to coalesce into anything coherent. But coherence has always been a distant concept that cannot be found in words alone.

The archangel Michael was quiet. That voice of conscience, recognizable for its silence that said more than words and its seraphic quality, remained quiet. He just looked on.

The woman threw the paper clip and the piles of dust into the bin. She folded her arms in front of her and gently rocked back and forth. The things she was looking at had slid into a vacuum behind her, while all the things she wanted to hurl about stayed put in their place. She raised her head. "There are three lines on my forehead, lines that are waiting to be written. Those lines are new, like lines in a notebook. Yet there are piles of empty notebooks here. I've been waiting for the right time to start on them, but I don't write in any of them."

"Why? You're perfectly capable of writing on your own." The archangel Michael's words touched a nerve deep inside her, threw light on an insidiously painful spot as yet untouched by anyone.

"I'm never going to see him again," she said, her face crumpling with sorrow. She traced her fingers along the furrows on her forehead and down each side of her lips. She couldn't cry, yet the rims of her eyes were burning. So were the roots of her hair and eyebrows. She ran her hands through her hair, and a few strands remained in her palm.

"The person I most wanted to live has died. What's more, he didn't die, he was murdered." She took a breath, something she sometimes forgot to do. The sudden gasp for breath made her heart hurt. She heard the sentence she had just uttered as if it were someone else's voice, someone else's life, someone else's pain. She had been her own audience for so long. It was a situation, a reality that she was unable to comprehend. There was absolutely nothing she could do about it. And she thought she was creative. She found it impossible to describe things to other people if she hadn't understood them herself. This archangel was her only confidant. He kept rattling the huge key to her inner self.

"Terrible things happened on the day he was murdered. Like a far-fetched screenplay. I mean, if I wrote it down, people would say I'd made it up and it was all fiction. But it was true. Almost farcically, sickeningly true. For the first time ever, I realized that for certain things, words are simply inadequate and that life is five times more powerful than literature. My mind, heart and pen just stopped."

Archangel Michael smiled. "Then write that down and start from six.'"

Six

Who knows how many times I've passed over you,
Sung songs to you
One day your place will be my grave

—Turgut Uyar, *Monologues on Death* [2]

Alive or dead, he was still in that city, which had remained the same

---

[2] *Ölüme Dair Konuşmalar*

yet was somehow different. In that city which called itself Istanbul, the Istanbul that was watching itself disintegrate into different entities, like pieces of a kaleidoscope. The Istanbul that was, rather than an eternally living city, reminiscent of a theater set on which the same play is performed time and again.

If only someone had stopped time. But nobody did. Yet for one person, it stopped very suddenly. He'd become embroiled in that fatal sequence of moments, which he would have preferred to rewind and have no part in. That's all.

An Istanbul of indifferent people, all living in their own time once again. Measuring that time impatiently by their wristwatches. But her heart was living for the moment. The heart does not see a year as a collection of life experiences, but as a series of moments. Moments, eternal moments or momentary eternities, etched into scarred hearts. Winking at the sorrow of a person in the life of a city. For Istanbul, death is merely the grime on its hands. Palace intrigues; boiling oil poured from city walls; centuries of different types of torture developed in cold prison cells; lonely corpses putrefying on sofas; traffic casualties who, thinking they'll be home for dinner, end up under some vehicle; bombs that blow the world into smithereens and bullets that rain down on the world—Istanbul has seen it all and is fazed by nothing.

She wasn't as experienced as Istanbul and was shocked by the sight of the pavement. That pavement which is still there as if nothing had happened. Time and Istanbul flowed through her as she looked at a man gazing in a shop window next to the entrance of the apartment building. The feet of this total stranger were encroaching on her time, her Istanbul. "Why did he have to be just there?" she thought. But why not, it's only a pavement?

They had gathered up the candles, flowers, pomegranate seeds, photos and newspapers, because enough time had passed since the murder. Time, in its impatience, wanted everything cleaned up, things that kept pursuing it, never in harmony. When the candles, flowers, pomegranate seeds, photos and newspapers, and the flood of visitors disappeared from the setting, there was no sacrosanct void left behind. And if there was no void, then the body that had lain there as if branded on the pavement could be forgotten. The spilled blood was cleaned up, the shop window redecorated.

And so the seasons passed. Babies grew bigger, hair grew longer, nails were trimmed, and the display of sunglasses in the shop window changed. A few exams, sporting events, holidays, elections, meetings and disputes came and went. Comments were made about *dolmuş* queues, the cries of street vendors, one-day markets, football games and other intolerable things. How else should it be? In the morning, as she ran through all the things in her life that sickened her, the young woman sounded like a stuck record. The moment she woke up, she remembered. Either she remembered because she'd woken up, or she woke up because she'd remembered. Her spirit had died.

She had to get through this nightmare. He didn't die, he was murdered. The days had no name, no order or connection. Each day of her life felt isolated, filled with the same emptiness. Life never stops, so if the internal clock of humanity stops for a moment, it becomes incompatible with this life. If all other clocks continue to move on, then your clock is malfunctioning. And of course, malfunction is not acceptable. Better if she kept things to herself and didn't bother the world with it. Despite everything, the world has to carry on, indifferently, dragging you with it.

Saturday doesn't follow Friday; it's what happens after a void, a time of harsh realization. That was the first day she went back to the newspaper office, to the place outside the office where it all happened.

Yes, it was here. It was all so familiar. Here? Is it possible to get through these crowds? She felt as if her small body had been hung up like a piece of meat, unable to move backwards or forwards. Then she caught the eye of one of the youths standing by the door. She had no idea how she knew him. Couldn't remember. "Clear a way through," the youth said, extending his arm to part the crowd and pull her inside.

The office should have been there at the top of the stairs, or perhaps not. Once through the door, lots of photos of a familiar man, candles and tears.

She stopped in the middle of the candles and photos. She wanted to tease him, saying, "I didn't know you were so popular. Your pictures are everywhere." And she wanted to hear him reply, "Don't tease me, you little minx." So solemn and warm, yet, with only photos of him there, so distant. With everyone else, she gazed at that familiar face from a distance. As if she'd never known him, as if she hadn't spent all those years so close to him.

People kept coming up to her, shaking hands and offering condolences. She knew the faces, but was unable to remember the names. Someone took her by the arm and walked her down to Elmadağ, then up to Şişli. When did this street become so diminished? She walked and walked, but none of the roads led anywhere.

Istanbul used to be a time and a place. A place covered by a time that was lost. Now, it was without time or place but, strangely, the city was still called Istanbul. Yet the name was changed when it was conquered. Over the centuries, it had had so many names. Now, in her own century, what should the city be called: Belabul[3], for instance?

Istanbul used to be a room filled with human warmth. It was a fantasy of fresh starts in dilapidated buildings. It was lives that on the pretext

---

[3] A word play on the city's name which could be translated literally as 'find trouble'.

of news were hunted out in forgotten parts of the city or respectable meeting halls. It was a place where horizons expanded to their utmost.

Was this void the price for all that? It seemed that, at any moment, he would arrive, just walk in. As if he were about to say, "What are we all doing in here? Come on, back to work everyone." She realized that she hadn't accepted his death at all, but felt a sense of hope that she would see him again. Her weakness amazed her.

This is a grief that makes people feel more isolated from each other. Maybe that is why, despite the crowds, it feels so lonely. Nobody wants to look anyone in the eye. Or recount memories. Referring to the past enables people to accept what has happened. But rather than accept it, she preoccupies herself with what happened a few hours before. "She needs time," they say.

What she most wants to ask is, when she comes back months later and these crowds are no longer there, when the piece of pavement is merely a piece of pavement and the shop window is brightly lit up again, how long it will take for her see it all without feeling a jolt? As the effect of her drugged state during the first few days wore off, the emptiness intensified. Didn't they say it would pass with time? Time for the most part passed all by itself, crushing those unable to move with it. The crowds at the funeral, during that week, on the fortieth day of mourning, eventually they all dispersed. They had things to do and they were impatient. Everyone wanted to get back to normal. "You are feeling better, aren't you?" she was asked, because they longed to offload their own sorrow, to find a way to relax and lighten up without being judged, because they longed to enjoy themselves again. They didn't have what it took to carry such a burden, nor did they wish to. That was when she first noticed how egotistical life was. After a certain point, if you were unable to live your life, then it was your problem. There were medications to anesthetize the pain, therapy groups to join. What would they anesthetize? What would they say? She was living in a void.

Life seemed to jump out at her like some big joke. Those closest to her seemed as distant as strangers, while people she'd never met before felt like friends. Relaxation was a forgotten art, while work was less tiring. Grown adults understood absolutely nothing, while babies seemed like mature beings. Nothing surprised her. After a while, she accepted everything.

But she had no idea how, months later and sitting in that room again, she would be able to face looking at the things around her. A half-used packet of scented tissues, for instance, that she'd given to him herself, and this and that… items, each with different words and times associated with them, conversations that had been absorbed into the walls. How long had it taken for so much to accumulate?

It was as if there was some magic word like 'abracadabra' or 'open sesame'. As if finding that word would mean everything could be turned back.

That was why she was disillusioned with writing. She and her life would change according to what she wrote. She would write lofty words like, "What I write lives, so I write what I live." Even this was derived from some other piece of writing. Literature was a constant in her life. When did life turn up its nose at literature?

Impossible, says a voice inside her with the stubbornness of a child, a sulky child. Impossible, because people die but life never dies. A man who is the essence of life, when so many living are dead, is a man who summons life from within; a person who embraces time, who lives and breathes life into others. He never dies. Anyway, he didn't die, he was murdered, she says to herself. And then there are funerals to go to, weddings to dance at, arguments to have, meetings to go to, journeys to commence, mistakes to put right, regrets to feel, bursts of laughter to let out and tears to shed. That's what she thought and that's what she believed.

When there is nobody left to go down to the waterfront with, she feels dejected and abandoned, like the objects left behind in that room. Was Istanbul like her, a room crammed with depressing objects? Would it, like her, become a place without roots? Like a fugitive who never seeks shelter from anyone?

She went out of the building into the street. It was time to get to grips with that pavement. Before stepping on it, she couldn't help but look at it again, long and hard. There were stains on some of the stones. Were they bloodstains, or was she just imagining it? Right there, as he looked in the shop window, he'd smiled at her. How long ago was it they'd walked on that pavement together? How long ago? With their own hands, they had carried their belongings and their hopes to this place. How long ago was it?

Istanbul was a pavement. First walked upon and then bled upon. Her own little life was squeezed between those two events. Istanbul had ceased to exist.

Four

Every office has a story
Every promise has a story
My love hurts

—Turgut Uyar, *It Hurts* [4]

There were teams of police and those dark crowds. They were swarming round the door of the newspaper headquarters, swearing at you and at

---

[4] *Acıyor*

our endeavors. It was like they were talking about somebody else. They wanted to hang a label on you that contradicted the noble ideas you'd stood for all those years. How tall you were, how well-built your frame. You don't fit into such small-mindedness. From your beautiful writing, they pluck out a sentence and, claiming that you denigrate Turkishness, twist it into something monstrous. You and the world you've established; the world I was a part of, too. It was a world that we reestablished every single day with the purest of words; a virgin world that we created from nothing. That troubled, diffident expression is constantly before my eyes. "It's not fair on the shopkeepers, we've unsettled everyone…"

You know how if there is the slightest crack in an aircraft, everything gets sucked out in a vortex of air. In order to protect others from the effect of such cracks made by shameless people, you appropriated their shame.

Shame is the key to the door of conscience. If you don't turn it and open up your conscience, you inevitably create a darkness that is beyond human comprehension. Shame provides a wall of forbearance. Without a foothold on that wall, you can plunge headlong into evil. You can become blind to human worth. You might hurl accusations at someone, but you will be beholden to that person. Shame is the price of being human. If you don't have enough of it, you can destroy yourself and everything around you. Inability to recognize the dimension of a crime is the most powerful weapon against the ability to feel shame. If you have no conscience, you can destroy anything that will fill that void of shamelessness. That is why you keep getting so agitated, completely without shame…

What can I say now? Whatever I say, someone will come out and dispute it, creating the impression that there was a mistake that needed explanation. There's no mistake, maybe he felt shame on the street, who knows?

"It's not fair on the shopkeepers, we've unsettled everyone," said the man, as he paced endlessly back and forth. I feel as if, unwittingly, he is trampling over me. Paces within the four walls of a prison, a single cell; a prison that cannot be shared.

I witnessed the captivity of someone with the most liberal heart and mind. "It's not fair on the shopkeepers, we've unsettled everyone." Those words left me feeling crushed. I couldn't find anything to say. So I said, "Come on, let's write. We need to prepare a press release."

Your fingers clattered on the keyboard as you wrote about everything that was bothering us. "Move over. Let me see," you said and we changed places as always. We read and revised. But shame cannot be rectified like writing. That shame was bound to be exposed to the country like a shadow unable to escape once the sun had risen. Life would now have to be lived under that fateful shadow. We have no slogan to shout. The pure-hearted words recede quietly into the distance.

A crowd of television cameras had arrived without warning. It was like a raped woman being told, "You were dressed too provocatively." No one was held to account for this harrowing injustice.

The press release was finished and the pacing started again; back and forth, the sides of your shoes brushing against each other. Trampling over me, again and again. Then you suddenly say, "Sometimes I really miss village life." Meanwhile, I'm thinking of our old Saksı Han[5]. The same innocence and simple yearning in different lives. We'd moved the office from Saksı Han to Sebat[6], but in truth I was tired of Sebat and what it stood for. I was tired of learning so many things, reading between the lines, maintaining a balance, and especially feeling so much emotion.

---

[5] Saksı Han is the name of an apartment building. The literal meaning of the name is 'conservatory'.

[6] Sebat is the name of an apartment building. The literal meaning of the name is 'perseverance'.

After everything I've been through over the years, I'm no longer the girl who first ventured through that door. I just want to be an old-fashioned flowerpot. I want to stand in the corner of our old balcony and converse with leaves that quiver in a gentle breeze. But of course, I say nothing of this to you.

"Come on, it's time to go," you said. How many times had we locked that door in the evening before leaving the building? Outside, the air felt claustrophobic. We made no mention of the pain we felt. Just at that moment, the lights went on, making the road seem like a dead end to me. Like a theater set. You looked at the shop next door and said, "The shutters are down, it must be very late." And then that remark that tears at my insides: "You go on ahead if you want." Goddamn whatever made you feel you had to say that. We walked along the pavement together.

Two

Istanbul, a city in darkness
Took the moonlight and tore it to shreds,
Scattering some to each of the streets
Like a deity—God forbid
But that's what it wanted, that's what it did

—Turgut Uyar, *The High-Wire Acrobat* [7]

School seems so distant now. Roads once trodden, rows once sat in every day of the week are like shadows of someone else's life. There are places of learning other than school. Working for this newspaper is a constant learning process.

She likes the balcony best. When she spreads out her arms, she feels

---

[7] *Tel Cambazı*

as if she is about to take flight with the pigeons that perch on the rail. She has never felt so happy, energetic or free.

Once, a tiny mouse decided to visit the office. During the day, when it was crowded, it would try not to be seen. But it made its presence known when it ran at top speed from one corner to another. They called it Mıgır. Later, in the silence of Wednesday evenings, when the paper had finally taken shape, Mıgır would realize the coast was clear and start running about, skidding on the stone floors. The man calls out to Mıgır, with a great big grin on his face. "Look, look! How sweet he is," he says excitedly, "his eyes are like little beads." And the girl looks with curiosity at the tiny grey body and gleaming eyes. Between her two duties, she learns how to love a mouse. There's a round dining table with velvet-covered chairs. No office furniture. That's why it's like a home. Baron Seropyan, who prepares the Armenian pages, is telling some amazing stories and anecdotes of Anatolia, with its stones and earth, ancient grandmothers and craftsmen who he's never met.

Three people are eating their meal together, just like a family meal. She remembered the table of her childhood. After clearing the table, she used to cover it with a tablecloth and open her green file. During the years of nothingness, that green file was a treasure chest in which she kept all the good things of her life. Now, she is diving eagerly into a different chest every day. When she clears the table, she makes coffee for one person, tea for another. And then she sets to work on her writing. How things have changed.

She tries writing in Armenian, because the man believes in it. She learns to write news items, columns and captions. About history, philosophy, the Turkey of her infancy, Anatolia, Armenia, songs, and about the animal kingdom, its universe and philosophy.

Through the window, she sees pigeons perched on the windowsill opposite. The man talks about them, their feather-scattering fights, their rich love lives. Then, one day he takes a picture out of a drawer. "Look, this is my Bozo," he says. He was sitting on a grubby sofa, his arm round a donkey as if embracing a friend. Never mind that it's a donkey. Bozo is an old friend, not to be shown to everyone.

When she left the office, her feet felt as light as feathers on the pavement. This was her first home on dry land since leaving her nest and the ferry. She hadn't realized that Istanbul was so limitless.

Five

The world is an altar,
in time even its scribes are sacrificed
my blood is there
but flows no more

—Turgut Uyar, *The Altar* [8]

One can't help laughing about certain things. Idiotic things. For instance, wanting to tell you what happened when you were killed, thinking that no one but you would understand. It was an attempt at self-healing.

I called you that day. There was an exam and a meeting at the university and I'd just reached Kadıköy. Otherwise, I would have been with you then, as on the previous Friday. But I had so much to do that day. There was loads of time, of course. At least, that's what I thought.

I called you when I was on my way. You were preoccupied. As always, I thought. I even felt irritated. How long had my life been taking second place? As if I had no concerns of my own but was just part of an anonymous 'us'. So much effort, so much devotion. "Hey, I wanted to

---

[8] *Sunak*

talk to you. Just let me sort this out, then I'll call you," you said.

I walked for a bit. I needed to do some shopping. I'd just come out of the butcher's, carrying some meat when the telephone rang. I got excited, thinking it was you. "Good afternoon, Karin Hanım," said a voice from one of the television channels. "We've lost Hrant Dink, God rest his soul."

Five or six words, but together they are something monstrous. Nonsensical... "What are you talking about?" I said. "We were talking just now."

Yes, I know, my reply was stupid. Everything happened at once, that's all. But goddammit, some things shouldn't have happened.

I could deal with your being too busy to talk to me. All you needed to do was give me a ring and let me know; we'd talk later. But they don't give me a chance to call. The phone keeps on ringing, familiar as well as unknown numbers. I don't answer any of them. Then suddenly, I found myself surrounded by a pack of five or six stray dogs. I hadn't noticed them while I was trying to make out the numbers on my telephone. The dogs have smelled the package in my hand and are all over me because of course I'd just bought meat. They're enormous. I want them to go away and let me leave. It's all too much: dogs, packages and the constantly ringing telephone. Something ominous is going on. The packages are heavy, and the dogs' mouths are open. They'd be afraid of your rich, strong voice, if only I could reach you. Come on, shout! Make them go away.

I was stuck, with dogs all around me, a constantly ringing phone in my pocket and a package of meat in my hand. I shouted for help. There was a grey-haired man on the other side of the road. He just watched. Nobody else came to my aid.

The phone was still ringing. The dogs were snarling. And the packages weren't getting any lighter. I threw away the meat and began to run. "Hrant is dead," I yelled as I ran. Believe me, at that moment, I understood everything. I understood that your life and what it stood for would be greater than any literature.

They dragged me in through the door. Then I saw you on the screen on that familiar pavement, lying prostrate. If you were very tired when you reached the office in the mornings, you used to stretch out like that on your stomach. Fine, but why lie on the pavement? In the shop window behind you, there are rows of spectacles and clocks. All around you people stand looking petrified. Why can't they get you up?

I keep asking if it's true. They don't reply. There's something thick on the ground where you lie: your blood. I keep asking if it's blood. They don't answer. "Did they make you bleed like that, my lovely man?" Then some people came to clean it up. Nobody will ever wipe away even the slightest trace of you, let alone a bloodstain. Let the detergent brands compete over this, if they really believe in themselves. You know those stupid ads, when each claims to wash better than the other without naming the competitor.

Nobody came to my aid when those dogs surrounded me. If I wrote that down, people would take it as a metaphor. "Surrounded by dogs. Really? How crude," they'd say, "what forced symbolism."

Yet it would never have occurred to me to invent anything like that. And if I had, I couldn't have written it. Even worse, it's not a nightmare, because it starts when I wake up and ends when I go to sleep. It takes over my mind, running through my ears, my nose and my mouth. My legs are as useless as those of a marionette, and I can't move my tongue inside my mouth. My brain is going nonstop. "Just let me sort this out, then I'll call you," you said. They didn't let you sort it out, my dear Hrant. They didn't even let you live. This can't be Istanbul. Someone should change the name of this city.

Three

I've spent a long time among
Vases, small tables, and stones
My troubles could have swelled a river
Built a town from whose streets
a world uprising could have erupted
—but suddenly I feel afraid

—Turgut Uyar, *You Permeate My Skin* [9]

With pretense of excitement or an excited pretense, the girl sets out for the new place. They emerged from the side streets into the main road, right by the corner building. A historic building, called Sebat. She entered an elegant caged elevator, unlike the proletarian elevator used for heavy loads in the Saksı Han building. But this building weighs heavily. For a start, there are no balconies. That means more square feet, but it isn't more spacious.

There isn't a round table in the middle anymore. Everybody is in their own space. People have their own tiny rooms. "This matchbox is just right for Karakaşlı," says the man, as he shows visitors round the new place. One day he turns up carrying a small filing cabinet. "Take it, a box cabinet for a box room." The next day, he lays a carpet with his own hands. "Well, not bad." The girl covered the cabinet with stickers and put her books and files inside. The carpet made it look like a nest again. If only it had had pigeons and a balcony.

There were visiting delegations: foreign newspaper reporters, consular officials, party representatives and community administrators, as well as youngsters doing their homework and adults talking about their

---

[9] *Üstüme Sinmişliğin Var*

grandparents' villages. Local madmen. The girl says they're like monks and hermits, and the man laughs. There's less time to laugh now, he's very tired. When the room gets too full of visitors, he comes into this matchbox to play the horses. "Quick, pick a number from one to five!" "Three," she said.

There's a lot of work to do. But never mind the work, there are lots of problems too. Everything is written in a backstabbing way; so many things to study for impartiality or hidden meanings. The boss doesn't leave her alone in her little corner to comb the press for cultural news. The first page is like an ice rink. She learns how to skim through the lines without falling. And the man keeps going away on trips now. "The paper's in your hands," he says. "What, another trip?" she asks and gets a cuff on the back of her neck.

When everyone comes rushing out of their corners at once, or when things get too difficult, she goes and rummages in the bookshop next door, sometimes buying a book of folktales, sometimes stationery. Growing up means seeing all kinds of sordid things. This world has expanded a bit too much. Sometimes she goes back to Saksı Han. Even takes that ancient elevator up to the seventh floor and sits in front of the indigo-blue metal door. "Where did you disappear to again? You're like a cat," says the man, but she says nothing so as not to upset him. She missed the old times.

One morning, they met at the entrance to Sebat Apartments. The man was gazing in the shop window next door. "Hey, boss. Getting yourself some designer shades?" she asked. He smiled warmly where he stood on the pavement. "Watch your tongue, young lady," he said, wrapping his huge arms round her. It was still the Istanbul she knew.

One

First there was Istanbul, he was not there
Then one day he appeared
And found all the doorways

—Turgut Uyar, *The High-Wire Acrobat*

I know both Istanbul and myself from the ferries. Istanbul is like a country within itself. Not just because it is large, but because the people in all its different quarters know nothing about each other or how they live. A ferry doesn't scare anyone. It's familiar, like a nest rocking on the sea. In the open air with winds from afar blowing through my hair, I clutch a glass of tea, warming my hands. But every ferry is bound for dry land. And if you have to step on a gangplank leading to a land never visited before, it makes you feel strange, inadequate. All sense of belonging stays behind on the ferry.

I'm from the opposite shore. I used to take the ferry to school or to see friends. This was the first time I was venturing in to such an unknown. That was clear from my sweating palms. Actually, it was a totally different world, not just a new, unfamiliar environment. One day, months before, a man had come looking for my house. He had a deep rumbling voice and he sounded excited. "Young lady, you've won an award in the short story competition. I heard about it from the owner of the bookshop. Congratulations," he said. I had no idea what sort of man he was. He knew nothing about me. He seemed very fond of me, like a relative.

Later he came to the award ceremony. A huge man holding a large journal that matched his size and that he held out for me. "This present is almost bigger than you are," he said. I laughed at his natural bluntness. "We're setting up a newspaper," he said suddenly. It was to be published in Turkish and Armenian. "I'll let you know."

Some months later, I go to his office, a tiny room in Dolapdere. Things are piled on top of each other. He doesn't waste words or ramble. "Come and work here with me," he blurts out. Actually, my intention is to study. I'm not looking for work. I'd come thinking he just wanted a bit of free writing done. But I always think like that, no one had ever offered me work before. This is the start of a new episode in my life and it happened of its own accord. The rest was up to me. Either you find the strength to do it, or you say you have other plans and slip away into some protective cocoon. "What time shall I come on Monday?" I asked. He laughed, looking at me intently. His laugh was the warmest I'd ever heard. "You're the boss," he said. "Whatever time you want." Then, in a very sincere voice, he added, "I'm going to expand your world, you'll see." I got up. He opened his arms wide. "My little dark-haired lady," he said as he embraced me.

When I came out I looked confidently at this area, which I didn't know at all. Watch out, I'm on my way. I ran and ran along the pavement like a child. Istanbul is such a magical, miraculous city. While you're making your plans, it brings another destiny to you. And a good thing it did; at this moment, I wouldn't want to be anywhere other than Istanbul.

Making Marilyn Laugh

Şebnem İşigüzel

Translated by Amy Spangler

There is no substitution for love.

—Wong Kar-Wai

I was nervous, waiting, looking out my office window while I waited. I had described the way perfectly. I told her, "You get off the metro at Karaköy Square," and I even managed to squeeze in a short history of the metro. There was this pleasant look she would get on her face, an expression of approval, and she wore it then. I told her, "Look straight across when you exit the metro." That's why I hadn't opened the blinds, but just parted them, while I waited. I didn't want her to see me waiting like that. My secretary kept popping in and out of my office. She'd understood that I was waiting. But waiting for whom? My ex-wife was paying her. Not even money though, but perfume, a pair of leather gloves, a designer scarf, even a box of chocolates now and then—desirable gifts in those years.

My secretary, unable to contain herself any longer, asked, "Are you waiting for your American guest?"

Was that any question to put to such a seasoned man of the movies as myself? "No, why? Has she arrived?" I answered.

My dad used to say to me, "Boy, you can tell a forty-tailed lie standing on one leg. Film is the perfect industry for you." The guest I was expecting asked, a couple of days earlier on our way to the Pera Palas Hotel, where we would be staying, registered under false names, of course: "So were you very passionate about becoming a filmmaker?"

There, opposite me, she was like a tornado sucking me in; like a beam of light I couldn't bear to open my eyes and look at. The first question she had asked me in America was: "Does it snow in Istanbul?" Where on earth had that question come from?

How happy she'd been when I went to visit her later at the clinic. It was in North Dakota, the clinic. The latest trick pulled by her psychoanalyst, Ralph Greenson—the conniving prick's real name was Romeo something-or-other. That all happened in 1960, of course. Two years before she came to Istanbul. The clinic bit is important to me because I thought I'd never see her again after that. Who the hell was I anyway that they'd let me in, that she'd agree to receive me? I could very well have been one of her fans. Besides, I already knew the names of all the people she'd turned away in Los Angeles, about how she didn't want to see anyone, how she'd put on the men's pyjamas her manager had sent—her own choice—and slept, or been put to sleep. But she received me. Everywhere was covered in snow. Odd isn't it, the memories that stay with us! There was this big window in her room. Then I realized that it was a sliding window that extended down to the floor. I'd started out studying architecture. But then I became a filmmaker. Hence the interest I took in the buildings, the skyscrapers in America.

I'd taken flowers to her at the clinic. I was good at that sort of thing; I'd trained myself well, refined myself. The bouquet was supposed to look as if it were made of flowers randomly picked from a garden or the woods. Nothing grand, just natural flowers of the region, like a bunch put together by a child. But I got into an argument over the bouquet with the peevish woman from whom I bought it. Picking it apart in the front seat of the car and then putting it back together again, I got rid of all the carefully placed greenery.

She really liked the flowers. She was sitting on her bed. One of her bare feet dangled over the edge. Her men's pyjamas were buttoned all the way up. Her hair had big strong waves and it was messy. She wasn't wearing any makeup. She was pale. Her eyes were swollen, perhaps from sleeping, perhaps from the drugs. Since I'd always seen her in clothes and since she always wore a corset—or must have—I got lost in the curve of her swollen belly. She too looked at her stomach. Then she slowly placed her hands together on her lap. There was something odd about her, a light that only God could have created. A light so powerful that those who burned inside it could not possibly control it.

That's how it was. Thinking I'd lost my mind, I whispered to myself, "Rıza, son, know that this is the happiest moment of your life." I was so happy my eyes welled up with tears. It had started snowing. She turned her head, like she'd felt it. For she had her back turned to the view as if to the world. In her state, she couldn't see anything, she could only feel it.

She had such a gentle voice, you wouldn't believe it.

"No one's touched the snow in the garden, no one's stepped in it," she said. "There are only the footsteps of the sparrows I feed and the crows. Look. You see?" I didn't see a thing. To be able to see the marks left by the claws of a crow or of a sparrow on such virgin snow one had to have given up on life. Or the opposite: to be desperately clinging to it. My head was like a pendulum, out of bewilderment and excitement. Though she'd seen me once before—and do you know where?

At a party the studio gave on June 1, to celebrate her thirty-fifth birthday. The truth is, it was pure coincidence that I ended up there. I had a meeting with one of the managers of Twentieth Century Fox, because we were going to buy a film from them to show in Turkey. I expected no more than to be casually introduced and shake hands, if that even… But then, something much more significant happened. I ran into Edwina, the woman I had stayed with as a boarder while studying in America. Oh, Edwina! My crazy landlady who'd developed an unhealthy sensitivity to the language of running tap water! The only thing I recall from the tour she gave me of the house, in one room of which I would stay, was the fierce burning sensation in my bladder. What was in that tea? As if reading my mind, Edwina had said, "There was an herbal mix in the tea." And later, "When I heard you were Turkish, I looked at the map, found your country and thought you might be fond of drinking such things." After seeing my room I said to her, "If only it had a big, empty bookshelf." At the mention of books her eyes opened wide. "You know what, my son is a playwright!" When I heard his name, I immediately lost interest: Thomas Lanier, blah blah blah blah. Then, banging her hand against her head, as if it were an obstinate radio, she told me her son's pen name: Tennessee Williams. I nearly fell down the stairs! While touring the living room, which opened onto a garden designed in the style the French once referred to as 'imperial', her eyes fixed upon the shadows of the broad leaves of the paulownia trees which had extended past the threshold to invade the space inside. Edwina explained that it had been named by an indifferent linguist after the patronymic, mistaken for a second name or surname of a harmless lady, Anna Pavlovna Romanov, daughter of Pavel, nicknamed Peter-minus-Paul, the botanical Zemski,

I'm going to scream, I thought. Wanting a bookshelf in my room had simply been an excuse for me to wriggle my way out of this boarding deal, but things didn't work out that way. They didn't work out that way because I'd learned that this was the house where Tennessee Williams was born and grew up. Maybe Tennessee, who'd won the Pulitzer that year, would stop by. But he didn't.

At the said birthday party, though, he was there with his mother Edwina. Or rather, Edwina was there thanks to her son. If you're listening to me, thinking, "What an old, senile buffoon," well, I'm going to tell you who it was. But then that's why you're listening to this story—but then really it's wrong to call it a story, what I'm telling you, I mean, isn't it?

That's how I met her, Marilyn Monroe, on her birthday! While waiting to possibly be introduced to her, while, as chance would have it, having run into the chatty Edwina. I was thinking about how the authoritarian mother Amanda, who lived with the dreams of her past in *The Glass Menagerie*, the play in which Tennessee Williams tells the story of a poor southern family, must actually have been Edwina. I imagined Marilyn Monroe, if the play were to be made into a film, playing the role of the shy, crippled Laura, who waited for her mother to find an appropriate husband for her amongst the curios that she collected, when I felt myself being drawn to something, like a magnet to rusty staples fallen from a notebook swollen from humidity. Marilyn Monroe was right next to me. I was so nervous when Edwina introduced us that I told her about what I'd been thinking.

"Yes, I could play Laura," she said as if I was the producer and I was seriously offering her the role. Yes, she was insecure. She conveyed my offer to Tennessee Williams, as if I had sanctified her acting. He was about to say something, but then she turned to Arthur Miller, to whom she was married at the time, and said, "What's a gal to do, Daddy, they always write pretty girl roles for me." Odd, that she called him 'Daddy'. I'd introduced a topic that gave Big Mouth Edwina an opportunity to start yapping.

"You," she said, "I simply cannot imagine you as Laura! And even if you were to play her, they'd put a pair of thick-lens glasses on you and place a hairy mole on your cheek. People would only laugh at such a Laura!"

"In my language, Turkish," I interjected, "we have a saying: If one crazy person throws a stone into a well, forty wise men can't get it out."

"What?" her 'daddy' said.

When Marilyn's 'daddy' came to Istanbul, to my country, in 1985, to give support to Turkish intellectuals when it was under a dictatorial regime, I told him this, exactly as I'm telling it now, and immediately he said, "I used that. I used that saying in one of my plays."

And then he asked, "Is it true? Did Marilyn come to Istanbul?"

Once I'd finished telling my story, I had mind enough to ask him how he knew. And you know what he said?

"She told her makeup artist."

She had explained the bruise on her chin that the makeup artist had tried to cover up during the shooting of *Something's Got to Give*, which remained unfinished, by telling her: "It happened in Istanbul. My hands slipped while I was trying to board a skiff and I knocked my chin on it."

That scene immediately flashed before my eyes. As if it were a scene from one of the films I had produced. I'd been telling her, Marilyn, something just then. I'd be able to remember it word for word, whatever it was I had been saying to her, if my memory didn't play so many tricks on me. Whatever it was I said to her though, it made her laugh. Now how did we end up here? Remembering is sometimes as impossible as rewinding an old movie camera. Yes, you could find my name in those registers, the clinic registers I mean. The nurse had written down my name when I visited her. In fact, she'd had difficulty spelling my last name and so I'd had to take out my passport.

"Bay Rıza," she had said upon seeing me. She pronounced my name so beautifully it was almost shocking. And then she murmured one of Laura's lines:

"I know there's a future for me, but I can't wait for it."

I told her exactly which scene and which act that line came from. She smiled. The recording, the film of that moment remains in my mind, can you believe it? That ephemeral moment of just a few sentences... "The flowers," she said, "they smell beautiful, don't they?"

And then, out of the blue, "forty-one," she said.

I was taken aback at first. I hadn't removed my coat yet. It was just something I'd bought on the way there anyway, and I wasn't used to it, I'd sweated, and I was even more surprised by her saying 'forty-one' like that because of the distress caused by my sweating, or I had appeared more surprised, more shocked, being sweaty as I was.

"There's a weird fountain in the garden," she said. Lifting that divine index finger of hers. Sometimes I take my hat off to memory, impressed at how it could possibly retain that single, precious moment. Marilyn remained frozen, as if listening for something, Marilyn, that legend for all of humankind. There, at that moment, she was alone with me and there really was a sound, the sound of a device that needed oiling.

"When the device in the mouth of the fountain fills up with water, it falls to the ground," Marilyn said. And at that moment, the sound of the metal mouthpiece descending was heard, I think, for the forty-second time.

"And there's a tiny pool where the mouthpiece falls."

Marilyn stopped. And so we heard it hit for the forty-third time.

"Maybe the water in the pool has frozen. That's why there are so many sparrows in the garden because they drink from the pool. And the crows scare them. One day, I went out and scared the crows."

Now, as I'm telling this, I'm wondering what would have happened if I had told all of this earlier? It would have been fodder for the glossies and perhaps made its way into some fictitious biographies, that's all. I could very well have taken this secret with me to the grave: that Marilyn was here, that she came to Istanbul. She was my guest here on the Island.

Then, something utterly unromantic happened during my visit to the clinic: the nurse switched the lights on, *pow!* Just like that. The lights were fluorescent and utterly repulsive. I gave Marilyn my card and thanked her for remembering me despite our brief time together and for receiving me.

"And I am grateful for the pleasant conversation." she replied.

I wanted to ask, "What conversation?" Had no one talked to her, listened to her before, or did she think her entire life had been one long monologue? I saw that she was struggling to read the information on my card, fighting off the fluorescent light that had suddenly filled the room.

And it was then, at that moment that she asked: "Is it snowing in Istanbul?"

I left Marilyn there in front of a snowy landscape, inside something like a toy, like one of those snow domes when you turn them upside down, beneath a crappy fluorescent light. Next to the nurse who had let me in stood a man I knew I'd seen before, but where? I'd seen his photo in the papers, but he wasn't a filmmaker. When I reached the end of the hall, it dawned on me: Carl Sandburg, the author of the biography, *Lincoln*. Marilyn hadn't received him. He was following right behind me.

When I exited into the garden, I heard that sound made by the weird device in the fountain again. I stopped. I turned around and looked. Her large window was visible, secluded amongst the trees. Marilyn was there.

She came to Istanbul two years later. She told me on the phone in a rather weary voice, that her trip to Istanbul had to remain top secret and that she trusted me to make sure it did.

"Don't give it a second thought," I said, thinking I was having a daydream. When I hung up the phone I was doubtful about whether or not I had really had such a conversation. Using some excuse or another I called my secretary into my office.

"Who was the person you just put through?"

"The woman on the phone said I only need tell you it was Marilyn," she said.

"What, does she think she's Marilyn Monroe?" I laughed.

It couldn't have been a joke. I hadn't told anyone that I had met Marilyn, that I had visited her at the clinic. It was she who had called and who was coming.

I picked her up myself from the airport. I'd worn the band of my watch extra tight so that I wouldn't think the moment was a dream. I had such poor circulation that my doctor had described the precariousness of the situation by saying that wearing underwear that was tight around my waist, wearing a belt, or even socks that weren't pure silk, "would be like putting a noose around your neck and kicking the stool out from under you." By the time I saw Marilyn, who had a turban wound around her head, my arm was already numb. Again, she was without a corset. She was wearing pants that left her ankles exposed and a short-sleeved shirt. And she carried a bag pressed under her arm. She wasn't wearing any makeup. Even in such an everyday state people stared at her. And who could blame them, for she was a superhuman being.

"No one could even imagine that I would come to Istanbul," she said to me on our way to the city.

I almost ran off the road. With my Marilyn at my side, I nearly flew into the sea, off that road that Menderes had filled in the sea to build.

I settled her into her hotel myself. Under a name I'd made up. "We forgot her passport at my office. We'll send it to you tomorrow," I lied.

"I have a house on the Island, come and stay there, you'll be more comfortable," I said.

"As long as no one finds out I'm in Istanbul," she replied.

I was offended. We were sitting in the tea parlor at the Pera Palas. She was leaning over watching the street and drinking tea with milk.

"I got this habit thanks to Arthur," she said.

When she told Arthur the same thing he'd corrected her, "From my mother, a habit she picked up from my mother, Isodora."

Marilyn had just taken a sip from her tea with milk when she heard the voices of some Americans who'd plunged into the room, and she froze. Like a rabbit that's had a flashlight suddenly fixed upon it. The cup in her hand remained suspended in the air, as she listened to the Americans who settled in directly behind her.

"I can't let them recognize me."

No one could have recognized her, because she was playing someone other than Marilyn Monroe. A shy, timid woman, who, unable to bear it any longer, had escaped from home, but was happy to be where she was. No one recognized her. That night, I took her to a run-of-the-mill Turkish *pavyon*. This time, she'd gathered her hair, in an unusual way. She wore a bit of lipstick, nothing else. What was it that made her so different? That she was missing the false eyelashes, the corset, the blonde curls? No.

"Anyone would recognize her at the first opportunity," Arthur Miller had said. I had offered him a sip of cognac and Miller had gone on. He must have known better than I what had happened to her in Istanbul.

When the belly dancer took the stage at the Turkish pavyon, Marilyn's mouth gaped in amazement. On the way back to the hotel, she perked up quite a bit. She broke out in a couple of moves that she still recalled from the ukulele, or in other words, Hawaiian dance lessons she'd taken for the movie *Some Like It Hot*, while the two of us were walking together, next to each other, on the sidewalk.

It was on the following day that she wanted to try coming to my office by herself. She could have gotten lost. Marilyn Monroe lost in Istanbul! Who knew that she was here? No one. Her secretary, May Reis, knew that she was on a short, secret trip, that was all.

"You're going to finish the movie when you get back, alright?" the producer had said.

"He asked that question over and over," Marilyn said when she told me. It was at such moments of unhappiness when she became her real self, when she failed to play her role.

"That lady," the person walking up to us said, "looks a lot like Marilyn Monroe." It was a well-known contractor who spoke those words. I saw him often at the Pera Palas Hotel. "Does she realize that?" he asked, nearly squeezing the hat in his chubby hands into a ball.

"Yes," I replied. "It's her line of work; she makes a living from the resemblance."

"Do the newspapers know about it?" he asked, the cunning fox. That's when I recalled that I knew his swollen face from somewhere else. He was one of the MPs from Menderes's party, when Menderes came to power in 1957. And so they were all over the papers in ads leading up to elections.

"Yes," I said. "The papers know about it."

"I," he said, nearly beating his chest as he pronounced the words, "I agreed with what Eisenhower said: America's interests are in the world's best interest. But just look at what's happening now!"

I slowly leaned toward the man. All the while he was expecting me to translate what he had said to Marilyn. "She's not American," I said. A clump of sweaty hair stuck to the back of his neck, he quickly swung his head around. "Really? Where's she from?"

"She's Swedish," I said.

The man rose from our table and stomped off in a huff.

I would have to take her to the Island as soon as possible.

That's where we left off now, isn't it? I was waiting in my office. She had insisted on coming over from the hotel on her own. I had drawn a detailed map of the road from the Pera Palas to the small metro station at Tünel Square. Nevertheless, I still thought it possible she might get lost and disappear. When I saw her emerge from the Karaköy station I nearly jumped out the window because she didn't know which way to go. I opened the blinds. I wanted her to see me but she didn't. There were a couple of jerks trailing behind her, drawn like moths to her flame. Wearing a floral-print dress in a scuffle with the wind, she was dangerously beautiful.

Then I lost her. It happened all of a sudden. I was at the office window, but Marilyn was neither where I had last seen her, nor crossing the street or walking in the opposite direction. In desperation I opened the window and looked down, but she wasn't at the entrance to the building either. That powerful beam of light into which I could not bear to look was directly behind me. Marilyn later said to me, when recalling that moment, "Your pupils were spinning like mad."

"My blood pressure," I said, "low blood pressure, plus a clamp in my chest and besides, I have poor circulation."

She looked me in the face, as if she hadn't been the cause of all of this. We went downstairs, to Baylan Patisserie. Back then there was a Baylan Patisserie at Karaköy Square. We had a Coupe Baylan, the house specialty ice cream dish. Ask the owner, Hari Lenas, if he's still alive that is, if I didn't show up there with a mesmerizingly beautiful woman. But I don't have to prove it to anyone, the time I spent with Marilyn in Istanbul.

Back then, I was plagued by a single question: You see, to the firm she worked for, Marilyn was a goose that laid golden eggs. She couldn't very easily just up and vanish. But she told me very strange things. If the same had happened to me, I would have done whatever it took to disappear. It turns out that when I had visited her at the clinic, the producer, who'd run out of money and was unable to finish the film, had forcibly had her admitted. And a bunch of other things like that. Why hadn't Arthur Miller been able to do anything about it, I wondered? Why hadn't anyone been able to protect this woman? I told Miller that too.

I didn't want her to be unhappy. Because when she was, she was like her real self. Whenever she got a bit teary-eyed, it was as if her entire body lit up, as if she were covered in flashing neon lights that read 'Marilyn Monroe', and that's when she was noticed.

"C'mon," I said, "We've got a job to do, and it's going to be a blast."

You'll be shocked to hear where we went!

To Florya Deniz Köşkü, the mansion where presidents stay when they come to Istanbul. And why, you might ask? Because the projector there was broken, the projector we'd supplied them back during the second president's reign. Back then, in addition to producing, I also imported such equipment. Why, I wondered, had the projector broken?

We went, and Marilyn was in awe of the mansion, which stood directly on the sea. I introduced her as my wife. My American wife.

When I turned and told this to Marilyn, though I'd only whispered it, she got upset for some reason.

"Don't do any such thing ever again," she berated me.

They had us wait on the veranda. The president himself was nowhere in sight, but he had some guests about. And, what would you know, they were British! I curled my lips. After all, wasn't it President Cemal Gürsel who had fallen prisoner to the British on the Palestinian Front? Anyway, Marilyn smiled. I realized that it was a conversation at the next table that put the smile on her face. One of the Brits, the short, stout, melancholy one, had started talking about the menu. Florya Deniz Köşkü had a menu, just like a hotel!

"I'm going to start with the bananas," the Brit said.

"That's not bananas, it's *ananas*—pineapple, pineapple juice."

"Oh, I see. In that case, bring me some meat broth."

The strange thing is, that short tête-à-tête at the neighboring table melted the ice between Marilyn and me. We each had lemonade. We chatted. "I'd like to adapt Nabokov's *Ada, or Ardor* for the screen," I said. They'd prepared the projector, like a patient about to undergo surgery. I fixed the problem, which had been caused by humidity. Someone dashed off to deliver carbonated water to President Cemal Gürsel, who was suffering from gastric bleeding and couldn't manage to fall asleep for his midday nap. I thought I saw him, at the end of the long hall in that ship-like mansion. The papers had written that he'd had a mild stroke.

"Quite the lovely lady, congrats," said the pint-sized servant, who'd caught my attention and whom I'd seen before—when we delivered the film camera, when we did routine maintenance on it and when I'd come to remove the film that one of the National Chief's sons had gotten jammed.

"Give the lady a tour of our mansion," he said. And then he riveted his gaze upon me. A strange, strange man. I mustered up a perfunctory smile. My great grandmother used to say that some people saw with the eye of their hearts; they know things before they are told, see things before they are revealed, read the unwritten.

We took a tour of the mansion. Oh boy, the stories that servant told us! About how one day the mansion popped off the beams that propped it up above the sea and took flight, how one day, when the National Chief just couldn't be woken from his beauty sleep, the servant found himself entertaining the Italian commercial attaché. How one day a sea lion gone astray landed on the pier connecting the mansion to the sea, stood up and walked like a human and then, frightened by the people who had come to the veranda to see what was causing the mansion to shake like that, instead of just plopping back into the water, surrendered himself to be delivered to the Gülhane Zoo, and then one day...

I translated each story word for word. I made Marilyn laugh. Not that servant with the nonsense stories he told, but I myself, with what I had allowed her to experience. Later, I took her to the Island. I accompanied her the last summer that Marilyn Monroe lived.

If the readers would like a piece of advice, if they expect one, I'd like to tell them that when you lose your memory, you lose your immortality. And then if you end up in a mental hospital with your pillow and your bedpan, they won't give you Shakespeare or Ayhan Işık as a roommate; you'll be left with retards and street performers.

I think that suffices to explain that understanding happiness and love is as simple as understanding whether or not it's going to rain. I had a few days on this earth that were worth it all, worth everything. Now, I continuously swoop back and forth over those days, buoyed by that swing called memory, filled with the same love and happiness that filled me back then.

She didn't stay with me on the Island for long. But if you ask me to continue, I can go on. A short history of another brief couple of days; a gallery suffused with flowers; an embroidered ceiling; an amorous frolic caught upon the forget-me-nots next to a bird bath; the butterflies on the shore of a sea of love; the butterfly orchids on the slope leading down to the sea; the sight of it from the marble stairs, draped in fog; a gazelle feeding in the garden of our family mansion, bought to make her happy as she gazed upon it and so much more, so much more...

The Silence of Sevinç Duman

Semra Topal

Translated by Abigail Bowman

It doesn't matter whether the earth was created in one day or seven; back before anything human-like even existed, there was history. And ever since then, that ancient history has been remarkably tolerant of all monstrosities. In the city of Cannes, invaded by celebrities back when it was just a fishing town, an Eastern woman clasps her Golden Palm and with the grace of Madame Butterfly, proclaims: "The world is a beautiful place." And so, in that moment, it was.

In those days, rallies for the Republic were being held in Istanbul and the Anatolian towns that shared its fate. Flag sales had rocketed and the skies were cardinal red. The flag was the king of every demonstration. This time, Atatürk's girls were brandishing flags in protest of women with headscarves. In short, the world wasn't a beautiful place, it was a bloodthirsty one.

At the time, I was staying in a very old apartment building in the Galata neighborhood, in the home of a one-legged man with a heart of gold. When I woke up each day, the first thing I saw was the Galata Tower, rising before my eyes like a giant phallus. For some reason, over time that giant historical dick merged with the one-legged man and they became the same thing. This man, sentenced to one leg for life, had strengthened his muscles with bodybuilding and grown a beard like that Christian symbol of goodness, Santa Claus. And so when this one-legged, dark-skinned and golden-hearted Santa walked across a wooden floor, it was like stampeding horses. He'd travelled more places and seen more sights than anyone else; in fact, at one point he almost left his crazy country behind for good, and when he returned was dumbfounded to see all his acquaintances appearing on television. So every now and then, he'd leave time behind and sever all ties, without realizing how lucky he was. After all, he was lucky, and it wouldn't be harsh to say his house was a shithole. He'd exhibited the same slovenliness throughout his escapades extending from Georgia to China. His mind was a mess and not once did he make an effort to pull himself together. As for me, I was slinking around the house like a snake, the spitting image of a Lilith preceding Eve.

Tons of famous people lived in the apartment building. The singer T. was there; he must have found the sadness he was searching for in the huge, strange rooms where seagulls screeched in our brains. Santa Claus called T. a good kid, but then we saw overly good kids wherever we looked. The rallies for the Republic were the work of good kids, and since a singer's job was to excite the population, they, along with university professors, had jumped at the opportunity to lead the people, addressing them from podiums. This was clearly taking advantage of the situation. The historic apartment had accumulated within itself those things particular to Istanbul, and was harboring a few well-known and recognizable journalists and actors in addition to T. Upon all those who passed through its door, a thousand tiny, invisible bird mouths issued forth breezes of blood flow, brother murders, and a little happiness too. In short, there was something sanctified about it; you could go crazy if you stayed there too long. Thankfully, I was a transient in this apartment.

I wasn't really a guest, or a tenant, a lover, a whore, or someone's wife. Maybe I was suffering from an abundance of opportunities, like everyone was. Back then women would say: "If only I'd been created to cook meals for a good man."

T., who spent mornings in his studio and evenings in the bars of Kuruçeşme, would sit and drink tea in the cafeteria behind the apartment when he woke up. There was never any noise apart from a few old men playing Rummikub at a far-away table. Sometimes T. would sit there alone in the darkness of the night; perhaps he was stricken with melancholy like everyone else. Though he was attracted to crowds, I sensed there was a side of him that had never been socialized. T. was always terrified of banality, and his main problem was women. It was well known how he ran from one woman to the next, and it was evident from his music videos that try as he might, he just could not attain the *desired*, or how should I put it, *the ideal woman*. In one of those videos—set in Beyoğlu, where the crowd goes wild 24/7 and there is no such thing as sleep—packs of dog-like women in gothic makeup were frantically trying to steal T.'s heart. But it was all in vain, because our singer would open his arms to them one minute, then reject them all the next. His constant sorrow was clearly that of a man desired and satiated to the extreme. After sex he would howl in the dark like an animal; he didn't know that howling is all that humankind can do. I used to say T.'s heart would be the death of him for sure. Sometimes he'd surprise us and his pain would be reborn in a comic book hero wearing shorts and looking just like him; but otherwise everything was the same. The taste of tea, coffee, cigarettes was all the same. The newspapers were saying that some blind man had butchered his wife in the bathroom with a cleaver, slashing the air at random in the pint-sized space. According to the blind man, the woman's crime was that throughout their marriage, the whole time she'd been having sex with him, she'd also been having sex with her ex-husband, Beytullah Kansandık. His wife's confession, "There's enough of me for both of you," had been enough to drive the blind man to murder. Behind her back the blind man said of his wife: "She's a nymphomaniac, she kept me erect all the time." The same newspapers reported that pictures of a TRT anchorwoman in only her underwear had been posted on the Internet. According to the anchorwoman, the person who posted the pictures was the professor husband she had divorced. As for this character in the story, he said of his divorced wife: "You can ask my friends, she was frisky."

One way or another, everything was coming to an end. Suddenly, even things we'd deemed impossible became possible within the span of a single day, so to speak. My days in Galata were quickly approaching their end, and it was like I was condemned to experience everything at a breathless sprint. I knew that after Galata, the Tünel neighborhood would entice me with its mysterious light, drawing me into its motherly embrace. But right now, let's fast forward to the last night I spent in Santa Claus's den.

THE LAST NIGHT IN GALATA:

I had gone out shopping like I always do, paying no attention to the rally-filled atmosphere (thankfully I was able to get my hands on some money somehow). Since there was no supermarket or anything in the area, I had to procure our daily food from small neighborhood shops. The only downside to this was exposing myself to their gabbing. And you could never tell for sure if someone had woken up on the right side of the bed or not. Santa Claus was an incomparable chef; he could put together incredible meals using whatever ingredients I set before him. That night, like every night, we planned our meal with meticulous care. It was all simple fare: lentil soup, aubergines with ground beef, rice, a cold

yogurt and cucumber dip, and just as we were moving on to bread pudding with ice cream, the singer T. came. I noticed a joy in him I'd never
seen before. He wore a white leather jacket, with a whisper-thin white
shirt, probably made of silk, fluttering beneath it. Below that he wore a
pair of skintight pants, the kind they say can render men infertile. He
was amazingly cheerful. I can't remember how many beers he drank with
us on an empty stomach. In short, he was bursting with happiness and
booze. We were already quite used to his standoffish attitude towards
food; he was forced to watch his weight to the point that he was a veri-
table corpse. The fitness trainers he employed were going to pull him out
of his human suit—if we lived long enough we'd see it happen. At the
head of table sat Santa Claus with his massive paunch and his one leg,
patting himself down to find a match like he was playing a lyre with his
dark, delicate fingers; it was a special quirk of his to constantly smoke
other people's cigarettes.

"I could never live anywhere outside of Istanbul. This place is my
temple, my native land, my mother…"

We didn't pay attention to what he was saying. He would get
emotional from time to time and blurt out this kind of thing, and we
were forced to believe what he said because he'd travelled the world; he
had achieved a victory that neither T. nor I could ever measure up to.
He was a financial wizard who could live without dipping his hand into
his pocket. I don't know what his talent would have amounted to over
time, and it was already clear he was slowing down as he grew older. I'd
observed him growing slower day by day; nothing had escaped my notice.
Even his coal-black beard had gone grey. Soon his teeth would start to
fall out one by one; the toothaches that poisoned nights already besieged
him. While T. was howling with spiritual pain in his songs, Santa Claus
was howling from physical pain. I had probably accumulated a lifetime's

worth of howling in Galata, and so naturally I lost it myself every now and then. The speakers on TV used to say that the only thing we needed was reason.

T.'s white pants were soon covered in crazy stains. He'd gone to the bathroom repeatedly; in the blink of an eye, he'd soiled himself with beer and piss. The night flowed along in this way when suddenly one of the girls Santa Claus used to bed showed up: Sevinç Duman. Two or three months earlier, after an argument with her mother and good-for-nothing brother (whom she loved more than anyone else in the world), she'd decided that she couldn't live in the same house with them and moved into a crumbling building in Kuledibi with a girlfriend. As for Santa Claus, he was a mentor for Sevinç Duman both inside and outside the bedroom. You know, that sort of thing. There was only one word to describe the girl: melancholy. Melancholy made even the least mysterious people seem mysterious; this was the costume worn by Sevinç Duman, who was now doing wardrobe design for soap operas. There was mild acne on her cheeks and her hair shot out from her scalp, bursting with femininity. She would have been happy to talk until morning in her soft and dewy voice; she was one of those women who when she spoke, it mattered not one wit what she said; it seemed that her sole mission in life was to relish this privilege.

Sevinç Duman, who only knew T. by reputation, was meeting him face-to-face for the first time, and the be-stained 'T-eity' couldn't contain himself: he laughed and laughed, showing off his pearly whites. I don't know what was causing his peculiar drunken delirium that night, but it was truly difficult for him to curb his energy inside this Galata den. As soon as Sevinç Duman set foot through the door, she had a rude awakening about T.; or rather she'd gone into shock for a few seconds. In her own words, it was like a cold shower, before she even knew what hit her; as for me, I was perfectly happy with T.'s presence. Only seconds after they'd met, T. was calling her baby. Naturally, he'd left a bad impression on the girl; God knows why girls were always doing T.'s bidding. Some sudden something had offended Sevinç Duman. Meanwhile, Santa Claus had broken out in another one of his refrains: "In Istanbul you get together with people you wouldn't otherwise ever be able to see, not in a lifetime, this doesn't happen anywhere else in the world…"

We were forced to believe him; Istanbul was his greatest passion, he'd talk about it for days on end if we let him. According to him, Istanbul stood for deep Freudian feelings and love. Determined, he had searched every corner of the earth, but in the end had come running back to his Istanbul, a city that knew how to mete out compassion and cruelty just like that mother he never stopped mentioning. There was nothing to say. It was as if Sevinç Duman and Santa Claus had started a smoking contest between the two of them, a contest with no rules. T.'s stain-covered white pants could have been recoated with cigarette fumes. What if that black smoke actually swept away everything, I said. T.'s eyes bulged with fear and he spoke: "Baby, anyone who does this to their lungs could stomach anything, oohhh…"

This time even Santa Claus was roaring at the top of his lungs, smoke belching out of his ass: "In my whole life I've never seen a creature as pure as you. We love you dearly, but compared to us, you're like a teething baby. You're something from another planet, an angel even…"

T. had suddenly taken on a kind of asexuality thanks to Santa Claus. There might have been tears in Sevinç Duman's eyes; there was no way we could have known what caused her such constant inner pain. There was no sign that we could grab hold of and pull on. Soon she would be leaving for the Southeast to make costumes for a soap opera about Anatolian tribes, because such series were trendy and filmed on location.

It seemed people were obsessed with honor and manliness. Once someone starts to give a speech, it's nothing but honor, because according to rumor (the tragedy of it is that rumor can turn into scientific fact), all of us originally came from tribes or something, I don't know. We breathed this sweet air, taking it in with pleasure, and every particle of it was filled with the drivel of honor and glory. At times it seemed as if T.'s unbridled joy might rub off on Sevinç Duman, but each time it instantly abandoned her beautiful body like a seed renouncing undesirable soil. Really, her body was like a masterpiece of mystery, and all this time a giant mouse was waddling around the house and no one even noticed the creature. These beasties were one of the unchanging facts of life for us; one could form an immediate attachment with them, as with cats and dogs, if only they weren't so stomach-churning. Every day when Sevinç Duman looked out her window in Kuledibi she saw legions of these animals; perhaps it was necessary as well to take inspiration from them in the great struggle for survival.

After a spell, T. and I found ourselves outside buying beer and cigarettes together. T. was already burning like a lantern in the night. The people in the street were wallowing up to their necks in love: we could see it in their cat-like expressions. And it was like pointed horns had already sprouted from their foreheads. So, holding hands and singing songs like the Hansel and Gretel twins, we set out to rustle up some provisions. T. may have caught on: Santa Claus and Sevinç were now fucking on the floor, on their beloved cushion. The plump, stark white legs freed from Sevinç's jeans, on that floor cushion full of fleas and mouse shit, juxtaposed with the one leg of Santa Claus, the single leg he got by on after losing one hideous leg in childhood due to a mother's mistake: even innocent T. could probably picture it. He'd kicked us out, allegedly with utmost discretion, and now he was screwing the girl in all his leglessness;

a bodily state which was the cause of his extreme aggression. The girl on the floor cushion was a mysterious work of art, and her pimples only made her sexier. The girl was as hot and bothered as a rabbit.

As Hansel and Gretel, we stopped by a few jam-packed bars in Taksim. Boys and girls alike were hitting on T.; maybe it was their haircuts, maybe it was their way of gliding around, but the boys seemed prettier than the girls. Each one was a god in his own right, ephemeral and erotic. Their heads were drained and empty, consisting of nothing but flesh. It was the stupid songs that ignited these gods, such silly songs that confronted us, songs that it would be meaningless to listen to in the daytime. At that moment, in someplace where a fishing net was hung over the ceiling and walls, a group of girls and boys at T.'s feet was shouting: "Eeaat us, T., tear us apart!"

"Ma cherie, let's get out of here before this shit gets out of hand."

In the place with the net, his white shirt was ripped apart, riddled with bites; one of them bit him like a dog. Another guy grovelling at T.'s feet tried to pour straight *rakı* on the bite; perhaps that's how they did things in his family. At that point everyone said, "fuck off" something-or-another, and we got out of there. I don't know how many hours it had been since we left the house; when we returned to the den in Galata, we found Santa Claus and Sevinç Duman biting their nails because they couldn't find anything to drink. They snatched up the cigarette packs and bottles like mice and didn't pay any attention to T.'s bruises. The smell of Sevinç Duman's pussy was everywhere, on the floor cushion, on the ground, in the sky. While we were out, an insect had bitten the girl, or so they said; our Santa Claus spoke, as if on autopilot: "In Istanbul, all kinds of crap can happen to you…"

While the girl scratched herself with a vengeance, Santa Claus went over to stand in front of the mirror and have a stretch, free of worries and cares. He'd shaved off the hairs on his chest so as to better observe his growing muscles: how silky smooth was the man before us! T.'s fierce, wolf-like grins were also reflected in the mirror, his savagery in that moment almost unbelievable. Sevinç Duman only knew him by reputation, but T. didn't seem much like a hopeless romantic hero. She thought, is this the T. with those great big misty eyes, ever pursuing an endless quest for his ideal woman? The girl, made even more sensitive by the bug bite, asked herself questions whose answers she'd never know. We were in a day and age when everyone was as miserable as caged tigers. Towards morning I snarled from within a bright red kimono: "I'm beat, T."

Santa Claus was still up to his antics in front of the mirror. At any moment a voice from the beyond could have called him up to the stage for a one-man circus act; to tell the truth, no one would have been surprised. But he lacked the wisdom required by the circus world: weirdness alone served no purpose. T. was swaying on his feet, covered in filth. We were in a place where bedtime stories for children were superfluous. But the patron saint of those children, that victim of a mother's mistake, was saying, "It's hard to find a place as cosmopolitan as Istanbul, not to mention the good sex, the good philosophy, the good highs…"

"It's a delusion, baby, you're all hearing a delusion now," T. said; he'd suddenly decided to clean off his white boots with toilet paper. He was stamping on the wood floor like the flamenco dancer Joaquín Cortés. He was in the mood for a small private showing for friends: there was no music, no words, but there were T.'s legs; truth is, there was no need for anything else concrete. Sevinç Duman's increasingly misty eyes were a piece of her insanity. Suddenly, her face turned as bright red as the half-open kimono I was wearing. For a moment I thought she would spew out everything she'd eaten—who were we to know what disease she'd inherited from her ancestors. Persisting in his Joaquín Cortés impersonation, T. spoke to her:

"Come on, baby, release that dog inside you."

From atop Santa Claus's old hairless back I said, "T., you could never order anyone around."

T. was howling with laughter. It occurred to me that he ought to be pitied; after all, he made his living off the woman problem he couldn't solve. Santa Claus was saying tipsily, "You meet the world's most beautiful women in Istanbul, we're sitting on top of a goldmine…"

It seemed he was set to carry on until morning about this inheritance bequeathed to men; I was thinking the time had come to cut and run. Sevinç Duman was shooting me hysterical looks, like she could read my thoughts.

Rearing up on his one leg like a horse on a rampage, Santa Claus spoke: "Sevinç Duman is a schizophrenic. Come on, tell them how you're God's beloved woman. Tell them how you're a soon-to-be Turkish Mother Mary. Soon she'll give birth to Christ without ever having had intercourse with a man, but of course the child won't be anything like Christ, apart from his birth. He'll look like John the Baptist; we all know how John was more beautiful than anyone. This is a woman who's carrying out all of God's wishes and will soon be rewarded. We will see for ourselves how a Muslim woman is rewarded…"

After this revelation, T., of all people, seemed to have settled down. Towards morning, no longer drunk, he gave us an impersonation of Santa Claus: "Istanbul is full of female traps."

I sat there in my red kimono that had shamelessly slipped open, saying, "In Istanbul, women belong to either God or men, no wonder we're always getting sharp things shoved up our asses…"

I said this as if it were the truest thing I knew; and in the early morning hours, fate was turning me into a schizophrenic maniac and I suddenly wanted to cry. I was sitting in my half-open kimono growling like an old dog and listening to the Muslim Sevinç Duman howling in a convoluted syntax as she prayed in a corner T., completely sober in these wee hours, was asking, "What's she saying?"

"Religious stuff, it's really magical…"

T. shouted as if he'd been betrayed: "Why's she doing it in front of everyone!"

Kneeling on the small carpet she'd appropriated for a prayer rug, Sevinç Duman howled with her hands raised to the sky. Santa Claus's naked body had broken out into a sweat, whereas T., whose outfit was no longer legitimately white due to the crazy stains, would not for the life of him cease with his refrain: "What's she saying?"

"Really magical stuff, words you couldn't figure out without first improving yourself or going mad…"

T. was dying to get his head around Sevinç Duman's words. I think it was the first time in his life that he was forced to take a woman seriously. It would be hard for him to talk about love after this, I said. I saw my eyes in the mirror: they had slipped to one side just like the kimono I wore.

A Question

Müge İplikçi

Translated by İdil Aydoğan

A bench between two fountains. Three old women sitting on the bench. One's wearing a purple dress, the other is blonde. One's name begins with an N. One's name ends with the letter K. The third one has snow-white hair and wants her name to be mentioned with someone called Kenan. The total age of the three women seated together is 195. Almost two centuries. Easy to say! What's more, together they embrace two centuries not just with their ages but also with their sentiments. The age of the one whose name ends with a K, is 10 less than N, and 10 more than the one with the snow-white hair. Together they keep opening the fountain taps, and then forgetting to turn them off.

Şehnaz was stuck on this last sentence for a while.

Just when she had found the ages of these three women. One was 75, the other 65, and the third 55. In fact, in her mind, she'd even figured out their names: Nur Hanım, Dilek Hanım and Sisyphus Hanım. This was just when she'd worked out the love between the butch Sisyphus Hanım, the tough woman of tough rocks and slopes, and her life and love, the tough man of tough moments, Kenan Bey.

But the question didn't ask the ages of these women. It wasn't an age sum or a logic problem pretending to be an age sum. It was a pool equation. But it didn't quite pose a question related to the pool. Şehnaz sensed that the women sitting on the bench between the two fountains, the taps of which they had forgotten to turn off, were looking at her, and she shuddered. Her shudder would be replaced by despair within minutes. Because the question was also not about how many hours it would take for the pool to fill up or how long it would take for it to flood.

Şehnaz was confused.

She lifted her head up and looked away from the booklet in front of her, trying to perceive the classroom she was in, the smell of early summer trying to penetrate the windows, the sharp colors of the Bosphorus.

Şehnaz is in a damp-smelling Student Selection and Placement Center, abbreviated ÖSYM in Turkish, level 2 exam room of 1984. On the green board, a notice written with broken chalk reads 9:30–12:30; the mark of blunt limestone looms over the numbers. And it partly reveals the character of the person who wrote it. This was the writing of a hand whose presence had been conscribed to random appointment, being moved about like a checker piece, or fate. Who were they... Young teachers in Indian print skirts, standing in front of the desk. Every now and then they check their watches with leather straps wrapped around their delicate wrists, escape through the door that opens to the corridor, to the drafty, sublimely long hall, and then retreat back inside, only to drift off elsewhere, to the view of the Bosphorus that Şehnaz too was gazing at a moment ago. Escapist teachers these are, escapists; nothing but young idealists, the romantic types.

If Şehnaz hadn't wanted to be a doctor, she could have become one of those weird romantics that were now extinct. But her biology teacher had told her on several occasions: You could become a teaching assistant when you graduate; you could be a teacher and a doctor at the same time...

Şehnaz was convinced and satisfied by this idea, and she prepared for and entered the ÖSYM exam with this plan in mind. And with the belief that the saying 'things don't always go as planned' was just a saying, an old saying belonging to the past that had long lost its meaning. Fate is in one's own hands, she had said to herself. One can achieve whatever one desires.

According to the reassurances of her biology teacher and the future plans she had set in her mind, there was just one question Şehnaz needed to solve to win acceptance into medical school, and this was the pool, age, logic question. This question was an obstacle in itself. Şehnaz had aced all the questions up to this one. But in the face of this question, all her weapons dropped; she waited. Simply because she was not facing a logical question relating to the two fountains these three women were sitting between: It was an incoherent, inconsistent, utterly ridiculous question.

In contradiction to the complicated situation she was currently in, the question was actually simple. But, grave and stubborn, it stood there, clinging to the small black letters on the white booklet.

The question was a 'What happens next?' question, but the five multiple choice answers did not hold the option 'None of the above'.

It must have been the way Nur Hanım, Sisyphus Hanım and Dilek Hanım were sitting, accompanied by the bold view of the Bosphorus that the Beylerbeyi Halide Edip Adıvar High School, founded in this precious district, had inherited from life, that caused Şehnaz to ask herself the exact same question: 'What next?'

And years would go by.

What next: Şehnaz had never calculated this. After passing the exam on that day, she believed that the headscarf she removed when she entered the building and put back on when she left would never be an obstacle to her registering for and pursuing her studies like any other quiet and ordinary medical school student, or to her becoming a teaching assistant after graduation and staying on at the university. What's more, who could know what the future had in store for her, and what did it matter since she was eventually going to have to face it anyway.

From that moment on, 'What next?' was a question Şehnaz might think to ask herself frequently. But she would never quite find the words to express it. Because in the worst of memories, as in the best, some things are impossible to recount, like that question on that day.

For seven years, Şehnaz resisted dropping out of school. She would have to pass through seven doors and surrender an item of clothing at each one.

And she would break down: first because of the headscarf, then for the insults, then for being denied, for accounting to nothing, for being forced into being someone she wasn't, for being ignored... She finally dropped out of medical school, leaving it behind like a belonging forgotten on a bench.

What now?

What happens when and if someone is simply pushed aside?

Şehnaz and her headscarf would be in dissertation topics, essays and footnotes, but Şehnaz would never write her own dissertation, her own essays or footnotes.

What next? Things didn't always go as planned. Şehnaz the MD would still end up as a housewife. She would make wishes, pray that the nimbus of the universe would rain down on her, yet her fate would always match that of Sisyphus.

In the damp-smelling room of 1984, Şehnaz looks at the supervisors on whose flutter reflections of the colors of the Bosphorus seeping in through the window. And it is there she notices for the first time that the clues the future has to offer us are hidden in today. The power of the today that foretells the future, with a question, a color, a smell; for the first time. The day she was to leave the university not as a graduate but with the broken heart of being rejected entrance into class, for some strange reason she would run to Beylerbeyi, and as she sat on a bench pondering what made her like others and what made her different, she felt that the navy blue of the Bosphorus and the parade of colors reflected in the navy would burn her eyes. Only upon looking more carefully would she realize that she was in the garden of the Beylerbeyi Palace, sitting on one of the benches between the two fountains.

"We see the future, but at what cost?"

That is when she heard this question.

She wasn't the one to ask it. Even though it was a question she had wanted to ask, she hadn't heard it in the tone of her own voice.

Looking closer, she noticed that the question was posed by one of the three old women sitting on the bench right next to her.

—Seeing the future can sometimes change everything, she calls out to one of the other old women.

The old woman hadn't directed this question to Şehnaz and so didn't look to her for a response. She sat motionless, her eyes fixed on the fountain.

—You are sunk in thought again, Sisyphus Hanım; what is it? asked the woman sitting on the other end of the bench.

—Oh, don't even ask, Dilek Hanım, sighed Sisyphus Hanım.

—The color of the water is so dark, said Nur Hanım.

—Oh, oh! sighed Sisyphus Hanım. And then she added: Seeing the future can sometimes change everything...

—The elixir for the future is hidden in today, said Nur Hanım.

—The water is dirty, said Dilek Hanım.

—Oh, Kenan, Sisyphus Hanım went on sighing.

—You left the fountain tap open again this morning, Sisyphus Hanım. If it weren't for the watchman, we'd be in trouble, said Nur Hanım, a little reproachful.

—We know what her problem is; she thinks she'll be united with Kenan if the waters of the fountain flood, said Dilek Hanım.

—But if the waters were to flood, all the dirt would be washed away, said Sisyphus Hanım. There will be no more borders once the waters flood. Then Kenan will be a country, a name for hope, not a nightmare, a lover who deserved to die.

—Hah, said Dilek Hanım. A nightmare is a nightmare, and dirty water is dirty water.

—We can't really be sure, said Nur Hanım.

—Of what? asked Sisyphus Hanım.

—Whether the water will be cleansed or not, said Nur Hanım.

—It isn't that simple to cleanse dirty water, said Dilek Hanım.

—We can't really be sure, said Sisyphus Hanım.

—I don't know, said Dilek Hanım.

—Well, what next? asked Nur Hanım.

—Nothing has meaning anymore, said Dilek Hanım.

—Well, what next? asked Nur Hanım, insistent.

Şehnaz was stuck on this last sentence.

There was a bench between two fountains. And three old women sitting on the bench. One had a purple dress, the other was blonde. This seemed to be the summary of years passed. One's name began with an N, the last letter of one's name was K. The third one had snow-white hair.

Şehnaz was stuck on the last sentence. That was all she remembered.

"What does this question mean?" she had asked the supervisors in Indian print skirts, who after reading the question carefully alone and with each other, then turned their hands up in desperation and said: "We don't understand either; you might as well forget about this question…"

The question was forgotten. Just like all questions in the past.

Was that why Şehnaz had become so forgetful? Was that why she felt so tired and old?

That day, as the only remaining visitor of the day, she slowly walked out the Beylerbeyi Palace, laying the question 'What next?' aside, like many of her sex. Leaving behind her two fountains, their dirty waters flooding, as heavy as time, as old as life.

Tubbynana's Istanbul

Gönül Kıvılcım

Translated by **Kerim Biçer**

It was a cozy ground floor apartment in Fatih. Istanbul was small enough for its full view to be seen through the not so wide living room window of her jerrybuilt house. Perihan Hanım or Tubbynana, as she was known by her grandchildren, aged watching that narrow and dusty street in Fatih, whose dawns, twilights and evenings she knew like the back of her hand.

It was a street where the sky was not visible. No trees or flowers, but it was also merry, as one street peddler's voice followed the other. Fish, fruit and vegetable sellers…Once Tubbynana heard the yell, "Fresh fish!", she'd roll up her knitting around her needles, find a spot to place it on the low coffee table in front of her, and stop the peddler before he disappeared from sight. Fish scales and shoals of anchovies: all that reminded her of the past, of the Black Sea that would fill the house with a blowing breeze.

It's now evening time. The *fasıl* begins on the radio in the three-story Greek house. A day in the past: Tubbynana pushes her wicker chair beside the window, singing along with her voice, which matches just the sound of gramophone records. She is engrossed in the far-off sunset, the sun that is setting the sea ablaze in Tirebolu. Ruddy sunsets form a background for the five healthy children, each hungrier than the other, sitting at the table munching away. A huge kitchen with an ottoman inside, a large oven with a brazier and stove, each with a meal cooking, wild waves, maritime pleasures… They are all history now. What, the view from the house in Fatih, did you say? The roof of a rundown outbuilding stuck between two apartment blocks. The view of the waves she couldn't stop watching had now been replaced by some ragged old belongings dumped on the roof of this derelict building. And the joy in a family home, visits from friends and grandchildren, were all exchanged for a flickering television screen.

It didn't matter what was on, television meant sound, a sound that never abandoned her in this small and conservative neighborhood in which she was trapped. Perihan Hanım was all alone, but she didn't complain. Despite her negligent children, her pelvis fractured when she fell while queuing to draw her pension, and the fact that she has to walk with crutches for the rest of her life, she holds her head up high.

Imagine a volcano ready to erupt any minute, under whose constant threat you live and whose shadow you feel on your back, but who is still a friend. A friend, because no matter how difficult it makes your life, you still cannot do without it, and it is your source of income. Thank God tourists come, attracted by its charm. The volcano is part of the scenery you have outside your window. Its presence in the horizon reminds you of how meaningless your ambitions are, and that everything you have bled yourself to make flourish could turn to dust, melting in a sea of lava.

The presence of a grandmother who is eighty-odd years of age, is likewise a threat for us. An index finger that is always pointed, forbidding, drawing the line.

Something had happened to her recently, something even her index finger found difficult to describe. A dream! For the first time in many years, it was not the house or the furniture or even the layout of the furniture in her house that she was seeing, but a true dream. A bright light had filled the apartment. The whole place seemed to be lit up. It wasn't a kind of light she had known before. It was a strong, radiant, penetrating light that blazed in each and every dark room and dim corner. This must be an imitation of heaven, thought Tubbynana. The furniture seemed erased in the violent light, and not a single defect to upset her or disturb the order of her home remained.

It was death that was approaching her. She understood this when she saw her husband's body leaning backwards, his mouth wide open.

She froze holding their morning coffee on a tray. Tubbynana encountered death in her flannel dressing gown and with her floral-print slippers. The day Sait Bey died, his lively voice still echoed in the house. She was pleased that the Turkish coffee she had made had plenty of froth, just the way her husband of forty years liked it. "Perihan, no one can make it like you do. Go on, make me a strong cup of Turkish coffee," he had said, flattering her and sending her away to the kitchen. He knew very well that Perihan would never forget his morning coffee. But just in case! Death was right there, in the body of her husband of forty years. When Tubbynana came in, Sait Bey was already in death's command; death, whose place and time is never guessed, had taken her husband. She searched for signs of life in his already heavy arms. She understood upon touching his feet, death had descended upon Earth with all its coldness and unpredictability. This was something she could not handle alone. She called her ungrateful daughter who lived in the city.

On the walls of Tubbynana's house in Fatih were damp stains, plaster cracks and layers of soot from the central heating, which built up more and more each year, just like in all old houses. From the outside, it was an apartment building from the Sixties with a mosaic façade. They had moved here after Sait Bey had gone bankrupt and sold out his haberdashery. There was no longer any sign of the old wealth or splendor. Whereas in the past...

The whole family would visit Istanbul altogether, traveling in luxury cruise ships with pianos playing in dining halls, entertainment on the deck, and poker in the casinos until three o'clock in the morning. They would pull up in motorboats alongside the cruise ship anchored offshore in Giresun, and while expandable suitcases and provisions were carried on board one by one, passengers would rush to board the boat, excited about the voyage that was soon to begin. Everyone would prepare for the express cruise to Istanbul as if it were a fashion show. If the ship was not bobbing up and down on the wild waters of the Black Sea like a nutshell, people would eat in fancy dining halls, play games of chance, poker, pontoon or conquian all night, until they crawled back to their cabins. But on stormy days, they were deprived of these pleasures; seasick, they would wait in their cabins for the storm to subside. In Istanbul they would stay at Hotel Meseret, eat out at Konyalı Lezzet Restaurant and dress from the best tailors in Tarlabaşı. Tubbynana would have almost all her dresses sewn by Tailor Hayriye, whose fabrics and designs were matchless. Hayriye's atelier was spacious and located between Taksim and Tarlabası. Her styles were so amazing that once the adventure was over and Tubbynana had returned home to Tirebolu, everyone would rush to her place to see them. She was the talk of the town—Perihan's scarves, Perihan's dresses, Perihan's coats...

There was a different nightclub to visit each night, and they enjoyed the world of entertainment until the early hours of the morning. Tepebaşı, Cumhuriyet Nightclub; with Sait Bey's cash-heavy pockets and Perihan Hanım's jewelry from the Grand Bazaar, they chased after their favorite stars together. All that was left now was awaiting death in this dim house that no one ever cared to visit.

No one knew how lonely she really was. No one. Not even the loners of Fatih Park, who walked even slower than she did and whose eyes shed no light. At a snail's pace, leaning on her crutches, Tubbynana would walk to this park on the main street, which had a playground in one corner: this was the meeting point for the lonely and those who longed for green. She'd go and move closer to someone sitting on their own.

"So what is your home like?" she asked the woman who, like herself, had false teeth.

"Two bedrooms, a sofa, a hob, a stove. I don't even have central heating." They were both there to complain. But Perihan Hanım had to give her son his due.

"Bless him, my son had central heating installed in my house," she said.

"You see, yours is grateful."

"Oh yes, he is... If only his wife would let him do more."

"What does your daughter-in-law do?" asked her bench friend, wanting the conversation to go deeper, happy to have the gossip continue. Without answering the question, Perihan Hanım complained about her false teeth. "It's as if I have a second mouth in my mouth," she said. The lady did not seem to be interested in her teeth at all. Had she known that for Tubbynana food was equally important as her daughter-in-law... Life meant eating, drinking, tasting, watching cauldrons boiling, laying generous tables, throwing and attending dinner parties. All of this was now history. All that remained now was a park, a street and a window.

"So, you were talking about your daughter-in-law..."

The loneliness in the park grew each time of her companion said 'daughter-in-law'. Tubbynana criticized her daughter-in-law partly just to amuse her companion.

"To hell with my daughter-in-law," she said. "She does all she can to make a fool of me in front of my son. She is jealous of me. She wants him to love no one but her, that's what she wants."

As the two women conversed, seagulls flew over the onion domes of the mosques in Eminönü. A little boy fed the pigeons; ferries that smelled of history moved closer to the pier in Karaköy. Perihan Hanım dreamt of watching the sea from the courtyard of Süleymaniye Mosque: the Bosphorus looked deeper from there. To tell the truth, she greatly missed the sea, even in the city of the sea. She once was a well-off girl, of the sea and of abundance.

Now all Tubbynana did was nag. "How will we die? How will we be buried underground!" It was to such an extent that whoever heard her nag would think she believed the more she nagged the longer she would live. "All is vanity. If there is death, all is vanity," she kept saying.

"Oh mother, that's enough! You can't die just because father has." It was when her youngest daughter İdil last visited. She hadn't knocked on her door for nearly three months. Her rich and capricious daughter, who lived on the opposite coast and thought the neighborhood where her mother lived was so below her standards, she'd make her driver park the car on the next street to prevent anyone she knew from spotting it. The lives and secrets that Istanbul harbors! Without welcoming or pampering her daughter, Tubbynana turned her eyes away to the television and grunted, "I'd been waiting for the news." İdil held in her hand a plastic bag full of sea breams and green apples. Tubbynana's face lit up when the silvery fish were laid out on the worktop. As her daughter gutted them, she did not watch idly. She tied a piece of cloth to the end of her crutch and cleaned the living room windows.

Then she took her false teeth out of their box so she could bite an apple. "If they weren't in this box, I would never ever be able to find them when I need them," she said, gesturing with the confidence of a politician. Yet she detested these false teeth. "These are like railroad tracks with stakes in my mouth," she said. But no matter how much she hated them, the case was always there in its place, in the top drawer of the bookcase just above the divan. Not only the dentures but every object in Tubbynana's home had its own unmistakable place. She designated a place for every object with the fastidiousness of a landscape architect who plans precisely the order and arrangement of the flowers to be planted in a garden. Her keys, pictures from her youth, her prayer rug, all lived happily in their spots set many moons ago. Moreover, Tubbynana's mirrored wardrobe, antique clock that rocked the whole house every hour, and the chairs placed at each side of the table in the living room, all perfectly balanced each other. If they ever slouched instead of standing erect, it was enough for Tubbynana to raise an eyebrow.

But death! Tubbynana told her daughter over and over again about that day when it rained continually, and the moment she was caught unprepared by death. They searched for a place to put death in the most remote corner of the house, over and over again. But it didn't work. There was no place for death in Tubbynana's plans. She kept speaking to herself for days and days. Each time, going around in circles in vain, she ended up talking about death again.

According to Perihan Hanım, death must have been amused to see people breathing their last breath, just as it was amused to watch cars sliding on icy roads. She recounted over and over again that day with heavy thunders and rain, the moment she was caught unprepared by death. They searched every corner of the house knowing it was all in vain. There was still nothing. There was definitely no room in Tubbynana's world for the unknown.

For Tubbynana, the map of the objects in her house was clear and detailed. For example, Sait Bey's briefcase was always where it was supposed to be. It was hung on the coat stand once he got home, would be placed on the table after dinner, and before he went to bed, it would take its place on the coat stand once again. She could not help it: she had thought of places for her merchant husband and his personal belongings in the house, as well. In the early years of the marriage, Sait Bey would occupy the dinner table once he got back from work. In the evenings, she'd put his dinner at the head of the table, and when he had finished and it was time to do the dishes, her husband's newspapers, bus tickets and all the other various items in his briefcase would be scattered all over the dinner table. Every time she looked inside the briefcase, she'd feel dizzy. But her map of objects would not allow her to fiddle with the content of the briefcase.

When her husband confessed the shop would be closed, "Your place is ready," she said. "Don't you ever worry about where you will go once the shop is closed."

She allotted him the room that overlooked the walnut tree in the back garden. With difficulty, she'd deliver Sait Bey's coffee to his room twice a day. A coffee with no sugar, while he was reading the morning newspaper; and another right after his midday nap. It was easy to see they were not the same age and Sait Bey was getting closer to the threshold called 'death'. He was fifteen years older than his wife. There were also signs his heart was growing weak: The back pains at nights. The tremble of his hands. The puffing and panting worse than a steam train as he climbed the stairs. The pills he took. Cutting down his coffee to one a day. Phone calls informing her that he was just taking a rest and that he'd be on his way shortly, whenever he was out.

Tubbynana, despite all these warnings, could neither find a place for the inevitable, nor calculate it in all the plans she made. She was unprepared. However, death was gradually materializing, becoming as real as her home furniture.

The day arrives when life makes all the plans we hold in our hands unusable. For Tubbynana, that day had already arrived. They lay Grandpa Sait down on the bed, which for Tubbynana, was the source of life.

Death was in life's bosom.

But life, despite everything, refused to give in and kept showing itself in curious places. It wasn't even a week before the local authority had planted hollyhock seedlings in this barren street in Fatih. Tubbynana was over the moon. She was now the guardian angel of the saplings; the kids didn't stand a chance. She was horrified that hard footballs might knock down the saplings. And when one day the saplings suddenly bloomed, she felt elevated with joy remembering Tirebolu, moments of happiness, life, which continues despite death, and her children, her children who had forgotten her. The brass bed on which she had become pregnant with her two daughters, the children she had given birth to in the same bed, pushing in excruciating pain. The younger weighed four kilos, she remembered as if it were yesterday. Tubbynana had screamed for two days until her bones widened. Abal Güz—she'd never forgotten the midwife's name—had pressed cooked eggs on her wounds.

Tubbynana watched the hollyhocks from her window, and waited for the night to come, when she would turn her face to the past. One evening, as the dark began to fall, for the first time in many days she didn't turn her lights on. The house was pitch-black, so pitch-black that her own house suddenly scared her. This familiar space was now frightening. What if something unexpected would come in her way and make her trip and fall? The city lights were left outside; they couldn't find their way in. Neither could the streetlights and the moonlight that stared strangely from the sky. And the bedroom? Would Tubbynana be able to make it there? Perhaps death was faster than her. At the same time, the caretaker and his family were in their apartment breathlessly watching an exciting action film and had completely forgotten about her. But they were all ears when they heard the thump that came from upstairs. "Here, even the loneliness of the streets is dusty," thought Tubbynana as she fell to the floor.

And in those final seconds just before she shot off like a shooting star, "Death in Istanbul," she thought, "death in Istanbul is a little hasty, a little doleful, but very lonely."

Whereas, she said to herself later, *while loving, wearing fancy clothes and breeding mountain-high ambitions, one ought to make room for death too.*

The Button to Activate Forgetting

Nazlı Eray

Translated by İdil Aydoğan

I'm in front of the mirror. I comb my hair, cleanse my skin with lotion, apply navy blue mascara on my eyelashes. I give my lips the slightest touch of a number 146 light color lipstick.

I'm wearing a half slip and a black lace bra.

You, the size of my little finger, are sandwiched between my left breast and bra cup. I placed you there myself.

You lie slightly stretched over my breast; your arm dangles down from the edge of the black lace.

You have this sluggish morning drowsiness in your eyes. You lie in my bra motionless, as if resting in a hammock, right on my heart.

I carry on getting ready.

"Close your eyes! I'm going to spray my armpits with an antiperspirant!" I said. You closed your eyes and buried your head deep inside my bra.

I sprayed my underarms with the Pinky deodorant.

I applied light beige powder onto my neck and breasts, using a huge powder puff. You choked and coughed and started sneezing.

I talked to you while I put my jacket on.

"You're comfortable down there, right?"

"Yes, I am. The smell of perfume has slightly befuddled me…"

"Perfect. That's why I wear it!"

"Is it Armani?"

"Yes, it is."

I button up my cardigan, leaving one button open so you can breathe.

I slip my boots on. Wear my coat and leave it unbuttoned.

"I'm going to my friend's for a cup of coffee. You won't be bored down there, will you?" I asked.

"No, no, I won't. I might take a little nap," you said.

* * *

I got out of the cab, hastily climbed the stairs to Gülben's apartment, and knocked on the door.

Gülben opened the door.

She looked at me.

"You're better. You're looking beautiful today," she said.

She gave me a hug and a kiss.

For a minute, I was afraid you'd get squashed between us! I took my coat off and went into the living room.

Ayten had arrived before me. She had lit a cigarette and was sitting in an armchair by the window.

"How are you?"

"Well, slightly better, I guess…"

"Any news?"

"No".

"How many days is it now has it been now?"

"Twenty…"

Gülben came in from the kitchen and sat opposite me.

"I wonder why he doesn't come and talk to you?"

"He's running…"

"Perhaps he believes he's already said everything there is to say."

"These are terrible days, girls…" I said.

Ayten: "You've got to press the button to activate forgetting!" she said. "Press it and free yourself! Let time start ticking. You're stopping time, because you still hold hope within you. You're wearing yourself out with every passing day. Every day he doesn't call, you fall to pieces all over again. Listen to me! You've got to press the button to activate forgetting!" she said.

"I can't believe it, Ayten!" I said. "I can't believe that he could do this to me. Or rather, I don't believe it. And it's not exactly easy to believe…"

Gülben: "He must have had dilemmas," she said. "When he went, he must have had dilemmas… and his family probably put pressure on him too. Flattering him because he's now a doctor, a professional who earns good money, encouraging him to find a suitable bride," she said.

"Yes," I said. "And he couldn't present me to them. He was afraid of the rumors and gossip that would spread. His family, their small circle in the country, nosy people… Isn't it just terrible? The deep love we've had for each other these three years, and such a perfect relationship—it can't just end this way!"

Ayten was harsh.

"But it has," she said. "Why do you still refuse to see the truth? You'll be free the moment you do. You're going to hate him. He left you! That's not what you deserved!"

"But I don't want to hate him," I said.

"Enough! None of this is real!" you shouted from inside my bra.

Gülben and Ayten stared back at me, shocked.

"What's wrong?" Ayten asked.

"Nothing. Don't mind me. I'm a bit tense. I don't know what I'm saying,"

I said, and stared at the African violets and ferns in the windowsill.

"I hate men! I simply hate them!" said Ayten. "Years ago I found this really ugly one, skinny like a walking stick. Single. Younger than I was. They snatched him off of me too. Really, I didn't care about him being ugly, as long as he gave me peace of mind. He walked in one day and told me he was marrying a twenty-three year old. Oh! How I felt at that moment! Goddamn them all! I was there when the marriage ceremony was taking place in the marriage office. I walked about like a ghost. I fainted. Collapsed onto the floor. They lifted me up. 'He was my husband,' I said. What else could I say? I cried for months in an empty house, all on my own. I kept visiting the *hodja*. Once the hodja asked me to bring a black rooster! Another time some water from the *hamam!* We filled up a bottle of water from the hamam! But none of it was any use."

She was so sincere in how she told her story, I started laughing. I looked at her cute blonde bangs, black beady eyes, lively spirit, and laughed.

"Yours was simply ungrateful," I said.

She laughed.

"And what about yours?" she asked.

Suddenly you started screaming at the top of your lungs from inside my bra.

"Enough! Enough of you women! Enough of your nonsense! I don't want to listen for another minute!"

I didn't know what to do, what to say.

The two of them stared at me, surprised.

I didn't know how much of it they had heard or understood.

"My heart has started pounding terribly, girls," I said. "Forgive me. I'm suffering from depression. I don't know what I'm saying!"

"I know exactly what I'm saying!" you screamed.

I pressed my hand against my chest. I was trying to keep you quiet.

The doorbell rang.

Ayten went to get it.

Two people were standing at the threshold. Confused, we looked at the newcomers. A young woman and a young man. It seemed as if they'd popped out of an old snowy winter's day and appeared at our doorstep. I recognized the girl immediately. It was me, seventeen years ago. And the young man next to her was my ex-boyfriend who I'd split up with after deep sorrow and serial arguments. They were so distant to me, and I was such a stranger to the things we had lived through, to those past days; I shook their hands coldly.

They had clearly just had an argument. Perhaps they had quickly made up outside the door and were stepping in to my life out of the blue, at this most turbulent, painful moment.

The man sat on the sofa. It's obvious how he's upset the girl; in other words, me. He is a real thug, you can tell from his every move. It's incredible how the girl can't see this. The sorrow in their faces, as if it was the end of the world.

"What's going on? Isn't that you?" you whispered. "Who's that man with you?"

"Hush," I said. "That's me seventeen years ago; she's here with her boyfriend. Quiet."

"So, how is everything?" I asked the newcomers just for the sake of conversation, raising my voice.

I didn't like my old hair. It was dark. Too long. And the cut of the trousers I was wearing: they were simply hilarious! How fashion changes…

In fact, how everything changes. Why on earth am I wearing those low-heeled shoes? Clearly we've been roaming the streets idly. We must have just arrived from Istanbul.

How strange, these two people sitting in front of me. I can't find a single thing to talk to them about; these two people who are a part of my past. I felt miserable. I was already heartbroken.

The girls proved to be friendlier. They started conversations about this and that, and offered the newcomers coffee.

I look at my old self, unable to decide whether I was attractive or not back then.

The man was an idiot. He could hardly string a sentence together. He must have had issues. He used to drink: that's what I remember. I don't even remember the details.

I sit still, bored to death.

"Forgive me, I've got to be somewhere," I said.

I left the old lovers with the girls and rushed out of the house.

You began questioning me on the way:

"That was the guy you loved?"

"Oh, I don't know. It's been so long. I'd even forgotten what he looked like."

"You were so gentle in the past."

"Am I rough now?"

"But that old you, so gentle towards that guy...You gaze into his eyes."

"I can gaze into yours. What are you trying to say?"

"No, that's not what I meant. But see how you cherished even that worthless man."

"I did because I loved him. Are you jealous?"

"No, I'm mad."

"And I was mad at myself. Didn't you see, I couldn't stand sitting in front of them."

We walked without saying a word for a while. I knew: my feet were taking me to Dream Street.

I had just turned into Dream Street when I heard the noises of two people running after me.

I turned to look.

Oh boy, the old me and her boyfriend who we had just left in Gülben's apartment had run after me and caught up with us.

"Can you help us? After all, you do have more experience and knowledge compared to us. Something is happening to us. We're suffering. You're the only person who can understand. Please help us," said the girl.

I always find myself in the strangest of situations.

You started fidgeting about inside my bra.

"Guys, you're so young," I said, "what could possibly come of your relationship? Besides, look, you're together. Go out, roam the streets, go to parts of the city you've never seen before. Everything will pass; it will be better. I'd try to do something if it were any other time, but believe me, right now, I'm in a far worse situation than you are."

I look at the girl. She's grief-struck. She has bags under her eyes. Clearly the inconsiderate jerk who's meant to be her boyfriend is upsetting her and making her cry.

I look at the man. A type that hasn't settled down yet. How did these two people find each other? How did they ever fall in love with each other and, most importantly, how do they manage to cause each other such pain and grief?

Don't we do everything we do just to be happy?

Whatever…

I can't believe it!

I look at my old self in amazement. I pull her aside.

"Do you love this man?"

She looks at me, her eyes shinning bright, but in agony.

"I do, I really do." (How naive, how very naive…)

"Does he love you too?"

"Yes, he does…"

"So what's your problem?"

"We hurt each other. We can't be together or apart…"

"What does this young man do for a living?"

"He's currently looking for a job."

"Does he have money?"

"His father is rich…"

"What does he give you? I mean, what do you love about this man? He doesn't seem very amiable to me."

The old me felt offended. Her eyes watered up.

"I like what is disagreeable about him," she said.

"Couldn't you find someone else to love?"

"…"

"Why don't you choose someone that's right for you, someone who can make you happy…"

All of a sudden you jumped out of my bra. Like a heart that had popped out of place you shot out in an arrow and landed in the middle of Dream Street.

You were your normal size.

You stood right next to me, as solid as a door.

The me from seventeen years ago and her boyfriend looked at you in astonishment. You were fuming mad. You turned to the man:

"Hey, why do you have to be so stubborn and keep upsetting this girl?" you shouted.

The man opened his mouth. Said something. We couldn't hear what.

You punched him in the face! His nose started bleeding. I was afraid.

The me from seventeen years ago tried to intervene. You pushed her aside.

You turned again to the man:

"You going to marry this girl? You got good intentions?" you asked.

To my surprise, he answered back:

"None of your business, man! Who the hell are you anyway? Who do you think you are? Mind your own business!"

The fight flared up, with both of you kicking and punching each other. He gave you a left blow. You gave him a wallop on the side.

The old me and I were rushing around the two of you, screaming.

You shouted:

"Like hell it's none of my business! I'm the last man this woman loved! I'm a part of her world, okay? I can protect her!"

And he shouted:

"And I'm this woman's past. Don't you undermine me, you jealous bastard! You clearly made this woman unhappier than I ever did. Get lost..."

"How dare you speak to me like that, you shadow from the past!" you shouted.

And off the two of you went again.

Fists flew in the air.

I was horrified in case one of you pulled out a knife.

A watchman's whistle was heard from afar. "The police are coming!" someone shouted; it was your cousin Asım.

The branches of the trees trembled. There was a disturbance on Dream Street.

Asım had climbed up onto the wall.

"Ali Abi! Hit him, kill the thug!" he shouted.

"Stop it," I motion to him. He provokes you even more.

"Hit him, Abi, give him a taste of your fist!"

We, the two women, watched the fight holding each other, mortified.

A police car appeared in the distance.

The team had arrived.

You leapt up, shrank in the air, and hid inside my bra.

Four police officers had come out the car and were looking around.

"Where's the other man?"

"What man?"

"Wasn't there another man?"

"No, there wasn't!"

"Yes, there was."

"What are you talking about? What man?"

They put the ex-boyfriend and the me from seventeen years ago in the car and took them to the station to take their testimonies.

Dream Street fell silent again. Everywhere, in the bushes near the edges of the walls, in the ivy winding around the houses, it was evident that winter had just arrived in Ankara.

There was nothing else to notice.

As I walk, Dream Street slowly diffuses around me.

I talked to you, quietly.

"I never knew you were so short-tempered."

"I couldn't bear it," you said. "I couldn't bear that jerk upsetting you like that... Never let anyone upset you like that for as long as you live, okay?"

"Okay," I said.

Tears ran down my cheeks.

No, I won't let anyone upset me like that again.

Dream Street was gone.

I was surprised to suddenly find myself at the seafront. A bright blue, shimmering sea stretched out in front of me. I knew right away: we were in Bodrum, near the pier. It was the early hours of the morning. There was a slight summer mist in the air. You were holding onto the tickets you had placed inside our passports. In front of us a convoy of tourists had formed a queue.

In a moment, we'd pass customs, board one of the Meander ferryboats, and sail to the Greek island which lay straight ahead.

I pulled out from my pocket my red-rimmed 'punk' glasses and put them on.

We quickly passed ticket and passport control and walked onto the pier to board the boat.

This was the first time you were going abroad. You were excited and eager. I was as eager as you were. We climbed up the stairs on the side leading to the upper deck and sat on one of the lined-up benches. You had pulled out your camera and were taking pictures of Bodrum, me, and the boat.

The tourists had filled the deck. They chattered livelily amongst themselves.

The boat moved.

It maneuvered and made its way out of the harbor.

Leaving foam white bubbles behind, it set out towards Kos.

Bodrum slowly grew smaller, the white shapes on the shore becoming unrecognizable.

A while later, a gigantic dark mass appeared in front of us.

We had almost arrived in Kos.

In the Melancholy of Wisteria

Suzan Samancı

Translated by Amy Spangler

I am a pendulum in the tangle of voices that destroys my dreams. A bitter-ish taste in my mouth. The drone of a slumbering city, the mysterious scent of wisteria... The sun seeping through the slats of the shutters is foreign, as are the voices. My very being feels foreign; and as I toss and turn in bed, as if I am trying to rescue myself from my body, I don't know what to do with my hands.

Istanbul absorbs all sounds. A flowing river, wild pansies, an ethnic joke... I scatter them like a string of pearls on the hard surface of my memory. While the lavender scent that fills the room reminds me of my freedom, I cannot escape the acrid smell of the humidity that was my companion for twelve years, nor can I, in this state somewhere between wakefulness and slumber, pass from one thought to the next. Not a soul came to meet me when I was released. My legs were rusty scissors, my arms walking canes. I was taking refuge in the salvation of my backpack, getting lost in the crowd and trying to follow people I thought might be the right ones. I was taking a breather at bus stops, reading signs, and when I asked after an address or the time, the words would get knotted up in my throat. The eyes of the man sitting on the bench twitched. "It's obvious you're not from around here!" he said.

What torture not to inform me of my release date! When I heard the sound of the sloppy-mouthed warden, my wish to have committed a crime worthy of a life sentence was more than a mere passing thought. "There's a big ol' roaring world out there!" the other inmates laughed. The headcount that struck you like the vilest swear word, the door of rusty iron, the drippy faucet…

I don't recall how long I sat at the stop. I kept getting lost in thought, staring at the skyscrapers, the huge billboards, images that travel from the other side of that foreign wind. I was watching the hurried steps of all those people with their telephones to their ears and their synchronized arms, and I felt I might suffocate. That's how they release you: just toss you out, just like that. If they'd let me know the day beforehand, my sister would've come. When I got on the bus, I took the twenty lira bill from my pocket and held it out, asking, "How much?" The driver's bulging eyes became crossed and he shook his head saying, "Good heavens, have you been living under a rock! You need a ticket, a ticket!" A red-headed woman sitting in the front row spoke up: "I've got an extra." I sat down next to her. She looked at me from over the rims of her glasses and smiled. "Hmm… You're from the countryside, I imagine!" No matter where we go, our identity is obvious; they read it in our voices, in our faces. As I concentrated on the groan of the bus and the gaze of the young men with their tattooed faces, sounds exploded like tiny pieces of crystal in my mind, and birds of yesteryear began beating their wings in my heart. I shut my eyes. The lean horses pulling fancy phaetons pass before them, planes dives into blue eternity… Houses with earthen roofs, skyscrapers… A cow bellows on a yellow plain, the limbs of the trees on the hilltop shake. I'm aboard a ship. Across from me, the Maiden's Tower! Pharaohs with kohl-lined eyes wave their hands. When I realized that I had given voice to the correlation between the violence which has alienated me from what is mine, and those who had put me in this situation, I shot straight up as if I'd swallowed a pole. Those behind me giggled, "She must have escaped from the clinic!" While the woman next to me, a benign smile on her face, said in a low voice, "Go to sleep. Just go to sleep."

When I got off at Taksim, I didn't know which way to go; as I looked around blankly, children selling handkerchiefs and gum stuck to me like ticks. I asked them what their names were. "Rojda, Mizgin, Welat, Şilan…" One of them laughed as she yelled out, "Sister, this one's name is Ajda, Ajda!"

The evening rush, Istanbul with its huge, droning belly! A shiver went down my spine. In a state of mind like those who long for freedom yet recoil from it, I headed for the phone booth. When I had trouble using the card I had bought, I asked the people in line for help. "You're putting it in backwards," one of the men grumbled. My breathing grew quicker. "Hello," my sister said. When I told her I was in Taksim, my voice cracked; I swallowed. I sat down on the bench next to the flower sellers. The boisterous Romany women with big breasts and swinging hips were raising a ruckus, smoking cigarettes, foxily observing their targets. I smiled at their brazenness, as they swore like sailors. Words that I was hearing for the first time fluttered in the darkness.

The last time we'd seen each other, my sister had been in poor spirits. I didn't ask her what was wrong. I knew it was Sinan, the conflict between them, their inability to get along. Yet how sincere and protective she had been when we had first set out to overturn the system. She'd met Sinan one night at a memorial. In his baritone voice he'd read poems by Cegerxwin and Nazım. When my sister started coming home late, all hell broke loose. My father told her to get her act together. "First school, then marriage!" he said. When she'd been taken into custody and released, he jumped all over her. Sinan was hanging out in front of our home, putting notes into matchboxes and tossing them onto the balcony. That day, my sister began living with Sinan's family. "I disown you," my father said. "I won't have a daughter like you!" My mother pounded the pavements of the neighborhood where they lived to be able to see her daughter; she sent food, warning her, "Whatever you do, make sure your father doesn't find out."

Women who abandon themselves for the sake of marriage or children. Such a pity...

My eyes are dazzled by this atmosphere, which flickers, full of laser lights. As I pondered the overwhelming distance created by luxury, my sister cried out, "Ayten!" I froze. She embraced me, sobbing. I buried my face in her neck; it was the scent of my mother. I looked at my sister out of the corner of my eye. Is this my sister? I asked myself. She'd gained weight, her hair had thinned, and her face had grown wrinkled before its time. As if reading my thoughts, she said, "I'm a total waste." As we walked down İstiklal, I kept tripping. I didn't know what to say. The lights, the crowd, they were frightening. Young people were joking around, taking rhythmic strides to the music playing in their ears. My sister told me that Sinan had a successful textile business, that he'd expanded and gotten into export. And then she sighed, "Money changes people, it changes them a lot."

We stopped in front of a building that looked like a piece of Roman architecture. As stills from black and white films cracked open the door to my consciousness, I suddenly got the feeling that I was living in a different time. The high, decorated ceilings, the encaged elevator, the marble column, all said so much. I stuffed my hands in my pockets and rose onto my tiptoes. "The building must be really old," I said. My sister, with an irrepressible tone of satisfaction in her voice, replied, "A hundred and thirty years." I sat down on the armchair. "Why don't you take a shower? You'll feel better," she called out from the kitchen. As I relaxed under the hot water, I thought of the cesspit—the pressurized water, the fat cockroaches and the time I had bathed in the tub. My sister had worked for an architect while she was in college. We'd spent the night at their home once, to look after their kids. It was the first time I'd ever seen such a beautiful bathroom; what fun we'd had while bathing.

At the dinner table, our voices grew softer as we spoke about our childhood, prison days, and the military coup. We were at once so close yet so far apart; the thin silence between us was one of suppressed pain and anger. I opened a window. "It's quite a nice view but, well…" she said, like a hostess trying to salvage a tense evening. My gaze caught on her nicotine-stained hands. She smiled and shrugged. When I cried, "It's not like I have a life, Sis!," she let herself go, like a clock whose coil has snapped. "You know what, you're the one who's really living! Not being able to be yourself, continuing a relationship for the sake of the children… life with Sinan, it's…" Her eyes wandered until they fixed on a spot in the distance. "Dad never forgave me, not even on his deathbed."

She was telling me about how miserable all of her friends were—the group of them had migrated to Istanbul en masse—when the doorbell rang. It was Sinan. He hugged me enthusiastically. How much he had changed. His clothes, the weight he'd put on. A consummate business-man. With an easygoing manner that bordered on snobbery, he headed for the liquor cabinet, as if walking over to embrace his enemy, and asked, "So, what's up with you these days?" His face, heavy with market ideology, grew broad and his 'colonial governor' posturing annoyed me. In his eyes, I was a creature to be pitied, someone whose life had been stolen from them. "Sell-out!" I thought to myself. And then I lost it: "You best just go to bed, or else you and I are going to have it out!" My sister hung her head, as if to say, 'Please, don't.' Sinan was getting slobbery, his tongue too big for his mouth, and he was speaking nonsense. It was the feeling of guilt that drove him to action now, that much I knew.

My sister sat down on the edge of my bed. "Where could I have gone, with two kids, and not a cent to my name?" My mouth was full of words, but I didn't want to hurt her. "Just let me be," I said. She scurried out of the room. "You don't have the guts, you…ah, you…" I mumbled after her.

The thousand-and-one-faced night of Istanbul echoed inside me. Hearing the whisper of my loneliness treading at the window, ships that had cast anchor drifted forward like brides ready to greet the conquerors and weep at the defeat of heroes.

I woke to the sound of voices coming from the kitchen. The sea quivering along the opposite shore filled my heart with hope. I stretched. I thought of my friends back in prison. We would have been having our seminars at that hour. My sister smiled. "Good thing Sinan left," she said. "Where are the kids? We rarely see their faces around here. They come home late and leave in the wee small hours for work," she said. "They're grown up now," I said. "And we're old," she mumbled, as if expecting consolation. I looked at the photograph of my smiling nephews. "Do they know how much bread costs?" She responded, "You must be kidding," as if speaking from deep within a well, her mind on her sausage and eggs. I couldn't tell my sister that her voice had lost all trace of her roots. In her attempt to repair the rift between us, she resorted to motherly compassion. "Eat some of this too. How about shopping? What about a trip to the baths?" As she considered a rant about Sinan's absence and how pathetic he was, her double-chin trembled. "Eat, eat," she said. I stepped out onto the balcony. The warm breeze dallied in the melancholy of the wisteria. I thought of the incompatibility of my arms and legs, and a fear stirred on my skin. I listened to the voice within me. I grabbed my bag and dashed out into the street. "Where are you going? Where…?" my sister cried after me. I walked up the hill. I inhaled the optimism emanating from the centuries-old houses along the narrow, cobblestone streets. I heard the sound of morning folk tunes coming from some of them, gossipy women joked as they watered flowers, old people enjoying the sun by the front doors shaded their eyes as they watched passersby. When I reached Galata Bridge, my steps grew less hurried, my arms and my legs were not mine. I leaned against the bridge railing; my passion for freedom dissolved in the blue of the sea. I trembled at the thought of the mountains and the pastures of my homeland. I walked to the intersection. I hailed a taxi. "To the bus depot!" I said.

Solmaz's End

Nilüfer Açıkalın

Translated by İdil Aydoğan

Istanbul was a matchless precious jewel, sprawled across God's table. Bright and radiant it shone in the night, under the full moon.

I had been on the road for nineteen hours. Sixteen hours of this was in the air, not counting the six hours I spent at Munich Airport. In an interval of six hours I had seen the full moon twice, on two different continents. When we began hovering over Istanbul, my spirit which had abandoned me until then returned and settled in its place.

It was as if I were a dream, slowly coming true.

I was like foaming coffee, about to be poured into a cup. Someone was sure to tell my fortune.

How I had missed everything…

No, I wasn't going to make a list.

What I had missed the most was the way everything was happy-go-lucky, so susceptible to change at any minute.

No, I wasn't going to make a list.

A city that was alive; that made you feel alive and constantly reminded you of mortality; left you astonished at the unpredictability of the world; a city that inhaled and exhaled, that gave life, took life, and carried life till the end; a city you could sacrifice yourself for.

I wish I hadn't made a list.

When I travel beyond the borders of this country the whole landscape transforms into a stage, and it is as if the play ends when I set foot on my land again.

As if the citizens of other lands had long become people of their roles, not people of life, but our people were forever backstage.

In my country, everything is excessively real.

I admire my people's shameless sullenness. They wander about all day with confidence, each posing in their own triumphant airs, having absorbed all their anger. Each is a bomb, ready to explode. No one bows down to anyone. There are no pretentious smiles. There is no law, no rules, no fear. If a shop assistant isn't in the mood, she won't even look a customer in the face, a grocer won't give you bread before he's finished on the phone, civil servants will snap at you if they're in bad spirits. People are open to argument, up for a row, but if someone were to trip and fall, they'd quickly catch them and raise them to their feet. Words are magical in my language; multiple meanings can be deduced, no word has a single meaning, not one. Meaning alters according to intonation and even the simplest sentence is open to interpretation.

Families go on teaching their children words that reside in dictionaries. They maintain their customs adamantly, persistently.

After so much longing one looks with such favorable eyes; surely this must be why everything appears so beautiful.

I really am happy to be in such a lively city, among such lively people, and to be one of them.

I had a huge portion of kebab. There's nothing like knowing what you are eating. Now that I'm back in my city, this brings an end to studying menus at restaurants. Simply say the word and get the dish. *Köfte* and *piyaz*, fried eggs, *kokoreç, ayran, dolma, kelle-paça,* beans, soup; all familiar tastes.

I have missed olives most of all.

The sound of the tram; the joy of the children holding on tight.

The faces of lunatics had slightly changed. The fallen had fallen deeper, adding to their numbers, while some had disappeared completely.

There were always discounts in stores. Products were half price at every season. Everyone knew that they were on 'sale' at their true prices but everyone had the tendency to swallow, digest and then forget the same lies over and over. To learn, know and feign ignorance and then forget has almost become a rule. Of course this rule also applies to tabloid journalism, the media and politics.

Men eye up girls unremittingly, girls craftily pretend not to notice. Everyone is happy. So it seems.

The İstiklal Bookshop. Oh, I've missed you so. New books, used books, reprints and discount CDs…

Preparations to build an unnecessary new shopping center on this magical street are being carried out at full speed. Capitalism presents those with capital the opportunity to change whatever they desire; and capital itself in the hands of the capitalist only produces capital again. What the magical street needs isn't a new shopping center but a new theater, a new cinema, a new exhibition hall, a new bookshop. Of course those who already possess capital don't care in the least about art and culture: all they care about is making more money.

I'd presume that as soon as one sought a reason to be angry it would be readily available, but it turns out this wasn't quite that simple. Everything is beautiful, simply beautiful. Throughout the time I was away, I had tried to understand another culture, but thanks to my obstinate refusal to adapt, I had never felt like one of *them*. And this helped me respond to every mistake I made simply by saying, 'So what!', therefore I am much calmer. Yes, I always found it difficult to adjust. I deserted my city as if I was fleeing something, and I still remained an alien in that far-off place where I landed. Time and again, I was shocked at the multitude of rules; and the more I noticed how they strived to conceal their biggest fears behind feigned respect, and how exhausted they were from trying to avoid stress and conflict, the more I retreated.

What we need to do is rip off the habitual smile that has seeped and settled into the faces of all Americans. But, alas, this is impossible. I couldn't possibly trust people who smile at everyone they come across, each and every passerby, anyone standing next to them, everyone their eyes meet, and then realize that afterwards their grins deflate like a burst balloon. You don't need a mask like that in my streets. Everyone can look at each other; there is something we call the 'eye's right'. They look, and carry on their way. If one day a passerby were to say to you, "Good day!" or "Hello!", first you'd be amazed, then you'd stop for a minute and think, "I wonder if I knew him from somewhere? I didn't say hello, how rude of me," and that would be the end of it.

There, someone just walked past and said hello, and I said hello back. I just arrived this morning and no matter how noncompliant I am, I would certainly respond to a greeting accompanied by a true smile. Before I understood this habitual greeting thing I probably said hello to at least five hundred people in the States. Now I said hello for the hell of it. Just for the hell of it.

"Solmaz!"

"Yes?"

"It's me!"

"Yes of course, it's you! Forgive me, I'm a bit absent-minded, I didn't notice you."

"You nodded hello!"

"I did but I didn't mean it, I mean, I just got back, just this morning. I'm a bit bewildered and preoccupied, please forgive me. How are you?"

"Fine. How about you?"

"I'm good too. Great, well, take care, I'll see you later."

"You too. See you."

He's gone. What was the guy's name, what was it?

"Solmaz! Solmaz!"

"Yeah!"

He's back. What was his name?

"I've moved, babe. Not far though, just one street down. You know my old place, the one on Simsar Street, behind Mecnun's, right?"

"Uh-huh…"

I don't… I can't remember… What was his name?

"Now I live right opposite Mecnun's, the yellow building, number seventeen, the loft. We're celebrating tonight. Osman, Naci, Şefo, Melda, and there's the new drummer for the band, and then there's…"

Now I remember.

"What happened to the old one?"

What happened? What happened to my love, Ömer?

"Oh, you mean Ömer?"

"Was that his name?"

"Ömer. He left the band but he's still coming, I mean he is invited. Join us too if you can."

"Alright. I'll see. I'd love to but I've got a couple of things to do. As I told you, I just got here, I've already told you. I'll try to make it though."

"It's number seventeen. Catch you later!"

"Bye."

I walked all the way to the tunnel thinking about Ömer. One month before I left, we grew closer unexpectedly, no strings attached. I concealed from him the storms that brewed inside me, and he never said a word to me. We didn't speak once about what had gone on between us, our feelings or thoughts. It seemed it was better that way. When he found out I was leaving, either he wasn't upset one bit or like me, he hadn't let on. You know how we take everyone to be like ourselves... Well, what was done was done. Tomorrow night I will go to that address, and if there is anything more that needs to happen between us, well, I'll take it from there; if not I'll just go on my way. What else can one do?

I had to stop by to see my doctor. My test results were back; we've got to talk, so he said.

Okay, I'll see him. But first a top-notch coffee, Turkish coffee, with sugar, a proper one.

I drank it.

I went to the doctor.

Big news: I've got cancer.

Strange... I feel so strange.

"I'm so sorry to say this but, you've got cancer," the poor doctor stammered, while I let out a deep sigh of relief upon the revelation, at last, of a case that seemed always to be known to me.

That's the spirit, doctor: relax, take a deep breath, and give us the full details. No no, forget about treatment, there's no need, I don't want to be treated. I dunno, in my case that would be a waste of medication. After all, what are my chances of surviving? Is there a possibility I might be cured? You're just going to buy me some time, and a whole load of torment with it. Has this pestilence spread everywhere inside me? It has. It has spread across my whole body and wrapped itself around me. So, it loves me! Tell me, how long have I got to live? Just tell me that, and see that I don't suffer pain, that's all I ask. Don't say you can't, you damn well can, and that's the end of it.

What a doctor! Cold, sullen and such a pain in the you know what. As if it's him who's got cancer. I think he felt slightly humiliated too. What good to him is a patient who refuses his treatment? If I were him I'd kick me out. Besides, I must be getting on his nerves with my increasing positivity. He says he's never seen anyone like me. Neither have I, quite frankly.

So I'll join the great majority in three months if I don't receive treatment. That's the spirit, let's hear it! Will I suffer pain? Yes I will. Of course I will; I'm used to it, aren't I? Never mind, let's not dwell on this; it's just a simple, common condition that so many people suffer from; I'm just one of them.

Lung cancer; just like my grandfather.

I left the doctor's surgery, bought a packet of cigarettes, quickly lit one and puffing away at it, dialled the one I loved. The man I had believed loved me. If I hadn't just received the news I had, it would have been impossible for me to call him. I admire the courage granted by knowing when you are going to die. The more conscious I become, the more I will enjoy my every moment.

"How are you?"

"Great! How are you?"

"I'm great too, really great."

I took another drag of my cigarette, had a couple of outbursts of coughing, and then we picked up the conversation from where we'd left off.

I didn't mention the cancer or anything. What's the point anyway? I'm not going to tell anyone.

I think my condition is going to present me with a deeper understanding of things.

"So, what have you been up to?"

"Nothing. I just got here this morning. Look, I'll just ask you straight: have you told anyone about what happened between us?"

I asked him this out of the blue. The most sincere answers are those received after asking the right questions at an unexpected time. And here we have his answer:

"Between us? Which one?"

"Oh, I was thinking the fifth occasion!"

"I beg your pardon?"

A hell of a curse passed my mind but I didn't voice it. I took another drag of my cigarette: no bud, just plain tobacco.

"What went on between us. The private stuff!"

"Oh, that. Listen, let's forget it ever happened. We were drunk, we weren't really thinking right, it was an accident, that's all."

"If you say so!"

"Don't you agree?"

"I do!"

I hung up. So did the man with the beautiful eyes whose crooked smile crawled from the corner of his mouth all the way up to his dimple.

And he carried on drinking.

We were drunk, we weren't thinking right.

I tumbled down the Italian Hill, down to Tophane.

So that was it! What happened between us was an accident.

Everything was simply accidental and…

Therefore it needed to be forgotten.

We must forget, presuming that we escaped without any harm done.

Well, who is going to stop me mentioning it?

The air smelt of the sweet *lodos* wind. I had a slight headache but I didn't let it get in my way. I've got cancer, my friend! I'm not about to be defeated by a headache!

Suddenly, a cold sore began to grow on my lip; it's more than welcome to come, to settle and nourish in its spot since there will be no kissing from now on.

An accident! I should have asked how many times the same accident needs to be repeated in order to not count as one. Surely he must have an opinion on that. He could lecture you on any given topic for hours and hours, but this time he probably would have fallen silent.

Fuck him and his answer...

I didn't order myself a narghile or anything. The clicking and clanking sounds of backgammon pieces echoed in my head. I decided not to sit down and went on my way.

Kabataş, Beşiktaş, Ortaköy... I walked. I felt like calling again but I didn't.

One day, a while after we had met, he had kissed me. The instance was a crash; the damage was great. Everything had altered and we had gone from two distant strangers to almost one united entity. The time we spent together afterwards was so brave and passionate that if this really was an accident, then we were shattered to pieces. I thought I knew so much about him. What a delusion!

I grew tired not of walking, but of my thoughts. So I decided not to eat myself up inside; there was already something doing that for me, it didn't need my help.

I jumped into a cab and gave the driver the address.

Istanbul, howsoever do you manage to preserve your bloom when being used so recklessly?

There's nothing quite like knowing you're going to die. You adopt an overtly relaxed state of mind, and are filled with unexpectedly huge courage, becoming insusceptible to life, assuming a wry attitude, laughing at things both appropriate and inappropriate. It's not that there are fewer misfortunes; it is your reaction to unfortunate events that changes.

The driver suddenly took a turn into a side street and the peculiar excuse that followed was this:

"*Abla*, I'm sorry but I really ain't in the mood. You see that traffic, if I get stuck in that I'll go completely bonkers! There's this wanker at the cabstand, excuse my French, he keeps winding me up. Now if I don't get back and beat the crap out of him, I won't be able to cool off. If you don't mind, I'll drop you off so you can take another cab. I don't expect you to pay, seriously, you understand, abla, right?"

He understood that I was pretending to understand. I quickly grasped and accepted the situation, which was by no means understandable, and got out of the vehicle.

Right then and there, for the first time, I felt like someone who was going to die anyhow, not like someone who had got out of a cab at a ridiculous spot for a ridiculous reason. The ridiculousness instantly became humorous.

I climbed a couple hundred steps to Cihangir, and from there I slowly made my way to Taksim, to the Magical Street.

Istanbul, as I stand an inch from parting from you for eternity (whatever eternity is), you play your most enthralling tricks on me; as if you need me, as if you'll refuse to let me go. But I did all I could; I took good care of you, I treated you well to the best of my capacity, I helped the needy I could reach out to. Even if I didn't really fix anything directly, I did at least change some small things for the better.

I wrote what I thought were my victories on the wings of a butterfly; she flapped and flew away.

I've been up and down this magical street God knows how many times. Its every spot, dot, comma, ellipsis and parenthesis I know by heart; all its positives and negatives, multiplications, divisions, fractions, all its other names, nouns, adjectives and pronouns unite with new words to create more and more phrases inside my head.

Each step breeds a new incident.

How is a municipal police officer supposed to understand a glue sniffer? The kid's on a loop, they're making him scream. And people are watching, staring as if it were on the evening news. Among them I am the only one who is shaking. The boy's screeches cut the street like razors. The bulky officer is just a numb wall he is crying at. As I draw close, I spot the tears marking clean waterways down his dirty face. Very young and extraordinarily beautiful eyes, an extremely well shaped, completely shaven head. Over and over he repeats, "Give me my glue, give me my glue, give me my glue…" It's fairly simple; a fairly simple request: he wants something that belongs to him. The municipal police officer wouldn't know how to handle the boy; he's bound to remove him as he would a street vendor's stall. Unable to see the importance of using his mind and heart, he thinks his strength will suffice. The motorcycle police will be here any minute, but if the boy carries on screaming like this, the municipal officer's fist will land on his face like a loose brick from the wall.

"Okay, dear, calm down!" I tell him and suddenly realize how close I've got. I thought he wouldn't hear me. But I was wrong, he did; I'm sure he did. He stopped the weeping and wailing for a minute to listen, searching for the direction of my voice. I quickly repeated:

"Alright, dear, it'll be alright, just calm down!"

What power the female voice holds.

I felt the eyes of the whole crowd on me. Faced with compassion, it seemed the poor boy feared being stripped of his power, so he responded to my unwelcome voice by screaming louder. The municipal officer lost his patience at this sudden outburst and grabbed the boy's twiggy arms.

Oh, how the boy bent like a cardboard box in these careless hands; how, how pitiful!

"Oh, oh no, no, don't hurt him, don't, don't you dare hurt him!" I said.

In perfect timing and at the perfect spot, two motorcycle police parked their bikes and snatched the boy off of the municipal officer's hands. They were like two statues, living and breathing statues shaped from the same mold. Holding the boy between them as if the three were friends, they walked him all the way to the mosque wall. I followed. I was afraid he might get beaten. One of the officers leaned him against the wall and began speaking to him in a calm and quiet tone. I got close enough to hear what he was saying.

"Son, you're a regular, so what's all this whining? It don't suit you, I'm telling you. Come on, pull yourself together. We know you, you're strong, you're brave. Come on, sober up. Chief is going to have you registered at a school, Chief Officer Sami. You can even become a police officer if you like. Don't you know Chief Sami, boy? Hey! I'm talking to you! Burak, look at me! Look at my face! Chief Sami… Come on, boy, pull yourself together. You know, right?"

"Right, alright, *abi*, alright."

Yeah alright. I'd heard what I had wanted to hear. I walked away with the rest of the crowd.

It was time to pull myself together. I made my way towards the Mevlevi Lodge in quick steps. It was closed. For renovations. The interior needed complete refurbishing. Why? Because it was old. How can you close down a Mevlevi Lodge completely? Well, they had.

"Come, come, whoever you are. Now go now and come after the renovations have finished."

I sat in the garden for a while. There, I was still close. I shut my eyes and gently sunk into a prayer.

In a corner I spotted a bunch of kittens play fighting.

The sunset in the Tünel resembles the scent of an *akide* candy. A sweet parade of colors.

I walked to Kuledibi. My feet were dragging me to that address I knew.

I knocked, feeling uneasy. He smiled as soon as he opened the door. I was relieved. I placed a kiss on his dimple and went headfirst into the conversation. I'm in a hurry, as you know, with one foot in the grave, I have no time to lose.

"Go on, then," I said, "tell us about this accident."

He laughed. He was terribly drunk.

"I will, but you'll never believe me."

"Still, go on, tell me!"

"I'm a member of an organization," he said.

"No shit! Who is your boss?"

"Nimet Şanoğlu."

I fell silent this time. You could tell from the expression of regret in his face for having shared secret information that he wasn't messing around. He went on. He was a Special Teams officer. They'd call him for certain assignments when he was needed, and he'd go.

"And?"

And then he'd close in on his target. This wasn't a matter of bringing someone down, it was destroying the target. It didn't matter that the target was a human being; a target was simply a target. He said he was an excellent gunman. He could shoot bull's-eye from as far as three kilometers. His commander was a key figure, one of the most important men of state.

"What good to them is a drunk like you?"

"We're all drunk," he said, "we're all high." He had broken his chin five times. I knew his chin was broken but I thought he fell off his bike when he was a kid. That's what he had said. He was lying. He had to lie.

So who were his targets?

"Kurds, Americans… it doesn't matter really. Anyone causing the state trouble."

Maybe he was lying, maybe he was telling the truth. It seemed more like the truth. Drunken saliva dribbled down the corner of his crooked smile as he said he had assassinated people. If his intentions were to jerk around and deceive me, why on earth would he choose to do it like this? I began to see him differently. He now seemed more real. As the tone of his voice grew wilder, his behavior slightly changed: faint twitches touched his face and strange shudders passed through his body, and his perturbed existence was gaining meaning in my eyes. The excitement of seeing that a person is much more than the person you thought him to be makes you forget everything for a minute.

How can you live a life playing the drums in a no-name band a couple of times a week in a side street bar? Judging by the miserable life he was leading, but with no financial worries whatsoever though he was unemployed, the story he was telling perfectly fitted the man. A living and breathing weapon who would be summoned when needed. Introduce the target, mark it, and then exterminate it in some godforsaken corner of the city. A life that would never lead anywhere. The way he would sometimes disappear and then turn up as if nothing had happened; how he'd be pissed drunk, unable to stand on his feet, and how he'd be healthy and sober on his return. A whole load of details to confuse you. As soon as he got back he'd start drinking from where he'd left off, and he wouldn't stop until his whole system failed.

"What good to them is a drunk like you?" I asked a second time, realizing he was offended by this question.

"Look…" he said in a calm tone befitting a professional killer, and surprised me once again:

"Three days. They'll take me into the Kuşlu Armenian Hospital for three days and clean me up. The drip, medications, you know how it is… (I did). Then they'll have me picked up by this vehicle. I'll be taken straight to the camp. They'll inject me with a full syringe of red liquid and I'll pass out then and there. When I'm conscious again it will still be the same day. They'll take me out on this terrain to run and I'll start running but I'll collapse before I've even run a kilometer. When I fall they'll start kicking me so I'll have to get up. They kick you but this is solely for your own good, it gets you going, reminds you that you have a mission, there are people who care about you, you're important, you feel this every minute. The next day they'll inject the same liquid into your vein. This time you sleep a bit better and run better when you wake up. You'll still fall though; you will fall and they'll kick you again. They're on your side. Everything is for your own good, for the indivisibility of the nation. It's the same routine when you wake up on day three. A syringe full of red liquid. I know you're wondering what's in it. Honestly, I don't know. Who cares anyway. You can't ask, and even if you did, you wouldn't get an answer. But it does you good, and that's what you should be content with. That day you won't fall when you're running. You'll be ready in a week. They'll show you the target; you go and take it down. That's all there is to it. And therefore, if a man like me is dealt his share of romance, it can be nothing but an accident, darling. And you are an accident."

"I don't believe what you've just told me."

I had to say this. Although I did believe him, I had to say I didn't because I needed to know more; I needed to know all there was to know.

"I'd call them for you here and now but that would be wrong. That would be unacceptable."

"Go on!" I said. "Go ahead, ask them to take me in too. Don't they have women? I bet they do. Why wouldn't they? I want to serve the nation too."

"Could you kill someone?"

"I couldn't. I don't know. Perhaps I could, if it'd do anyone any good…"

The ignorance in what I had just said. What good could it do anyone to kill a person? Plain stupid.

"You could never kill someone!" he said, as if he could read my mind.

"I could," I said stubbornly. I wasn't lying. I could. I could at least kill myself. But that won't be necessary because I've already got cancer. Hurray! I've got cancer. Well, could I kill someone else? As I thought about this, visions of the people who had betrayed me, harmed me, been hostile to me went running through my head; none were worth the trouble. Was anyone really worth it? Of course! Say for example a war broke out and the enemy had entered our lands, I'd grab a gun, and each and every one of them one by one I would…No I wouldn't! I'm more of a massacring type. I couldn't kill them one by one. I wonder if I'm a potential murderer. I'm not, but what if they're trying to trick me? I wouldn't want to be defeated. As if it mattered. I couldn't convince him. He was driving me insane. Who wouldn't want to have a secret mission, to work for their nation and offer faultless services? Who wouldn't?

"Go on, please, I want to be part of the organization too!" I had become childish in begging him. I was whinging in a baby voice, insisting as if what I wanted was ice cream.

He looked so attractive.

I began drinking with him. I drank, and I drank…

I got so drunk I recall completely forgetting for a moment where I was and what I was doing.

I passed out.

When I woke up in the morning he was sitting by my bedside, stroking my hair.

"You're a baby," he said, "a baby!"

"Did you believe my story? You're so naive. Forget everything I told you, I was just testing to see how gullible you really are."

And that's when I snapped, and wherever he was in my head, he sank into darkness. He became not just invisible, but also unnoticeable.

To be gullible, to be deceived, to believe, to be convinced, trying to understand, to accept, to respect, tolerance, patience, compassion, all my good feelings went up in smoke, mingled with the wind, dispersed, vanished, disappeared.

I might have had a chance with him.

To cling onto life again, the tiniest reason would be enough for me.

But not with a liar, no way! Never again.

I placed a final kiss on his dimple and…

"Bye," I said. "Just imagine I died in that accident."

"Bye."

I left, and walked away.

I wandered into the side streets of the tower, and as I stared at the old buildings which smelt of history, I was thinking God knows how many people over the centuries had been filled with feelings similar to mine as they passed by and passed away.

I too would join that unknown realm before long.

Three months, four months, what the hell mattered? For a minute, this time felt long.

Change this thought, my dear, change it. Life is what you make it. I walked all the way to Karaköy, I went to Köprüaltı and sat down at a café, leaned back resting against the Bosporus and began watching Pier Loti.

There are those in Istanbul who perish without setting foot in Hagia Sofia or Süleymaniye. There are those who live a whole life without seeing the Topkapı Palace, the castle, or Yedikule.

We live here in this city, in the threshold of civilizations, and become trapped as postcards in the album of time. We are at a passage where seas meet; if we aren't grateful for all we possess, we'll be deemed to play only the role of victims.

These were the lands on which all the beings of Anatolian civilizations had been raised and had walked from antiquity to today.

I never thought there was such a great difference between trying not to be unhappy and simply being happy.

Everyone has a different way of perceiving things. Some use visual memory, some auditory, and some act according to their kinesthetic memory. I have a strange memory of scent; this might be another reason why I am so passionate about this city. This scent. What is love but a mere scent anyway? I love my lover by inhaling him. If he's near me and I'm inhaling him, I'm in love. If he's not with me, his scent is the thing I miss most.

Why am I a lonely person?

Don't think about it; drive negative thoughts out of your mind.

It is a wonderful feeling to know you are going to die. The shorter your time, the faster your speed. I'm talking about the speed of thought; I'm still at Köprüaltı and haven't moved my eyes from Pier Loti.

At one point I shed two drops of tears. Only two drops, but they were sharp and fast, warm and piercing.

Thus, I relieved myself of my wrath and tried to focus on positive thoughts.

What a strange life it is; the more I live, the more surprises I find life has in store for me.

I come across, meet, feel, understand so many different people, and still find everyone and everything awkward. I just haven't been able to master the art of communication. I haven't been able to jump on the swing of destiny or enter the whore's amusement park. Whenever I step inside, it is packed. Everything is already taken. From the slide to the seesaw, from the swing to the rollercoaster, from the ballerina ride to the giant chain swing, to the bumper cars, everything, even the circus mirrors (I'd never expect it but even them); they were all taken. People emerging even on the backs of those buckled up laughing look at themselves and laugh too. They fall, they rise, and they carry on. There are queues for every ride. Those queuing are so impatient that the people on the rides cannot enjoy themselves. This place which looks like an amusement park from the outside is actually nothing but a battlefield once you step in. There is only one difference: battle is replaced by play. They are fighting for play.

What a strange, shameful, nauseating situation. Everyone is breathing fire. Each to finish their turn rushes back into the queue again, over and over. Some are after the same ride; others keep changing rides. The most important thing about them is that they all constantly want to play.

They're players.

Since they are not children, they can hide their wrath. If we were to imagine they had all regressed to age seven and gathered together in this park, the scene we would see might then resemble a battlefield.

Whereas we would promote play.

What a simple idea.

They would never be content. Play isn't enough for any of them. Even when simply being in a playground should be enough, it just isn't.

They only have one aim: to play again, again and again.

In the lush green countryside adjoining the park, only the souls of deceased players roam beside those like me who refuse to join in, and we are very few.

Imagine how difficult it must be for a person searching for someone who refuses to join in to make friends at an amusement park. It might be possible to make a new game with a friend like me, but life, full of coincidences known only to God, never gives you what you expect.

But what can I say, that stroke of luck never arrives. And if you really want it, you can keep struggling in desperation. If only fate herself, that whore of a park keeper, would show herself, if she would not remain so invisible, perhaps I could make friends with her, make her my partner in a new game known to no one else, and play; but she never does.

I guess the best thing is to sit underneath an august tree, leave hope to wither and seem void of expectation. Only then maybe fate will grow bored, change her mind and choose to play with me. It's not that I don't feel sorry for her, really. All the carefully chosen machinery she put in place so perfectly, and along came humankind with its ambitions, primitive egos and sins, invading this place of amusement. A quarrel, a conflict, a relentless tussle... Players who won't let go of the chains they're holding onto, who crash and crash bumper cars and crash them again for not smashing up, who make the swings dizzy, the merry-go-round nauseous, who drive the chains crazy and make them tremble, and always want to carry on.

How lonely I am in this park.

If only someone would come... Perhaps a friend. If we could make up a new game and play together.

There was someone. Oh, yeah. Who was it? Who was it?

Time to scan through my phonebook.

But first I must find that august tree and caress it for a while.

Before I die, someone must promise they will plant a tree by the head of my grave.

I'm going to go home, wash, freshen up and rest. No, I have no intention of preparing for death; on the contrary, I intend to benefit from all sorts of social activities I have avoided until today. Let's see what I have missed.

I will begin the expedition by seeing a few old friends. It was tonight, wasn't it, the party at that guy's house whose name I couldn't recall. The building opposite Mecnun's, number seventeen.

I no longer have any expectations from life; let's see what life has to expect from me.

I went.

It really was a strange night.

Should I recount the truth? What is the point in mentioning truth that struggles to conceal lies but can never suffice? The best thing is to console oneself with lies.

I met a brand new person. Someone who was too scared to utter the word 'love'. Someone you could tell was hurt. His heart punched and pierced, his time faded, his turn done. Someone who had worked hard besides idling about, but who apparently wouldn't have idled at all if he weren't unemployed.

He was smart. I've already told you he had a hole in his heart; this was his other distinctive quality. He walks about with a hole in his heart. Nothing happens, apparently, he just has to be a bit careful sometimes. About what, did I hear you ask? I don't know, all sorts of things really. He mustn't exhaust himself, mustn't run, mustn't fight. But he has a temper too; he's a little neurotic. He has a dimple. That night I realized that all the men I've ever been interested in had dimples. While this new man, Sami, spoke of things I wasn't listening to, in my mind I made a list of lovers. An embarrassing score for an Eighties generation rocker:

a very short list of seven men, and all seven had dimples. I popped into the kitchen for a minute and shared this with one of my oldest female friends. "And you think you can preach to me about men, get lost," she said, and we had a laugh.

"Bang Sami tonight. What are you waiting for? Seriously, don't come to me tomorrow if you haven't made that eight by the end of tonight," she cautioned me as we walked out the kitchen together.

Apparently, the guy really liked me.

I sat down next to Sami.

Cold winds blow on the road formed by his rigid smile, stretching from the corner of his mouth all the way to his cheek. I find this interesting. With a stone cold gaze and simple tone of voice he tells me that love is lost to him. He tells me that he can no longer recognize love. We are all under the influence of the night. Double joints are being passed around but we give it a miss. There's a hole in Sami's heart, and I've forever suffered from a crack in the head. I'm not messing around, I'm seriously done with drugs; I grew bored, I quit. The mixing, rolling and smoking turned into torture after a while. Besides, supplies became so easily accessible and incredibly cheap in every way; the quality went down, the ingredients changed. Pleasure should never be that cheap; it should never be within such easy reach. I'm not talking about addiction, I'm talking about greed. The room was smoky. It felt as if we had gotten closer. Like we understood each other better.

As he spoke, the rough winds blowing over the cold smile of the dimpled man transformed first into a sweet chill and then a mild breeze.

Kids build up their relationships while playing games. Their futures, their steps, their goals, their paths, their decisions, their characters, their ideas, their feelings, their relationships with humans, animals and objects.

"I was never the cowboy when I was little," he said. "I was always the

Apache."

He was the Apache. So was I. He had grown up in an orphanage. I fell silent.

"So did I," I should have said, but I couldn't. If I had, this would have been followed by a full list of other facts: I had cancer, I was infertile, I was a bastard child...

There was no need to ruin this beautiful night. Besides, he wasn't asking me anything anyway, he was telling me his story. And so I just listened. He was the Apache and he'd give out all his marbles. A lying Apache. Who had ever seen marbles at an orphanage? They'd all disappear as soon as they arrived. Toys were treasures, true treasures. To spend a couple of minutes playing with a marble, I had once traded my lunch cake at lunch, weeks before it was to be served. Anyway, tell me my dimpled one, tell me, but please cut the crap.

He had never cared about winning! Now look, that's reasonable, I can relate to that.

And when he says, "Games are played to be lost!", I freeze.

This hopeless, worn-out and immersing thought that everyone laughs their asses off at is my thought too.

It's the first time I've ever come across someone who agrees with me on this one.

I wonder if I should jump and kiss him.

I think it's better if I just stay put. Because the night has almost come to an end and we are soon to fall out onto the street like raindrops from the same cloud, splattering onto different spots.

Oh! Oh careful! It is raining quite heavily, let's not skid on the roads. The roads are dangerous in this weather.

He offered to drop me off when he realized I wanted to go home. Melda heard this too; she winked at me and giggled.

"Come on, guys. Where are you going? The night is young! I've still got a wonderful surprise for you all," said Joy, whose real name I still cannot recall.

We stopped for a minute. I quickly caught up on what was happening. Even if I couldn't remember his name, by observing his behavior and words I could pretty much guess what kind of surprises would come from him. Joy and his house have always been around, since the craziest days of our early youth. His house that moved frequently. You can tell he is from a very wealthy family but there's never a mother or a father around. I've always felt a bit sorry for him. But I don't believe he is a good person. Everyone may get what they deserve in life, but sometimes fate puts people into strange ordeals, introduces them to the wrong people and puts them to the test. Ones who go their own way win, and those who join with the devil don't lose but find themselves in a labyrinthine path.

Just as I thought, he pulled out a new supply from his stash.

Melda jumped up and grabbed out of Joy's hand the limestone-like, matt white rock, as big as a table tennis ball yet not as smooth, that he had pulled out of the secret compartment in the drawer.

"What the hell is this, man?"

Joy has always been annoyed by Melda's reflexes, quick as a squirrel's; and I, by her soft spot for drugs.

And I am irritated by how Joy uses everyone, absolutely everyone who has this weakness. He's the one who started Eso on heroin. Then what happened? The girl was found dead in some dump, and he beat the rap.

I grabbed the stone-like object from Melda's hand; in the end, I was the one who was sober.

Joy held out his hand. I felt obstinate; I pulled the stone away.

"Seriously, what is this?"

"Give it here and I'll tell you!"

"Tell me and I'll give it!"

Meanwhile, I was trying to feel and examine the thing I was holding in my hand.

"Stop squeezing it, it's going to chip! Oh, give it back will you, girl! Look, come on. Cut it out, that's enough!"

I was a bit closer to Sami. I looked at the stash in my hand, and as I brought it closer to my nose I saw him mouth the words, "Don't smell it!"

Joy kept circling round and round the living room.

I was growing bored really but my curiosity hadn't fully subsided.

"Go on then, take it," I said, holding it out this time. And just as he reached out I pulled my hand back again. The air got even tenser. I felt a little embarrassed. "Okay okay, just kidding. I'll give it to you. I will, but on one condition…"

I didn't say what my condition was, nor did he ask. He thought he knew what it was. As soon as he had it in the palm of his hand, he became extremely careful, as if he didn't want to injure a rare and delicate plant. And like a professor ready to introduce an archaeological finding to his students, he held it where everyone could see it, and began his lecture. I wasn't sure if he was showing off, pranking us or doing his sales, but I remained interested in what he had to say. Even though what was really crossing my mind was to leave with Sami, I wasn't willing to leave Melda behind. She had lost her father three months ago and no matter how well she could manage to hide it, I knew that she was actually emotionally very weak, and I really loved her.

I had met Melda after I had left the orphanage and started looking after an old Armenian lady. We were only eighteen back then; we became friends. Melda's mother was Madam Mari's neighbor and they were close friends. I owe it to Melda's mother that this old woman eventually adopted me and supported me in university. Friends shape our lives, and no one could beat Melda, the cherished only daughter of her family, at picking the wrong friends. I knew back then that I would always, for as long as we lived, be watching out for her and I've never grown tired of this. I never will.

Joy sat down in the middle of the wooden coffee table. He opened one of the drawers, and without missing the chance to show off his knife collection, he pulled out a cut-throat razor. He sliced a piece the size of a single lentil off one side of the crooked ball, held it delicately with the tips of his fingers and lifted it up into the air. "Guys, tonight's surprise is called 'stone'!" he said, rising from where he sat.

"Methamphetamine, ephedrine, whatever you will call it. What the crank shaft is for the engine, that's what the stone is to us. Even a tiniest piece of this is very, very precious."

As he toured around the living room like a vendor singing the praises of his goods, he made us watch the big stone and its tiny particle. Once he had finished what he had to say, he went into the kitchen, humming a tune.

"Is this guy a queen now?" asked Melda, while we were waiting for his return.

"Where did you get that?" I asked.

"Can't you see he's prancing about. Oh, you're so naive!"

"You're the one who's naive. Melda, I'm telling you, if you lay a hand on that shit, I swear I will tell your mother. This bastard must have heard about your inheritance and he's trying to catch you in his net. Look, I'm warning you!"

"No way, girl, I might be crazy but I'm not that mad."

"Prove it!"

Joy came back with an empty plastic bottle and some aluminium foil. He picked another knife out from the drawer and pierced a hole in the bottle.

He placed the aluminium foil over the open mouth, pressed it in a little and put the shit he called a stone right there.

"Man, if it's taken in such small amounts, why the hell have you got a massive lump? Are you dealing or what?" I asked, unable to hold my tongue.

"Why shouldn't I? You'll know what I mean once you've had a taste of it!"

"What did you say it was?"

"Stone, it's stone. My father's latest discovery. Crystallized cocaine. More effective, plus cheaper. The high it has to offer is indescribable; you'll have to experience it for yourselves. I'm telling you, pretty soon, each and every one of us is going to be flying, what else can I say!"

My heart began racing, my hands were shaking. I regretted this filthy bastard wasn't an ounce cleaner. There was no way I would smoke it, but I was curious. I was angry. I had again found myself in a situation I didn't like. I looked at Sami. He was watching quietly. When Joy went into the kitchen and while I was talking to Melda, he sent someone a text message, and I felt a strange sense of suspicion. Maybe he had a lover, or a wife. Who cares! What difference would it make even if he didn't; it wasn't like we'd be happily wed and raise our own little family; I was going to take my exit at a convenient moment anyway. Right, good thing I remembered that. There can be no harm in my giving this stone thingamajig a try now then, can there?

"Come on, Joy, light the thing up already. What, you want us to say prayers or something! Stop messing about and get on with it!"

He struck the lighter, placed his lips on the hole in the bottle, lit up the fuel and simultaneously sucked in the air in the bottle. The bottle filled with smoke. He inhaled half of the smoke and with his eyes rolled up, staring at the ceiling, he held it in.

"You're under arrest, pal!"

"What? What?..."

I observed everything without moving my eyes from that single spot: the ringing of the doorbell mixed with other sounds, Joy in a coughing fit, and Sami shooting up, grabbing Joy and tossing him onto the ground, Sami shouting at Melda to get the door, the police entering and moving about like live statues, their calling Sami "Chief!", Melda shrinking in fear and sitting by my feet.

As they packed Joy off, I wanted the last iota of smoke escaping the bottom of the bottle to mark my mind. Everything had happened in less than a minute.

"What about the women, Chief?" asked one of the officers, motioning towards us.

"They're with me. They're clean," Sami replied.

Everyone left, except for us.

Oh, Istanbul, what games you are playing on me again.

I reached out, swiftly grabbed the bottle, and sniffed it. A gourmet by profession, I have engraved in my memory all sorts of smells; but forget all of them: my extremely sensitive nose and all my senses could never define or describe such a smell—even though I was in charge of the chemistry lab at university, too. It really is an indescribable smell. The word disgusting would be repelled by it. Perhaps it is the smell of space; perhaps an atmosphere without oxygen could smell like that. The smell of danger; it's briefest definition. Either you smell it once, understand the potential danger, and flee, or you'll end up craving it until it finishes you.

"How did it smell?" asked Sami.

"There was no smell, it's all gone," I answered.

"Are you testing me or something? Don't even try it. I won't stand for any tricks or games. Don't hurt my feelings, because I wouldn't want to hurt yours."

"So what would you want?"

"A friend who can plant a tree by the head of my grave when I die."

"I could do that, if I'm still alive."

"You will be, don't worry."

Melda was walking by my side quietly; she put her arm in mine and said:

"Girlfriend, is this guy really a cop, do you think? I thought he said he had a hole in his heart. On second thought, don't bang this guy tonight. I won't be able to stop worrying about you. Why doesn't he drop us of at my place; you can stay at mine tonight."

We arrived at the house where Melda lived with her mother. As we parted, he pulled out a pen, held my hand and wrote a number on it.

"Don't wait until you die to call. Let's have breakfast tomorrow morning at Saray. You never know, we might not have much time, let's not waste it. Besides, we can talk about that tree of yours, alright, babe?"

"Fine, okay."

He left.

I knew I was at the brink of a wonderful love story I could live until the day I died, and in the center of the city of love.

I was filled with appreciation, with gratitude for life, for the night, for Istanbul.

Compassion, Love, Innocence, Etcetera

Sabâ Altınsay

Translated by Nilgün Dungan

When the train they boarded in Samatya stopped at Sirkeci station, after passing through Yenikapı, Kumkapı and Cankurtaran, they got off. Walking through the well-trodden streets of Eminönü, and in front of stores that sell electronic appliances, imported goods, books, stationery, mobile phones and sports equipment, they plunged into the crowd in front of the Yeni Mosque.

The crowd of the last Saturday before the *Bayram* holiday had descended upon the ferry ports and buses, the courtyard around the mosque, the interlaced passages of the Spice Bazaar, the square that backs onto the florists. People went in and out of these places, the station court, bus stops, side streets, inside the Sultanhamam, streaming like pieces from the mouth of a tyrant who spits out what he eats, people changing places with new arrivals every second and disappearing into completely different neighborhoods.

The father and his son, who was still thinking of the goalkeeper's strip he just saw in a shop window, walked into the Spice Bazaar's buzzing crowd, holding a list that had kept getting longer and longer as the necessities for the house were jotted down. Peppercorns, candy for Bayram, coffee, cologne, holiday shoes for the boy... His mother crossed the last item off the list. "You won't know what to get, I'll take care of it," she said.

His mother was a brown-haired, plump person who lost her temper at anything, and smiled at everything. She was a textile worker. She was unstoppable both at home and at work; it would be okay if she were the only one running around, but she loved to put anyone around her to work too. They made fun of this way of hers at home. If the boy were to laze around a little, his father would crack a joke saying, "Your laziness will be marked as your mother's sin."

Their house was on Arap Kuyusu Street, which, meeting with the railroad tracks, turned into a blind alley in the cramped neighborhoods of Samatya. Framed wooden houses with low roofs and blocks of apartments covered in mosaics were lined up on both sides. Children used to make noise playing football on this street until late hours during summer and early evenings of weekends in winter; housewives would throw long cardigans on their backs and run to the corner store in mid-morning saying, "Detergent's finished, right before laundry time."

In the summertime, the smell of scrambled eggs with tomatoes and green peppers, cooked in a hurry, and freshly cut watermelon would come out of open kitchen windows; the curtains of those windows would delicately blow and swell with the warm, calm breath of the wind to accompany the peace of the afternoon naps to be taken shortly.

In the springtime, the distorted sounds of cheap plastic recorders played by children doing their music homework would float through the windows left ajar. Then amateur versions of the famous song "Samanyolu" would be heard, and that song, mixed together with the coughs of the elderly who are pleased to have made it to spring, would carry the sounds of spring from one house to another.

To the right of Arap Kuyusu, almost all of the buildings of Işgırlak

Street were covered with posters left over from elections, reading, "There is No Rest for the Weary" and "Standing Shoulder to Shoulder against Darkness"; moustaches had been planted on the pictures of the leaders by children catching their breath between two games, and cigarettes were drawn on the mouths of some and flowers behind the ears of others.

It was a warm, modest and familiar street in Samatya.

As the train left the streets of Samatya behind one by one and advanced towards Sirkeci, the father was calculating how much everything on the list would cost, and the boy was pleased: pleased that it was Saturday, that the weather was beautiful, that they were going shopping; pleased with the crowds, his father and Bayram.

First they would stop by the seed man and look for pepper seedlings. Hasibe Teyze's peppers turned out to be hot last year. This year his father would buy the ones that said "sweet pepper" on them; otherwise, he couldn't eat them because his stomach would ache. The other day he took the day off from the factory, which meant he must have really been in agony.

The father and son walked, making room for themselves in the crowd. It was hot. As they turned towards the Seeds Market, the boy was dying of thirst. Florists spread out in the courtyard of Eminönü Mosque and the backyard of the Spice Bazaar, seed sellers, pet vendors, soil and flower pot vendors, pesticide sellers, seedling vendors, men with rabbits that draw fortunes, shrewd Kurds posing as falcon trainers, children gathered in front of snake cages, children selling water, adolescents, housewives, loud budgerigars, disgruntled and sickly dogs, noisy monkeys, retired soldiers, bird lovers who can pick out goldfinches that could sing and those who can't pick them out but try to learn from the others, purse-snatchers, petite young girls, undersized young men who thrust out their shoulders left and right all the time trying to protect their 'halal' girlfriends with tightly- wrapped headscarves on from the horde of men around, people strolling just for fun, hundreds of plants with and without pots, flowers of all colors, tall saplings, mouse traps: they all fascinated the boy; it seemed that each eye looked in a different direction and he simply could not put the two together. Even his father, obviously confused in this crowd, stumbled twice.

They caught their breath before the pepper seedlings. The roots of the seedlings were kept in soil so that they wouldn't wither, and they were lined up next to each other for support.

"Do you have any basil seeds?" his father asked just for the sake of conversation.

"No, mate, you can't find them anymore."

They didn't dwell on the fact that there were no basil seeds.

"Are these hot?"

"They are. If you're looking for sweet ones, look at these here."

When the store owner reached for the seedlings, his arm hit a cage placed over the big packages on some makeshift shelves on the right. First the rows of shelves, then the cardboard boxes and finally the bulky cage tumbled down altogether. A few boxes of pesticide and packages of birdseed followed the cage.

Boxes of vitamins knocked down by the birdseed fell on top of the cage, now at the bottom. Just as the dust was thought to have settled, a few more boxes fell off the shelves and scattered right in the middle. Then silence befell. Peace…

The cloud of dust that blew off the sacks of seed spread in the air in waves. The store owner hurried to the door, blinking, and loudly sneezed twice in the direction of people passing by. He found a wrinkled handkerchief in his pocket and wiped his nose.

"Excuse me, brother. What was it you wanted?"

Instead of a response, there came a faint meow from the depths of the cage boxed in sideways between the shelves. The sound was so weak that the only way to figure out where it was coming from was to bend down and look carefully. As they were looking for the source, another meow was heard. Harboring not even the least bit of anger or threat, the sound was that of complaint at most, or more of fear. In fact, it was a whimper.

Possibly, it was a kitten, too small and insecure to scare anyone but its own peers. Its secret whining would stir great compassion in anyone who heard it.

"Oh dear, we frightened the poor thing. Take that cage out of there so it can get out."

"It can't get out, brother. That kitten's for sale; it'll run away then."

They did not insist. The store owner straightened the cage. A white kitten, a tiny ball of fur crouched in the corner, came into view through the bars. Starting from the middle of its forehead and spreading down to its cheeks, a black patch drew a thin line around the edge of its mouth; as if its mouth, rather than its eyes were lined with kohl. Standing up on its hind feet, the kitten tried to get its paws on the store owner's fingers holding the cage.

"Looks like it's hungry."

"We give it food every now and then, but it doesn't always eat."

"It must be bored in the cage."

"Of course it is. Wouldn't you be bored if they put you in there?"

"Then get the poor thing out of there."

"Buy it then, so we can get it out, mate, if you want it out that bad."

"Are you kidding me? You don't pay to get a cat!"

"Honestly, a lady dropped it off last week. She said 'sell it' and left. And we're selling it."

The boy, who had been quiet all along, jumped up and tugged at his father's sweater.

"Hey, Daddy, please let's buy it, please, Daddy."

"Hold on, son, we came to get peppers, drop it. How much was it for the peppers?"

"Three for two liras."

"Give me thirty of the sweet ones but do it as four for two."

The seller smiled meaning to say, "That's not really on, but so what." He counted the seedlings, put them aside and wrapped them in newspaper. He handed them to the father.

"Is this a purebred?"

"No, but it's house-trained. Knows about the litter box and stuff."

"Why should a litter box be necessary; so far as I know, it can go in the garden."

The boy did not miss the opportunity and butted in: "We'll put it in the garden, Daddy, it won't go in the house, I swear it won't."

"Hush, son, don't make me mad now."

He stopped speaking. If he made his daddy mad, that would be regarded as the end of the world. In a world that ended, neither cat nor pepper would be left. His father would take him by the arm and drag him back home, both of them looking dejected. When he thought of going back home, he got scared and gave up. "Okay, we won't buy it then." His father was still turning peppers over and over; he was lost in thought. He was surprised as if he heard something new. "We won't buy what?"

"I'm saying we won't buy the cat."

His father laughed: "Were we going to buy it anyway?"

The store owner did not miss a thing. "You were going to buy it, sir, but we could not agree on the price."

"You don't say so! Where is this cat, let's see it, too."

The man brought the cage forward. He opened its door slightly. A snow-white paw clawed the bars of the cage. Then a half-black nose sniffed the air at length. As the dazed, shy and slender body pushed its head outside the cage, it got startled, and hissing, it ran back inside. They laughed at its antics. The boy was bursting with excitement. As he was about to open his mouth to say something, he changed his mind and just gulped.

"Is this male or female?"

"It's a male, a month and a half old, that's what the woman who left it here said."

"Why did she leave it here, anyway?"

"She could not take care of it; she didn't find it in her heart to put it out on the street, that's why she brought it."

"That's true, poor thing could not survive on the street."

The boy gulped again. "Let's buy it, Daddy, look it's so tiny, please let's buy it."

"Hold it, son; did I say we'd buy it?"

"You'll buy it, mate, don't hurt the child's feelings."

He reached into the cage and got the kitten out. Gripped with fear, the poor kitten tried to scratch the seller's hands with its thin claws and left small, harmless marks which would turn red later. Holding the cat by its neck, the man placed it in the boy's arms. The kitten soaked up the warm smell of a human. It nudged its head into the crook of the boy's arm, rubbed its moist nose on his skin, and settled in the shelter of his arms. Where it buried its head, it found warmth similar to its mother's. Kneading the inner part of the elbow with its small white paws, its mouth moved closer to the skin, and with the drunkenness of having found an illusive nipple, it began to suck while purring from the bottom of its throat.

The boy's father reached out, found the little black and white head from where it was hiding, stroked it backwards from its forehead, and petted it reservedly.

"Little rascal is cute, too."

"Give me fifty lira and it's yours."

"Get out of here, streets are full of these."

"That may be, but look, this one likes your son."

"Fifty's just not on, if we tell them we paid for a cat, they'll make fun of us."

"Let them, sir. Which one of them will snuggle up to your boy like this one?"

"Honestly, I won't buy it."

"Come on, mate. You'd save this poor thing's life, too. Is that so bad?"

"Not bad, but look what you're saying."

"That's what its owner said, so what can I say?"

"Then let go of the cat, son. We'll pick one up from the street, you can find cats anywhere in this country. Put it back in its cage."

The boy had a hard time pulling the cat away from his arm. As its head was pried from the illusive nipple just found, its ears went back, the weak paws tightened their grip, tiny claws protruded; and suddenly separated from the human warmth and sense of security the warmth created, the kitten let out a long, deep groan. This sound was so sincere and heart-wrenching, like a little child lost in the marketplace crying for his mother; it was more than enough to pain those who heard it.

As the boy put the kitten back in the cage, he could not endure the tightness in his throat. He was unable to hold back the tears that rushed to the tips of his eyelashes and rolled down his face. He looked for a handkerchief, a dirty rag, or at least a crumpled piece of newspaper to wipe his nose before anyone saw it, but he couldn't find anything. He wiped his eyes with the back of his fist. Fresh tears quickly replaced the ones he wiped away, trickling all the way down to his neck. He could not bear the powerful grief rising from the depths of his chest, so he finally let go and sobbed.

"Look here, mate, you made the boy cry."

"Oh, son, you're a fine one! Is this something to cry over, now?"

He turned to the seller. "And you, you ask for something more reasonable then, let's not make a laughing stock of ourselves."

"Alright, mate, give me forty, and take it."

He took the kitten out of the cage once again. The boy immediately snatched it. He rested the kitten against his chest and put its little head under his chin. A strange, unfamiliar smell filled his nostrils. He sank into the warmth of the soft neck with white fur. He kissed the middle of the little ears right by his mouth. The kitten felt the tide of love emanating from the kiss rush to its face, body, puny paws, tail and white belly. Just as a warm drop of milk would go through his soft teeth to his throat and from there down to his belly, the joy of the boy's kiss, of being kissed, spread all the way to his bones. He felt the same desire to lick himself as he would after drinking his mother's milk to his heart's content. Suddenly, he started licking his front paws. The boy grinned and kissed the kitten once again, pressing him to his heart.

"Come on, son, you've done it again. I'll be damned if I come here with you again."

He turned to the seller. "Are you going to give us the cage, too?"

"Well, they left him with the cage."

"You got me all confused now, how much do we owe you?"

"With the kitten, it's fifty-five."

The dad took out the money and counted it. He counted again and handed him the money. He turned to the boy and said, "Come on, take your kitten and let's go. Hold the cage carefully; make sure you don't knock it about."

He smiled and patted the shoulders of the boy whose eyes grew wide with delight.

The father and his son placed the cage outside the door and then stepped out themselves. They walked side by side. The crowd was coming at them. The cage would get people's attention, and as they were looking at it to try to figure out what was inside, they'd pass by without noticing the boy and his father.

Yet if they did, they would notice on one of the faces an enormous joy, the like of which has never been witnessed by anyone since the beginning of the world, a measureless excitement like that of almond blossom bursting out of buds in spring.

It was as if this huge Eminönü Square, or even the entire population of Istanbul, was bubbling up noisily in a cauldron and this bubbling sound entered into the boy's blood, the almighty din into his heart. If the passersby pricked up their ears, they would hear the pounding of his heart.

He wanted to show his kitten to everyone. He thought about carrying him in his arms, but he changed his mind, thinking he would run away. If he had wings, he would fly home. All of a sudden, the thought of his mother crossed his mind. What if she got angry as soon as she saw the kitten, barring him from the house or kicking him out? What if she insisted on saying "I don't want a cat in the house"? What if she got mad at his father too? Just as his father said "Everything's settled", what if his mother said "No way"? His feet got heavy. He felt too weak to take another step. His blood drained away. The loud beat of his heart crazy with joy now turned into a numbing splutter, like running a nail along a plaster wall. He stood aghast.

"Dad! What if Mom says 'I don't want it'?"

His father stopped, too. It was as if he suddenly heard the name of someone he'd long forgotten and could not remember where he knew her from; he blinked. He stared uncomprehendingly.

"Really! What if she says 'I won't let it in'?"

"I won't let go of my kitten, Dad. I'd see somebody in hell first."

"Hold it, son, hold it. Don't confuse me now."

"We'll tell Mom we paid for him."

"If we told her we paid for a street cat, she wouldn't let us in either."

"Then we'll tell her we found the kitten on the street."

"She'll say 'Well then, let him go.'"

"I won't let my kitten go. I won't"

He started crying.

The man thought. He took a few steps, thought again. That failed; he returned to the boy. Turning things over in their minds, the two walked aimlessly towards the steps of the mosque. "Let's sit down here," his father said. When they did, they put the cage right by them. The kitten was crouching somewhere in the cage and could not be seen. The boy bent down to check if he was there. He was. He was sitting alertly. He was waiting.

Pigeons were landing and flying off left and right in front of them. Some would come all the way to their feet, walking around to see if they would give them some birdseed, looking inside the cage hesitantly and darting away. Children were tugging at their mums' arms to get them to buy some birdseed, and as soon as they persuaded them, they would take the wheat kernels in handfuls and jump in among the birds, pretending to run at them and scaring them away.

From the Yeni Mosque, a poignant voice sounding almost like a wail called the faithful to afternoon prayer.

They did not talk at all. The boy almost opened his mouth to speak twice but changed his mind and kept quiet. Any idea he came up with to keep the kitten, he could also find the response his mother would give, quickly abandon his thought and start looking for another. Presumably his dad was doing the same thing. While sitting, he would put his hands in his trousers pockets and then take them out, crack his forefingers, and extending his hands, he'd look at his nails. When he was done with his hands, he'd pick the fluff off the arms of his sweater, frequently wrinkling his forehead and looking in the distance. Suddenly, he came to with a start and jumped to his feet.

"Get up, son, let's go home."

"What are we going to say, Dad?"

"We'll say we got him as a Bayram present for you. You know she was going to buy shoes; she said she'd go herself and get them. She doesn't have to. 'We got this,' we'll say."

"You think that'll work, Dad?"

"What else will, son?"

"Hurray, Dad! You're the best! My dear father!"

He stood up, or rather jumped up, ran and hugged his father's legs, wrapping his arms around his hips and resting his head on his belly. "My Dad, my dear Dad…" He kissed his belly over his sweater.

They took a few steps. He realized that he'd forgotten the kitten. He nearly panicked. Like an arrow, he turned and grabbed the cage from the steps of the mosque. A tiny meow came from inside. He shuddered. He thought that his joy would overflow from his chest, become a sound and burst out of his mouth.

He came running. He moved to the right and held his father's hand with his free hand.

He stuck his chest out. It looked as if he were walking while holding hands with God.

The father and his son walked slowly towards the station, merging with the crowd and leaving behind the Spice Bazaar, to take the black and white kitten they paid forty lira for home.

The sound of the Samatya train came echoing from Sirkeci; after filling the square with a shrill, it went streaming on to other neighborhoods.

City of Borders

Cihan Aktaş

*Translated by **Daniel Rosinsky-Larsson***

In those last few days, I had started to board my usual ferry two departures earlier, as this would mean gaining a half-hour's time. He would be waiting for me at the dock. Crossing over the footbridge together, we would walk up the hill. We would stop for lentil soup at one of the small restaurants on the left side of the street. Then he would walk me to work, and go to his own job. Every time he left me and went away, I felt like I had been abandoned forever. He's finished studying. Soon, he'll go back to his homeland; he'll enter the war. He'll settle into a life without me. I won't ever see him again. He'll probably go soon, but I couldn't ask him not to leave, not to join the war. The southern part of his homeland was under military occupation; the city he was born in had been turned to ruins from the bombardment.

I would walk down to Üsküdar and take the ferry to Beşiktaş. He would be waiting for me at the dock. We would sit in a cafeteria together and he would give me the latest information about the war. He didn't think the reports published in the newspapers about the ongoing battle could be trusted; his opinions were shaped by the reports he received from his family. I didn't let him hold my hand while we talked. Actually, he never tried. If he held my hand, we wouldn't be able to part again;

we both knew that. Since he'd completed his Master's degree, it was important that he not squander any more of his time around here. As we crossed the Galata Bridge together, I saw his eyes tear up.

If someone is going to make a sacrifice, why should it be you? asked Zeliha.

Because there's a war in his homeland. That's why he wants to go. He's more tied to his home than ever now. And if he stays here, don't you think his whole family will think he's afraid, that he is hiding away?

Sometimes on our way back home in the evenings, Zeliha and I would meet at the Üsküdar dock and walk together to Harem. Hotels that would change the city's silhouette were under construction on the European side opposite; the construction on some of them had been halted. But Üsküdar wouldn't change so easily. Zeliha was infatuated with Üsküdar, and the Bosphorus. None of the skyscraper hotels under construction on the other side could completely change or close off the familiar view of the Bosphorus. I couldn't lose myself staring at the view like she could. The worried face of my lover covered my horizon. I felt that if he went to his homeland without me, he would die in the war or be lost.

You can't get by in those places, Zeliha told me. There's not even a lake in the city where you're going, let alone a sea.

There's a river that runs through the city, and a dam half an hour away.

Comparing a small river and a soulless dam to the Bosphorus...

But I can't imagine I'd be happy even if I saw the Bosphorus every day, not without him by my side. I don't see the same landscape that you do right now. When I'm crossing to the other side on a ferry, it doesn't even enter my mind that I'm on a sea where two continents meet.

You're forgetting that there's a war over there, the war of the cities.

But he's going soon, and I might never see him again.

My sister also asked me what kind of future I could have with him while there was a never-ending battle in his homeland. No one around me approved of this love that was going to take me to a country at war. That's why I kept stalling the moment of decision.

II.

When leaving the Istanbul he dearly loved, instead of photographs, postcards, lemon cologne or paintings of the New Mosque or Galata Bridge, did he want to take with him as a souvenir a girl who would carry inside her more of the city's life? What was it that he really loved—a person, or a city? There was no sense in these questions as far as he was concerned. When we love someone, our feelings shouldn't change when their context changes. I thought his explanation was logical, yet I tried to put some distance between us; but that didn't last long. When he told me that his departure date had been confirmed, I felt that I had lost him, as if he had left forever and I would live the rest of my life in mourning. I began to cry. This time it was me running after him, doting on him. I always forgave him, every time for the same reasons: he's confused, his homeland is under occupation, his home city may fall victim to the war.

One time at the Beşiktaş dock, on New Year's Day, I waited for him. He was going to come from Sarıyer and we were going to go to Anadolu Kavağı. The new year; drunks passed in front of me; I waited and waited but he didn't come. He forgot that we were going to meet there and went to my place to pick me up; there weren't any mobile phones at that time.

As I waited there, rather than being angry at him, I was surprised to find myself feeling anxious about him, about the life he would live without me.

III.

He watched Istanbul through me, for many years. And during this time, Istanbul was for me a destination reached at the end of long bus journeys. In the first few years, departing Istanbul by plane or bus felt like entering a dark and endless tunnel. Time went slowly until the day that I could return to Istanbul; that's what it felt like. I would wait in line by the border crossing with a baby in my arms. A signature or a stamp would be missing or there'd be some sort of mistake, and I would find myself at the end of the line again. Thermoses full of hot water. Roadside restaurants where I would look for a place to change the baby's diaper. Dripping sinks. The commotion of quickly repacking luggage torn up, searched by customs agents on both sides of the border. Filthy toilets without water. Long lines. The destitute youths with dark, melancholic faces who would watch our bus the whole way and rush around to sell cigarettes and alcohol, or offer to exchange money.

I filled a cup of tea from the thermos by my side and gave it to the young man next to me. We began to chat. He was preparing to go to Istanbul. It seemed to be big enough to hold all the border cities' populations.

Most of the other cities I lived in besides Istanbul all resembled each other. But any city where I lived had to have a river or a lake that I could reach by car in two or three hours. The road from a city is always shortest to the place you'd rather be. Plane trips are good for returns: the trip passes in a rush yet it goes more gently.

Even in my limited days in Istanbul, I always end up seeing those youths wandering about with melancholic faces. It's as if I carry the border with me. The days slip by quickly, a season is a short time. In the two- or three-week trips, when making big plans, I am led astray by small plans, or the opposite: small plans get lost in the commotion of big plans. On returning, I remember the past days with remorse: Istanbul days should be spent discovering silent, hidden corners and conversing with friends in green gardens. I should gone to the places I went when I was a young girl in Yakacık, to the tea gardens where the winds blew in, that overlooked the islands, where the Judas trees start taking on their color towards summer; but once again I hadn't. Each time, I always found I was somewhere other than that tea garden. Istanbul's borders were constantly expanding. When I returned, it felt like a month had gone by like a day.

I had to be more careful and keep to a planned schedule. A line of notes in my planner:

A. To do this time in Istanbul:
Take a walk on the Üsküdar shore with Zeliha
Wander the back streets of Süleymaniye
Search for the "lost box"
Explore the used book stores on both continents

B. To get this time in Istanbul:
Salt-free olives, thyme
A few half-kilo boxes of *lokum*
Kemal Paşa and *Şam Baba* desserts for Ramadan

C. To see this time in Istanbul:
Zeliha – the shore of Üsküdar…
Süleymaniye Mosque complex
The tea garden in Yakacık
Streets of Sarıyer

D. To visit this time in Istanbul:

Süleymaniye

Nuran, who just had her fourth baby

Leyla, who bought a house

Some possibilities turned up on both the "To do" and "To visit" lists. I absolutely have to call Zeliha. We'll take a thermos of tea and two *simits* on a ferry up the Bosphorus and chat. How many years has it been since we last saw each other…which one of us was the last to contact the other? Zeliha, my dear Zeliha, this year we certainly should see each other again.

How many years has it been just talking on the telephone and extending our hopes to see each other again?

The years that have passed add up almost to the fingers on both hands; the years I've lived in a city that rests against the mountains, almost six hours from the sea. My closest friends, the neighborhood store owners. In the war years, my job was to wait in the coupon lines; one had to take the risk of waiting for hours in order to get milk, chicken, eggs or oil. Maybe it's due to those years spent waiting at the end of lines that I now stay well away from all the subjects, undertakings and procedures that made queuing necessary.

The grocer, the butcher, the corner shop owner, the baker, all express astonishment each time I stop by: How could anyone ever abandon a city like Istanbul?

Everywhere was dark; it became darker, rockets rained from the sky. Because the war of the cities continued. I took shelter under the rickety staircase of the apartment where I lived, situated above a bakery; it was an unreliable shelter, broken and unsteady. Five hundred meters away on the other side, I heard a hospital being fired on; a fallen soldier's funeral passed by on the street, accompanied by lamentations and prayers. We had visited a large cemetery on the fortieth day anniversary of the return of a neighbor's body which had been sent back from the front. A fountain stood right beside the cemetery gurgling red water. Soldiers' mothers who had heard no news of their children sat around the fountain and cried.

IV.

Istanbul was a ferry flowing up the Bosphorus from afar, and a document. Documents unlikely to be found in their places. Mother, you knew that that drawer was mine!

How was the cleaning lady to know; the documents and papers in the drawer had been mixed up during the spring cleaning. I went through the dusty piles of paper again and again, but I couldn't find what I was looking for. To get a document like that again…how many places will I have to wait in line, bureaucratic procedures to endure, questions to answer, do you know, Mother?

Since I couldn't face the thought of getting into line at those government offices, I had taken a lot of care to protect my documents. I placed the most important ones in a handmade wooden box. Thinking that my brother was tidier and more organized than my sister, I had left it in his care; but the wooden box probably got lost in the turmoil of his move. That box meant more than the world to me! I screamed. My brother suggested I was exaggerating the loss. I said, even if it doesn't seem important to you, there were a lot of things in that box that are valuable for me. Things I had saved that helped me feel I was still tied to Istanbul and the memories of my past: diplomas; old report cards, postcards, letters, even expired contracts and legal agreements, a diary from my high school years…

That summer when I couldn't find the document where I had left it at my parents' house, even my sister remembered that I had gathered my important documents in the wooden box and handed it over to my brother. Yet my brother continues to say that that year when the earthquake happened, when he was moving from his damaged house, he had given the box back to me. And when our argument carried on longer, he argued that in all the years it was at his house, I hadn't once asked for it. Okay; maybe I never wanted to see the contents of that box all those years, but I knew that they were there, that I could go and find any one of them when I felt the need. Moreover, I don't think I ever took the box back; why would I? Where would I have put it if I had? As far as he's concerned, I must have forgotten it somewhere I travelled to. But I'm sure that I wouldn't just leave a box in any old place…It was a small box, true, but not so small that I would just lose track of it.

We went to my house and searched for it together. See! It's not at my house, the box with my diplomas, report cards, those petty little contracts and my photographs—lost! On visits, I haven't unlocked my own little apartment for a long time now; since the earthquake to be precise. Sometimes I stay at my parents' house, sometimes with my siblings. I have avoided staying at my brother's house since the box was lost. I can't say that I feel comfortable at my sister's house, though. She always wants me to stay with her, and I'm wholeheartedly open to it, but then I start to feel stressed after a few days with her because I feel like I'm under investigation. Where am I going and why now and why doesn't she know about it and for how long and why is it necessary to go to those far-off places in this heat…She wouldn't hear any objections about all the visits piled up during the year that we were obliged to make together, in the precise order she planned.

One death, two births, two marriages, moving, congratulations for property purchased, visiting sick people, visiting our aunt from England,

and our cousin returning from the Umrah pilgrimage...

I have to set aside a day for Zeliha.

We haven't seen each other since the earthquake, Zeliha, have we? I usually come to Istanbul in the midst of the summer heat, whereas you save your annual leave for then. Why can't you come and stay with me for just one night...I'll come one night, we can meet at the ferry dock and walk along the shore. You and I always walked together, do you remember, following the minibus road from Bostancı to Kadıköy, our walk took exactly forty minutes; and from Kadıköy to Üsküdar following the *dolmuş* route, that walk took twenty-five minutes. Well, can't we meet this Saturday? Impossible, said my sister, this Saturday we promised Suna Abla, she called before you came, she invited us to breakfast in Salacak. I would love to have breakfast in a tea garden in Salacak with you both. But is it okay if I miss out just this once? No, that's out of the question. Suna Abla delayed the date just so she could invite you. But I haven't seen Zeliha in years...Well, that just proves you can survive without seeing each other for another week. You were always like this, preferring your friends over your family. Suna Abla isn't even part of our family...She's a family friend; she counts as family. Besides, every time you come, you either call Zeliha or you want to call her, but she hasn't called you once. Because she never knows I'm coming. If she called me once in a while, she would know when you were coming. We communicate through the Internet, we've gotten used to that. Admit it, you've always considered your friends more important than the people in your family. Look, you've still never been to our only brother's new house; let's go there next weekend. Okay, maybe; but only on the condition that we don't stay overnight. Don't you think you've made too much of a fuss over this box issue? No, I don't think so. Do you have any idea what it means to not find something where you left it...

V.

We took transfers to Harem, my sister, her daughter and my little girl, first on the E-5 highway, then by minibus. Walking on the shore there, I drifted away from the conversation and got lost in the view of the Maiden's Tower. Thinking of why it was built, it had to be unreachable; but as you look at it from here, you think you could reach it in just a few strokes. When I was a student, passing close to the tower by ship or ferry, I'd look up at it and think about the imprisoned princess. How would she spend her days; with what hopes would she start a new day? Was she able to escape the tower one day or was this where she lay down for her eternal sleep?

My sister called me back from the realm of legends into the real world: You almost fell! If I hadn't been holding your arm, you would have fallen into that pothole there! A meaningless, black emptiness, right beside where I had stopped. What could it be doing here? These days they're busily working on the sidewalks, said my sister, and she went back to discussing my attitude about staying over at my brother's house the following week:

A document, a box, it can be lost at someone's house. And why are the documents in that box so important for you, I really don't understand...

Because you're not in my place, you've lived mostly in the same house ever since you got married. I remember when you were on the other side, in Bakırköy, you couldn't get used to that house; you moved back six months later.

We don't always find everything where we left it, either, you know...

When we reached the tea garden, Suna Abla had just arrived and was unloading her bags from her car. This invitation hadn't been for open buffet, so Menekşe, my sister's daughter, was fretting, expressing shame for not bringing anything.

Although the Salacak tea garden didn't let you bring drinks from outside, they allowed food, and so Suna Abla would bring her summer guests here. Two tables were brought together and a lace tablecloth was spread over them. While I watched Suna Abla unfold it, I felt as if I were seeing her departed mother decorating a table at the tea garden in Yakacık, and my eyes teared up. You see, said my sister, family friends are like relatives. We have shared memories, we've seen some good days together. While Suna Abla ordered large glasses of tea for some and small glasses for others, Zeliha appeared, with a bouquet in her hand. She hasn't changed at all; actually, she has changed, she looked younger, maybe because of her casual clothing. First, we shrieked, and after she had handed over the bouquet of daisies wrapped in white, we embraced each other in turn... It's been at least five years since we saw each other, hasn't it, five whole years. My little melon, how much she's grown, she was still crawling the last time you brought her to me. Was it the year the earthquake happened that we saw each other? It was the year my mother passed away, you and Zeliha came to give your condolences. Yes, I remember, we spent the night at your house...

I'm full of surprises ladies, said Suna Abla. She and Zeliha had become neighbours recently.

The tea came, half in large glasses, half in small. Menekşe pushed her chair back from the table, away from us and ordered an orange juice from the waiter. I didn't drink anything from mugs for years because I had heard that our Prophet never drank out of anything with a handle, said Zeliha. She had had a bad marriage. It took her nearly ten years to break up with a husband who would start fights with her because she had most of the covers, or the lettuce was chopped too big, the teapot lid had been placed upside down, his shirt hadn't been ironed properly; a man who saw himself as a literary genius and believed those close to

him needed to live by this opinion and support it especially in public...
Sugar for the tea. Wrapped in paper. What a waste. Not at all, it's better
that way, untouched by human hands. It's a bad thing to protect yourself
so much, though... The daisies smell wonderful, like they were real. They
are real. I didn't mean to say that, flowers these days look beautiful but
they never have a scent. I never buy flowers from Gypsies, I know what
they do to keep those flowers looking so fresh, they have buckets full
of dirty water somewhere. Okay, but we can't remove the flower-selling
Gypsies from our lives because of that... Then poems just wouldn't be
complete, songs would lose their persuasiveness... Don't make such a big
fuss over everything, girls, it's no good! Look who's talking, coming to
a tea garden with a white lace tablecloth. If I don't use this white lace
tablecloth for you, who would I use it for? I have piles and piles of them
in cupboards and chests, my mother was always crocheting lace table-
cloths for my dowry almost until the day she died... What can I say, this
girl used to wash the lettuce with detergent when she was making salad.
That's how she was but now she's taking pills for a cleanliness obsession.
I'm not as picky about everything as I used to be, but I still have to try to
ignore some things. What sort of things? Ah, Istanbul, Istanbul, we can't
walk your streets anymore because of those southeastern hicks. That's a
very crude judgment, Suna Abla, don't you think? Not at all. You need
good manners to live in this city, if you immigrate here, you need to do
something before you deserve to live in one of the world's most beautiful
cities, like take a six-month or one-year course; our esteemed ancestors
kept a spittoon nearby on their walking routes. Oh come on, what kind
of a judgment is that? If a man migrates here, do you think he comes for
the fun of it? This isn't the time or place to be discussing this...

How many years has it been since we've seen each other, hmm? Come
on, tell me, my little homesick swallow, you first. I don't think we really

need to talk. Let's just watch; let's watch this marvelous view and sip our tea. The glasses are clean, the tea is blood-red. It's like this every time I invite guests here, I come here with plates and pots, the waiters know me by now. I mean, they allow this here at this tea garden. Let's go to the tea garden in Yakacık one day; this time I'll prepare everything. I was working back then, when April came, you were always going to Yakacık, and my dear departed mother would tag along with you. It wasn't tagging along, we would invite her. My mother had a childlike spirit; she'd go to your place, nearly every afternoon she'd go. If she came at a time when you were getting ready to study, this would never make you happy, but the two of you would still clown around, you'd pull a few tricks. I'd warn her every morning before going to work, I'd tell her to stay at home for once, that you girls were studying, don't go and disturb them, I'd say to her, don't be a nuisance. She'd try to hide it from me but I knew she'd still go, she couldn't bear loneliness, my late mother. When it comes to frying aubergines and peppers without oil, this is a secret which includes my homemade vinegar, but you mustn't forget to add sugar. I was such a domestic goddess that I ended up becoming a spinster. Suna Abla, you were the first in a line of women who did not marry because they loved themselves. But I was never stuck at home. For years, for at least thirty years, I was one of those who would set off on my way at six-thirty in the morning. I've been making the most of home life since I retired. You had a man who was in love with you, the typewriter salesman in Sirkeci, that was where I got my Silver Olivetti. We all thought you were going to marry him. You were madly in love with him, weren't you? He wasn't able to trust me, I'm sure you'll make a magnificent wife but you're way above my league, he said in the end. He thought I was stubborn and too independent, that's what he'd imply, but the real reason was different, I knew that. If he married me, three people would enter his life: it was clear that I wouldn't leave my mother, and my sister had just started university. We had got off the train at Haydarpaşa, and were walking towards Kadıköy. There were still rocks by the shore at that time; we sat hidden by the rocks. There was a line in front of the Meat and Fish Directorate, I wore sunglasses in case there was anyone in the line who would recognize me. He had wanted me to take off my sunglasses; he said they looked too good on me, that I was attracting attention. That's how jealous he was. You might ask how I can remember all these details after so many years. I think so carefully about the past that I miss many details belonging to the present. Just look what I did today; I left home in a hurry and forgot to bring the *sarma!* Just think about it, last night for two hours I was rolling leaves with such enthusiasm, and in the morning, I forget them at home and come to Salacak.

Everything's really great, but just tea and simit would do for a breakfast here. These are the rules at this tea garden: you can bring your own pots and plates. Let's come here again in the summer, but this time, we should be inviting you.

I don't think I'll ever go anywhere with you again, said Menekşe, holding a wad of Sudoku puzzles cut out from the paper. She was sitting at a distance from the table, as if she wanted to show that even if she was here with us, she was still different from us.

It's my insomnia that makes me so forgetful, said Suna Abla.

She has an anxiety which makes her lose sleep; she doesn't mind sharing it with us. She was alone at home on the holy night of Regaib. Her newlywed brother, Süha, lived in the apartment right above; he was her only sibling. I've said on several occasions that I didn't marry because of him, that I worked to give him the chance to study. We're all human in the end, but the rumor that his first marriage didn't last because of me, or that I interfered too much with his life, I simply don't agree. I get involved, I can't say I don't. And if you call that being difficult, I couldn't care less. Look, my only brother just passes by my door but doesn't even stop just once. I couldn't control myself; when he was halfway up the stairs, I opened the door. Do you know, Süha, that's exactly how mother would wait on Bayram days, with her hand up in the air saying, 'My son and my daughter-in-law shouldn't be long now'. You have a sister living downstairs; you can't not have seen that her light was still on. Really, sister, I'm terribly tired tonight. Well alright, go and rest then. He walked away. As soon as they got married his wife kept her distance, and Süha went along with it to make his marriage work this time.

What's going on? Where are you going, leaving all at once, sit down, we've still got the beans to eat.

They really look delightful, but I can't eat beans at this hour… In that case, let's go straight to my place, our sarma is ready there.

We'll come another time, Abla, but you should come too, you never do.

Are we out of wet wipes?

Go wash your hands, the rest room is clean, I've checked.

So have I, they don't have any liquid soap. I've got a couple more visits to make today, I can't be too sweaty.

There's a demonstration in Fatih, I'm going to go there now, you should come, too, said Zeliha.

Stay like that everybody, don't move, I'm going to take a photograph. The view is beautiful, but the chairs are plastic. The chairs are plastic, but the tea is wonderful. There's a tea garden on the way to Çengelköy, its chairs look antique. What's important for me here is the view, not the chairs. It feels like I could touch the Maiden's Tower if I hold my hand out. I used to pass right by it on the ferry when I was a student, sometimes I took a small ferry, It'd get very close to it, and I'd wonder what was inside, as if I could find the traces of a girl hidden away from a snake by her father the king. Just imagine, it has a history of at least two thousand four hundred years, maybe even longer. Apparently this isn't the original building. As far as I know the original was destroyed in an earthquake and a wooden building was built as a lighthouse in its place. It was a former prison, a prison which created fairytales and legends; then it started to be used for military purposes, and today it's been opened to the public as a restaurant and cafeteria. Shall we go there next week? We could do. Oh really, my sister interrupted, what about our plan to visit our brother together next week? I didn't promise, did I? We can even go to our brother's during the week, but Zeliha works, we can only make plans with her for the weekend. The Maiden's Tower isn't going anywhere either; you can go the following week…

The thought of entering the Maiden's Tower overwhelms me; I would have wanted to see it in its old state, unchanged for hundreds of years. Who knows what it was like, the place where a princess was hidden from the evil of a snake. The walls were thick, it seemed impenetrable; yet the snake would still sneak in, in the king's flowers.

According to one legend, the king had built the tower to keep the girl away from a fisherman she was in love with.

A fisherman would have been able to reach the foot of the tower easily from this coast.

Even if he was able to swim, he probably wasn't able to enter.

In the past, this coast was always crowded with people who were fishing.

We used to go on picnics to the dam in Ömerli. We would fish on the banks…

We're supposed to have water shortages this year. I wish we could get away in the second half of August. A desert heat is going to descend upon us. They said the same thing last year; we didn't suffer that much but this year they're saying we're going to see a serious water shortage. In the past, in the 1970s, when the water was cut, we'd go to Yakacık to get water. You know I told you about the tea garden there, I really loved to go there, sit, and read a book. Should we go together one day? It had to be when the Judas trees were in bloom, at the beginning of May, the fuchsia cyclamen flowers and light and dark colored Judas trees covered the mountains and hills. I'll most likely be on annual leave in August; we'll go when I return. Let's find a quiet little corner like this where we can sit and talk, there's so much to talk about…We could walk from Eminönü to Saraçhane; that would have been nice but our time is short, we have to catch the demonstration…

Seeing as we came here together, shouldn't we go back together, asked my sister. We had discussed this at home. We were going to stop by Kadıköy and look at university preparatory programs for Menekşe.

We can go to Kadıköy during the week anyway, but there's not a demonstration every day.

They must be like a way for you to never get old, demonstrations. Well, go, but don't be late.

We had cleaned the table and started to put the bags in the trunk of the car, but the car keys were missing. We opened all the bags, searched them; we searched our own handbags; there was no key. Some of us should stay and watch the car. Suna Abla can take a taxi home, get the spare key and come back. You come with me, my dear Menekşe, I can offer you some sarma, you can spend the night at my house, the Bosphorus under our feet, we can enjoy the balcony together, said Suna Abla. Menekşe wasn't too keen. I want to go the demonstration with my aunts, she said. "I've never been to a demonstration in my whole life…"

We took a small ferry to Eminönü and from there jumped onto a minibus. There was no sign of the crowd we had hoped for at Saraçhane. The only evidence of a crowd was at the park entrance; the demonstration had broken up. It had lasted a short time, just long enough for a press statement. We were late too because we had been looking for Suna Abla's car key. There were still a few banners floating around, brochures on the ground: "Don't Stay Silent, World!", "We Won't Stand for Imperialism in the Middle East!"…At five o'clock, a friend of Zeliha's who we had run into at the park invited us to a literature forum that she was going to take part in. Passing shops that sold leather clothing, shoes and bags, exchange bureaus, small hotels, restaurants and tourism agents, we reached Zeliha's workplace. It was her day off, but the literary magazine forum her colleague was going to would take place nearby, so we decided to stop by to relax. Her friend at the office, a warm, likeable girl, turned on "Rain" by Feliciano and offered us mineral water.

Zeliha didn't want to attend the magazine meeting; she didn't like literary types. Menekşe, though, was excited. I've always wanted to go to a literary meeting, she said.

VI.

I handed the postcard I slipped into my bag before leaving home to the greengrocer at the store where I usually shop. This is an old postcard of the Galata Bridge, but the bridge back then looked a lot different than it does now. My greengrocer friend slips the postcard into the side of the large framed photograph hanging on the wall behind him; a fellow townsman who was world champion in weightlifting, a photograph taken with him, like a guaranty document for his customers.

Istanbul's a beautiful city, isn't it, very beautiful. I've gone there two times; I'd still like to go again. The Bosphorus Bridge. The Islands. The Blue Mosque. The Galata Tower. The hotels in Laleli, night clubs, leather goods stores…

When I think about Istanbul, what do I remember? The pigeons in Beyazıt Square. The cool green path at Dolmabahçe palace. Sitting in the cafes around Sultanahmet and listening to the mosques take turns singing the call to prayer. The open tea garden in Yakacık. The *medrese* in Çemberlitaş. The Süleymaniye Mosque complex, too. A ferry drifting up the Bosphorus and the second-hand book stores that would take my breath away as I wandered around, diving into a sea of books…

Why would someone want to dive into a book when the real sea is right next to them? Istanbul was a city surrounded by the sea, a city decorated by lit-up minarets with messages hanging between them.

Istanbul's not just one city anymore, I said. There are women living there who've never seen the sea, not even once in their lives. There are homes at the top of the hills that don't have water or electricity.

Those don't count, said my grocer friend. Those don't count as part of Istanbul.

VII.

Night. The Maiden's Tower. Live music with a prix fixe menu. We sat at a table on the first floor.

You can see Salacak from inside, right there.

A group of businessmen opposite us ordered food for their German or Austrian guests. A picture on the wall: a youth, madly in love, trying to fight against the waves to reach the tower; he must be the fisherman we talked about in the tea garden. Inside the tower is a commercial air, stranger than the fairytales that had inspired me from the outside. Legends always overrate love anyway, said Zeliha. Love is always such a strange flood of emotions, and because you let yourself go in that flood, now you're sitting here across from me with the discomfort of a guest. The reason for my discomfort is firstly because I'm disappointed, I said. It is narrower than I thought it would be inside the tower, and very confusing, I mean, it's a lot more confusing than I thought it would be. Is it possible to find a trace, a single trace of the girl who lived locked up in this place for years, among all this furniture? We can go up to the mezzanine, said Zeliha. They sell gifts on the mezzanine, we can have a look. Never mind, I said. Let's sit here a little longer, then we'll leave. Let's have some dessert, said Zeliha. *Keşkül* pudding or Şam Baba, perhaps. I'm going to buy a few packets of Şam Baba for the *iftar* parties. I still haven't gone shopping; actually I've barely done anything I had planned to. My sister insisted on going to my brother's new house this weekend and bringing my own girl along. With every passing year, the distance between me and my siblings grows a little more. But tell me, when you entrust something to your sibling's care and it goes missing, can you really put aside strange feelings?

Zeliha took out a wooden box from the bag she was carrying around with her: Could this be the box you said had gone missing?

Oh, yes, that's the box, of course! My goodness, when did I leave it with you, I don't remember at all.

You used to come and stay with me every now and then that year when the earthquake happened, you remember…

Why did I forget leaving the box with you?

Maybe because of the earthquake. It was a bad year for all of us.

It was. I couldn't spend the night at my own house because of the deep crack in the wall. I went from house to house with my daughter, who was still a baby then. I usually spent the weekends at your place.

Aren't you going to look inside the box?

I want to look later, when I get back home. Everything looks different when you're far away. I don't want Istanbul, or the life led by my family and friends here, to change in my absence. Every change seems like a sign of loss to me. The box that had disturbed my peace of mind was smaller than I had thought; it was ordinary. Now my important documents seem to have lost their importance; there you have it! All these years, I haven't had to queue in front of state offices because one of them was missing.

If they weren't important losing this box wouldn't have upset you so much...

Of course they were important, but I had definitely overreacted in some ways. I guess after I've taken a look inside at home, I can leave it with you again. I might consider taking it with me too. Otherwise, it can stay at my sister's for a while. I don't want to talk about that box anymore. Let's talk about you; you tell me about your life. What's changed in your life since we last saw each other? How have these last few years treated you? Come on, tell me.

Stripped of My Bikini by Poseidon

Handan Öztürk

Translated by Kerim Biçer and İdil Aydoğan

When I first arrived in this city I was dressed as thickly as a whale-hunting Greenlander.

The fact that I was feeling chilly had nothing to do with the farewell rain pouring down on me at the station that resembled a World War II film set, probably because it still maintained the spirit of colonialism. Neither was my heart's shiver caused by raindrops brushing past the feelings this callow young man had buried deep inside himself, as I watched him being pushed onto the train before ours, amid cries of joy, to join the military.

And I was not aware of the delirium that would come during this journey into the unknown that I had embarked upon, just after the young man who had soaked under the rain on the same platform with me and who I had lost with the departing whistle.

Perhaps the chill came from the rising fear I felt because of my father's sudden decision to migrate, dragging me and my troubled transition to adolescence along with him to an unfamiliar setting. Could God be the only one to blame for the conservatism of a small town adolescent girl who, breaking out of her cocoon and terrified by it, had transformed the abandonment of her childhood and the place that shaped it into deep sorrow? Even at this age, I have difficulty separating the memories that emerge from my excavations into my mind's depths as I search for answers about my past and my future, and the schizophrenic attacks that lead to convulsions in my subconscious; and so the two end up bubbling in the same cauldron.

During the journey, my body responds to every young man I see! And I feel certain that they will carry my messages to that particular young man who I saw at the station and whose whereabouts I do not know. In my mother's eyes, I am just a girl whose little black box hasn't yet been opened. I am her pillar of pride; a casualty of her rooted aristocracy, deemed to be silenced as I learn to speak my mind.

As I searched among all the boys I came across, like an old pervert, trying to find the handsome novice soldier—his face drenched as he stood among the friends seeing him off, his growing impatience to meet the archetypal warriors of his dreams only heightening his innocence in my eyes—I was still holding my mother's hand. She was guilty of aristocracy; I, of mighty desire.

The shivers, which started when my mother and I were holding hands, were the malady of my attempt to fit my passage from childhood to adolescence into one train journey rather than enacting it an unfamiliar place. It worsened as the train approached Istanbul. Faced with my shivers, which quickly became life-threatening, my mother instantly resurrected her post-natal nightmares; then she called up the compassion she had felt during my infancy and tried to protect me, with stories. The panic I felt as I struggled to grow up in one journey was overcome by her urgency to tell me stories about the dangers of the big city. And because in those days this vast city was in a battle against cholera, her stories settled into a background of disease, with thick black smoke and bubbling lime cauldrons.

Before my mother could finish her stories, the train dove headfirst into the Bosphorus from the Haydarpaşa Terminal; or so it seemed to me when we moved into the platform on the very left, which almost formed a border with the sea. I poked my head out of the train window and gazed at the enormous city that stood before me; I knew I would never be able to settle in here, knowing now the stories my mother told me. Perhaps that was why the provocative grandeur of the Roman, Byzantine, Genovese, French, German and Ottoman architectural styles was unable to overwhelm my fears or console my heart. The indifference I felt to this vision partly owed to the magic of the raindrops I had left behind. I should take into account as well the disillusionment I felt as all the magical places I had squeezed into my childhood world tumbled down, diminished to dust with a sudden earthquake. I believe this can explain to some extent too the apathy I continue to feel towards buildings and objects. It could also explain the dervish in me; wearing the weight of the world like a tattered cardigan. Perhaps, together with the influence of nihilism in my soul during my forties, it could even be the reason why I renounced every kind of physical elegance, which I believed created nothing but oppression.

By burying my head in the books on my father's shelves and those at the county public library, I had read and digested all the delicacies and cruelties of Hagia Sophia, the Sultanahmet Mosque, Topkapı Palace, Sarayburnu, the Galata and the Maiden's Towers, the Basilica Cistern and the Dungeons of Yedikule, long before I set eyes on them. All the knowledge gained from this quick but committed study retreated to a dark corner of my mind, and I never went looking for it.

I had arrived at the grand terminal, leaving behind everything I knew at a slippery wet and moldy suburban station. The face of the novice soldier I was keeping, as if in the palm of my hand, suddenly filled the platform.

But his unique face lost all meaning as it duplicated into various colors and shapes here in this huge city, so I was now as lonely as the devil. Once I sensed that this feeling of homelessness which had embraced me was going to last a lifetime, I began to shiver again. My mother tried to warm me by telling me about our new home. "Well, it's not a mansion, and of course it doesn't have a garden. But it's an apartment, so it's modern," she said. That's the first time I placed a question mark beside the concept of modernity.

My shivers worsened. As we stepped off the train, my mother wrapped me in a new story. This one was about a different rapist.

I shivered despite my burning body; aflame with a budding desire to which I was stranger. I could have frozen to death in front of the eyes of all in this huge city into which I must have fallen from the clouds. Although I knew he had long got off at some unknown stop, my eyes still searched for the young man who had seduced me with the innocence that his warrior spirit was trying to destroy. Instead, I bumped into his clones, rushing about in amateur excitement. The hundreds of young men we traveled behind in consecutive compartments, and with whom in silent pacts I had committed my adolescence, asked for the addresses of the military headquarters to which they were to report. So many of them; my body is bewildered by the lust awakened and growing it.

As a family, we leaned against the railing on the deck of the boat that connected Asia and Europe; dazzled, we watched this intercontinental passage, smiling at each other with the joy of completing our journey. Because it was the only moment in this chaotic trip that made me smile truly from my heart, whenever I read an article that belittles or ridicules this metaphor of passage, I immediately fall out with the author. And when I look back and remember that fragile moment, which doesn't only represent an intercontinental passage for me, but the transition between East and West, my childhood and my youth, my past and my future, I resent myself for not letting go of my mother's hand. Each time I weigh my weaknesses, I always place this cowardice in front of me and ruthlessly use it against myself.

The glory of the Byzantine and Ottoman palaces, the entertainment venues frequented by sinners in search of heaven, the cafes with their static elegance and clienteles, seeking out new regulars: none of these could bring back the magic of the places of my childhood, which perished into dust during the earthquake. So I flung myself into the city's streets, which seem to reproduce as I paced them. In the narrow, dim medieval and modern streets intertwined, where even the wind lost its way, I searched for my past and my future together.

I let go of my mother's hand when I joined protests, shouting anti-militarist, anti-fascist and anti-imperialist slogans. I still find it amusing that I dealt her the heartbreak she deserved in an arena in which she was a total stranger. I don't know if I need mention that my anger, which subsided by screaming these anti- slogans and gave over to the romanticism of protest, united me with my fantasy of the novice soldier I had lost at the colonialist-spirited station. And my hand, which was now free, I held out to other young men walking beside me joyfully.

If our experiences can ruin our dreams, I am definitely someone who is not in fate's favor! Despite this, the golden blonde hair and green eyes of the young man I fell in love with as a university student blurred the image of my novice soldier with rain dripping down his raven-black hair, and my shivers subsided. It wasn't just the flasks of warm tea he prepared each time he took me to the seafront in Moda or Salacık in his old VW Beetle, as if he had sensed my chronic shivering, that warmed the caverns of my heart. It was partly owing to the Bach cantatas we listened to in his car, which reached the bubbling cauldron in the heart of this small town girl and made me warmer with him. And the lust that had drained from me at the Haydarpaşa Terminal years ago gradually rejuvenated…

I now began to dress thinly. My summery clothes added a new air to the songs I sang, the poems I recited; I was strange and new even to myself. The shivers passed on to my mother, and the turn to tell stories passed to me. No new story I learned was enough to warm her old heart. This is how my mother got her revenge for the time when her stories were unable to warm me on that long journey of migration. Prologues to freedom, women's rights, equality, imperialism, fascism, poverty, democracy and love were enough for her to block her ears to what I had to say before I even started.

That is why, on one beautiful summer's day, when Poseidon stole my bikini on the beach of Kilyos during my first time making love, I kept this secret from her. Yet my mother's frightful stories about the big city were recycled, coming from my lover's lips. And in contrast to my mother's naive narratives, he presented them to me in macho slang. Just when I was beginning to make peace with its streets and shores, someone had come between me and this ancient city once again. I quietly relegated to my heart the feelings of being exiled into fear for the second time in this city. I handed back to this jealous lover all the slogans of freedom and equality he had taught me; and as I walked away, alone with my broken heart, I remember as if it were yesterday being overcome by an intense feeling of freedom. Maybe in part because I was bold enough to take for myself the meanings of the slogans.

I mentioned the narrow and dim intertwined streets of this city. And I think it is time to tell you that, once experienced, the pleasure of getting lost in those streets, tagging behind strangers, becomes highly addictive. I also explained as best I could the reasons why the nihilistic relationship I formed with buildings and all things related to physical appearance had made me rebellious. This must have been why I could not find an inch of land where I could express my emotions physically; so I chose the sea. With my new lover, who I felt shared not just the slogans of freedom but also their meanings, on the hidden piers of mansions, above the soft waves stroked by the shadow of the Bosphorus Bridge, facing the whole city, I sanctified my body with childish games. On a small rowing boat, when I lost my jeans to one of the strait's playful waves, I realized that I had formed a strong bond with one of Istanbul's most important qualities that made her who she was: her nature. With the intoxicating bliss of having made up with her, following a wild winter *lodos,* I found myself on the Island.

Alas, as I crossed more boundaries and became more independent from my mother and her infamous stories of Istanbul, my lover seemed to be developing new habits. For example, since he considered a visit to the Island akin to a trip to the Australia, he feared that his lifestyle entrenched between Cihangir, Beyoğlu and Etiler would slip away forever. And it was left for me to discover that the freedom he babbled on about was restricted to his own habitat.

I was in love and stark naked. In this city I arrived in with clothes so thick I was ready for the Arctic, I was now bare enough for the hottest places of Africa. At that moment, under my increasingly transparent skin, my heart could be seen under my ribs. This simplicity and transparency I had engendered in myself transformed me into a glass girl. And it was right there, in the ebb and flow of an Island night, that Eros snatched my heart away, just like that! And I was still innocent enough to believe that as soon as I had lost it, he would return my heart unharmed. Now I take my revenge on Eros by whispering into the ears of all the young girls I meet, how his arrows that seemed like love slyly pierced my heart.

This makes me mischievous. And I fall in love with the idea of turning my glass body into a magic mirror by rubbing into it the secret silvering used by magicians. I wish to be a mirror for the people crunched by the metropolis's half-grown teeth. The mornings I wake up with the feeling that my wish has come true, I climb the highest hill on the Island. I reach the Aya Yorgi monastery through a route people walk twice a year, entrusting all hopes and vows to colorful devotional strings. Facing Istanbul, which lies ghost-like before me, I sit boldly on the highest rocks of a steep cliff, poised like I am the world's largest mirror. As the first rays of morning sun coat the sins left over from the night, the huge, befuddled city awakens yet again. I am old enough to know that not even the coffeehouses and teahouses carrying the aromas of the Orient, nor the cafés preparing to sell their industrial concentrates would suffice to make this ancient city rise and shine! People get out of their beds and slowly get dressed for the journeys they will make into their own daily lives, their inner worlds and the souls of others. When I see their reflections on my silvered surface, once again, after years, I feel the same old shivers I had suffered throughout that long train journey. As the doors of houses open in the narrow, dim, perplexing streets of this mysterious city, where even the wind loses its way, along with the countless stories left idle because no one is willing to listen, I shiver. This enticing city of historical and natural wonders selfishly appropriates the stories people bring with them from the four corners of the country.

It must be because no one is allowed to tell their full story to anyone, and no one really listens to anyone's story wholeheartedly that this city wears so many different styles of clothing and concealment, I begin to think, when that freezing cold chills me to my bones again.

I'd better head back home and put on some clothes.

The Bostancı Garden Tree

Gül İrepoğlu

Translated by Nilgün Dungan

If it was just a coincidence that she was looking out the window when the municipal work crew arrived, she never knew. She just continued looking, keeping perfectly still.

A mechanical lift inside a truck, the kind that could go fairly high. And two men, the kind who could do anything that requires strength.

Neighbors had filed a complaint a long time ago about the tree, as if it were a criminal, saying that it had grown really old, completely dried up, and unable to cling onto its roots, would fall on top of them during a violent storm. God forbid, the things they heard about—branches injuring passersby, limbs falling on top of cars—could happen, couldn't they? They were absolutely right; it was true as the blue of the sky, which the sycamore once brushed with its thick foliage.

The tree had no life left in it; in fact, it had shown no sign of life for a very long time. It must've been the oldest tree on the street. Still, it stood there, like it didn't have the heart to harm the honeysuckle that climbed and embraced it. Actually, it could probably have lived a lot longer, but the big sycamore had become ill. Getting ill wasn't its fault; it did its best for years: didn't waste the sunshine and rainwater it was allotted, started producing green foliage at the onset of spring, and tried to hang onto it until the very last days of autumn. It always tolerated the lovers' names carved into its thick trunk. Its roots used to be inside a garden, but after rezoning they ended up being on city property that lead to a sidewalk. Its duty, first and foremost, was to offer caring shade to those passing by and catching their breath under it, and to embellish the street with its greenery.

But some extraordinary things happened. When new cobblestones were laid around the tree, so little soil was left that it couldn't breathe, its roots trapped between the artificial, cookie-cutter stones. And perhaps because this confinement overwhelmed the tree, its demise was hastened.

The honeysuckle that it carried so conscientiously was still full of life, though helpless in the face of what was happening to the tree it had been holding onto for so long.

The men tackled the tree with the indifference of just doing their job, yet with a determination commensurate with their experience. The metal lift with the man inside went up, stopping first at the lower branches, and the electric saw began churning with its horrible noise. These lower branches, signs of the older days the tree had seen, fell to the ground one by one. As the lift rose, the falling branches were younger and younger. Those at the very top must have thought they had a long time ahead of them when they began their life, not realizing how old the body they were attached to actually was. And they must have tried to stretch upward in order to see the sea, not realizing this was in vain too, because it was no longer possible to see the sea, blocked as it was by grim buildings.

The huge trunk was next.

The trunk was thick, its bark peeled off in places, and it bore the scars of many years. Now with all of its branches cut off, its old body stripped naked, the tree was self-conscious but could only stand there helplessly.

It seemed to have surrendered. Yet it also held within it a final fight.

The men could not work the saw easily on the trunk; trying a few different spots and grinding hard, they injured it badly.

Then perhaps because it could no longer bear looking uglier and uglier, the sycamore suddenly submitted to its fate and took in the steel. The men relaxed and proceeded more enthusiastically, though not more roughly, with their metal might. Naturally, many people had gathered to watch with a strange pleasure the whole course of this cutting—people would always be wherever spectacles were, and it would always take special effort to keep them a safe distance from the scene—and these onlookers now breathed a sigh of relief, as if they had accomplished the task themselves.

The street was rid of the old sycamore! And how convenient: there was now firewood for some. Anyway, the loves carved into the tree had already faded...

When the truck drove off with the once majestic, now chopped-up tree, the woman at the window gaped sadly, as if watching the funeral procession of an old, beloved family member, noticing much later the tears streaming down her face.

The things that this departing tree had witnessed! Or rather, what hadn't it witnessed? It had seen the most pleasant times of Bostancı: Those carefree times when it was the seashore resort of Istanbul. The times when the district was exclusive and was described as 'classy'...

The best times of her childhood, the most trouble-free and least responsible parts of her youth. And then the further stages of her life as she matured. First intermittently during the months of winter, then uninterrupted...

The first grandchild of a large family and thoroughly spoiled, she must have been very little when she passed underneath the tree for the first time. Perhaps the tree was very young back then, too. The times when gardens were quiet, streets were desolate, and squares secluded... when nights were dark...when only a few large gardens would fit onto a street...when small buildings in the gardens were completely hidden by the trees...

The times she went to the beach as a little girl, carefree and full of joy...when there were a few sandy beaches and one ice cream vendor at the seaside in Bostancı. The residents of the district knew that the dilapidated bridge on the road to the beach was the historically famous Bostancıbaşı Bridge, and that entrance to Istanbul had been controlled from this bridge for centuries. The times when buying calico for dresses from the fabric store on the corner would be enough to make the little girl happy...And the time she was surprised when seeing for the first time a declaration of love carved into the trunk of the sycamore.

That big sycamore was there when she became a teenager; when she wished to grow up and become beautiful yet was moody and never happy with the way she looked; when eagerly she was "going out" to stroll up and down Bağdat Street then sit in the patisserie; and at the end of the summer when she was "going down" to Istanbul, sadly bidding farewell to the beautiful garden.

Later, when she was a university student running to catch the Beşiktaş bus with a T-square in her hand, it was there too. Every evening, the tree would shield her from the windows of the house when she innocently hugged her boyfriend as they parted. Or with its leaves shed, it allowed her to wave at her boyfriend from the balcony for longer.

Now Istanbul had the Bosphorus Bridge, and people lived all year round in Bostancı; and there was no garden left to bid farewell to: they were all replaced by multistory buildings. The more she thought about it, the better she understood the important place this sycamore had in her history. She walked on the same road as a young married woman, going to university to teach; when she held the hand of one of her children as the other one walked by her side, and she daydreamed, imagining every little detail about them was perfect.

For years, stepping on the cobblestones of the same road, tired but still thinking she was young, she passed under that sycamore. Disregarding, not noticing its old age…

There was no end to her memories: some faint, some very much alive.

The changes in the city had silently accompanied the changes in its residents.

Holding her very young mother's hand and skipping, a little girl in a ponytail—because her father likes her hair best in a ponytail—is going to Bostancı Station to welcome her dear grandfather. Her grandfather, as soon as he steps off the train, will run agilely towards her, hug her, recite the tongue-twister that belongs only to the two of them, give her the paper bag full of pistachios that he brought, and sometimes an umbrella-shaped chocolate too. Together they will go home unhurriedly, climbing up from the underpass and walking past the coffeehouse amidst the trees in the square just behind the station, and greeting all the shopkeepers along the way—everyone knows her grandpa, Cemal Bey the chemist, the owner of the mansion "Cevizli Köşk". Let no one be fooled by him, passing by with a humped back: with the keen gaze of his dark green eyes, he notices everyone but only sees those who he wishes to see.

Their garden was big—big enough for a young child to call part of it the "lower garden" and to be afraid that the kind of alligators seen in books might live there. Their house was wooden, three-storied, with an attic above the other two stories, with balconies and carved banisters. Wrapped around the balcony, which overlooked the sea nearby on one side and Kayışdağı in the distance on the other, was honeysuckle, her mother's favorite flower, whose fragrance she called exquisite and inhaled deeply as it came into the room while she played the piano... Honeysuckle intertwined with wisteria, which was her own favorite flower for as long as she could remember, almost fully wrapped around the house. The trunk of the wisteria was so thick and twisted, she rode it like a horse as she played and travelled far, far away to imaginary realms. One of its branches reach over far enough to cover the wide gazebo, like a curtain that illuminated with the slight movements of the leaves.

The patio with wooden columns that covered the entire front of the house was her favorite place; its comfortable armchairs were painted blue and had colorful floral print cushions. Just a little further away were birds that furtively drank from the fountain basin of the ornamental pond with water lilies on it. And a grandfather and grandchild were there; they knew every single tree and flower in that garden and made the most of everything. Other members of the family surely loved the garden, but strict devotion, now that was something else... How many children were there whose grandfathers would make an iron step for them climb easily to the fragrant apricot tree and dream for hours in their special place there, where the branches forked and created a natural seat?

She still reminisces about how, when they decided to tear down the house and garden to erect apartment buildings in their place, despite her childish defiance, and it was finally time to say goodbye, she silently caressed every single flower and tree, every wall of the house, especially the white-washed one where the wisteria found a way to enter from the window, and how she smelled the honeysuckle, scattered at the end of the summer, in order to hold it inside. Because bidding farewell to places lived in is only possible by holding on tightly to the memories and keeping them alive inside you.

The crowd and pleasure in the garden are unforgettable; long summer days when the garden overflowed with friends of her mother, father, beautiful aunt, and uncles; when large pots of food prepared by her long-suffering grandmother and her helpers were consumed; when the music from her younger uncle's 45s, later her own, was interrupted only by the playful screams of her siblings or clinks of a backgammon game; and when the long summer nights were enlivened by open air cinemas. Evenings when heart-wrenching love stories, exaggerated war scenes, and images of faraway countries were watched with excitement in Bostancı Deniz Cinema, on wooden chairs whose nails scratched legs, occasionally interrupted by the sound of trains passing on the nearby tracks; when soda pop was drunk out of green bottles; and when sleepy children wanted to climb into their parents' arms during walks back home at midnight.

No one knows whether it's the smell of the vermilion-colored velvet roses or that of the pink roses used for making preserves that prevail in her memory. Or is the smell of fried aubergines and green peppers more evocative? Or is it the taste of the luscious fruit picked fresh from the tree, which lingers on the palate, especially that of red peaches or of those tiny strawberries that she swallowed with dirt still on them… Or is it the unique color of the black mulberries shaken from the tree onto snow-white sheets that touches her deeply? The excitement that she felt on the day when she was old enough to take the minced meat *börek* on the big round tray covered with newspaper to the bakery at the end of the street to get it baked. Could the burn to her hand caused by carelessness when she was so excited to pick up the pastry from the bakery still be hurting? Perhaps this, accompanied by the dirt that scattered as she kicked it up from the ground when she was riding on the swing that hung from the most solid branch of the blue pine, and by the rustling of the great pine trees taller than the roof of the house…

Is it this place, gone forever, where now only block after block of apartment buildings rise and where she herself has found a place to live, that once embraced all that splendor? Those who can testify to it are becoming fewer and fewer...

It was as if all of this was engraved in the memory of that sycamore.

As if the holder of these dim memories wanted to revive all of them, all at once as it was being chopped up and taken away. Just like someone who is dying is said to see their life flashing before their eyes...

Life flashes of a city, a district, a living creature of the world, or all these intertwined with each other...

Those finished and revived. Side by side with those that continue...

The roots of the honeysuckle held firm even though it was deprived of branches to hold onto. It wrapped itself round the crude fence of the apartment block garden. The woman noticed it the next year, just as the smell of blooming flowers reached her nose when she was passing by. She could not have known that one day she would embrace the flowers of that honeysuckle with intense sorrow.

Years went by and her mother became ill like that sycamore and lay in her death bed. When she realized that her mother's time had come, she went out and picked a few stems of the honeysuckle and set them on both sides of her pillow. She knew her mother liked that very much from the way she held her hand.

She could not lift her head up and look as they were taking her mother away, wrapped in her sheets, but the next day when her mother was about to be washed before burial, she went inside the *gasilhane* one last time. The sheets were opened and honeysuckle petals fell to the ground. The honeysuckle petals of Bostancı, the Old Bostancı, that had kept the "Lady" of Old Bostancı company during her lifetime.

The cycle on earth did not change as the dried-up trees left this earth.

And new saplings were planted in place of the trees that had been cut down, just like the tree full of leaves that they planted in place of the holder of memories.

And now that spindly body is trying to grow as much as the concrete slabs surrounding its roots allow, to witness the histories and future memories of the people of the city, of the neighborhood, and maybe of her own children…

Close to the honeysuckle tree, very close. No one knows when they will meet, but one day… If only the street stays where it is.

Transaction

Menekşe Toprak

Translated by İdil Aydoğan

The city gave her a strange sense of perpetuity: it was ungraspable, it was reckless. It harbored all dreams and opportunities, and every kind of evil; it could overthrow both beliefs and disbeliefs. The city couldn't care less that she had taken this baby step out of her safety zone. It seemed to greet games with a warm welcome. And she was the star of such a game that night. An ambiguous game in which it was partly possible to make out the next move and when it would come, and she believed she would have control over those moves. She didn't quite know the ending. There would be a boundary where she would stop. She thought she would be the one to set the boundaries and the one to lift them. Like she was both the actress and the spectator of a play.

But she should have known better, and she did. Everything in this world has a cost. Nothing can remain unreturned. Not love, nor a meaningful glance, nor a hand trying to hold yours. Everything had a price and a gain. A man her father's age had expectations from her young, tender body, her raw fire. And as he waited, he grew bored. If he could smile at her so sweetly while tolerating her inability to converse, her childish shyness which she struggled to hide behind her joy...

She didn't think about the price for this. She thought she was in control of the night, of the man and herself. And she didn't think she would cut the game somewhere, that she wouldn't go all the way. She was a little blind and naive. Without realizing that silent acceptance was a pact, and that every drop of alcohol downed together had a price, she sipped her *rakı* after every bite of her sea bream. Under the man's admiring gaze she took a fork of *meze* to her mouth coquettishly. She kept her eyes on the man. Sometimes he looked at her like he was grooming a little girl, brushing aside strands of hair that fell on her forehead, or like he was her older brother, or perhaps her lecturer at university.

The man asked her if she had a boyfriend.

"Yes," she replied.

And she believed her own lie. She was a normal, natural young woman. Balanced, lively, fair, usual—maybe even ordinary. She always slept well. She drank a glass of milk every night to keep her skin clear and glowing; she ate plenty of apples, and she sometimes dieted. Her teeth were white, her gums were pink and hadn't receded a single bit. Her boyfriend would send flowers to her workplace every Valentine's Day. In short, she was in harmony with life and at peace with herself.

She was sure this was who the man perceived her to be, and now she could flesh out her lover for him, however she wanted. Someone like Cenk, for example. Could she justly talk about him without mentioning why he hated this city so much? According to Cenk, this city was a whore; its men lived and consumed love like it was bought with money, and its women were confused, angry, and hence lonely. Can you tell me why is it that men who suffer from love open up to another woman and not to their male friends, she could have asked the man now. Do men your age fall in love? Have you ever suffered from love? Cenk has. Cenk hates this city you live in because his girlfriend cannot part from it, whereas I feel sorry for him. His girlfriend is right. Cenk isn't a man you would want to fall in love with; he is a safe island where you could seek refuge. The air about him is heavy and depressing. When he sits opposite me in front of his computer with that helpless and pained look on his face, like he was shouldering the weight of the world, I sometimes feel like slapping his face. 'What do you expect, if you are so good, suffer so badly, and beg so desperately in your whimpering voice,' I feel like telling him. Cenk definitely should have been a writer, not an engineer. He is melancholic like them, and obsessed... Perhaps I should portray someone like Kağan. If she were to describe him without giving his name, would he figure out who it was? No way. How was he supposed to know a man who had listened to him alongside hundreds of others at a five-day conference? And how well did she know Kağan anyway? No! She needed to be more cautious about Kağan: she mustn't yet allow him to grow inside her, preoccupying her fantasies.

But the man had no intention of finding out about the Cenks and Kağans of her world, or listening to the details about her life with her retired civil servant mother who, after the death of her father, had aged on her own, her body sagging while untouched. He wanted to get to the point without wasting too much time. He knew life well enough not to postpone his desires. Now, as his intentions were so blatantly obvious, she would either have to respond fully or lie about having promised to meet someone so she could escape. Or she could go to the ladies room and call one of her friends or Cenk and ask them to call her on her mobile, so she could slip away telling the man she had to be somewhere. She could put an end to this game without provoking the man.

Darling, wasn't it very awkward of you to mention literature, cinema and art while discussing marketing strategies for the new surgical products imported from America by the company? Do you really carry in your head a massive library, as you would have everyone believe, or are you one of those who has memorized only titles? Or one of those who believe they are living a wrong life in a wrong world, with the wrong people? I can spot a white mark left on your finger by a wedding ring. Will you reveal your marital status? This is none of my business really. Just like the fact that I have a boyfriend is none of yours.

Of course, these questions were ridiculous and unnecessary. "Take it easy," she said to herself in English, an expression they had worn out at the office. That's what she was doing. Light, the world was extremely light. Life was a long way away from her mother, who had hidden her own youth in steamy bathrooms, aged it in broken mirrors; way beyond the embroidered white handkerchiefs she had lined up for her daughter, the clean towels saved for special nights and the pure silk nightdresses. She carried no fear: none of the fear taught or preached or tossed upon her shoulders. Why should a lively young woman like herself reject a spontaneous invitation? What a coincidence, she thought. If her mother—who wished even more than her that one day a clean-cut young man would ring their doorbell with a box of chocolates and a bunch of flowers in hand—hadn't called her the minute the conference was over, rambling on and unnecessarily delaying her exit from the conference hall, she wouldn't have bumped into this man who she would hate for treating women in their forties as if they were already old, and she wouldn't be sitting here with him now.

"You know when you caught my attention? It is truly impossible for you to go unnoticed, really, but anyway... Yesterday when you were going through your bag, I noticed the book you placed on the table. First I thought, hmmm, a charming young woman who is interested in literature. And world literature, as a matter of fact! John Updike is an author I discovered while I was doing my master's in America. In fact, there's a story in that book you are reading. It's absolutely marvellous! I have an audio recording of it too. A superb story about how male sexuality depends entirely on the pleasure induced in the female."

She felt herself blush but she tried to hide it. "I haven't read it," she said. "I just recently bought the book from a second-hand bookshop to help improve my English. I'm only on the second story. What did you say the title of the story was?"

" 'Transaction'."

"Forget it," said the man, when she reached out for her bag to get the book. "You can read it later. I have a tiny apartment in Şişli I hardly let anyone into. It is my private space, my hideout. I listen to music there, read books, watch films, and especially, I close my eyes and listen to the audio books I have ordered from the UK and US over the years. In fact, if you want, we can go there now and listen to the audio version of the story I'm talking about, together. It's marvellous! Sexuality can only be described with that kind of appetite, with that kind of passion."

She ignored the man's sexual references, his invitation to his private apartment. All she could say was that she didn't really know Updike, she had no idea what kind of an author he was, while she was actually devising a way to leave the table to go to the ladies room and thinking of who she could call to ask to phone her back.

But she didn't. She was tipsy; in fact, she was slightly drunk. She'd lighten up when she felt this way and laugh a lot.

And now as she laughed, she got even lighter. The crowd in the restaurant became blurry and transformed into a single drone, and time became an incalculable moment. The man's joy was rapturous, his gaze lustful. When she was a young girl, she would watch herself in the mirror and imagine how the man she loved or could very well fall in love with wouldn't be able to keep his love-struck eyes off of her, like the male characters in the romance novels she read. She was watching herself in that mirror again, admiring herself through the man's eyes.

But was it because they didn't speak the same language that the man kept bringing up sex as a discussion topic? Was he actually bored of her? Did he believe that the bridge between a man and a woman, who were to him unequal, could only be built with so much body talk and the brute force of sexuality?

The man dwelt on Updike's women, explaining how he so masterfully portrayed the way middle class Americans found the most exciting and truest love outside their mundane marriages. His thoughts led him to the film, *The Last Tango in Paris*. He said she reminded him of the young woman in that film, that she, like her, was charming and full of life. Then he asked if she had seen *Night Watch*. Oh, she simply must. He had the DVD. The film showed the boundless pull between man and woman at its most intense.

While he talked, she saw his eyes divert to her breasts, his suggestiveness, and figuring this was just a game, she didn't listen. When the man took her hand and brought it to his lips, she thought this must be the climax. And when he placed kisses on each of her fingers and then took her little finger between his lips, she felt on her finger the wetness of his mouth, the texture of his tongue and the pressure of his teeth. She sensed the man's skin, his raw flesh for real; her gasp hung in the air and clung to his breath. She shivered. She felt suddenly removed from herself. The setting became more tangible. That distant monotonous drone was pierced with the rattle of cutlery, a woman's buoyant laughter, and noises that rose and fell. She felt on her the curious looks of the brunette sitting at the table opposite with another woman. She turned away from those looks; instead she fixed her eyes on the broken lights of the city reflected on the dark quilt of the never-ending sea beyond the restaurant window.

She gently pulled her hand away from the man's palms.

"It's late, I should be going," she said, trying to pull her eyes away from the man, who became doleful, like a big child whose toy was snatched from his hands.

"So that was it! Oh well, it will have to suffice," he said disappointedly. "But don't be silly," he went on, "I'll drop you off."

Throughout the journey, the man talked in a resentful tone about when the next conference would be, how bored he was of his life and job, and how the only bearable space in this crowded and shrewish city was his private apartment where he could be far from everyone and everything. Meanwhile, she was thinking about the group she had agreed to meet the next day for a tour of the city, and Kağan, who was in the group, in particular. If Kağan discovered she had been out with this man who was the coordinator of the conference, would he still be interested in her? Did Kağan really like her? Or was this just a delusion? It aggravated her that he had made do with shy passing glances when this man could be so forward, approaching her with impunity. People should be different in a city by the sea. She just couldn't determine exactly what that difference must be; in the spirit of the storm coming from the sea perhaps or in the sensation of the incoming tide for example? The sea must expand and make us forget every glance that fixes on its gentle rippling and then withdraws, and every sorrow predisposed to become self-pity. The infinite sorrow of the sea should overpower everything. The view of the Maiden's Tower opposite, adorned with lights; it winked coyly like a little girl. If it were any other time, she would envy this city, its people, its mosques, its white mansions overlooking the Bosphorus, its historic stone school buildings, its old vision, which its authors hadn't been able to expend for centuries. The crowds... The crowds were flooding out of coffeehouses and into the streets. The droning was a reminder that this huge city was awake tonight and in pursuit of something. Young, very young faces. The man's breath smelled of rakı. Was his hand on her arm? Young faces… they seemed to be looking at her, and then at him. Their looks seemed to be asking, was this the best you could do, a man your father's age? She was ashamed of her own thoughts. Was that why she was unable to turn him down? Or was it because she didn't want to hurt his feelings?

She was sure of one thing: she would go to her room shortly, empty her souring stomach, and return to her own routine, safe world. This was all she believed.

When they drew closer to the hotel where she was staying, she tried to loosen the man's grip on her arm, but he held her even tighter. The uneasiness she felt inside was amplified. When they had reached a quiet leafy corner, "We're here, thank you very much for tonight," she said, and pulled her arm from the man's clutches. And now the hand was stroking her; starting from her earlobe moving down to her neck and around to reach her nape. Unable to look the man in the face, in an instinct of self-preservation and concealment, she shrank her shoulders, bent her neck, and buried her head between them. She wanted to run and hide, to lock herself up in her room.

Suddenly she found herself in the man's arms, her back pushed up against a tree trunk. "You're driving me crazy, you can't just leave me like this now," the man said and pressed his mouth on hers. His tongue pushed, trying to pry through her firmly sealed lips. She felt the weight and power of the tongue. For the first time in her life, she feared she could be raped, and she understood herself now how a woman being raped wouldn't stand a chance against a man's strength. She was terrified. She struggled desperately to save herself from the man's hands and mouth.

The man withdrew; he stared into her eyes that were widened with terror. His astonishment was visible in his face. The man turned his back without saying a word; his body tense and nervous, he walked away in hasty steps.

They were planning to visit the islands the next day. They might ride in a carriage. Perhaps Kağan would open up to her. In fact, excited by this, she was also planning to walk around the İstiklal Street area in the early morning, before it was overcome by waves of people. But both the city and Kağan were distant and repulsive at that moment. Like all the men she had known and loved. She thought, "The grizzled old bastard has taken all my joy away from me, my desire to spend a weekend in this city, flirt with a man who I've only spoken to on the phone before and whose face I've always had to picture in my imagination. I find it hard enough to flirt anyway. I find it scary enough to think that any promise given has the potential to lead to a suffering heart."

That night, she cried more than she had in a long time. She actually cried because she couldn't be as easygoing and cheerful as everyone else. She cried because she couldn't grasp the lightness of life, because she couldn't know boundaries, because she so feared rejection when she put boundaries in place.

The next morning, when she boarded the bus to return home and throughout her journey back, her self-recrimination did not cease. In the city she lived in, she would never have done what she had. Cenk was right: the people of this city really were different. This city was fast, it was hard, restless and insensitive.

After she returned home, whenever she remembered that night she spent with the man, sometimes she was angry at him and sometimes at herself. She didn't tell her mother, or Cenk, with whom she shared most things, or her greatest confidant, an old friend from university who now, two years into her marriage, was expecting a baby. Her rage was fuelled even more after reading the short story the man had recommended. The narrator, a middle-aged man, told the story of a night he spent with a very young prostitute. While the prostitute's concern was to get the job over and done with, take her money and leave when his hour was up, the man longed for an ounce of compassion from her. And thus, the roles were reversed, and instead of the woman serving the man, the man's struggle to give the woman pleasure began. The detailed description of sex bordered on pornography, and the fact that the story was about a prostitute and her client drove her absolutely insane. She was furious at the man's bravado, at the message he was sending, that he had intended to get her into bed that very night, and the fact that she, knowing exactly his intentions, had almost gone all the way with the game.

Over time, her anger subsided and the memory faded. At work she shared an office with Cenk and watched his never-ending romantic suffering. She witnessed how drastically he changed with a single text message from his lover. Sometimes she listened to him, thinking maybe he wanted to be closer to her to help him forget his suffering. As usual, she spoke on the phone to Kağan, who was responsible for projects at the central office, about business; she had lost her former chirpy enthusiasm. She returned home after work, and as she ate the food her mother had prepared, she watched soaps on TV. Life was passing by as it always had. She made herself believe that nothing had really happened, and nothing she ever encountered with could ever distract her from her routine. So why this vexation, this loss of appetite? Why couldn't her mind stop racing? The soaps were sleazy, the words of the most exciting novels were heavy and foreign: her mother's often needless usual reproaches. Why did her list of potential grooms upset her so much? This emptiness, this idling of the soul...

On one sleepless night, as she lay in bed reading a book, the words sliding out of reach, her eyes became fixed on the long rising shadow of her folded quilt, illuminated by her bedside lamp. She likened the shadow to a hand, a hand with large, long fingers. She remembered the man and shuddered. Pleasure, which she had long forgotten, spread across her flesh and pierced her groin. She wanted to drive it away. She clutched onto the quilt, but the shadow stood right where it was. She tilted her head to the side. The shadow stretched out and fell beside her. It came closer. It grabbed her hands, thrust them against the wall behind her head; she couldn't move. And then with his fingers he unbuttoned her nightdress, grabbed her breasts violently and squeezed her nipples. Her nipples became dark and erect, bumps emerged on her areola. The hard, persistent mouth parted from her lips and slipped down to her breasts. His tongue passed her bellybutton, went down in between her legs. It revealed her privacy, leaving her exposed and defenseless. "You whore," said the man. She groaned. "You easily let anyone fuck you. Now it's my turn." She screamed. "You want it, go on, take it in your mouth," said the man. "My love, my love, my man," she screeched. "Are you going to be my whore?" the man asked. "Yes, yes," she replied. "Just for tonight." "Yes, just for tonight," she moaned.

But one night wasn't enough. It was revived with every phone ringing; she opened every beeping text message, every new e-mail received on her computer at work, with the hope that it might be from him. Weeks had gone past, and she now believed that he too was thinking of her and making love to her secretly. For nights on end, she visited his dirtiest fantasies. She listened, unrelentingly.

But the fantasy wasn't enough.

One day, she picked the phone up and called the man. He didn't recognize her immediately; or he pretended not to. Or perhaps she really just took it however she wanted to. He took her number. He was going to call her that same evening.

The man wanted to carry on from where he had left off weeks ago.

He started by asking her what she was wearing.

The woman described the black velour tracksuit she had on. The man wanted to know where her hands were. She told him she was playing with a piece of paper, and that she had just made a paper airplane with it, with one hand. The man asked if she had been thinking about him. "Would I have called if I hadn't," was all she could say. "Tell me," the man insisted, "how do you think about me?" "I imagined you were an amazing kisser." "What else? What else can I do?" "I can't tell you on the phone," she said. "Oh don't," complained the man. "I'm an old man, you might be disappointed if I come to you." "Are you old?" "Aren't I? Isn't that why you turned me down that night?" She laughed; she made the most of feeling unattainable. For a minute she understood the irreversible, unforgiving distance between old age and youth. So, that meant she was still holding the reins. She always had a chance. She had the right and the time to play hard to get.

"We haven't touched each other before; we're not yet close enough to have phone sex."

"Okay," said the man, "say something sweet that will help me sleep tonight and put the phone down."

"When are we going to make love," she said, and hung up.

The next day, she went to the beauty salon. She ignored the recommendations made by the girl who did the waxing that she should wait for the hairs to grow a little more and she had them removed. She had a manicure and pedicure and her hair cut short, in a style that would make her look even younger than she was. She strolled around in the house with her mother's special face masque on, which was comprised of tomato puree, yoghurt, oatmeal and mint leaves. She bought expensive moisturizers and creams. She picked lace thongs and chiffon bras, as she shuddered, willing to spend half her wage. She waited. She answered every phone that rang, opened every text message that beeped, with her heart racing. She counted the minutes, hours, and days. She lost her appetite, lost sleep, lost joy and spirit. Sometimes she waited faithfully, sometimes hopelessly. She never heard from him. Then she thought she had done the playing hard to get for too long and that it was her turn to make a serious move. So she decided to jump on the bus that weekend and visit the man's private apartment. Confident that her number would be recognized by the receiver, she dialled his number. There was no answer. She waited for the man to call her back. And as she waited the hairs on her legs grew, grew so that they were just right to be waxed. The cuticles around her nails reappeared, she picked them reluctantly, making them bleed. Her body had fallen for pleasure and passion; it stiffened, her skin hurt. To ease the pain, at night she decided she would seduce Cenk and make love to him, but come daytime she forgot all about this. In the event that the man did call her, she decided she would not answer her phone and that she would make him wait at least as long as she had waited.

Finally she convinced herself that the man must have not heard his phone, and that even if he had seen her missed call, he probably wasn't able to work out who the number belonged to. This time, she sent a text message.

When?

Dilan

Jale Sancak

Translated by **Kerim Biçer**

TARLABAŞI. The Zerdali–Sakızağacı–Dernek Street Triangle.
Özlem Turizm. Good news! New Midyat Travel. Attention please:
Our 3pm bus travels all the way to Dargeçit every day.
Mardin Midyat Dargeçit

Vay lele[1]…A poignant folk song sung by a woman with a husky voice
fills the street…Dilan is alone in that musty smelling room. She is a
stranger in front of the mirror, doleful at the edge of the window. Dilan
is one of many girls carrying the scent of Mardin who sit outside their
front doors on the street. After all these years, here in its very center,
Dilan is still distant to the city; she is still in Dargeçit.

Tarlabaşı. Fast and dark-skinned Senegalese roll hastily down the
Sakızağacı slope. A sad old homosexual who hasn't been on the job for
a while now, handy only for those asking for directions. A boy with a
pocketknife in his hand, musing. And a gang of glue sniffers and outcasts
that dwell in the night…In other words, these are the 'others'. A carpenter
carves the long necks of ouds and cuts chord pegs; none can be an inch
shorter or longer than the rest. He is master of his craft. He's not from
around here, he's from Cidde. Unlike the others, he earns his living. Has

---

[1] An expression of lament, common in many Kurdish folk songs.

a house and all; he's well off now. His shop is the ground floor of a building that used to be a hotel. The hotel was first run by the French, then the Greeks. The carpenter had long learned the ways of the city. There are no French or Greeks anymore. Gangs control everything now. Everything is a gravy train. A tawny cat lies in the doorstep.

The last murder took place the night before.

The double staircase with engraved banisters in the center of the high stone courtyard was two hundred years old; the stairs had absorbed every footstep over time. In the large rooms, most of the glass in the double-paned windows was broken. God knows when the metal-leaf on the ceiling had begun defoliating: the roses were pale and the leaves had already been touched by fall. Dozens of pigeons stood motionless in one of the rooms where the wooden flooring had been ripped off in places. There were bags of weed in another room, a little bit of angel dust, a gun, a skewer, and a straight razor. Cops had entered the ramshackle house, breaking open the safety lock on the iron gate.

Tarlabaşı is all angel dust and imprisoned pigeons.

Dilan slowly descended the stairs to the cool stone courtyard; she hesitated for a minute amid the noises. Dilan was inside a pointed gun. Vay lele, vay! The African boy who saved her from being run over by a van was no longer around. Her father spoke that same proverb he did after every murder: "The water jug will break on the way to the water fountain." Her father smelled old. He was the owner of the secondhand furniture store a couple of streets down. He was a man who smelled of a wood frame sofa with springs bulging out, a century-old cabinet with a mirror, a man who smelled of musty chests. The *pide* seller who smelled of heavy oil and always had to have the last word, and whose counter was unfortunately betrothed to a filthy dishtowel, was also there in Zerdali. Meryemce had been craving some pide. It wouldn't be fair for Dilan to keep the poor bedridden woman waiting, now, would it? "I'll break your legs," her father had said after the last murder. "Don't be out on the streets."

The reflection in the dusty window of the pide store belonged to an old woman, an old woman immersed in thought. Her hair and eyebrows were hennaed; her eyebrows two henna lines. She is broke and starving, a retired madam who has been kicked out onto the street in her faded flannel gown. She once owned three houses in Peşirci, and a shop on the big slope which she let out to a Greek carpenter. She had a neighbor, a prostitute from Balat, who had beaten the life out of the carpenter for flashing his dick at the kids who were playing outside.

The hennaed madam lost all her properties one by one to her gambling lover. Now one of those houses was about to collapse. The other accommodated barefoot women who wash their rugs with running tap water in the doorway as they fling about their traditional scarves and headbands, and then relax in the same doorway once they have finished their daily chores. Rough male voices, mouths full of curses, children's cries, murmurs in Kurdish, all roam the rooms.

"Is this Istanbul, is this really Istanbul? This wasn't the city I saw on TV. We came here with such big dreams," one had said on her arrival three years ago, and today she struggled to feed her seven kids, one of whom had a hole in his heart. But she still believed "they could fix these parts if they wanted to."

"Of course we're scared of guns and murders. Who wouldn't be?" said another. "My husband was a peddler, they cut his leg off and he's been unemployed for eight months now," said another exhausted woman. "My sister lives in Zeytinburnu, but we can't afford to move there," said another who seemed sorrowful, and, "This house could cave in on us any minute," said a frightened woman.

Okay, this area was dodgy. The city was fury, it was rancor; it was besieged by blood. The young black man who was killed, he was dodgy too. When guns were pointed, no one dared look out their windows; they'd quickly draw their curtains shut. If it was fear, then Dilan was afraid too; horrified even. It wasn't her who had wanted to move here!

Dilan was the embodiment of compassion by the side of the bedridden woman, of indecision in the cool courtyard, and of cowardice in the street. But she still had to go buy the meat pide, without her father knowing, and make Meryemce happy.

Diagonally opposite the pide shop is a ramshackle Internet café that also served as a kebab house: what a strange combination. There are no customers inside. A man known as a swaggerer wipes the tables. On the lefthand side, before you reach the pide shop, is an empty field that has turned into a garbage dump, and just past the shop is Özlem Turizm. Just opposite was the shop of the antique dealer from Dargeçit who had left his homeland so his sons would not take to the hills and because it was easier to win bread in the city. As soon as you turn the corner, there is the carpenter's store. Oud makers could never do without him. A black boy was lying dead in one of the rooms that stored century-old smells.

Maybe she should go through the upper street, Dernek Street, then take the avenue down to Zerdali, so she wouldn't have to walk past the shop. It was okay if her father wasn't outside his shop. She should quickly get the pide and return home using the same route. Was Kasım Efendi worried that his daughter might run away from home just like her mother?

The Manastır Bar, where the discotheque scene in *The Bandit*[2]—one of the most renowned, commercially successful movies of Turkish cinema— was shot, was on the ground floor of a magnificent two centuries-old

---

[2] *Eşkıya*

stone mansion on Dernek Street, which was a convent in the past. A young man was breathing on the glasses and wiping them behind the bar. This place was now much more than a bar; it was a real film set. Upstairs, in the summer chapel on the roof, alcohol poured like water all night, young sinuous girls belly danced, shaking every inch of their bodies till dawn, sleepless young men exhausted their passion for punk and hip-hop all night long. On the other end of the large, dim, damp-smelling corridor was the small winter chapel of the convent, the new setting for commercials, TV series and fashion catalogs. In other words, worship and commerce went hand in hand here. And all that was left behind from the performing arts was a few free-floating spoken lines, long tirades and the curtain! The Kumpanya Theatre in this building lost its place to the Oyunevi Theatre later on. The plays that had been staged here: comedies, tragedies, avant-garde, absurd, epic...

Later on, the Oyunevi Theatre deserted this place too. Now only stage-struck would-be actors excitedly walk the floors of this corridor.

Alluring transvestites chose to hook up just outside the front door of the stone mansion which opened right onto the street; until the police arrived.

Police lay in wait day and night.

The young Senegalese man was shot during a gunfight with the police. One of the bullets hit a bystander, a teacher resting on her balcony after a tough day at work. Her brain splattered into a million tiny pieces, staining the white laundry hanging on the line with blood.

It is now bedtime for prostitutes in Tarlabaşı, time for pimps to count their money. A few adolescent boys are torturing an old dog. Lowlifes are on constant alert, monitoring the dangers of the street. Dilan slowly exits the street, which knows all the stories past; where timeworn houses, perhaps in longing for their good old days, lean against each for support, on final effort to stand erect. She walks past women screaming to silence their spoiled children. Nusaybin, Silopi, Cizre, Şırnak are all women, women like remote, deserted cities; women who are shot dead by a stray bullet when pregnant or while resting on a balcony. Her head hanging low, Dilan climbs up the slope slowly. Her Aunt Meryemce had been bed-ridden for three years now. The grocer and real estate agent are playing backgammon. Dilan's aunt was like a mother to her. Meryemce had never married. Obeying an order, she had brought up her nieces and nephews instead, lavishing love on them. On both sides of the slope are lines of laundry. There are green, blue and red iron doors. On the walls are fine embellishments, archaic and alien to the present. There is a reeking smell of sewage, of mold, food, of filthy skin and rotten breath. Self-deception, hunger, fear, fury. Weed, pills and heroine. A boy, too mature for his years, playing with a pocketknife, is plotting a night burglary. Dilan takes the turn to Dernek Street and keeps walking with her head down, not sparing a hello to the hennaed madam, ignoring the gypsy violinist who is a friend of her brother's.

But curiosity is a strange plague. Although she looked away and kept her head down, the convent was calling out to her. Dilan didn't know why. The church, the bar, the theatre… This must have been the strangest place on earth. She never forgot the Assyrian church in Mardin where she went with her mother to make votive offerings. Dilan didn't forget anything. She had seen bars and discotheques on television. But what about theatres?

Forget about the theatre now, Dilan, don't forget Meryemce is waiting for her pide. The avenue was lined with shops, their windows advertising in red letters. Red is the color of eroticism. Dilan, you concentrate on the pide. There's an increasing number of 'erotic shops' with dildos, Dilan. What does 'erotic' mean, what does 'shop' mean, forget it all; the man who spared your life, the guns that were pointed, the slaughter, these streets that lead nowhere, the red letters, Dilan. Pide sells fast. Don't forget the pide, they may sell out. Never mind, let the carpenter stare and eye you up all he wants.

The other side of the street is Beyoğlu, Dilan. Beyoğlu and what's left of its noble Beys is only a stone's throw away. The sounds, colors, lights, Dilan, both near and far. They say everyone is free. Everyone does whatever they want here in Beyoğlu. Forget about this too! Just forget it! Don't forget, Dilan, you may later resent a black eye, the gift of his fist!

But Dilan never forgets anything; even though she obeys orders, and walks on, her head hanging low…

Fig Seed

Feryal Tilmaç

*Translated by **Ruth Whitehouse***

After many months, we are finally in the house where I was born and brought up. This view I had looked at for so many years seems different today. The sun paints fiery streaks on the water, and on the windows of Silver Water Apartments. On the opposite shore is the Maiden's Tower, which seems to have leapt out of the legend where the unfortunate princess was bitten by a snake gliding out of a basket of figs…

All around is unusually silent, even the gulls that fly from roof to roof. Perhaps it was still too soon for us to come here. But here we are. I know that when everyone assembles it's not going to be easy. I knew that right from the start. Everyone has unavoidable moments, meetings in their life… But no, I don't have to apologize to anyone. If there's anyone who deserves an apology, it's me. I shall just say, "Well, here I am. I've come." But what if I find myself frozen to the spot, my stomach contracting, my head throbbing… It will all pass. I'll wake up in my own house again and everything will go on just as before. I smoke a cigarette patiently with my back to them. They approach. Neriman nervously replaces my ashtray and disappears. Gently, I reach out for Asım's hand. His fingers are unwilling; our hands touch and separate.

"Müge, how nice to see you."

My mother is perfectly contained as usual. Her hair is immaculate, like she has just come out of a salon. Her makeup is the same. As always when she wants to appear young, she is wearing jeans. On top she has a smart white shirt, on her feet a pair of black stilettos. I approach her apprehensively. She offers me her cheek.

"Hello, Mother."

I take Asım gently by the arm and try to push him forward. His feet seem to be embedded in concrete. I hope he doesn't make things difficult.

"This is my husband, Asım."

"Do sit down."

My father mutters something. This isn't talking. He too is in jeans. They're definitely making a point. Okay, we know you're still young. He wears a checked shirt and has a cigar in his hand. Neriman places an ashtray near where he sits. Crossing his legs, he lounges back. He tries to give the impression that, despite his youthful looks, he is master of this house. If only they would speak openly, so that we could all feel more at ease. Oh, Daddy, I can hardly stop myself from throwing my arms round your neck and kissing you, but I am so mad at you. This time you went too far.

"Hello, Müge, lovely to see you."

Burak is totally indifferent as usual. He comes and shakes Asım's hand. Deep in his eyes there is a devilish smile. He never allows anything to get to him. Once again, he is wisely refusing to get involved. He sprawls out on the sofa in front of the television and reaches for the remote control. Ignoring my mother's glare, he turns the television on, finds a documentary and starts watching it. Apparently some fossilised remains of a half-man, half-ape creature have been found in Africa. The top half is ape, the lower human, or the other way round. I catch snatches of the commentary. People think these remains belong to a three-year-old. Burak watches with total concentration, letting out cries of amazement. Like nothing had happened. Like everything was just fine and we were paying an ordinary family visit. He must find the theory of evolution more interesting than family matters. I don't blame him. If only we could get this over and done with. If only we could all get on with our own lives.

"Hi, Müge, good to see you, and you, sir."

Grandma enters the living room. My father pulls himself together. Uncrossing his legs, he straightens up in his chair. Cheers for Grandma! She leans towards me and holds out her hand. I'm supposed to kiss it. Nedret Hanım seems determined to show Asım just who we are. She wears a cashmere shawl over her shoulders and silk stockings on her arthritic legs. This play-acting has to stop. She's the only one I thought might back me up. I kiss her hand. The Dutch diamond on her finger touches my chin, then my forehead, pricking me like a thorn. There's no way out, we'll have to show Asım who we are!

"Asım, darling, this is my grandmother, Nedret Hanım."

"How are you, *Hanımefendi*?"

Asım reaches out and kisses her hand lightly. Asım, don't put her hand to your forehead. You'll ruin it all— like a whole sack of figs, as the expression goes! He doesn't. My grandmother smiles, but it is a flirtatious smile and most inappropriate. I feel embarrassed at what my husband must be thinking. I know what he thinks of large mansions and luxury lifestyles of so-called aristocrats. But he seems happy to have found a potential ally. Neriman must have been waiting for the moment of my grandmother's introduction. She appears with a silver tray laden with a set of colored crystal liqueur glasses. Crème de Figue, served with some chilled fresh almonds at the side. Hospitality never varies at our house.

Suddenly, I realize how much I've actually missed it all.

Burak seems to have lost interest in the apes; he is blatantly analysing Asım. I fear he might delay the speech I've been waiting to make all this time, by going on about some nonsense. Once he gets going— "What interesting bone structure you have. There seems to be a trace of Slav, especially in the shape of your forehead and nose..."—then congratulations to anyone who can stop him. As if she can see it coming, my mother takes over. "Müge says you're a doctor."

Grandma and Burak jump in simultaneously.

"An obstetrician."

"A gynecologist."

"Yes. I specialize in maternal medicine."

Asım stirs uneasily. My father must have been waiting for this very moment; I could swear he had prepared his next sentence beforehand.

"You are undoubtedly an expert on young ladies."

Got you, Daddy! You fell right into it! Thank you. I rest my case.

"Daddy, your photo in the paper was great, you looked very handsome."

He blushes. It's hardly enough. If only he knew how much he hurt me! I want to forget that day. We are at the breakfast table; Asım is reading the paper and I am reading the Saturday supplement. After a while, I realize that he has not eaten a thing, not even taken a sip of his tea, and I ask what's the matter. His face has turned pale. Looking confused, he tries to hide the newspaper, but unable to hold out against my insistence, he hands it over...

Businessman Osman Saran has announced that as far as he is concerned his daughter Müge Saran died when, without his permission, she married Doctor Asım Tezan, 25 years her senior. Special prayers were said for his daughter's soul at Teşvikiye Mosque. The ceremony was held in the presence of friends and loved ones, well-known figures from business and social circles and curious passersby. After the ceremony, the grieving father held a press conference at which he stated: "Doctor Asım is even older than I am; he should not expect any understanding from me. From now on, I have no such daughter. These prayers are the lament of a grieving father." It was noted that while Osman Saran had a red carnation and a photograph of his daughter attached to his jacket collar, the young lady's mother, Gülin Saran, did not attend the ceremony. This has been cause for some speculation. After the ceremony, all the guests were presented with dried figs instead of the traditional sweets.

At first all I can think is that everyone, everyone will have read this! If only the earth would open and swallow me up, if only I could disappear, become a particle of dust and just vanish into the city air. After reading that news a shell cracks open inside me. The larva squirms around freely. The monster of reckoning hungrily awaits my next words, the fodder upon which it thrives.

"Handing out dried figs to your guests was a very nice gesture. But you put the photo taken for my high school entrance exam on your collar. Couldn't you find a more recent photograph, for heaven's sake?"

The redness that started from your ears has already covered your face and is advancing rapidly towards your neck. "So, you wore a red carnation in your buttonhole, did you? Well, Daddy, how am I supposed to look my friends in the face? Did you ever stop to think about that? Did you put Asım down as a pedophile? You are lucky that he is mature enough to come to your house. It shows there's something good to be said for older sons-in-law." Burak laughs. My father slowly turns to face him and is just about to explode with anger when my mother comes to the rescue.

"Asım Bey, Osman is devoted to Müge and it's been traumatic for him. Please don't take it personally. You know how precious daughters are to their fathers."

In my mother's eyes, Asım's career clearly compensates for his age. Her tone of voice indicates that she is genuinely no longer upset. For the first time, I appreciate her worldly attitude. She changes the subject masterfully.

"You're living in Nişantaşı, aren't you?"

"Yes, Mom, we are living in Asım's house. There was no point moving somewhere else just for the sake of it."

My father pulls himself together. He offers Asım a cigar. Asım doesn't smoke cigars. He doesn't smoke cigarettes either. Note: This man takes care of himself. Relax. See, he looks younger than either of you. The passage of time doesn't affect everyone in the same way. Every person has their individual life cycle. When are you going to understand that? My father does not look in my direction at all. If only he would say he was sorry and shouldn't have done it. Then, I'd be prepared to forget all about it. But he continues to fire questions at my husband as if it wasn't him who brought all this humiliation on us in the first place.

"Is Müge going to continue her education? I'm sure you have no objection to her studying. She has two more years to go. Afterwards, I was thinking of sending her to France. If you like, she could still…"

Grandma does not miss the opportunity.

"Oh, my Osman is really keen on education, always has been. He was a wonderful student; never gave us cause for worry. If only her dear grandfather were alive, how proud he would be. It runs in the family. You see, *our* family—"

"Yes, I see. Müge will continue and finish college if she wants to. She will have my support if that's what she decides to do," Asım politely silences my grandmother. And he does a good job at it. Once she gets started on the family tree, there is no stopping her.

"Daddy, I'm going to finish college, but you can forget about France.

Would you like it if Mother went off to study abroad? I'm a married woman and I have responsibilities. Asım works extremely hard, so I have to take care of everything at home."

For the first time, he looks very sad, like he might burst into tears at any moment. It really is as if I had died. My anger subsides; despite myself, it simply melts away. When I have children of my own, I'll understand; in ten years or so perhaps. Could Asım wait that long? The pregnant me walks through the middle of the room. Even my grandmother isn't as fat as me. I'm wearing a robe with a smocked yoke, like the dresses Neriman wears. My abdomen is swollen, my ankles puffy. Holding my stomach, I rush out to the toilet to be sick.

"Müge!"

My mother's voice brings me to my senses. She says I look quite yellow. I don't feel well and want to go home. I just want to put on my pyjamas, sit on Asım's knee, and drink the milk he warms up for me. I want him tell me funny stories about his patients while I lean against his chest. I want him to stroke my hair while I fall asleep. It doesn't happen. As the afternoon draws out, it gradually seems to engulf the whole of our lives and turn into one never-ending moment.

My father and Asım start a rambling conversation about politics. Burak whispers something to my grandmother, covers his mouth with his hand and laughs. My mother goes to the kitchen, probably to ask Neriman to make some coffee. How at ease they all are. My insides heave, subside and once again…Oh, God! Nobody takes any notice. I want to exclaim: "Hey, look, I've been planning this meeting for months, moment by moment, word by word. It wasn't meant to be like this. Not so quick and easy, not so superficial!" My father asks Asım if he enjoys playing bridge. This is driving me crazy. Stand up for yourself, Asım. He humiliated you in the eyes of your patients. Don't forget that! My mother appears, followed by Neriman carrying a tray of coffee. Neriman refills everyone's liqueur glasses, starting with my grandmother's. Burak's mobile rings and he leaves the room to talk in peace. I take a sip of coffee and light a cigarette.

"Müge, darling, your skin will age prematurely. Look, your husband doesn't smoke."

With everything that is going on, my mother decides to fuss about the fact that I smoke. And as if that isn't enough, she uses Asım as an example. I inhale deeply, pout my lips, and blow smoke out in front of me. A tiny cloud of smoke hovers above the coffee table, like a jellyfish disintegrating into the ether. This amuses me, and as soon as it disappears, I exhale again. My mother's eyes and eyebrows implore me to stop. Grandma intervenes.

"She's been like this since she was a child! Never say 'don't' to her, Gülin, it just makes her obstinate. Leave her alone. She takes after my late mother-in-law, Atike Hanım. She was just the same…"

I stub out my cigarette and get up.

"Can I have a look in my room?"

Finally, I succeed in getting everyone's attention. My father and husband stop their conversation and look at me as if I've asked for something unfathomable. Nobody makes a sound. Mother looks out towards the sea, and Grandma rearranges her shawl. They're uneasy. I take no notice. I want to go to my room. For months, I have been dreaming about it. When I wake up in the middle of the night and realize I'm in a different room…My bedroom door is shut; I open it slowly. My heart pounds. As always, it smells of pine and Rive Gauche. Nothing appears to have been touched. I lie down on my bed. My books, computer, photographs, globe, stereo and CDs…Everything is in its place. So, the only thing they emptied was my wardrobe. How I cried the day Neriman came to the house in Nişantaşı bringing the suitcases she had so carefully packed with my clothes. I asked her to come in for coffee, but she said the driver was waiting outside and rushed away. When Asım arrived, my eyes were all red from crying. Someone knocks at my door. Good! They haven't forgotten my rules. Neriman enters cautiously.

"Don't pay any attention to them, sweetheart. You're the lady of your own house now, just do your best. It's alright. There's an old saying that goes, 'Marry a young man and he'll break your heart. Marry an old man and he'll treat you like a princess.' My late husband was twice my age. And we got on just fine. I mean, we struggled to make ends meet, like everyone else, but he always treated me good. What more can you ask for? He *is* your father; he'll come round. Just play along. And don't stay away so long again. Your grandma, she's really missed you too. You know how we've always thought she only has eyes for Burak, well, she wouldn't stop talking about you. She kept going on and on at your father. Osman Bey was really angry, otherwise ..."

"Thanks, Neriman. No reason to get upset, we'll come by more often from now on. My mother's calling. You go or they'll start wondering."

Now I'm all alone I ponder what Neriman said. She said she was happy. Yet I know how difficult her life really was. Her husband was ill and bedridden for years. She married off her daughter, but her son-in-law's been sponging off of them for as long as I can remember. Her son didn't go to school. It means that happiness between man and wife must be about something else. So, am I happy? Every so often this question comes to mind, but I brush it away. Asım does all he can. He smothers me with presents. We go wherever I want to go. No need to ask permission, no need for explanations. I'm free. We reserve tables and dine at the clubs where my friends go to drink and dance. Sometimes we meet them and stand around talking. They are always dying to meet

Asım and are fascinated by us, by our marriage. I feel somehow different, important. I want to maintain the respect I have gained in their eyes by standing up to my family. I feign reluctance when they ask to meet up. After all, I'm a married woman now. I like this game, or rather, I used to like it until we came here. They're confusing me. The way they accept Asım so quickly makes everything I've done seem so ordinary. I feel sick and tired. I want to sleep in my own room tonight. Someone knocks at the door again. This time, Neriman doesn't come in but just pokes her head through the door.

"Gülin Hanım is asking for you, Müge. They're wondering if you're still in your room. Apparently you're staying for dinner. The food's all ready. I made *börek* this morning, spinach, your favorite, since I knew you were coming. If there's anything else you want, tell me now so I can have it ready in time for dinner."

"No, Neriman, I don't want anything. What's Asım doing?"

"The Doctor is playing chess with your father."

"Fine, tell them I'll be down soon."

I don't want to go. I just want to sleep. A deep, deep sleep. When I wake, I want to get up, ask for a milky coffee in my room, start up my computer, chat to my friends on MSN, plan my day, decide what I'm going to wear, and rush out of the house, mingle with life, become Müge again, and feel the relief inside me with every breath. I throw off my shoes and get into bed. I put my hand under the pillow. In that coolness, I feel for the lavender sachet. My fingers find it. Right where it has always been. I inhale the scent of my pillow. My head becomes heavy. My thoughts become cloudy. It won't hurt anyone if I sleep until dinnertime.

The Uninvited

Sezer Ateş Ayvaz

Translated by Nilgün Dungan

And in the morning, I will tell all this to myself one by one
Inside of Yakup, growing again into a void

—Edip Cansever, *Uninvited Yakup* [1]

Should I call Yakup, she thought. Would he hear me, would he respond to my voice?

Nadide was in a cozy tea garden wrapped in autumn colors in a district that had just become a part of Istanbul. Tables and chairs thrown on the grass, and in the middle, a deep blue decorative pond swans swam in, and around it, unscented flowers of all colors.

The Green Valley Tea Garden, separated from long, wide avenues and multistory apartment blocks by a line of trees grown from seedlings brought from outside of Istanbul. Underneath the trees with large, heart-shaped, nervate leaves, it was cool. Yet the late September sun was reminiscent of summer days, almost over.

---

[1] *Çağrılmayan Yakup*

In Nadide's head was a throbbing heat, in her ears, the murmur of songs…

Nadide, who had lived in many corners of Istanbul, the city of seven hills, without knowing, passes through the old neighborhoods of Istanbul, knocking on doors that will never open again.

First, through a rippling photograph, she journeys to Beyoğlu. All the colors come alive, people fill the street, assistant dressmakers and young students pass by her, laughing heartily.

Carried away with the bird of hope chirping inside but discrete as she is alone, Nadide is walking, having decided to be wise and to put a serious expression on her face.

The moment she arrives by the door, her cheerfulness will disappear anyway; her legs will grow heavier, a feeling of guilt will creep upon her and rest on her shoulders, and from there it will reach her hands, her hair and, lastly, her eyes.

Her eyes will become green with malice.

"You're here, at last?"

If she were to ask, "Am I late, Mother?"

"Hush," the angry, scolding voice would come quickly. "Hush. You made me worry and you have the nerve to ask! How many times have I told you? This is Istanbul!"

* * *

Nadide is now getting ready to go to sleep on the second floor of an old, nameless building with winged angels above its windows, on the same street as the Beyoğlu Police Station.

The smell of mimosas, Judas trees, and of scarlet sages, becoming one with the colors of spring, filling the night air from the coastal districts of Istanbul, cannot reach here.

Her mother, Adviye, has only geraniums in tin drums, without enough sun, spindly stems and sickly flowers, looking makeshift, in front of the window.

Nighttime. Very late…

The humming noise coming from İstiklal Street abated; the dark, narrow streets are quiet enough to amplify and echo footsteps, for now.

Rüstem: Her father has just come home, tired from walking all day on the streets that he's tried to make his own, and fallen asleep the moment he got into bed. He's kneading the meatball mixture, smiling, in his sleep. The more he kneads the better consistency it will have. The more he walks around, the more meatball sandwiches he sells, the more life will be Rüstem's. The desires flourishing from adolescence to adulthood will come true on the pavements he treads. Sirkeci, Taksim, and gradually all of Istanbul will say what a skillful man he is, that his meatballs are extraordinary. Women will talk about how young and handsome this Rumelian is; he'll have a reputation as tall and handsome Rüstem with deep green eyes…

Adviye is woken up by the first sound coming from the streets; she can't sleep peacefully in this city.

The sound leaves the police station, turns the corner, and echoes on the forlorn windows. It fills the room through the window left partly open right underneath the angel wings.

"Hey there! Democracy is here, democracy!"

Shouts, whistling, laughter… shouts of "Long live democracy!"

Adviye, this immigrant woman with a tiny little face and a flat forehead, pulls the curtain apart and first looks at the street with her eyes that resemble blue marbles, and then rushes to Nadide.

Get up, girl, she says to her. Listen! The bastards are running riot. They've won an election or something. All the good for nothings have hit the streets. No more wandering around for you, just so you know.

Nadide has her mind set on Yakup, that's why. Since her mother can't tell her to stay away from that penniless guy, she will ban Nadide from wandering all the streets that lead to that newsstand in Taksim.

If that doesn't do it, they'll move out of this house. She never liked it around here anyway.

With the help of their hometown friends, she'll find a house in Sultanahmet, an old, dilapidated, two-story stone house with a creaky stairway going upstairs. So what if there are cockroaches everywhere, even in the cupboards... She's not afraid. Her fears are of a different kind, they're multiple...

She'll exterminate them, get rid of the dirt and bugs. She'll plant roses and hibiscuses all around the garden; she'll have sweet williams of all colors. Every time she lifts up her head, she'll see the minarets; her feet will touch the earth, which will be sweet.

It would be close to Sirkeci, to the train, the ferryboat, she said when telling Rüstem that she wanted to move.

Rüstem didn't object to Adviye, his mind was on the looks the city gave him; who cared whether they changed house or not. He was in love with the night lights of the streets and avenues.

The city was a pair of eyes promising endless pleasures... One of its eyes was open, the other closed. Istanbul sometimes would look at him with its open eye. At that moment, the world would become more beautiful, opening its arms, embracing Rüstem. Jewish vendors taking cheap clothes, cheap combs and cheap scissors from Sirkeci to Anatolia, truck drivers, porters would say, come on, let's eat a meatball sandwich today. Meatballs packed on a tray would sizzle on the grill's flame, becoming smoke and smell, stretching five streets down. The world? You can keep it. With its grand sycamores and street lamps right next to chestnut trees, Istanbul is enough! He would go flying down the hills with the meatball cart in front of him, and he would let go of his breath as soon as he saw the sea from a distance. He would contentedly inhale the smell of gas from the streets. In the evenings of such days, his feet, having taken wings, could not make it to the door of the house no matter what.

Yet if the city were to look at him with its closed eye, Rüstem's luck would turn, and no one would see or hear him in this damned place. Meatballs, wrinkled and scattered tomatoes, peppers would just sit there on the trays.

During the nights of those days, Adviye's fears would grow and thrive. She would fear that Rüstem would die in this city; that Nadide would run away with that scrawny boy; that oil, sugar, water and electricity would run out; and that they would be left penniless.

* * *

She suddenly opened her tightly clasped fingers by the well in the middle of the garden.

A golden bead bounced and beamed in the air, and then the sequins, bright gems, and then the spangles…Breaking free of Nadide's palm, they scattered and fell into the well.

Good, said Nadide, good! There, my hands are all empty! She got close and waited contentedly for the sound to echo from the well, but the well was deaf. It didn't let on receiving the beads nor did it echo the name Nadide quietly voiced.

The sound came from someplace she was not expecting at all, from behind the garden gate. Getting closer to the gate! Are those footsteps? She was startled. Who could that be? My mom? Afraid, she jumped back from the well. How could that be? She'll go all the way to Mahmutpaşa, climb Mercan hill, and find the garment workshop. Dresses will be laid out on long tables. Are they embroidered well, flawlessly? As the boss, that crude fool, finds all kinds of mistakes so he can pay little, my mom, sour as vinegar, will sweat and then keep quiet, will sweat and then keep quiet…

Then she'll say, with a cringing voice, that she took great pains in embroidering them. I tried to make it better than usual…The boss will pretend not to hear as she talks. Her mom will know she's talking in vain as he puts aside the dresses deemed unsatisfactory. She wants to cower by the wall, to disappear and make herself forgotten, at least for a while.

When the boss is getting ready to leave the workshop, Adviye slides past the other women and asks him for new pieces to sew now that the damned man's anger has subsided. Her mother takes the dresses given and then asks for her money in a broken voice. She doesn't move a muscle, looks at the money offered but can't tell the boss how little that is; she quietly puts it in the purse tucked in her bosom.

No, it can't be her! She can't come home three hours early!

* * *

Halil approached like a tall, dark shadow from near the pink hydrangeas, those robust flowers. As if there now and then gone the next second…He stopped when he got in front of Nadide. Smiling, he approached the table and leaned over; waiter Halil's deep black eyes were exactly at the same level as Nadide's.

"Would you like something?" he said softly, and then he disappeared immediately. Maybe I should eat an ice cream, thought Nadide, to cool myself on this hot summer day…She felt the soft touch of her dress as it drew close to her legs and blew away. Then, she remembered the beads in the glass bowl sinking into the water. She looked at the golden yellow, pomegranate red and bright pink beads jumping up and down. She carefully counted the beads that were not in her hands.

Halil sweated in the steamy air of the tea house. Just as he was about to say, maybe I should turn off the tea water now; no one would come at this hour, "What about that one over there?" asked Hasan, as he dipped the tea glasses first into soapy and then into clear water. His wet fingers pointed outside the window, towards the woman sitting alone at the table. Most of the tables on the grass were empty. Only that woman was sitting there, staring into the distance, with a faraway look on her face and seeming a little sad. "One last glass, and let's take an ice cream to the poor woman too," Hasan added. The two friends had been serving the customers at the tea garden since morning, working side by side and joking with each other, and they were tired, their hands now weary and clumsy.

When she saw Halil, Nadide felt the bareness of her chest and tried to cover it up with her hands. She did not see that the lights of the tea garden came on and that some curtains were drawn. She casually looked at the apartment block opposite. One, two, three, four lights, one, two, three windows, red washing over her face, a heavy pressure over her head, ringing in her ears. From where she was sitting in the courtyard, she had seen the evening sun retreat and disappear, and the gate at the far end of the dimly lit garden open. She was thinking of Yakup with shudders that released and then started again in her brain and her heart.

She thought she was alone in the backyard of the apartment block at the end of the narrow street leading down to the sea, in Samatya; then her father came up right beside her, though she didn't hear him coming. Come on, I'll take you out for a stroll, he called out, and persisted when he didn't get a response: Come along, get up, get up, come on! What about Mom? she asked. She wouldn't want to come anyway, her father said. Cheerfully, Nadide went in and out of rooms; she looked at herself up and down in front of the full length mirror for a long time. She closed the door of the walnut wardrobe in a rage

It serves her right! She shouldn't come anywhere with us. Let her moan, The day has turned into night! Where is Rüstem and that girl whose neck should be wrung? Oh, let them spend their money on horse-drawn carriages, trains, patisseries, the seaside, the movies…Let them have fun all the time. This Rüstem has no sense of tomorrow, and neither does that daughter of his. All they care about is today! Let the damned two of them eat and drink on filthy streets! Like a couple of twigs, let them wander around without putting down roots anywhere. How will that girl know where we've come from, where home is, how beautiful the weather, water and fertile soil are…

Speaking of the filthy streets of Istanbul, Yakup's hands came to her mind—clean, warm, ready to reach out. It was those that first attracted her. She saw his long, thin fingers, then his face, his eyes, his smiling lips…Ankine, her friend from the neighborhood who walked right next to her, knew it…Her mom too…Nadide would look once, and then put her head down. Days later, Ankine said to her, girl, he liked you a lot; he can't get over you…

Clutching her purse tightly, Nadide was looking at the light on the balcony of the house opposite, without even blinking. The wind started, she felt the chill of the evening and was surprised by it. Inside the tea house, now all lit up, Halil and Hasan were doing the last chores of the day, getting the place ready for the next day. Satisfied and ready to go now, Hasan said, "Let's ask her now. Let's tell her that it's night and the garden is closing."

Nadide had no choice but to listen to her mom as she hastily cleaned okra in the kitchen. Is the wind chilly or what now? Seemed like her mom was cold on this hot summer day. Her face was pale, dried up, and her skin had taken on the color of a rotten weed, verging on yellow. Out of breath, coughing, she was still talking incessantly…

Just so you know, seven mirages have always existed. In every corner of the world…Both now and before…They exist! It's the biggest of all mirages, the most beautiful, the most pleasing, the strongest…A naive person is carried away by beautiful eyes. Seduced and enticed by one look. Eyes invite, yet the worst is the word, the most dangerous one! It's a trap! You think your heart is your mind, you think it tells the truth, it besieges you and locks you up, you say I want it never to leave my side, you say this is just what I have wanted and waited for all my life. You think love will last forever and those eyes will always look at you nicely…You think you are the only force in this world, in his eyes.

The girls have left, they're all spring chickens! They have all run… After love…

They were all wrong…This is why the name, unfortunately, of womankind is…Mirage!

Then they look and see that the eyes are not the same eyes, or the words the same words…They've changed with the hours, days, years… Two pairs of eyes have grown strange to each other. One day, they find that the word they so sought has become evil, the looks hostile, the life like the blade of a saw; pushing you against walls, it eats you up; the rooms you live in become your prison, the world a place of suffering. Ah! Mirages!

Those were the days! Look at your father, Rüstem!

These places look nothing like our hometown. Before long, you understand how it can change someone. Istanbul has enthralled even your father; he's long been lured by the night, no longer able to tell what's bad, what's forbidden…He's left pursuing pleasure in out of the way places.

* * *

Nadide didn't care; she left the window open in her room across from the well. Yakup's hands appeared with a slight brush of the wooden sill. In the heavy air of a hot, a very hot night he was so cool, so unhurried, so full of joy… His breath smelled of tobacco, his beard hadn't fully appeared yet, luckily, lightly grazing everywhere it touched. Towards the morning, Yakup left, leaving behind that beautiful smell of sweat, the smell of his skin filling up the room and slowly growing stronger.

After that night, Nadide always missed this smell when she and Yakup were apart and couldn't see him.

* * *

As she was sitting on the kilim laid on the ground just beyond the well, Hasan tiptoed through the clothes that her mother had tossed on the ground. He walked in front of the sewing box and came closer. Nadide looked at the face of the young man who suddenly appeared in front of her, staring in surprise. He seemed to resemble Yakup.

"Don't you have any place to go, mother?" Hasan said gently to the old woman. "Look, it's late now. Darkness has fallen all around. Don't you have any relatives?" "No," said Nadide, her cheeks rosy, speaking proudly while seeing the image in her mind. "I was my father's only daughter; he did not have the heart to give my hand in marriage to my suitors. I never married, son."

"My mom and dad passed away, they left me stranded. They left me all alone."

Halil was listening to them impatiently, standing two steps behind, with his hands in his pockets. He was looking at her with pity and thinking that they should take her to the police station.

The phone in Nadide's purse rang for quite a while. The old woman didn't take any notice of it, as if she didn't hear it. Hasan reached for it and answered the phone. The young woman who was calling sounded frantic. "Mom! Mom," she kept saying, "where are you? Where have you gone? Father is here with me too. You haven't been answering your phone for hours, and we've been worried sick." Halil was looking at Nadide from just a little further away; the woman was sweaty and preoccupied, unwilling to get up and go. Hasan handed her the phone, "Your daughter is calling you." He saw the fed up look on her face. He saw her weariness, her lack of interest in life; the arms of her old plump body were open but she looked like she was closed off from the world…She opened her eyes wide; she gazed at them playfully, with the look of a little girl, so innocent and spoiled…

Suddenly she smiled and then bounced as if filled with the joy of playtime. Nadide listened to her daughter's voice without recognizing it, "Who are you?" she said, "Who?" In a very high pitched, fragile and barely audible voice, "Which mirage are you?"

* * *

In the street that ran by the Green Valley Tea Garden, a light drizzle began suddenly, sleek cars passed by with songs ringing out from their windows. From inside houses, the light from televisions reflected on windows; passengers of the shuttle busses of mega markets got off into the rainy radiance in front of white headlights, their hands full of plastic bags. From somewhere afar, the whistle of a security guard was heard, shrill and echoing in the night…

"You pretend to forget, but you don't forget," said Nadide's daughter. She was tired and furious. Your memory is intact, actually…All you care about is making us sad…And then those beads you can never finish counting…

Anemone Flower

Yıldız Ramazanoğlu

Translated by Ruth Whitehouse

Their faces were a little flushed after climbing the stairs. Who knows what tribulations they had endured to get here. Glittering shop windows, flashy women, murderous faces, urban thugs bent on jostling anyone who came near them, jokers distributing hand-written notices offering money for 'work in the comfort of your home', weird items on peddlers' trays, babies turning their heads in curiosity, croaking frogs, plastic spiders and snakes thrown among pedestrians to attract attention; and yet they had persevered through all that turmoil in order to find me.

It was a first floor suite overlooking the street in the Tezveren office building. But I could never look out of the window because I was constantly dealing with clients. None of them understood a thing I said. They would listen to me in a state of total incomprehension, their trust in me increasing with every word. It was amusing to see their looks of gratitude, as if I had performed a miracle, before they had tested a single product. The same thing was happening now. I was looking at faces lit up by a strange gleam in their jaded eyes. It was the final session of the day. I would get away soon and escape from these last clients who were listening to me in rapt attention, without a hint of fatigue. Escape from the women intently monitoring my body language and sitting bolt upright to catch my every syllable. The one man present, whose wife I swear had dragged him up to my office, was so impressed by my endless list of services and asked so many questions about the active agent in each product that, despite the late hour, I was simply unable to pack up and go home.

"This product I'm holding here," I proclaimed brightly, "will boost your collagen. The addition of aloe vera means that it is easily absorbed and very effective. It's also good for hyper-pigmentation. And, since it's an herbal product, there's nothing to worry about. Its bio-select function also remedies dark circles under the eyes."

"Definitely an antioxidant for the gentleman!" I said. "As a former judge, you must have used your great intelligence to sort out and make judgments on so many incidents that have happened in our country. A hypoallergenic product is just what you need now. What about a 60-plus multivitamin? This product has been specially prepared for retired judges of your age."

"How soon will it produce results?" asked the man, with a nervous giggle.

"Well, it's a question of detox," I said. "Everyone has a different biorhythm. We might have to do a medical ozone diagnosis to stimulate the immune system, or we could use a product derived from shark liver oil. That way, we'd be eliminating the free radicals first."

They did not understand a word or else they were completely dazed by it all. My arrogant and slightly contemptuous manner left clients with no option but to accept everything I said, whether they understood it or not. After all, I was the expert.

"What about snails?" asked the woman. "You recommend snail cream, don't you? My friends are always talking about it. What are the benefits of snail cream, in your view?"

"Well, people have smeared these earthbound creatures over their bodies for thousands of years," I said, in a rather theatrical voice. "In ancient Greece, Hippocratic scholars with names like Zessos or Messos used snails for the treatment of skin problems and various other ailments. But eventually, people became greedy and started eating them…"

Nurten Hanım started muttering to herself impatiently. "It's late, enough about snails. Let's get this stuff off so I can go," she said in her deep, slightly coarse voice. "It's eight-thirty, Berrin Hanım. Closing time." Nurten looked as if someone would be calling her to account at home. If she had not intervened, the snail conversation might have gone on all night.

As my final offering and as a special favor, I told the lovely couple that these products were normally sold over the Internet, but we had made a huge investment and acquired the franchise so that our special customers could be saved from the effects of aging and regain the youth and beauty of their thirties. And that owing to our large discounts, we made very little profit from the sale of these products.

The woman gave her husband a remarkably saucy look. The very thought of increasing their collagen was already making them excited. If only the fire raging so crazily beneath their wrinkly skins could be captured and put into jars.

"You must focus on yourselves more," I said, as the final statement of the day. "Listen to your inner voice. Allow time for yourselves. Look in the mirror and ask how you might transform the jaded face you see before you into a picture of liveliness and joy. And if that's what you want, you've come to the right place."

"Couldn't we make a start on some ozone therapy, Berrin Hanım?" asked the man, making one last attempt. As a retired judge, I thought he probably deserved the ozone.

He wanted to reclaim the youth that had been stolen from him while he meted out justice. As if there were a magic formula that could erase scars caused by maddening years of dealing with reprobates, lying witnesses, hard-nosed criminals who got off with the help of bent lawyers, and poor wretches destroyed by unjust verdicts.

"Don't get hung up on the ozone thing too soon," I said. "I have major and minor hemotherapy in mind for you. We'll talk about it tomorrow."

Turning to the woman, I said, "I haven't discussed the wonders of the anemone flower yet, or powdered leaves from the rain forests. I have a big surprise in store for you." I tossed my bag over my shoulder and gave her a naughty wink.

"When you come tomorrow, we'll talk about this oil and look at your muscle ratio," I called out after them, sizing up their bodies carefully. But tomorrow, always tomorrow…

I had spoken confidently about the marvels of the anemone flower. But it was impossible for me to tell them that, as they regained their youth, they would utterly drain me by trailing after me with their inexhaustible erotic desires. Or that, despite being a hard-headed businesswoman, renowned for my expertise and sought after by every company in the beauty sector, I was rapidly losing faith in the business. That very morning, I had given a full account of my distaste for my profession at the quarterly meeting of the Support for Simple Life and Human Rights Association where, after five years, I had been made a director.

"Look in the mirror and stop focusing on yourselves, stop listening to yourselves. Just forget about that egoistic jangle of sounds inside you for a moment. What's the point of continuously investing in the body?"

"What does she mean?" said the expressions on the faces in the audience, eyeing up my chic suit and wrinkle-free skin and glancing at my expensive brochure.

I would tell almost everybody about my position in the association because it gave me considerable prestige. My activities as a member of a non-governmental organization added weight and impact to my words. In a way, I saw myself as the conscience of our clients. While some looked sixty when they were thirty, others might very well try to achieve the exact opposite. To be honest, this was simply because I was the one applauding it; I who knew everything and gave great importance to balance and harmony

Everything had been going well until recently, when something strange started happening to me. The laughter and happiness of others seemed to be breaking off and devouring large chunks of my life. Those people clearly had access to a secret of which I knew nothing. I had no energy for dealing with this world. It was a daily struggle for me to remain on an even keel and not feel even worse. I really did believe in the anemone flower. But what if I were to confess that I had used that highly recommended product only once, rubbing it on my face with the prescribed circular movements in front of the mirror? That I still made do with cucumber skins, lime blossom tea and Daphne soap, and that the beauty of my skin was all down to empathizing with the misery of others and lavishing my time on them? I'm certain they would have thrown me out of the company from which I had made a fair amount of money, counting bonuses.

Strange floating images of weird people kept coming into my mind. Rush hour; when the heavy evening air blots out all pleasure with a myriad of melancholies, when the city hums like a beehive. I didn't want to see either the real or the fictitious me in the mirror. It seemed that the more equality-promoting popular literature I read, the more bad-tempered, sharp-fanged and cruel I became. Would I ever be able to find my untouched, unsullied inner self? I needed a place to do this. That was why I had invented my cave fantasy. I was nurturing caves inside me. Somewhere beneath a trusty rock, where civilization would never find me, where no one could see me. A place where I could rise up like a great plane tree. A place where creams and vitamin pills, meso-therapy and lymph drainage rooms would evaporate like gas and disappear into the sky, where abused women with bruised faces and forlorn-looking refugees would cling to the tail of a kite and fly away.

Once you start to question life, you never know where it will end. I felt that something had let go of my hand and set me adrift. That was why I clung to the image of a plane tree. A plane tree that with closed eyes and raised hands was trying to feel the glory of God, and like a lunatic begging to be saved from the city's paralyzing brilliance, to be granted a breathing space for forgiveness.

Something odd happened today. I got up before dawn to get ready for the day. At the meeting that morning, I had intended to talk about a Red Crescent worker who had returned from a place in Iraq where there had been a huge massacre. I searched for the poor woman's name on the Internet and a page called 'Pompeii' appeared, as if she had attended some meeting or other in Italy. I was mesmerized by that petrified city. I read the whole article without pausing for breath, then read it aloud over and over again. When I returned to my work, I thought how strange it was that certain things come and seek us out when we search on the Internet. Typing in a name beginning with 'p' brings up a completely unconnected page which you end up looking at.

It was early and I was listening to an album I'd recently bought, to see what it was like and if John Coltrane went with what I was reading. It did. The morning was permeated with intricacies of sound, which, like an electric drill, penetrated and lifted the stones of Pompeii. While everyone else slept, the mellow tones of the saxophone wound like an analgesic around the computer screen and the piercing eyes of the cover girl on the magazine beside it.

I was now flitting from one thing to another. I had no time to do anything properly. I was piling up images of life like a stack of plates. I put the meal for the evening on to cook while I hacked away at aubergines as if with an axe. Handling the vegetables with no sense of pleasure at all. Feeling completely indifferent. At the same time, I managed to draft some email replies. But what I really yearned for was something to pin me to one spot like a great plane tree.

I bookmarked Pompeii and moved on. I'd have to look at it later. I'd give it a few minutes one day. A couple of minutes for everything. Coltrane had lost his effect. I closed the page as the playing finished. Faded and gone. I'd look at the Pompeii page next time. They went well together. The significance of dawn is best appreciated when accompanied by Eastern instrumental music. Very therapeutic. A special melody should greet those who rise at dawn to pray. The home should resound with therapeutic sounds.

I am very conscientious and, in this city, you have to set out very early to be sure of getting anywhere on time, so I was in İstiklal Street half an hour early. I found myself being drawn towards a multimedia shop. Why had I not immersed myself in a bookshop, or marveled at the shop windows? Or even spent the time sipping coffee and looking at passersby? Something was guiding me. That was what the mystical side of me said. I wandered around aimlessly until some force made me stop in front of the shelf of urban documentary films.

There were several documentaries about New York, Tokyo, Cairo and Sydney. In front of these was one that had fallen from its shelf: Pompeii. A tragedy of stone among all those vibrant cities. It had clearly been made to fall there right in front of me. I stared at the cover for a while. I could clearly read the curling font that resembled Arabic script. A city, once inhabited by happy and wealthy people, was petrified when a volcano erupted. I immediately bought it and put it in my bag. One day, its time would come. Or maybe it would join the unread books, unplayed musical instruments and CDs, for which the right time never came, in the rubbish bin. Or the whimsical collection of exercise devices, garlic crushers, apple peelers and egg slicers that filled the house.

Still, these strange coincidences had affected me. The city of stone became etched into a corner of my mind. What if everyone out there now in the street were somehow frozen? My imagination started immobilizing them in different positions. It was a process I could not stop. Clearly the item I had put in my bag and expected to forget about was not going to leave me alone.

My meeting didn't last long. We postponed dealing with the stack of problem files until the next session and went our separate ways. Everybody had busy, complex lives and it was a bonus to be able to leave a meeting without being lumbered with yet another chore.

I got straight back to work: A flirtatious glance for everyone. New products. Well-dressed women, retired ambassadors and young managing directors seeking us out while still in their prime. Selling them dreams with a thousand words they didn't understand. All very entertaining. It was just about time to go home when, as I went to take the office invoices from my bag to file them away, my hand touched that thing again. I wanted to have a quick look at this Pompeii before leaving the office, rather than adding it to the queue on the computer at home. I could tidy my things while I was looking at it. As I said, long gone were the days when I could focus on just one thing or one file at a time. It was normal for me to be doing three things at once. Folding laundry while following the news and mollifying people who castigated me for never calling them.

Unimaginable. The idea of being engulfed by hot lava while taking a bath, paying a bribe, slaying a man for the sake of a medal. I was in the middle of the film, of course. Totally alone, everyone gone. No time to mourn before, out of the stones, emerged a cheerful-looking couple. The couple I mentioned at the beginning of the story. They were asking about anemone flowers and waiting for news of snails. Clinging to life, or whatever it was, they had bubbled up from among the stones. It was impossible to deny what I saw; I had to take it seriously. I could no longer remain an observer, while life, with all its brilliant luster, was being sacrificed to the final reality that awaits us all.

When they had receded and disappeared, I got up, my head tingling, to find that my car keys were missing from the table. I hunted through drawers, in my bag and on the display stands until I eventually decided that someone in the office must have pocketed them by mistake when it was very busy.

Pondering how I would glare at people to make the culprit own up, I failed to search the top of my own desk properly. Who could it have been? I searched frantically for the key in the same places, over and over again until I almost had a seizure, and then gave up. I went out to my car and found it was still where I had parked it. At my request, the owner of the next door shoe shop opened the car door with unbelievable speed. He must have learned how to do it from car thieves. After all, car theft was a normal occurrence in our street and would happen in broad daylight. If might be difficult to prevent, but at least one could learn how to do it.

Suppose someone was lurking out there in the dark, waiting for me to leave my car to get help. He could easily make off with my car and was possibly at that very moment cynically watching me in my confusion, anger and helplessness. There was absolutely no question of my leaving my prize possession unattended. It was nine o'clock by the time I sent the young assistant from the next door Internet café to fetch the local car locksmith. I knew the proprietor of the Internet café well enough to do this. His place was always full of young people. Our political and social views may have had little in common, but I have to say I got on very well with him. The diversity of this city makes people find ways of getting along with each other.

I sat in the driver's seat and waited, feeling unable to go anywhere until the assistant came back with the locksmith. I really thought that the moment I moved away, someone would get in my car, hotwire it, put his foot on the gas, and disappear. I had spent so many weeks and months dishing out flattery and putting up with people for the sake of that car, when I'd much rather have been doing other things. I couldn't lose something in which I had invested so much of my life. Of course, the car was insured, but it would still take weeks to sort everything out, and they were unlikely to pay even two thirds of the market value. Finding the time to buy a new one would be difficult. Worst of all, the experience would make the city seem even more sinister to me. I would always be looking warily behind me. The humiliation of being conned and put in such a stupid position would stay with me forever. By seeing everyone as a potential robber, I would pollute the mood that hovered over the city. I would generate a clammy fog of suspicion that would defeat anyone believing an epidemic of goodness was just around the corner. It was almost a social responsibility for me to wait with the car. Over the last few years, some mechanism inside me had been trying to take a share of responsibility for everything. I would agonize over every woman whose wrinkles were not eradicated, blame myself for every man who could not be saved from his free radicals, feel guilt because this city had become contaminated by an array of misfortunes. I pressed the button and locked myself in. That was silly. Whoever had the key could easily open the door if they turned up. Still, it was a useful precaution against any marauders other than the thief. Any street gang which, as a matter of course, bent down and looked inside to work out the marital status, age and facial expression of a woman inside a darkened car would be more dangerous than my thief.

I waited nervously. It was an hour before the evening call to prayer. I looked in the side mirrors and the rearview mirror. Then I started with the right side mirror again. I checked behind me. People kept passing by as I waited for either the car thief or my locksmith. They all looked like me. Personifications of my state of mind. I sat there feeling like I also was moving inside those bodies. Even running. The flow was ceaseless. Even though I was stationary, my mind was with the people rushing past. As darkness fell, I became no more than a silhouette. My sexuality vanished. I became an unknown entity. Invisible. With nothing to indicate my femininity, the flow of people passed by as if I did not exist. I just watched them parade past me. As if I were operating a candid camera. I felt a surge of excitement as I watched a young woman pushing a stroller hurriedly towards the corner supermarket, looking much as I had ten years ago.

Some adolescents walked by, gesturing and making lewd comments about girls to each other. A couple by the right-hand rear wing of the car was embroiled in an argument that looked as if it could turn nasty. I watched anxiously through the rearview mirror for a while. As a director of a human rights organization, it was important for me to observe this. It can be beneficial to spend a few hours arguing and bickering; a way of letting off steam for people who are at breaking point. But the woman would not stop talking. Some might say it is a sickness of the times. Women never stop talking; they have views on everything. But then she did stop and was quiet. The man had the last word, won the argument, and suppressing his violence, stalked off home. Or wherever he was going.

The adolescents gathered in front of the Internet café, then dispersed and left. Among them was a young guy who I recognized, despite the spiky, gelled hair that made him look like something out of *Star Wars*. They recognized me. I regarded them as my natural protectors. Whenever they saw me, they would stop swearing and straighten up. Bless them.

I looked in the mirror again and, instead of being frightened by everything, began to sing a song. I sang it over and over again in a meaningless way: "She's only seventeen, only seventeen." A shifty-looking man in his thirties, leaning against the shutters of the now closed shoe shop, was staring straight at me without a trace of pity in his eyes. In the street, the safest thing was to keep moving. To mingle with the crowds, wherever they were going, and blend in with the flow of garments. It was very dangerous to stop. Even a moment's hesitation could be fatal. I needed to be able to read what the man had in mind. It was vital to read people's intentions. That's how life was there. But the man had gone. Vanished. Suddenly wiped off all the mirrors. I speeded up my little song. "Seventeen, seventeen, seventeen, seventeen..." The man appeared and disappeared with the tricks of light and shadow. I half expected to find him sitting right next to me. It was time for action. I needed the help of everyone who passed by, anyone who would turn and look when I called out.

The locksmith appeared from around the corner. He was with the young assistant. The locksmith had a kindly face. My heart leapt with joy. I wanted to throw my arms round him. He swayed from side to side as he walked. At last, a normal person! What's more, as he approached, he smiled in a way that I could trust. Apparently, it was impossible to get a key made immediately at that hour. All he could do now was to hotwire the car and send me on my way. I would have to do my best not to stop anywhere.

It was completely dark when I set off.

I would have to take the shortest route, taking care not to leave the main roads. You can't imagine how I managed to avoid stopping, but that is another matter.

From Edirnekapı to Fatih, nervously edging through red lights. A hefty fine for every hand signal, every curse. The road veered to the right at Unkapanı. Then the Eminönü turning. Missed it, never mind. Unkapanı Bridge. Old Tuyap. Pera was on my right. There was something eerie about that place. I would occasionally go up there to drink tea. Tarlabaşı. Don't leave the main road! I was forced to stop. Now what? Darkness. On the third floor of an unlit old-fashioned building, I noticed the silhouette of a girl standing on a balcony barely big enough for one. She was motionless, like a statue gazing down at the street. To the side, at the back of a deeper balcony, a middle-aged woman with untidy hair was looking across at a woman's silhouette in the window of the bar opposite. Were they mother and daughter? Two women in the same home standing on separate balconies, clearly unaware of each other. The image surprised me. A gift of the evening. That unforgettable image made me shudder. A hundred different explanations rushed through my mind. Probably none was correct. I watched them through the windscreen until the lights turned green. With one hand, I put on a CD, *The Kaaba Imam* by Sudais, a present from a friend. I may not have understood all the verses, but the power of his voice and words filled my eyes with emotion. Time was running away. The voice of Sudais rose to a trembling climax and, as if by arrangement, the woman and girl both disappeared inside.

Which way was I supposed to be driving? What was to protect me at that time of night? To keep my nerve, there were certain things I needed to see, and others to not see. Or at least pretend not to see. Pretend long enough and, after a while, you no longer see. But I couldn't do that. My eyes fell on a transvestite signaling to cars as she touted for work. I was mesmerized by her. She said something to me. I wanted to say, "Don't you know me?" But she was angry. Before I could say, "I know you from somewhere, sister," the traffic opened up. But she blocked the way. Then suddenly we lost each other.

My journeys home in the evening were like that. Always depressing. I would put on a show of cheerfulness all day, but then my spirits would droop. So would my face. I would be filled with an ingratitude quite unfitting for someone with my blessings and so-called quality of life.

We seem weighed down by stones. Everyone just keeps repeating what they know. By merely repeating things, we will all turn into stones. Like it is our single mission in life, we mold ourselves into our final form beneath the stones. I slowed down and a beggar lunged towards me holding out a child. But I couldn't stop, you have to understand that. The woman fixed her eyes on me. Her eyes were tearful and traumatized. So was her stare. She was in a nocturnal trance: urban delirium.

I arrived home safely. That much I managed. I leaned against the mirror in the elevator. Elevators should always have mirrors. People should look at their human image as they go out and on their return. As usual, I didn't ring the doorbell, so as not to disturb anyone. After all, it wasn't their father at the door, only their mother. No need for ceremony. The stress of keeping the car moving must have caused my blood pressure to drop. As I turned the key, I saw a vision of moody people. Apparently flying upwards, like hundreds of balloons. There was clearly something wrong with my eyesight.

I saw strange faces in the hall mirror. Despite her tender age, my daughter had plucked her eyebrows. They were pitifully comical and asymmetrical. She had tried to make them even and ended up looking like an aging film star. Oh well, she's growing up. Got the message.

That evening, my dear husband had come home early. He was buried in his newspaper, which interested him more than I did. No one asked why I was late. My precious son, always tetchy and rebellious, wanted to get as far away as possible from us. He couldn't wait to be devoured by the city. Everyone in my house was a marvel of design. A constant source of strength to me. Yet still there was a huge void inside me. How was I going to deal with this odd quirk of mine?

I greeted everyone, hopefully asking if they had eaten. They had. Hurray! A huge weight lifted off me. Bursting with joy at this news, I prepared a little tray for myself and sat down in front of the television.

Later, I'd take out the laundry. I'd smooth it out with my hands, one piece at a time, because ironing was only for essentials. If only I could repeat the miracle of survival by just getting up every morning. If only life could continue like that for a while. With everyone applauding me for being alive, still standing.

I suddenly became detached from the reality of our life together in that living room. Overwhelmed by the feeling that nothing could ever be the same again. The form and posture of everyone at home, my daughter's slender neck, the lines on my husband's face, they had all become alien to me.

The television was on low. No one was watching, but it continued to churn out the usual stuff. I sensed my son going into the kitchen, grabbing a piece of cake and biting into it. I knew that taste. The thing crumbling inside his mouth was made of ingredients I had mixed together the previous evening. In a flash. Four eggs, one glass of milk, a packet of vanilla, half a bag of flour, baking powder and a tea glass of oil, with a few walnuts and raisins, plus a pinch of cinnamon. Pour straight into a well-greased cake pan. One hundred and seventy degrees. Thirty minutes. And it's ready to eat.

I went into the next room to do some cleaning. I was tired, of course, yet imbued with a fresh spirit, the spirit of the past day. I would be leaving early in the morning and I wanted everything in order for those staying at home. At that late hour, I dusted with enthusiasm. I wiped the windowsills and tidied everything up, despite the amazed and disapproving looks of neighboring housewives. I watered the flowers. There was deliberation in all my movements, and composure as I tried to find my penultimate memory.

Ever since it was proclaimed that free radicals had to be fought as the new enemy attacking our systems, I had played a significant role in that fight. Who was the enemy? Who knew about the enemy? How was it permeating the city? Perhaps I'd come to my senses if I went into the kitchen and brewed some tea. I wonder if the staff ordered the anemone flowers? How long does it take to have a car key made from the original? Should I suggest shark liver oil to the young bank manager? Would St John's Wort pills made from golden hypericum cure Perihan Hanım's hypochondria? Who could have taken the key? Does car hotwiring always work? How much longer can I tolerate this interminable life?

Why I Killed Myself in Istanbul

Mine Söğüt

Translated by İdil Aydoğan

You know those holy cities in faraway lands to which people travel so as to die? You know how people lay down on filthy cushions in ruined temples situated near lakes and gravely await death? Like them, I came to this city from a faraway land, to end it... to kill myself.

In fact, if they had let me, I could very well have died in the town where I was born. When the time came, as a matter of course. But life prodded me with a rotten stick. It said, get up, tag along behind insanity, behind mindlessness, behind ambition; tag along behind disbelief; get up and go to that city, roam its streets, make love in its every corner; kill on its hills and die in its pits.

From the first day I arrived in this city, I've been in every guise, choosing one danger over another. In the quietest neighbourhood, in an ordinary apartment in a most ordinary building, with my ordinary husband and ordinary children. Even if I did lead a truly ordinary life, my red, blonde, black, brown hair would dangle down the window and danger would climb up my hair.

One day I am stabbed in the heart with jealousy, the next day I stab my husband in the heart. Always a black-handled knife in my kitchen. Poverty is deemed to smell of death.

I give birth to children one after the other. Some I raise, others I let out onto the streets. Fires break out in my house. Sometimes I fling myself into the flames to save my children; sometimes I get delirious thinking of the ones swallowed up by the flames. There have been a few occasions when my children and I were killed from the fumes of a leaking gas cylinder, or from smoke coming in from the chimney, cuddled up together in bed.

Sometimes I am a young girl who works at a hair salon. I take the hands or feet of the women with whom I will never wear the same dresses, love the same men, grieve over the same things, and place them against my skinny, trembling knees. And with scissors, nail files, nail polish, nail polish remover, soap, cream, pleasure, pain, and spite in my short pink finger nailed hands, I have a nervous breakdown. My manic demon turns against me and, silenced, she listens to their ceaseless conversations. One day she will escape from inside me and kill you, me or all of us one by one, I want to tell them. I fall silent.

When my silence transforms into a huge cry, I am far, far away. From all my relatives, everyone I know, from my dreams, my passions...So far... Let's say in a hotel room in Beyoğlu. I stand in front of the mirror and stare at my pale face. My makeup smudged, my pupils tiny. The dye of my split-ended hair faded, my faded soul's heart torn. I give myself a new name every day. And they'll all be flower names. A different name for every man. I am Rose, I am Violet, Daffodil, Jasmine, Forget-me-not... and sometimes Calendula.

There are times when I roam the streets all night. A liquor bottle in my hand, I sleep on the sidewalks. Sometimes I lean against walls, crouch down on stones, get into strangers' cars. You see me in trucks, with a smoke in my hand and a cursing tongue; there is always a violent wind above my head, blasting my fate around. I look out of the truck window.

A little girl sitting on the pavement catches my eye. Dressed in filthy rags, barefoot, with a snotty nose. I know that her mother is somewhere nearby. Crouched down near the bottom of a tree, her mother watches her secretly. The girl lifts her head up and stares blankly at passersby. With her tiny, invisible hands she clings to the legs of those with whom she manages to make eye contact: "Money," she says, "give me money." Sometimes she wets herself. Her piss runs like a tiny river down the road. I gave birth to numerous children who drowned in that river.

Sometimes in this city, I am a sixteen-year-old pregnant girl. I lie down on the sofa bed at home, or sit at the table, and cry. What if my husband doesn't come home? What if my husband beats me again tonight? Will the child inside me die? Will the child inside me kill me too when it dies? If I were to go to my father, if I were to ask to be saved, would he open the door for me? Would guns be pointed, would they stone me to death?

And then I'd give birth to the child at home, alone. Like a cat, I'd tear the umbilical cord with my teeth. It would cry nonstop for three days. The more the baby would cry the more my husband would punch the walls. Finally, he'd grab hold of it by its cardigan and fling it out the window. A mother whose baby has been killed; what would she do all alone in this huge city?

I'm the one who steals women's handbags on the streets and who lays under strangers in foul beds. The hidden pockets on my *şalvar* are full of pills. Centuries ago, I came to this city from a faraway land.

All that can be seen is darkness through the window in the only room that belongs to me. That is why I can't see my past or my future. In a pitch-dark life it is both crowded and lonely.

If you were to ask me, I'd tell you I actually like this city. It is huge, colorful and alluring. It seems to be filled with promises. But that is just a delusion. That is why I feel dizzy, I black out; my love and my insanity are both illusory.

I am sentenced at its prisons. Bombs covering my whole body and a gun in my pocket, I dream. What if I were to blow up this city that I was unable to defeat? If I were to shatter into pieces the men I haven't slept with. If I were to stab the children I hadn't yet given birth to right in their hearts. If I were to appear in court singing the songs of the mountains I came from. Who is mightier, the city or me?

Sometimes I barge into the dark neighborhoods of the city. The women are black as coal. Tumbling inside a celestial lie, one by one I visit all the graves. All the prayers I know become the rain and pour down on me. At that moment, I believe in everything…And mostly in hell, in the sufferings of the grave, and that I will never shrug my sins off my shoulders, not in this world nor in the next… That I myself am the embodiment of sin.

If I were to hold the city in the palm of my hand and, with a cloth, if I were to scrub, rub and polish it, would the city be cleansed of menace? Would the hundreds and thousands of forms of womanhood finally embrace a new fate?

This city has been a man for centuries and doesn't know how to love women. That is why, in this city, I kill myself over and over again each day. I explode like a bomb; jump off its towers, its bridges. A knife in my hand, I slit my body all over. All the ropes on the ceilings dangle down so I may hang myself. Cars cruise so I can jump in front of them. My unidentified body in its sea, its sewers, its rubbish dumps. My colossal courage would fit into the narrowest pits in the cemetery of the nameless.

Mihr, Mahr, Mihrimah

Berrin Karakaş

Translated by Kerim Biçer and İdil Aydoğan

Mihr, the sun, rises in the east as Mah, the moon, sets in the west. Mah rises in the east as Mihr sets in the west...

When Mihrimah's sundial on the wall illuminates the sea, boats edge in at the courtyard of the mosque, a ladder is propped against its hallowed walls touching the queen's skirt. In Mihr's tiny footsteps, Mihrimahs open their doors after years for the homeless to rest. With their twin names, they are lost in the wonders of history.

As Mihr and Mah move back and forth to the past and then to the future, boats are lifted onto the deck of the ship of history and the journey begins, higher than dreams, a journey into the sky...

Mihr, the sun.

Asia is the continent of neighborliness... Words cannot describe my loneliness since I was exiled to Europe. And on this yellow autumn morning, as the blood of my children merges into the past, my body is drawn to the opposite shore. I'm so far away from home and death...

Instead of cruising on such a beautiful sea, hiding away in an old castle with poetry does not befit a queen like me.

I'm a confirmed lunatic; my mind does not see logic... It's been the talk of the town for centuries now: "She must be crazy!"

If they hadn't been talking under my nose again last night about old houses and Althusser, I would simply be sitting beside my poetry. I wouldn't have come to this mortal garden. Now that I have, I've been to hell and back, I have no desire whatsoever for the past. There is no poetry at all left on this shore, whereas when I was a child, one could see the faces of stones. Now they are all covered with nothing but haste.

A traveler once hanged himself from a lamppost. My Grandfather Orhan told me before he died. And Grandpa Goethe had told him: "And you, O humanity! You are making yourself a refuge using the mighty ruins of the past. You are pleasing yourself on the graves of the dead."

In those old days, when the traveler had uttered these words, Istanbul was a city "with restless and lush horizons, colorful houses, elegant mosques boasting lead-coated domes and graceful minarets; a smiling and grandiose city that needed only promise pleasure-centric philosophies and sweet fantasies."

To suit all this grandeur, I put on all this bright makeup. My eyes are the color of autumn and so is my face…I cannot make out any of the colors in this crowd. Instead of sweet fantasies, the true voyages of untrue seas loom over me. A fear grows deep inside me, as if I too would soon drown in the dark waters of the Bosphorus like those sailors. As the old and new were born between these two, I was sure to lose my mind.

Where was that fierce and feminine mosque my dear Mah had shown my eyes? The noise, the bus, the tunnel; I cannot see a thing…

How come these pavements of my childhood are so young and so crowded? In coy streets amid screams, I seem to catch sight of my Grandfather Orhan, twisting the ends of his moustache.

"With its dusty roads, torn cardigans and fountains; vineyards, fields and tall old houses, Üsküdar was a garden that longed only for loneliness. Its ancient smell repelled all visitors and no one would pass through it.

So it had found its true home in the paintings of artists', choosing for itself the coziest spot," he had said, smiling.

My Üsküdar and all I have left is in the past now haunt me. The old traveler up on the lamppost speaks: "You see this place? This place used to be more modern than any spot in Europe. Slaves had their rights and the birds their nests. If you did not have a front garden for birds, two small bowls for dogs, you wouldn't be strolling in the streets with your head held high and humanity in your hands."

In those past days, as boats and peonies would edge forward towards the skirts of Mihrimah Mosque, I would be walking in the dark, in the streets of what is now known as Üsküdar. Like my Uncle Yahya once said, "Every morning we are surrounded by heartsick people, and people who have just awoken."

I run through them, racing, my bloody legs covered with the past, and arrive at Mihrimah's door.

Mihrimah's arms are wide open; she is exhausted. "Oh, thank God you've come," she says wearily. "I've been so lonely and in the dark."

Wait, my darling Mihrimah, let me take a drag on this cigarette, then I'll come running straight to your aid. You half-domed, me half-witted, together we will be illuminated at dawn. From Edirnekapı, from Mihrimah, Mah will rise in the morning. As you and I permeate through the two minarets, it will rise on the opposite shore. When we unite with that pale light beaming from Europe.

Hush. Don't say that. Sinan is the sole light of my face; he will save me no matter what, just as he built for me a twin-named, multi-windowed mosque. I wish he were here with me now so he could open the windows of this dark heart of mine.

When Mah showed me this mosque from the opposite shore, she told me how dearly Sinan had loved you. And then she added, "See!

That's how I love you: madly." But I already had a lover. It was poetry. That tied my hands. And my Mah departed.

Sinan was the minaret of my faith. Once he entered these doors, who would ever be able to stop my heart pounding? Could queens chase fairy tales? Queens became fairy tales, they could never be swept away by them. Beside them stood the truth, like a sharp minaret. The one they call Hürrem sits on the Sultan's lap, parting her skirt. How can the spell of a fairytale carry a queen away when history comes rolling, unfolding all its dirt, sweat, damp and treasures? My darling Sinan, when you ran off with my curse hanging over you on your final expedition, a vision of this mosque was all I had in my memory. A bridge stands in the distance, ornate with pearls and lights. What could match it: the stars that shine in the sky? And will the commandments of holy times destroy this decree?

Fathers and their daughters, my dear Mihrimah. Fathers and their daughters.

Mosques and their modesty, Mihr. Mosques and their modesty...

Mihrimah blushes. The sun sets. In the cool breeze of the evening, Mihr and Mihrimah hide in the most secret corners of graveyards. They are finally warm. They fall asleep in each other's arms, resting upon the graves of infants.

Mah.

As scents of the soil that inhales the morning dew merge into the breeze that rises on the opposite shore and, passing over Sarayburnu gardens, reaches Mah, upon the heights of Mihrimah in Edirnekapı, Mah shows her face. Had she taken Sinan with her? Did she lay him down under the city walls, alone and desolate?

One staring from darkness into light, the other from light into darkness, they remember the past.

Who chases Mah in this city and leads her to speak, out of breath?

When Mihr brought me the poem, with Elif's music in my hands, I had pointed at Mihrimah. It was on a golden morning like this that I had the power of the sun blown into my lungs. As I rose on top of the single-domed Mihrimah, so would he on the opposite shore, and Üsküdar would rise in Mihrimah. As the walls, waters and prayers would all be watching our beauty, soon would begin the fairytales.

Sinan, who wanders around amidst marble, stones and secrets, tells his dervish-like, cheerful vagabond companion about his compass first. He points to the leg of his compass in the courtyard of the mosque. When he is looking around for the other leg, he remembers Mihrimah once again. He speaks from his heart, whispering softly to his sultan: "I was thinking of you last night. Inside this single-dome illuminated through the windows, I mourned my solitude. I was searching for a remedy for my heart, which darkened amid all this light. Oh, if only I didn't have history as a hunch, crate and timber on my back, I would not hesitate to swim across to the opposite shore."

"Yes," says the wild Mah and rants on: "Instead of sitting here and doing nothing…You cannot escape the past, say the old. Here I am now, along with this full moon, to escape into the past while everyone else struggles to do the exact opposite. If you ask Mihr, it's my name that is to blame. And his mother and grandmother and those before them will all say the same; names and the past travel together." Mihr is luminous; that is his name after all, so he had to leave me. Poetry was overshadowed. She began mumbling to herself in the doorway.

The sun rises in Üsküdar, between Mihrimah's twin minarets. Poor Sinan recites the names of the cities he has seen in the East and West. Between the walls, he drinks to the good old days. The Mihrimah Mosque too is tired, ruined. There is no room even for Sinan to rest. As he nestles himself in pain by the walls into his solitude, he stares at the opposite shore for one last time.

Mihrimah is standing in front of him, dazzling and radiant.

If he makes bricks of these airs and graces and lays them on top of each other, would that mosque stand a chance? If love was a stable structure, would earthquakes ever suit its soil so?

Mihrimah.

Boats are moving towards the shore in Üsküdar, to the old stairs of Mihrimah Mosque. Mihr and Mah, Sinan and Mihrimah meet where the sun and moon, the moon and sun unite, Asia and Europe connect; among the ebb and flow of the tides, they embrace. The many Mihrimahs, domes and minarets sway with giant shockwaves. The shockwaves travel all the way to Edirnekapı. They snatch away the lonely single dome from on top of the mosque. The remains of ancient earthquakes meet with Üsküdar Mihrimah's sea-scented skin, in the waters of the sea. Dead babies with their mothers, the empire's executed heads with their bodies, all lovers with their beloveds meet with this last earthquake, in the sea. Not missing this opportunity, the executed wanderer roams the uninhabited hills of the city he dearly loves. Grandpa Orhan sips his tea in the coffeehouse while pouring out his grief to the dervishes and hearing theirs. A few surviving downtrodden shout: "Neighbor! Neighbor, have you heard, the city has been razed to the ground. What you call history is now salt in the sea."

An Ode to My Istanbul

Stella Acıman

*Translated by **Ruth Whitehouse***

Why, like a well, does the past draw us in? I know that I seek not its people, nor yearn for the times they inhabited. No, we care nothing for things of the past as such. It is the emptiness they leave behind that draws us to them. We seek in them a part of ourselves that we believe is lost, whether or not any trace remains. Nostalgia is a world of its own. It enables us to explain the past, and thus live more meaningfully in the present.

—Ahmet Hamdi Tanpınar, *Five Cities* [1]

As I sit writing these lines to you in the tea garden at Rumelihisar, I look across the Bosphorus at the dwindling number of Judas trees above your other shore. "At one time…" I start to think, but then remember those times were not so long ago.

I recall how, when catching fish on the still unspoiled Arnavutköy shore, I used to gaze up at the purple-tinted splendor of the Judas trees in spring. When did someone allow those trees to be replaced by the concrete apartment blocks that so brutally broke one of the chains binding me to Boğaziçi?

---

[1] *Beş Şehir*

Speaking of Arnavutköy reminds me of the magical scent I caught whenever I passed a greengrocer in that special season, inducing a sudden craving for the tiny crimson strawberries which, once eaten, left such a sublime taste on the palate. "Two kilos, please," I would say to the greengrocer. In those days, Arnavutköy strawberries were the pride and joy of greengrocers, who would arrange them carefully, like fine jewels, in hand-woven baskets lined with leaves, and place them prominently at the front of their stalls. "Arnavutköy strawberries! Unlike any others, madam!" they would cry in praise of these goods waiting to be made into preserves or used to grace dinner tables. The soil that once produced strawberries was already being concreted over. Some people tried to prevent their plots falling into the calloused hands of men with shovels, but alas, to no avail. Instead of heeding the mournful complaints coming from the earth, hungry eyes and strong hands opted to strike at its belly without a second thought. As the Arnavutköy strawberry plots disappeared, the size of the baskets diminished. They were still displayed at the front of the greengrocers' stalls, but their beauty now harbored sadness.

One morning, years ago, when buying a newspaper in Arnavutköy market, I saw an elderly woman sitting on the pavement with a little basket of strawberries in front of her. They had been cultivated in the garden of a small wooden house set between tall apartment blocks. It had not yet succumbed to the times.

The old woman said, "Every year, that little piece of land provides me with ten small basketfuls. Some I keep for my children and grandchildren: they eat a few fresh and use the rest to make jam. The others I put into these baskets and bring here. It would break my heart if people forgot these little strawberries with the big taste. After I die, my children will build huge concrete blocks on that fertile land and these delicious strawberries will disappear for good, I know."

It was the first and last time that I saw the old woman with her baskets of Arnavutköy strawberries, and I said then, "You, my Istanbul, are gradually losing the struggle."

While speaking of lost tastes, let me say more. Do you remember how much I loved artichokes? Of course, I don't mean the sanitized, pale yellow, bland artichokes we used to see swimming in multi-colored plastic bowls of lemon water on every corner before the season had even arrived. You must remember, because your face would suddenly become sad and you'd say, "Are those really artichokes?" What happened to you? Did you lose your spirit? If so, why didn't you chase after it?

Anyway, more of that later. I want to talk about artichokes again—Bayrampaşa artichokes. Bayrampaşa is known, especially by young people, for the prison within its borders. Nowadays, Bayrampaşa is a busy, fast-moving industrial area with a lot of unplanned housing, but at one time it consisted of fields producing strong, almond-green artichokes, with a wonderful taste that remained in the mouth long after eating and that should never be forgotten. I sense a fleeting glimpse of your face, on which time has left deep furrows of sadness. What a shame we cannot turn back the clock.

How many people were able to resist the appealing smell of freshly ground coffee outside the shop of Mehmet Efendi, the coffee merchant? These days, we pine for a cup of that coffee, lovingly brewed in a copper *cezve* over medium flame. While our children are reared on cappuccinos, espressos and lattes in the brash cafés that have sprung up on every street corner, our palates still yearn for the delights of the past. But you hide yourself away in a corner, silent as always, taking refuge in your tears.

I'm thinking about the happy days we lived through together, you and me. The unforgettable times we shared in Yeşilköy, a place of profound beauty in a city that felt young and fresh.

Do you remember how the cobbled streets came to life with our bright laughter and happy faces, the ever-blooming flowers, weeping willows and linden trees?

Do you remember how we rode our bicycles, pedaling against the wind as if in a race down streets surrounding mansions and villas, how we laughed a dozen times for every word spoken, how people all knew each other, greeted and asked after one another, how the breeze blew through our hair?

Do you know that our initials, which we carved in capital letters into the trunk of one of the centuries old pine trees in Röne Park, are still there, fresh as ever? Two letters inside an asymmetrical heart: I and S. As if waiting for us, the tree still hums, "Come, sit in my shadow, inhale the pungent scent I bestow on you, gaze at the vastness of the sky, whisper words of love."

You remember, don't you, the days when children used to play beneath those trees, stepping over sharp rocks to reach the choppy sea and calling out to each other in a mixture of four languages?

Turkish, Greek, Spanish, Armenian...

Ayşe, Necmettin, Sabahattin, Laki, Dimitri, Seta, Aram and Ester...

You used to look rather enviously at their affectionate attachments and friendships, which paid no heed to religion, language or race. The sight of them made you very happy. At that time, you prided yourself on our multi-faith culture, the *ezan* blending with church bells.

Speaking of the ezan brings back memories of that handsome young *müezzin* with the beautiful voice at Mecidiye Mosque. I remember how my dear departed mother and her mother, Fatma Hanım, used to sit opposite each other in wing-backed chairs by the sitting room window in the old mansion, praying as they silently listened to the morning ezan. He soothed our souls as he recited the morning edicts in his rich, even voice. I often used to wonder if he had admirers who sacrificed their sleep in order to listen to him. My mother used to say, "I bet that müezzin is a master at singing our traditional songs. He could run rings round any of our professional singers."

Do you remember how passionate my mother was about Turkish classical music? How beautifully she used to accompany herself on the piano? Her lovely rendition of songs that descended right down to the lowest registers? She never went for the easy ones.

In her last years, when she was sentenced to watching TV, she used to flick through the channels trying to catch strains of her beloved music. The sadness would fade from her lovely face and her eyes would moisten whenever she saw one of the old artists. She would sigh deeply, saying, "Ah, ah, what happened to all those big nightclubs and singers?" I understood from the way she puckered her face that she was missing the glittering days when applause would bring the house down the moment Zeki Müren walked on, or Behiye Aksoy, known as 'the voice of Boğaziçi', shimmered with her platinum blonde hair and chic evening gowns on the stages of places now vanished, defeated by time and culture, like Taksim Maksim, Casablanca, Küçük Çiftlik, Bebek Maksim, Taşlık and Çakıl Gazino.

If I said, "Mother, play something for my beloved!", she would go to the old Russian-made piano, and Refik Talat's "Mahur Saz Semai"[2] would issue forth from the black and white keys, resonating through the mansion's gardens, accompanied by the music of the sparrows and goldfinches that filled the branches of the acacia and willow trees.

When asked why she chose "Mahur Saz Semai", she replied, "It expresses the color and smell of my Istanbul—it has the right touch of melancholy," and continued to play.

My mother loved you dearly.

---

[2] A melody in the Mahur mode, a makam in Turkish music

One year, when you had started to lose your resistance to time, I sensed that my love for you was turning to hate, and I decided to distance myself from you to prevent that feeling taking hold of me. Where I went had nothing to do with being far from or close to you. I just didn't want to acknowledge the transformation that was happening. I was so angry with you that I wanted others who loved you to move away too. "See how lovely it is here. Why don't you come too? Come and live with me," I said to my mother.

"I can't do that. I can't leave this place, my dear. Despite all its losses, changes and setbacks, nowhere other than Istanbul can satisfy my soul. I'm not ready for homesickness yet. One day, maybe…" she replied.

That 'one day' never came.

It was in the days when Beyoğlu was known as Pera that my mother first greeted you. That was in Bozoğlu Apartments, previously known as Bukis Apartments, a building that had been constructed by an Armenian master builder in a street near Galatasaray Lycée. Bozoğlu Apartments was the name given by its new owners, who had broken out of the heart of Anatolia, after the building's original Greek owners were hounded out of the country in 1964.

Mother had enjoyed mingling with Pera's cosmopolitan crowds to sounds of *bonjour, kalimera, buon giorno* and *iyi günler,* and frequenting places now lost to time, such as the Tokatlıyan Hotel, Café Markiz, Lebon Patisserie and the Baylan and Niçoise Cake Shop. She waltzed and tangoed to the orchestra with her first love, later to be her husband, in the decorous ballroom of the Park Hotel. I vaguely remember being with my mother in the hotel dining room, now consigned to the pages of history, eating what the French called chateaubriand—thick slices of beef, half-cooked inside and covered in sauce. Just an image from childhood. In those days, it was inconceivable that that magnificent, elegant hotel would one day be replaced by an indestructible concrete eyesore. Years later, I felt a mixture of sadness and joy on seeing that the bar of the hotel was now part of the interior at Zihni Bar in Nişantaşı, where I was to become a regular. "I wonder what stories you have to tell," I thought as my fingers caressed the medley of rose trees that had been carved into the solid oak by an Italian master craftsman in 1925.

"It was built in the neo-baroque style. Garlands decorated the pediment of the arched entrance and at its center was an engraved clock. Above the clock, was a sculptured human head and on either side were cones overflowing with fruit…" wrote Jak Deleon in his book, *The Living Taste of Old Istanbul*. He was writing about Çiçek Pasajı[3], formerly the Cité de Pera, which collapsed with a terrible roar on the night of May 10–11, 1978, throwing Beyoğlu into chaos.

Çiçek Pasajı had once been pervaded by the scent of violets, hyacinths and mimosa, but after the 1940s it was gradually given over to cafés and bars that eventually outnumbered the florists. The building had been trying to say that it bore the fatigue of one hundred and two years, but no one was listening. Whenever I went to Beyoğlu, I would turn my head the other way as I passed by it, unable to look at its heartrendingly sorry state.

It reopened ten years later with its façade restored by Beyoğlu Council, but the old Cité de Pera was lost for ever. Çiçek Pasajı, with its identical tables and waiters in identical uniforms serving beneath rows of overhanging lamps that were merely bad imitations of Art Nouveau, had finally surrendered its soul.

"My eyes seek a familiar person or object to warm my soul and remind me of days gone by. I see Madame Anahit. No longer able to walk, she sits on a stool in the corner, an accordion hanging round her neck, trying

---

[3] Flower Passage

to fill the time by scrutinizing the people sitting at the rows of tables. For a moment, our eyes meet. She smiles with happiness at seeing an old acquaintance, and seems to press the keys of the accordion with more relish. We end that night gazing at each other and reliving the not so distant past."

Speaking of the past reminds me of Bab-Cafeteria in Yeşilcam Street. Between 1968 and 1970, during my favorite years as a young adolescent with childhood behind me, it was the most popular place in Beyoğlu.

What pleasure I used to derive from watching a film on the large screen nestling between the thick velvet curtains at Emek Cinema, which still manages to survive. When the film finished, I would rush down the gentle slope to where the spacious Bab-Cafeteria stood waiting for me on the corner. With its delicious meals and smiling staff, it played an important part in my life. Bab-Cafeteria used to be frequented by famous directors like Tavuz Özkan, Ertem Eğilmez, Ömer Kavur, Orhan Elmas and Memduh Ün, famous actors like Kemal Sunal, Fatma Girik, Adile Naşit and Tarik Akan, and Galatasaray's popular footballers like Yasin Gökmen. We used to put money into the jukebox that stood in the right-hand corner just inside the door and listen to modern foreign music on 45s. The owner of the place, Aslan Bey, used to travel abroad regularly to buy the latest records for us.

Bab-Cafeteria opened in 1963, and by the end of the 80s its popularity had begun to wane. It put up a struggle but, unable to withstand the dizzying pace of change, it succumbed to the fast food and *lahmacun* culture. We could not stomach the changes at Bab-Cafeteria and decided to consign the place to memory. Shortly afterwards, it too realized that it was impossible to fall in line with these changes and left, seeking romance elsewhere.

Once you were my love with seven hills, but you surrendered to the harlot in your soul and multiplied, sprawling across seventy-seven.

At first I was just an observer, burying my sorrow inside while you deceived me. I did not care if I was wounded by every sledgehammer that struck your beautiful elegant body, every bulldozer that rolled over you. You seemed to be pushing me away. You no longer sang to me the songs I loved: "Nights on Heybeli Island"[4], "Yesterday, I looked down on you from a hilltop, beloved Istanbul"[5], "Row away, my love, let's lie down on blue waters"[6] or "Kalamış"[7].

The dark shadows that started to appear on your beautiful face gradually pervaded your eyes and delicate body, which I still could not resist touching. Physically, you were no longer able to tolerate what was happening to you and, more importantly, I sensed that you were losing your spirit. The tears in your eyes and the pain on your face suggested that you wanted me to help. And what did I do? Instead of helping you to save the parts of you that remained healthy, I chose to sacrifice you to those visionless shovels. I fled.

"My soul hurts, my body burns…" you used to complain in those last years. While you were suffering, I was seeking ways of distancing myself from you, so that I could avoid witnessing the daily process of your body ageing a little more, your face fading and your soul wasting away.

That day when I said, "I'm going now, leaving you," your sorrow rained down on me, drenching me with your tears.

On the last day, while wandering round the parts of you I loved best— Sultanahmet, Egyptian Bazaar, Beyoğlu, Kuledibi, Yeşilköy, Cihangir, Nişantaşı—you showed me a newspaper article. You had marked a particular paragraph with a black pen.

---

[4] "Biz Heybeli'de Her Gece"
[5] "Sana Dün Bir Tepeden Baktım Aziz İstanbul"
[6] "Çek Küreği Güzelim Uzanalım Göksu'ya"
[7] Name of a district in Istanbul

Are your people from here
or elsewhere, my girl?
Where are you from
in Istanbul?

Polonezköy Mayor: Daniel Ohotski, fifth generation born and bred Istan-
bulite; Chairman of Istanbul Municipality: born in Artvin, Georgia; Şişli
chairman: born in Erzincan; Eminönü chairman: born in Malatya; Pendik
chairman: born in Sakarya; Üumraniye chairman: born in Balıkesir; Üsküdar
chairman: born in Trabzon; Kadıköy chairman: born in Muş; Gaziosmanpaşa
chairman: born in Kastamonu... Most famous restaurant: Konyalı! The great
Gazi Osman Paşa himself: born in Tokat.[8]

I remember looking at your face in shame after reading that article.

"You surrendered me to them," you said, seeing the expression on my face. The tea I was drinking refused to go down my throat and I choked. You were right. It was I who brought you to this state. I had failed to be true to my love. What we lost is now long gone for both of us. It is too late for the things we surrendered to the darkness of the past to be returned to how they were.

On my last night, I wept profusely as I gazed at the historic peninsula of old Istanbul from the terrace of my friend's apartment in Cihangir. In the silent darkness of that night, everything—the hazy view beneath the yellow lights of Topkapı Sarayı, the sirens of the passenger ships passing into the navy blue waters of the Marmara Sea, the screaming gulls that circled above my head—told me how much I loved you and how I could never really break away from you.

Overwhelmed by shame, I was unable to say anything to you when I left. In any case, you have never liked farewells and have always been

[8] Yılmaz Özdil, Hürriyet newspaper (September 8, 2007)

confident that people will return.

So, forgive me, my love, for all the wrongs I have done to you.

Wait for me, my melancholy city. This is my ode to you, my Istanbul. My beloved Istanbul.

A Leylâ without a Mecnun

Nalan Barbarosoğlu

Translated by Mark Wyers

"I can live without a face. I can do this."

That is what I thought when I looked in the mirror. Actually, I had seen the calamity coming, it was reflected in the faces of the doctor, nurse and Yakup when they removed the bandages from my face in that drab hospital room. I think that's what gave me the courage to take the mirror from their hands with such determination. Then I saw the monstrosity of the left side of my face. A calamity: half of a face that inspired just as much disgust as fright. In comparison, the right side of my face was a blank slate. Strangely, I wasn't even surprised. That monstrous face of mine seemed truly appropriate for this life. "Take me home," I said to Yakup.

Your ancestors said that the face is the reflection of the soul. I learned that from you. I listened to your voices clamoring on my hilltops that gave you life, where you migrated, camped and moved on for thousands of years, and I gave you repose in my waters that splashed in the shade of the redbud tree, and I counted your lives as my own. Did I ever withhold from you my past, which I have so painstakingly compiled? I hid the pain of your butchery within me when your violence overflowed into the world. I waited for the day when you would see what you had done. Now, you too bear the traces of carnage, in that window from which you peer. Is that your home, Leylâ? Do you see me?

My home? My sense of having a home was lost long ago. I see through the window: you are swathed in the color of rain. A squat tomb of clouds above you. As if it were protecting you from the rain. Later, the sky grows even darker, like the downpour has increased its violence. The clouds resist. Gathering upwards, they glimmer with their haloes of myriad hues of darkness and flitter above, from one edge of the sky to the other. As they drift about, the light of the sun shines through where the clouds have stretched thin, lazing across the surface of your waters. You become water and flow within me. You are the place where I was born, the place where I was nourished; the place where I kept finding myself and was lost. But the doors of the houses no longer open up for me. I move through the scents that spill out into those streets which have no meaning of the streets of my childhood and adolescence. I move through those scents of the homes of the impoverished and the middle class, and of the tacky homes of the wealthy. I ascend the hill. The scents do not accept me—not the scents of the shoddy grills set up on small balconies, nor the scents of the barbecues on large balconies; not the scent of onions sizzling in hot oil nor the scent of fried food that fills the landings in the apartment buildings; not the scent of mildewed laundry refusing to dry in the basement apartment, nor the scent of tobacco from the rooftop floor; not the scent of laundry detergent from the mezzanine, none of them accept me. I return to my father's home, which has been shuttered for years. The well in the garden has gone dry and the pump no longer works, and weeds wind around the trunks of the cherry trees. Yakup takes me home and picks me up. It is as if the house grows smaller day by day. Or maybe I am growing larger. I have been ravenous. Eating anything I can find. And of course I have been drinking too. Drinking just makes me want to drink more, and eating just whets my appetite. I want to gather into myself the entire barbarity of life. To overflow off the stages, to not fit into rooms! As I become fatter and fatter, I feel as if I am squeezing myself in under the fat; more, more, more. To bury myself, inter myself deeply under. To suffocate under the fat, and cease to be. But it doesn't happen! A resonance, the note 'la' quietly shifts inside me. It finds a way between the squelchy fat and hums inside me. It makes me hear myself. But I don't want that. I don't want anything to make me hear myself any longer. I don't.

I remember you as well, just like all the others who opened their eyes to the world on my breast. You were born on a starless night. On a night bereft of the moon. The waters of my straits, which your father gazed upon, were pitch black. He was in the garden. The northeast *poyraz* was blowing. As he smoked a cigarette, he glanced with fear into the dark shadows of the dark night, his ear turned to the sound of your mother's cries coming from within. It was as if the night would never end; he thought you would never be born, could never be born. But at the same time, he downed glass after glass of *rakı*. He ended up passing out, slumped against the trunk of a wild fig tree. Later, on recalling your birth, he would think, "That was a long, dark night…" You were born at the first light of day. When he first held you, you wailed and cried. When he embraced you, holding you to his chest, you fell silent. "Leylâ," he said to your mother. "Look at her hair, those eyes, black as the night we waited for her to be born. Shall we name her Leylâ?" Your mother, lying exhausted in bed, could only weakly smile and nod. Leylâ…When a child was born, your forefathers used to say, 'Let her live just as she is named.' Have you been able to live up to your name, Leylâ?

A question for which every answer will falter. The tragic tale of Leylâ, lover of Mecnun, who went mad in the desert when Leylâ was married off to another man. What does it mean to live up to a name, anyway? Does the giving of a name write someone's destiny? I don't know. But now, I think that I like nights best of all. I like how the night lightens the darkness within us and how the things we clutch within during the day can emerge, recklessly, in the darkness. I like how the darkness swallows up all that is volatile and gently illuminates anything that weighs on the soul and how, only at night, people can open their wounds and stroke the pain, like a cat licking a gash—that pain revealed in those 'human by day, wolf by night' tales. I love their dread and despair when the silence of the cemeteries they carry inside turns to clamor, their meek submission to the night, their intimacy when they remove wickedness' masks of domesticity and open them like fans in their hands. It was at night that I learned that nothing is as it appears. The meaning and meaninglessness of life. How everything only exists in opposition, how every thought which is devoid of emotion can be razed, how that which is called real carries within itself the very unreal. In short, I grew up in the night, and it was at night that I learned what life is. I don't know if I have lived up to my name, but my name can no longer live; I know that now. I lost my name along with my face. Only my voice is left, a relic of my past.

Leylâ, you are not the first nor will you be the last person who has had their face ravaged. I know that you know this. And also that you draw strength from this knowledge, and that it binds you to life. I have seen how you have cut out another life for yourself, placing faces over the face you lack. You drew existence from out of nothingness. Do not think, 'What kind of fate is this.' Leylâ, nobody allows anyone else to be themselves. Look, on one of my hills, a grader is flattening the soil of my butchered trees, snarling fearlessly. My face changes again. Can you say that I recognize my own face in the mirror of the Bosphorus' thousand shades of blue?

Do as I have. Paint over the mirrors. Paint over every mirror you see and destroy that face in the mirror. Breathe, without appearing to yourself; live, without appearing to yourself. Live, as yourself, with that face, the image of which you have erased from your vision. Know nothing of your image when it is perceived by others. Be content with that face that has been left to you, that is nudged to the edges of your memory. Can you be content? To what extent will you be content and protect yourself for who you are?

Don't make me laugh. The sun washes my straits in color. Just like the glimmer from the rays of the moon, the glinting phosphorescence of the sea, the night, the stars, and later, the rain. And the silken clouds, gliding like fluffed cotton. Don't you know for how many thousands of years I have looked upon my face? Can you not imagine how thousands of years have changed my face? Don't, Leylâ, don't pretend not to know. I know that you are full of anger, that you speak thoughtlessly; you are hurt, and you would like to hurt me. But you know that no matter how much your appearance changes, you are always you; no matter what, Leylâ. How beautifully your name echoes across my hills…

But still, I would like my songs to ring forth. In the melancholy melody known as "Hicazkâr". I would like to sing the songs of those who carry within them distant realms. Songs I wasn't able to sing. But there is no longer anyone left who can bear to listen to the songs I want to sing. Besides, I do not have the face for those songs. I paint onto my face the faces of women who are the most different from me. I transform

327

my monstrous face into a canvas and paint onto it the faces of women whose faces and songs are loved, women who are wanted and desired. I place their faces on mine, and pose for Erdal. Putting a glimmer into my eye which is not my own, I look into Erdal's lens... "That's fine," he says, "You look beautiful, just like Esra, that's perfect... Yaşar should see you, my God!" and he trots into the boss's office. In a dusty mirror that sucks the vitality out of the images it reflects, I look at that face which is not my own. Tomorrow, my face will appear on a poster of Esra Ecesoy, on the spot-lit door of the night club. That photograph of Esra Ecesoy will seduce passersby on that muddy street, and her songs will resound in their memories. For six nights I look at that strange face, that face that will ignite the imaginations of all who come to hear Esra Ecesoy sing with her alluring glances. During Esra Ecesoy's popular song "My Reproach for Love", my voice will trill, reverberate off the walls steeped in alcohol and fill the room, and the audience will sigh and they too will feel the sting of reproach shoot through them. Thanks to this face, they will indeed be in the presence of Esra Ecesoy. Esra's hair, eyebrows, eyes, mouth and nose will be all the more glorious perched atop her barrel-like figure swathed in gleaming black. A string of faux pearls around the barrel's rim, and above that Esra's face. If they just take two steps and reach out—Esra Ecesoy! Unbelievable. They will be dazzled. As if they were living in a dream. Esra Ecesoy, looking into their eyes, will sing "My Reproach for Love", and then back-to-back, "Cemetery of Nightingales", "Endless Lament in my Heart" and "The World is the Source of My Never-ending Sorrow". They will see Esra Ecesoy, woman of gilded realms, and think that it was all a dream. Even if you were to collect all of the money from their pockets, you wouldn't be able to send one of them to listen to Esra Ecesoy. Choose even the best-dressed among them, and they wouldn't even be able to get in through the back door of the club. With my made up face and voice, I would be a solace for those who have been crushed by life. Because of me, they will be men graced by the presence of Esra Ecesoy, just three feet away. Heedless of the headache pounding in their skulls, the next day they would boast of what they had seen as they worked at their lathes and countertops, scaled up scaffolding, worked under cars on creepers and scrubbed grease from under their fingernails with kerosene. Those who were not so lucky would envy them, and lament that they had missed such an extraordinary evening. Hope will fill their wan faces in the mirror and they will comb their hair with a flourish, looking into those eyes that too will have the chance to see Esra Ecesoy; from where could they squeeze a few more pennies? Perhaps they could get an advance, or borrow some money, why not? With that prospect in mind, they will go about their day, and evening will pass more quickly. They will not know who Leylâ is; for them, I will be Esra Ecesoy.

In fact, aren't all of you endowed with part of each other's lives? Aren't you augmenting your lives in each other's lives? Don't you die in each other's lives and come back to life in each other's? Try as you want to resemble each other; why can't you accept the differences in your lives which are so intermingled? You want everyone to resemble you, and you cannot bear those who remain different. I am sad for you. For thousands of years I have been putting up with difference. I have learned more about life from the rustling nature on my seven hills than from you. If you could just give yourself over to nature and see your ruined face through nature's eyes, perhaps you could make peace with yourself, you wouldn't consider yourself faceless. Suppose that lightning fell in love with a tree, became a flashing bolt and struck its trunk. The trunk would be cleft; half turned to charcoal for love, the other half spring-summer-autumn-winter. Simply an accident of nature. An accident born of love! Place your hand on your heart, and think…

You are my one and only, would dare I break your heart? If that happens, say it was an accident, just an accident. An accident brought on by Kadir. If you ask me, Kadir was an accident that came into your life. Those were the times when I sang my own songs. When my voice was mine, and my face was my own. I worked beside him, with the long-necked *saz* behind me and the melody buoying up from below. I was myself. I had fame. I acquired a following, of sorts, they filled the tables. I wanted to start working at a night club. That's youth for you. Perhaps I thought I would be a star. All of my friends pitched in and found a venue for me; it was a second-class joint, but still it was a club, and I was fourth in the lineup. That's nothing to scoff at. Kadir said, "This is not going to happen, I won't let you go." At that point I realized it was all just a fantasy; in his mind, we had gotten engaged, which was news to me. And he had children, his own family, and who knows how many girls on the side. I realized that it just wasn't going to happen; knowing I wouldn't get my due, I didn't go to work. He banged on my door, and having no other choice, I opened it. All I saw was the edge of the knife, and of course, he was drunk to the gills. "This," he bellowed, "this is my passion for you. Every man who looks at you will read on your face that you are mine. They will all say, 'That was the work of a real man,' and their knees will tremble in fear." Then he hacked into the left side of my face; nothing was left, neither vein nor nerve. The nurse later mentioned that in the operating room the doctor had gone pale at the sight and said, "How can such a face be made right again." And it couldn't, in the end. The wounds worsened under the stitches. "This is the last time," I said, on the way to the surgery room, where I had gone so many times before. "For better or worse, I won't let them touch my face anymore. All I want is for the pain to go away." But the pain lasted a long time. Does it still hurt? I don't know. Maybe it does. Perhaps I became so used to it that I could no longer feel a lack of pain, nor the occasional soreness.

In those days, my only thought was, how to find a way to live without a face. Any possible way, just a way; a way in spite of Kadir. And, I should never let anyone read on my face Kadir's passion. In the end, I found a way to negate that passion which obliterated my face, by creating other faces. I beat Kadir's cruel game, in which he thought he had ruined my face, and I just wanted him to pack up and leave. But the wretch didn't go. When he left me faceless, he didn't see how barefaced he was himself, he couldn't. In the beginning he was afraid I would file a complaint, but when he saw that nothing was doing, he was relieved.

For thousands of years, I have been witness to the innumerable love stories that you have lived through on my soil and upon my waters. I have seen so many 'loves' that drove people to produce novel sounds like the cooing of doves and that turned people's lives upside down, like the sentences they uttered. I have seen women and men, whose hearts were as sound as their bodies and whose words were in harmony with their thoughts, rent apart because of love, and what they said, and more so, what they felt, differed entirely. I have seen people take to the road, choose death and change their lives from top to bottom. Isn't this also love, Leyla? Isn't that face of yours, which you say doesn't exist, Kadir's love?

This time, *you* are making me laugh. If you ask me, if those bulldozers razing your trees and flattening your hills are love, then what Kadir feels is also love. Love was in the songs I sang, not in the places I sang them. I learned this at the very beginning. Love was just an excuse for the drawn knives, the bullets fired. It was a lie, an infidelity, a deception. Nobody asked me, "I want to be with you, but do you want the same?" On the contrary, men would get into fights, saying, "I wanted her first." Is there any place in this world where a woman gets her fair lot as the result

of such fights? I don't know. I hated it all. I hated the nylon carpets
they threw at my feet, the withered rose petals they poured over me, the
jewels, which in my eyes were as worthless as pebbles, that they tried
to drape around my neck, place on my fingers. I despised the practiced
gazes, the politeness they feigned until they got what they wanted, and
the rudeness, boorishness and violence that came after that got what
they wanted. I also despised the hypocrisy and insincerity of the women
who saw this but pretended they hadn't. I would get the urge to strangle
them for their perfumes, a single bottle of which easily cost the same as
feeding ten children for a month. I restrained myself. I always restrained
myself. I began to feign lack of understanding. I wanted only to sing
my songs. If I could only sing songs of lament, woeful songs, songs of
longing, it would have been enough. If they had let me, love songs would
have sufficed for me. I had long ago given up on love. Let's change this
topic.

Whether or not we change the topic, or talk about it till the end of
time, love has always been and always will be. I have been witness to
thousands of years of your lives; I have been witness to the myriad
loves in your lives. Who could describe a life without love among the
blossoms of my redbud life? Whether you name it or not, you have
always been in love. And you always will be! Leylâ, what difference
does it make, whether or not it is known? Is not love creative when
it becomes known? Doesn't it rejuvenate a person, from head to toe,
inside and out? Doesn't love cast aside the life lived, doesn't it play by
its own rules and take you over? Don't tell me you don't know, Leylâ,
do not deny yourself. Love is not in the songs that you sing, as you
have so claimed. Is not your singing love itself? For the record, I ask
you: What about Yakup? Yakup, who has not left your side for years?

Who is Yakup, who follows you step by step and never leaves, even when told?

He forced his story into mine. I didn't want it. I kept him as far from myself as I could. The way that he mingled my life with his own and stayed by my side seems to me like a kind of stubbornness. If you ask me, this is his way of self destruction. I put a lot of people between us whom I thought he would not be able to refuse; he understood neither kindness nor bullying. He never gave up. I grew weary of pushing him way, but he never tired. In the end, I gave in. And there he is, on the shores of my life. He thinks that he is watching over and protecting me, as if there were anything left of me that needed to be watched over and protected. I don't know what is on his conscience, what payoff he expects. Before my face was cut up, he never approached me. He watched me from a distance. Even then he was quiet like that. He used to come and leave with Sevim. She said that he was her nephew, but nobody really believed it. People talked, saying that she had nabbed herself another strapping young man. As time went by, despite his girth, his presence became unnoticeable. That night, it turns out, Yakup brought Kadir home; Kadir was drunk as usual, so Yakup drove. They say that after taking me to the hospital he went back and beat Kadir, and they struggled hard to pull him off; those who saw it couldn't believe their eyes. Where did that shy, misshapen sack of a man hide all that strength? I asked him numerous times if he had beaten him, why wouldn't I? He shrugged it off, saying, "Don't believe what you hear." He is strange. Really strange. Until now, I haven't heard a single word from him about his life. A lot of rumors floated around, of course, when he stayed by me. I tried, but it was no good. I gave up talking. How can you make someone talk? You would just run out of breath!

Together all of you, who are so different in word and thought, lie within my bosom; your sorrows have lifted, those sorrows so unalike under the same canopy of the redbud tree, illuminated in the dark of night by the same stars, illuminated by the same light of sun at the break of dawn, the beads of rain glimmering on the leaves of my thousand trees. Your sorrows are separated by the blue of water. How did Yakup get into your story? You mentioned how he entered the story of your life... This silence Yakup is enshrouded in...

Just as I lack a face, Yakup lacks a voice. Of course he has a voice, how couldn't he, it's just that he doesn't use it, so long as he doesn't feel the need to. He doesn't string together two words to make a sentence, he doesn't liven your spirits, or, I don't know, you just can't shoot the breeze, chat about daily life with someone like that. You just don't get the urge to talk about little things. Some evenings, if I am at home as the day is growing dark, he sits in that chair, lights a cigarette, watches the light beginning to shine on the opposite shore visible from beyond the garden. The expression on his face changes, as if he were bundling up the light and painting a different picture. I pour him a glass of rakı too. I want him to lighten up, to unknot his tongue, to tell me what he has seen. I sit on the arm of his chair, pull his head to my chest, try to hear what is going on in his mind. It is in vain, of course. As if a mountain whispered to you. The whisper would be lost in the mountain's rumbling. The meanings of all the words that you know slip away; the sounds of letters and the letters of sounds vanish; in the rumbling that you hear, the significance of any of those moments which you know as time falls away; the names you miss, the adjectives you love, the pronouns you know become stones and tumble down from the peak of the mountain. You feel nauseous and dizzy. This rumble is like that moment born from the nonexistence that a person leaves behind when they die; or, like the mysterious gap that a baby leaves behind on the earth when it dies in birth. Yakup's silence is a rumbling. The silence of a mountain. That's how it seems to me while perched on the arm of the chair. While his head is on my chest, I also watch the lights of the other shore. I become lost, like my face, in that darkness rent asunder by light. Then, it becomes morning. Then again, night. Then… That cycle we know so well. On nights that I work, when I return home Yakup walks two steps behind if there is someone with me; if it is just the two of us, he walks on my right, places his left hand in his pocket, and slightly raises his elbow; this is an invitation. I place my arm in his. We walk silently, in pace with my steps which grow heavier with each passing day. He always looks straight ahead; his gaze is fixed, as if there were a curtain before his eyes. It seems to me that he is looking within as he walks. Sometimes I get the urge to be his eyes and look inside, telling myself that I should have a look and see what is inside there. Of course that's impossible. Yakup is one of those who, with his massive body, destroys himself as he walks down the road. One of those who, seeking to conceal themselves from others, suffocates inside themselves. That's how it seems to me. Once, perhaps twice, a year he disappears for a few days. You don't know where he has gone, where he stays… On those days when he is gone, it is as if I am listening to the lament of the absence of his existence, like the absence of his voice; this is a lament that I will not give voice to, a lament that I will not sing on stage with another's face. In this lament, snow buries the roads. You pass through the heavy, sublime, embellished doors of forgetfulness. Your blood curdles in the frost of the courtyard in which you step foot, life closes over you, a pain is completed. From the courtyard sheltered by the shadow of the mountain, you observe the mountain. You unravel the language of silence, the words of silence one by one reveal their meanings, and you articulate the erasure of moments from the memory of life. The melody of nonexistence becomes a new sound. It drifts into a blanketless, pillowless sleep on your shoulder. You know that there is no longer a place for dreams in those bird-winged slumbers that settle upon your shoulder. The sting of the lack of dreams! When you look at the moon which has shunned you, the flowers in the mosaics bead with moisture in the courtyard in which you recline. Thinking that your dreams are in the mortar of the mosaics is mere consolation. And later, you see once again your body pulled into the whirlpool of forgetfulness in the shadow of the mountain. You are a heavy body which changes color like the shimmering of light on a stone that is tossed into water. The water swallows you. You let your blood flow into the water which swallows you. You drift from life in a whirlpool reddened with blood. As your last drop of blood swirls in, you wish to stroke that mind which dreams of heaven-hell. Your last desire. This is Yakup's silence. That is all.

Ah, Leylâ! In your lives which bear no semblance, there have lived Yakups who knew death like this face-to-face since birth, and Leylâs who lived pretending as though Mecnuns never existed. I shall harbor this. To the colors of the flowering branches of my redbud trees which are becoming fewer and fewer, I shall add every life that passes through me.

Remembering a City

Oya Baydar

Translated by İdil Aydoğan

Each city has its own unique color; its own scent, sound and sorrow. The seasons look different on each of them. Each carries autumn leaves, flowers of spring, the sun, snow, rain, joy and sorrow differently. Cities often change habits. They are different in the moment, different in memories, in victory and in defeat, at every age and every love.

New York is baby blue, Moscow khaki green, Athens the color of sand, Prague pale magenta, Madrid crimson, Parma yellow, Amsterdam silver, Ankara snow white, Paris French rose, Oslo grey, Berlin beaver brown. As for Istanbul, stretching all the way back to the times of the Byzantine era, Istanbul has always been the color of redbuds.

Some smell of newly mowed grass, some of seaweed, some fish, some rotten leaves, jasmine, linden trees, lilacs, some sewage, some soot, rain, snow, some of blood, carnations, tangerine blossoms, burnt oil, olive pulp, dry weed, incense, mold, herring, wallflowers; yet each smells of memories.

At twilight one night, as she watched the city of Istanbul, she noticed that cities also bore daggers that pierced through the human heart. The sky and sea had orange and purple ripples shinning across their navy blue surfaces. Towers, domes and minarets had been lit up, and the lights had begun winking in the twilight.

When she spoke the words, "This city hurts me inside. It pierces my heart like a pointed dagger," she wasn't after a fancy stanza or a pompous line. There, at a spot on the bridge with the best view of the Bosphorus, where on one side stood Sarayburnu, Galata, Üsküdar, The Maiden's Tower, The Islands, and on the other, the meandering coast leading to the Black Sea, these words had rather escaped her mouth as a cry. At that moment, the city really had pierced her heart like a dagger. She felt excruciating pain.

For years now the city had been a symbol of the hope to return, a refuge for both memories and fugitives, the last stop for trains awaited at foreign stations that were never to arrive. Istanbul with its side streets, cobblestone slopes, its piers beaten by the *lodos* wind, its redbuds ready to bloom, its street cats, its mosque courtyards overrun with pigeons, its hungry seagulls, its noisy markets, its full moon that illuminated beautiful babes, the fishermen under bridges, wooden mansions whose shadowy courtyards smelled of magnolia and pink roses with petals fit to make jam, the lively factories, the muddy shanty neighborhoods, the main streets bursting with wealth and goods, the outskirts, its city squares that carried the bloodstains of the dead.

"This city hurts me inside. All the cities I love hurt me inside. But this one most of all."

In front of the window which opened out onto Istanbul, she sat in her usual place, watching the city. The city was there, right in front of her, all around her, in the sea, everywhere; it rose in the twilight with its own inner light, shining with its inner radiance. Wearing the armor of the night it hid its purulent sores under its satin redbud robe, concealing all. The city was there, right in front of her; it was bleeding.

Right in the heart of the city, in front of a window looking out onto

Sarayburnu, the port and Galata, seated facing Istanbul, she remembered Istanbul.

The hills on the two shores of the Bosphorus were still covered with lush green trees, and the bridges had not yet been built. Redbuds would bloom at the end of April. It was then the time for violets, wild strawberries and thistles, hiding in the shade. In the gardens of the wooden houses of her childhood that smelled of moth balls, mold and apple peel, were still Japanese plums, magnolia and pink roses. From the porches of the villas owned by rich school friends, and practically anywhere in the city, one could dive into the waters for a swim. People would hurry to visit the islands before the mimosas withered, and with the arrival of September, they'd grab their torches and rush to catch bluefish in the Bosphorus. Late at night, as families drove through the back streets of Beyoğlu, mothers would cover the eyes of their children, shielding them from the pictures of the women at Abanoz, thus evoking the very first of sexual curiosities. Hamburgers had just arrived in the city; Coca-Cola hadn't yet won the battle against lemonade. *Gecekondu* houses really were impoverished huts built over a night around newly established factories.

As the city changed secretly from within, simultaneously changing its inhabitants, we failed to notice this change together with the change in ourselves. We lived the city just the way we lived life; rowdily, with the blunt recklessness of youth. We wasted the city, just like we did our lives; lavishly, carelessly, hedonistically.

From the countryside filled with the languishing smell of bright yellow brooms, through the beaches that led to deep blue seas we'd hurry, and plunge into the dusty and muddy roads of factories, workers districts, gecekondu neighborhoods. On our way to a cheap *meyhane* to meet with our friends, we would drift past the lit-up doors of luxurious hotels opening to different worlds and dream of the day when we'd open those doors to workers and villagers. Swept away by the winds of the period, we'd sing by heart the folk songs that had journeyed from the villages and arrived in the city to be sung at the tables of intellectuals; we'd be 'The bride in the grain fields', we'd 'Migrate from the Taurus Mountains with the Avşar', and then we'd 'Grind our axes'.

The city was there, right in front of her. She knew it was bleeding within, crying for innocence lost, fighting death; that, without even leaving a note, it had silently committed suicide.

There was a house with a well in Laleli. And there was Haydar. And you; the bright young man who always smelled of cloves and cigarettes. And a handwritten notebook of Nazım's banned poetry.

We should find that house first and reach the well. Then walk past the lumber yards in Aksaray that also sell drugs, and from there head down to the seashore in Yenikapı. There, sitting at a lousy table on the pebble stones where the waves can lick our feet, we are sure to find commoners drinking wine out of tulip-shaped tea glasses, and the arabesque song "Veremli Kızın Şarkısı" playing on the cassette player, will tell the tale of the girl with tuberculosis. We can even go to Beyazıt Square. We can ask who has been killed today. Then, in the back rooms of the union, on the ditto machine can print declarations that will change the world. Maybe one of us will get shot walking in the street, who knows! Perhaps we'll meet tomorrow at a funeral, if not in a strike, or a huge protest. I'll go to the bus station and wait for you there. We'll scatter across Anatolia in night buses reeking of sweat, bad breath and sleep. And each time, at the end of every road, we'll surely return to our city.

The city was intermingled with its lives, loves, wars and struggles. They'd love it like an old friend, bewitched by its weather, its beauties and riches, but they'd use it like a decorative ornament or a pretty frame. It was a natural part of their being, an extension of their existence. They did not yet know that cities had lives of their own, that they could not bear being abandoned, that they could devour their own offspring, that they could betray and commit suicide.

The house with the well is no longer where it used to be. Nor are the gecekondus in Hisarüstü. What is left of the dense woods on the hills of the Bosphorus, showing resistance, is a couple of green patches here and there, one or two redbud trees, scrawny mimosas and magnolias that no longer bloom. The domes, minarets, palaces are lost among magnificent skyscrapers, hotels and plazas. In a world where everything is put on the market, shopping centers are filled with all sorts of products from all over the world; television screens shuttle between reality and lies, making one forget what is real and what is not; streets with eye-catching shop windows line up on both sides; expensive cafes, luxurious restaurants, latest model cars, suspicious limos; the coarse, hulky and grandiose jeeps driven by an army of identical women with dyed-blonde hair and languid faces; the noisy and lit-up night clubs built on the sites of the old gecekondus, discos, and the new masters of the city who carry guns with silencers and fake IDs alongside their club and bank cards... The angry outskirts of the city surrounding its all four corners that have cut deep into its heart, ready to riot. And the security protected, gated communities that separate themselves from the other city with private bodyguards, wonders of technology alarm systems and high walls.

One day this city is going to freeze like a stone and collapse. Everything is going to collapse; we are all going to collapse. Only the legendary silhouette of the city—the sea, the hills on the Bosphorus, wall ruins, mosaics, marble, decorated ceramics and winds will remain. And just like it has after every conquest, every surrender and every destruction, it will rise from its own wreckage, and be reborn of its ashes.

For now, here in front of me, it bleeds silently. With the silence and patience of stone, it awaits its destruction so that it may be reborn in the hands of new people.

The city was there with its beauty that stabbed one in the bosom; a beauty that left one hopeless. The color of redbuds, flames and navy, its magnificent seven-arm candleholder that lit up when night fell; there it was. If it weren't so beautiful, she wouldn't hurt so much. If only she believed she could hold it once again, if she had the strength to sing the song "Wait for us Istanbul", she wouldn't be suffering such grief.

There had to be a keyword for remembering. A code that would open the city gates. A key that would enable her to return to the city.

She looked at the city surrounding her. The magical words escaped the labyrinth of her mind, travelled the streets of the city, its squares, hills, outskirts and years, and reached her lips: "Hope and innocence."

Hope and innocence, she repeated in front of the city. The city is deaf and dumb; a total stranger.

The code had changed. No one had told her.

The city hurt her inside; it pierced her heart like a pointed dagger. "I no longer hold the key to the city gates. I must leave."

She drew the curtains of her window tight.

Biographies of Authors

Stella Acıman, born in 1953 in Istanbul as the daughter of a Jewish family, is an author and business woman. She graduated from the School of Business, Istanbul University in 1974 and began working in the private sector. Her first novel *Bella* was published in 2002, followed by *Kırlangıçların Ömrü* (2003) and *Bir Masaldı Geçen Yıllar 1926-1960* (2006). She settled in Northern Cyprus in 2003, and her fourth book *Orda Bir Ada Var Uzakta,* which recounts her impressions of Northern Cyprus, was published in 2011.

Nilüfer Açıkalın was born in Istanbul in 1967 and studied theater at Mimar Sinan University State Conservatory. She has starred in many theater productions, films and television shows since 1987. She has published four short story collections: *Bıçak Sırtı* (1999), *Saklı Safkan* (2002), *Çocuk Oyuncağı Değil* (2000) and *İyiler Yalnız Gezer* (2007).

Cihan Aktaş was born in 1960 in Pınaryolu, a remote village in Erzincan. She studied Architecture at Istanbul State Academy of Fine Arts and graduated in 1982. She worked as an architect for some years and traveled in Azerbaijan. Her essays and short stories have appeared in various journals and newspapers.

Berat Alanyalı was born in Ankara in 1961. She studied Classics at Istanbul University, graduating in 1984. She has worked as a writer, editor and translator for journals, as a reporter and editor for television and radio, and she has written screenplays as well. In 2005, she started writing short stories, many of which have appeared in literary journals. Her first short story collection *Tin Kavuğu* was published in 2007, and her most recent collection *Ömrün Yazı* in 2012.

Sabâ Altınsay was born in Çanakkale in 1961, lived in Ankara and İzmir, and received her degree in journalism. Her travel reports and short stories have been published in various newspapers and periodicals. Her first novel *Kritimu-Girit'im Benim* (2004) was also published in Greece.

Erendiz Atasü was born in Ankara in 1947. She graduated from the Faculty of Pharmacy, Ankara University in 1968, and was a professor of pharmacognosy in the same institution until her retirement in 1997. Her short stories written with a feminist consciousness have been published in literary journals, and her essays and articles on literary topics, women issues, secular society and Republican reforms have appeared in journals and dailies. She has published five novels, eight short story collections, six collections of essays, and has received many awards. Her short stories have been translated into other languages and have been published in anthologies in the US, Britain, France, Germany, Holland, Switzerland, Italy, Czech Republic and Croatia. Her novel *The Other Side of the Mountain* (*Dağın Öteki Yüzü*) was published by Milet.

Esmahan Aykol was born in Edirne in 1970 and studied law at Istanbul University. She earned her master's in law from Humboldt University, Berlin, with her dissertation entitled, *Gender inequalities in German and Turkish Family Law*. Her novel *Hotel Bosphorus* (*Kitapçı Dükkanı*), the first of her three Kati Hirschel mystery novels, was published in English by Bitter Lemon Press and in eight other languages. She lives in Istanbul and Berlin.

Sezer Ateş Ayvaz was born in 1956 in Antakya. She studied sociology at Istanbul University, completed her MA in politics and her PhD in Turkish literature, and then taught sociology and philosophy. She has written essays and reviews on literature and culture for newspapers and magazines. She was awarded the Akademi Kitabevi Short Story Prize in 1987 for her first short story portfolio *Bütün Oteller İstanbul Palas*. This was followed by the publication of her short story collections *Aynalarda Yaz* (1988) and *Yeryüzü Taksim* (2000). Her third collection *Tamiris'in Gecesuçları* (2006) received the Yunus Nadi Short Story Award.

Nalan Barbarasoğlu was born in Adapazarı in 1961. She studied systematic philosophy and logic at Istanbul University, graduating in 1982. She makes her living as a script writer and editor. She began writing short stories in

1980, and her first story was published in *Argos*. She has published four short story collections: *Ne Kadar Da Güzeldir Gitmek* (1996), *Her Ses Bir Ezgi* (2001), *Ayçiçekleri* (2002) and *Gümüş Gece* (2004). She is editor in chief at the short story journal *Eşik Cini*.

Oya Baydar was born in 1940. Her first two books were *Allah Çocukları Unuttu* (1961) and *Savaş Çağı Umut Çağı* (1964). She studied sociology at Istanbul University and after graduation worked as an assistant lecturer in the same department. She quit writing literature in the 1960s to focus on researching sociopolitical structures and became an activist in the socialist movement, for which she was arrested and dismissed from her work. After her release, she wrote columns for the newspapers *Yeni Ortam* and *Politika* until 1980. She had to flee Turkey after the 1980 coup, and lived in exile mainly in Frankfurt and also Moscow until 1992. Her first collection of short stories *Elveda Alyoşa* (1991) received the Sait Faik Short Story Prize. Her other awards include the Yunus Nadi Novel Prize in 1993 for *Kedi Mektupları;* the Orhan Kemal Novel Prize for *Sıcak Külleri Kaldı* (2000); and the Cevdet Kudret Literature Prize for *Erguvan Kapısı* (2004). Her novel *The Lost Word* (*Kayıp Söz,* 2008) was published in Britain by Peter Owen in 2011. She lives in Istanbul and on Marmara Island.

Gaye Boralıoğlu was born in Istanbul in 1963, studied philosophy at Istanbul University, and has a master's degree in systematic philosophy and logic. She has worked as a journalist, copywriter and script writer. Her collection of short stories *Hepsi Hikaye* (2001) and her novel *Meçhul* (2004) both met with critical acclaim. In addition to writing for some of Turkey's most popular television shows, Boralıoğlu wrote the script for *Eylül Fırtınası,* a film directed by one of the country's leading directors, the late Atıf Yılmaz. Boralıoğlu's 2009 novel *Aksak Ritim* is being published in German and Arabic.

Sevinç Çokum was born in Istanbul in 1943. She writes poetry, short stories, novels and screenplays. Çokum graduated from the Department of Turkish Language and Literature, Istanbul University and worked as a teacher for five years before concentrating on her writing. She was editor in chief at the journal *Türk Edebiyatı* and wrote for the newspaper *Türkiye*. Her short stories appeared in numerous literary journals before her first collection of short stories *Eğik Ağaç* was published in 1972. Since then, she has published ten short story collections, eleven novels, three collections of essays and two screenplays, focusing mainly on social and historical themes.

Nazlı Eray is one of the most prolific storytellers of contemporary Turkish literature. Born in 1945 in Istanbul, she studied law and philosophy at Istanbul University. She worked as a translator for the Ministry of Tourism in Ankara, and after having a family, she devoted herself to writing. She has published 25 books since her professional debut in 1967 with her collection *Ah Bayım Ah*. Most of her books are short story collections, but she has also written plays, like *Erostratus* (1985), and novels, such as her latest book, *Beyoğlunda Gezersin* (2005). Eray's writing has received prestigious awards in Turkey, including the Haldun Taner Short Story Prize for her collection *Yoldan Geçen Öyküler* (1988), and the Yunus Nadi Prize for the Novel *Aşkı Giyinen Adam* (2002). Three of her short stories have been published in English translation, and a selection of her short stories appeared in German as well.

Müge İplikçi was born in Istanbul. She graduated from the English Language and Literature Department, Istanbul University, and received MA degrees in women's studies from Istanbul University and The Ohio State University. She made her mark at a young age, winning the prestigious Yaşar Nabi Nayır Young Author Award in 1996. She has since published four short story collections and three novels, as well as two books of nonfiction. İplikci is a member of Writers in Prison Committee of Turkish PEN, and she has been the chairperson of the PEN Turkish Women Writers Committee since 2007. Her novel *Mount Kaf* is being published in English by Milet.

Gül İrepoğlu studied architecture at Istanbul State Academy of Fine Arts and began her academic career as research assistant and PhD student in the Department of Aesthetics and Art History at Istanbul University. She became professor of art history in 1997 and served for 26 years before retiring. She produced and presented two programs for Turkish television channel TRT 2, *Şehir ve Mekan* (2005–2006) and *Sanat ve Mekan* (2006–2007). She is on the executive board of the Turkish National Commission for UNESCO.

Şebnem İşigüzel was born in 1973. She wrote her first collection of short stories *Hanene Ay Doğacak* at age 17. When published in 1993, it received the annual Yunus Nadi Short Story Award, but the Turkish Censorship Board promptly banned the book, deeming it pornographic due to its open treatment of incest. The book was widely praised and read, and she went on to write a second book of short stories *Öykümü Kim Anlatacak* (1994), followed by four novels. Her novel *Sarmaşık* (2002) was also published in Italian and Spanish, and *Çöplük* (2004) in German. İşigüzel lives in İstanbul.

Berrin Karakaş was born in Konya in 1975 to a civil servant father, spending most of her childhood traveling in Anatolia until the family settled in Istanbul in 1982. After graduating from the Faculty of Communication, Istanbul University, she worked on projects with film directors such as Yavuz Özkan, and journalists such as Tuğrul Eryılmaz. She spent two years in London, taking courses in photography, cinema and media, then returned to Istanbul to begin her career as a journalist. Her short stories began appearing in literary journals while she was still a university student, and since then she has published the short collections *Sidre* (2004) and *Tül* (2005) and the novel *Hayalhane* (2007).

Karin Karakaşlı was born in Istanbul in 1972. She studied translation and interpreting at Boğaziçi University. Her first book *Ay Denizle Buluşunca* (1997) earned a mention award in the Bu Publications Novel Competition, and she received the Yaşar Nabi Nayır Young Author Award in 1998. Along with her novel, she has published the short story collection *Başka*

Dillerin Şarkısı (1999) and the poetry collection *Benim Gönlüm Gümüş* (2009). She was editor, columnist and head of editorial department at the Turkish-Armenian weekly newspaper *Agos* from 1996 to 2006, and currently writes columns for the newspaper *Radikal 2.* She teaches Armenian at the Getronagan Armenian Lycee in Istanbul and is lecturer at the Department of Translation Studies, Yeditepe University.

Gönül Kıvılcım studied Finance at Boğaziçi University and pursued her postgraduate studies at Bergen University in Norway. She began her career as a journalist in Berlin, as the German correspondent for the magazine *Aktüel,* and she worked at German radio and television from 1992 to 1996. She has made documentaries for the television channel ARTE Culture, including one on the subject of child marriages in Turkey. Among her published works are *Kasaba ve Yalanlar* (2001), *Parçalı Aşklar* (2004) and *Suç Sarayı* (2011). Her Short story "Kasaba ve Yalanlar" was published in an anthology in Germany. She currently resides in Istanbul.

Handan Öztürk is an author and film director. She was born in Tunceli and raised in Istanbul. She graduated from the College of Press and Distribution, Istanbul University, then moved to Sweden, where she worked at Radio Förderband as a program producer and presenter. After studying cinema and directing at the Hamburg Film Institute, she returned to Turkey and made noteworthy documentaries and the feature film *My and Roz's Autumn* (*Benim ve Roz'un Sonbaharı,* 2007). She has also made series, programs and commercials for Turkish and foreign television channels. She spends most of her time traveling to different countries, journeying into new cities, villages and cultures.

Yıldız Ramazanoğlu was born in 1958 in Ankara and is a graduate of the Faculty of Pharmacy, Hacettepe University. She has worked with various women's organizations. Her first writing appeared in the weekly newspaper *Genç Arkadaş* under the pseudonym Elif Yıldız. Her short stories are collected in *Derin Siyah* (1998), and her essays in *Bir Dünya Kadınları* (1998).

Suzan Samancı was born in 1962 in Diyarbakır. She has published four short story collections, *Eriyip Gidiyor Gece* (1991), *Reçine Kokuyordu Hêlin* (1993), *Kıraç Dağlar Kar Tuttu* (1996) and *Suskunun Gölgesinde* (2001), and two novels. Her short story "Kıraç Dağlar Kar Tuttu" came second in the Orhan Kemal Short Story Award in 1997. *Reçine Kokuyordu Hêlin* has been published in German, Flemish, Spanish, Italian and Swedish, and the collection *Kıraç Dağlar Kar Tuttu* in German. Her story entitled "Perili Kent" was published in a Turkish–German bilingual anthology. *Reçine Kokuyordu Hêlin* was published in Kurdish under the title *Bajare Mırınê*, and *Suskunun Gölgesinde* as *Siya Bêdengiyê*. Many of her individual short stories have been translated into English, Spanish, French, German, Arabic and Sorani. Since 1995, she has been a newspaper columnist, writing for *Demokrasi, Gündem* and *Özgür Politika*, and currently for *Taraf*.

Jale Sancak was born in Istanbul. Her career as a writer began in 1985 with the broadcast of her play *Yitik Sesler* on TRT Istanbul radio. In 1998 she made the television program *Ateşi Çalmak* for TRT. Her short stories have been published in literary journals, and her story "Mırıl Mırıl Münevver" was adapted to film by TRT. "Bıçkın Melek ve Küçük, Önemsiz Bir Kayboluş" came second in the 2002 Haldun Taner Short Story Competition. Her short stories and collections have been published in several languages, including Bulgarian, Finnish and German.

Mine Söğüt was born in Istanbul in 1968. She studied in the Department of Latin at Istanbul University, completing her BA in 1989 and later her MA. She began her career in journalism in 1990, and worked as a reporter, writer or editor for the newspapers *Güneş Gazetesi* and *Yeni Yüzyıl*, the weekly news magazine *Tempo*, and the monthly magazine *Öküz*. In 1993, she was awarded an honorable mention in the News category of the Turkish Journalists Association competition. She was a screenwriter for the television documentary series *Haberci* from 1996 to 2000. Her writings and interviews have appeared in numerous newspapers and magazines, and she has published four novels, including *Beş Sevim Apartmanı* (2003) and *Kırmızı Zaman* (2004), both of which were translated to other languages, and the short story collection *Deli Kadın Hikayeleri* (2011).

Feryal Tilmaç was born in 1969 in Adana. She graduated from the Department of Economics, Boğaziçi University. Her short stories, essays and translations have appeared in print and online literary magazines and journals. Her short story "Trilobis" received first prize in the Altkitap 2006 Short Story Competition. Her first collection of short stories *Mevt Tek Hecelik Uyku* was published in 2007, and she received the prestigious Sait Faik Short Story Award in 2009 for her second short story collection *Aradım Yaz Dediniz.*

Semra Topal was born in Eskişehir in 1964. She graduated from the Faculty of Economics and Administrative Sciences, Anadolu University. She was awarded the Abdi İpekçi Peace and Friendship Prize in 1990 for her short story "Çaydanlık Tanık", and the Yaşar Nabi Nayır Young Author Prize in 1992 for her story "Bayan Mira'yla Ufak Bir Gezinti". Her short story collections include: *Mani* (1988), *Kürklü Gece* (2000) and *Salta Dur* (2003).

Menekşe Toprak was born in Kayseri in 1970. She studied political science at Ankara University and worked for a bank in Ankara and Berlin for four years afterwards. She has been working as a radio journalist since 2002, and divides her time between Berlin and Istanbul. Her short stories have appeared in literary journals in Turkey and in Germany, France and Britain. Her published books include the short story collections *Valizdeki Mektup* (2007) and *Hangi Dildedir Aşk* (2009), and a novel *Temmuz Çocukları* (2011).

Biographies of Translators

İdil Aydoğan was born in London and grew up in both London and İzmir. She completed her BA in English language and literature at Ege University and received her MA in comparative literature from King's College, London University. Her English translations of Turkish short stories have been published in various books and magazines.

Kerim Biçer studied English language and literature at Ege University. His first published translation (a co-translation with İdil Aydoğan) was the short story "Time Decay" by Ahmet Büke, which appeared in Transcript: *The European Review of Books and Writing*. He is currently based in London and teaches English.

Abigail Rood Bowman is a Fulbright Scholar in Istanbul, Turkey, where she is translating Modern Turkish literature. Originally from Johnston, Iowa, Abigail graduated magna cum laude from Princeton University in 2011 with a BA in Near Eastern studies. Her senior thesis, "The Legs of Şahmeran: A Translation of Murathan Mungan", received the Ertegün Foundation Thesis Award and the Francis LeMoyne Page Creative Writing Award. Fluent in Turkish and experienced in Azerbaijani, she is now learning Modern Greek. Abigail is starting an MA program in history at Sabancı University.

Nilgün Dungan is a lecturer and translator based in İzmir. She studied English language and literature and received her master's degree in management. She is currently pursuing her PhD in translation studies at Boğaziçi University, and she teaches in the Department of English Translation and Interpreting, İzmir University of Economics. She has participated in the Cunda Workshop for Translators of Turkish Literature since 2007 and translates Turkish fiction and poetry into English.

Daniel Rosinsky-Larsson grew up in Mankato, Minnesota. He studied Turkish and received a BA in international studies at the University of Wisconsin, Madison. He lives in Kadıköy, Istanbul, and currently works full-time as an editor for a global energy industry publication, in addition to freelance editing and translation.

Jonathan Ross completed his doctorate in East German literature at King's College, London University and now teaches in the Department of Translation and Interpreting Studies at Boğaziçi University. His research interests include the translation of film titles, and community interpreting in Turkey. Ross has also published English translations of several Turkish books, film scripts and articles.

Amy Spangler was born in Circleville, Ohio in 1978. She is co-owner of the literary agency AnatoliaLit, which she established in 2005. She is a lecturer in translation studies at Okan University and Boğaziçi University, and the translator of Aslı Erdoğan's novel, *The City in Crimson Cloak* (Soft Skull, 2007), co-editor and co-translator (together with Mustafa Ziyalan) of *Istanbul Noir* (Akashic Books, 2008), and the translator of many Turkish short stories and novel excerpts published in a variety of collections and journals.

Ruth Whitehouse completed her BA in Turkish and PhD in Modern Turkish literature at the School of Oriental and African Studies, London University. She is translator of Esmahan Aykol's *Hotel Bosphorus* (Bitter Lemon Press, 2011), Perihan Mağden's *Ali and Ramazan* (Amazon Crossing, 2012) and *The Last Tram*, a collection of short stories by Nedim Gürsel (Comma Press, 2011).

Mark Wyers was born and raised in Los Angeles, California. He first moved to Turkey in 2001, living in Kayseri and Ankara for several years. He then returned to the US to formally pursue his study of Turkish, supplementing his BA in literature with an MA in Turkish studies at the University of Arizona. He is currently the director of the Writing Center at Kadir Has University, Istanbul. His translations have been published in Transcript and by the literary organization Het Beschrijf. In addition to translating from Turkish and Late Ottoman to English, he is researching Turkey's social history, focusing on gender and marginality. His book titled, *"Wicked" Istanbul: The Regulation of Prostitution in the Early Turkish Republic* was recently published by Libra.